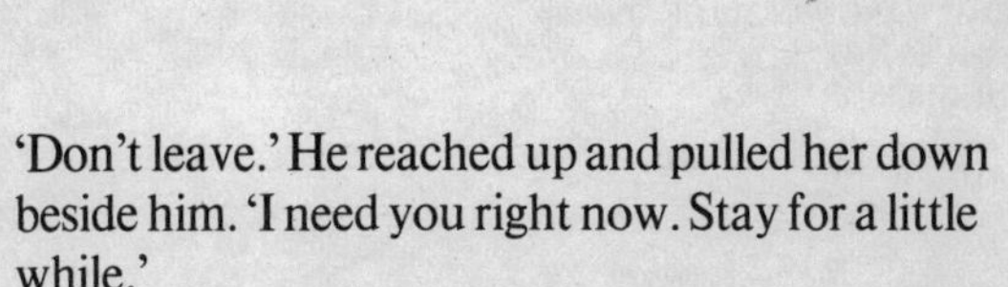

'Truly touching'
Publishers Weekly

'Don't leave.' He reached up and pulled her down beside him. 'I need you right now. Stay for a little while.'

Ryan reached up and turned her face towards his. 'I love you, Alys.'

The words came as easily as if he'd uttered them a million times, the thousands and thousands of times he'd thought them.

In another moment she was in his arms, and he was kissing her as long and passionately as if the world would stop if he stopped. His hands and then his lips were caressing her, and every part of her body responded to his touch. This was what she'd longed for . . .

Also by Barbara Ferry Johnson in Sphere Books:

DELTA BLOOD
HOMEWARD WINDS THE RIVER
TARA'S SONG
THE HEIRS OF LOVE

Echoes from the Hills

BARBARA FERRY JOHNSON

SPHERE BOOKS LIMITED
30-32 Gray's Inn Road, London WC1X 8JL

First published in Great Britain by
Sphere Books Ltd 1984

Published in the United States of America by
Warner Books, Inc., 1983

TRADE
MARK

Set in 9/11½ Plantin

Printed and bound in Great Britain by
Cox & Wyman Ltd, Reading

For David, who in many important ways is coauthor of this book.

His experiences while landing on Normandy, slogging his way in the infantry across France, Holland, Belgium, and Germany, and finally fighting and being wounded during the great Battle of the Ardennes provided the inspiration as well as many of the incidents for this book.

It is my hope that I have expressed in here the attitudes, reactions, and feelings of the men who endured the daily battles against fear, pain, death, and – yes – boredom while forging bonds of comradeship unequaled under less trying conditions.

This is not David's story, but this is his book.

These pages are also dedicated to all the men who fought in the infantry during World War II.

For David Ward, namesake of his grandfather and father.

Flowers in the Snow

You lie there – like a
Snow angel.
The price was paid for
Rock-strewn ground.
Was it just yesterday
You walked out in the
Sun – family proud –
And three-inch feet
Tripping and stumbling
Into the Light?
How short was the time
When you came in
With a flower in your
Hand –
Time eats away years
In consumptive fury –
The young man in
A new suit, looking
Down so as not to
Stumble over her feet,
And Glenn Miller playing
In the box.
You had no goal – no
Fury for the fight.
You came to do what
Was said – 'Go!'
Your body – the fallen
Angel in the snow –
Makes red flowers,
Red flowers,
In the frozen snow.

W. David Johnson

Echoes from the Hills

Soft comes the murmur,
Muted sounds ring down valleys –
The rivulets echo the sounds:
'Come back. Come back.
Stay here;
The greens and browns
Reflect your soul;
The thundering rivers, like
The storms and rugged peaks,
Remember your past.
Come back to the hills.
It is here you seek for
Eternal peace.'

W. David Johnson

CHAPTER ONE

i

Alys Prévou smiled as she settled her daughter, Minette, into the small pillion seat over the rear wheel of the bicycle and tucked a long knitted scarf around the little girl. The day, the hour, the success of her visit, all conspired to make Alys feel more jubilant than she had in a long time.

Before starting down the slope toward the road leading to the village of Ste. Monique, Alys paused. It had been snowing steadily until a few minutes earlier, and from the nearby fields to the distant hills and forests of the Ardennes, the undulating valley was one broad expanse of shimmering white.

Even as she gazed in delight at the beauty of the snowglazed scene, the late afternoon sun broke in liquid shafts of light through the translucent clouds and spread a golden roseate glow over the crystal landscape. Stepping through the frozen surface to the soft snow beneath was like biting into thick, soft frosting glazed over with a thin, crisp, glossy crust.

Alys was held spellbound for the moment by more than the shimmering beauty of the landscape. There was something mystical and unreal about the world around her, something captured in memory but almost forgotten. It was the silence that haunted her, a silence strangely underlined by the distant lowing of a cow and the music of its bell.

The peaceful serenity was like that of many late winter afternoons in her lifetime. The miracle was its being this way today – this particular day – in the midst of war.

There was irony in the miracle. The momentary calm was a false tranquility that seduced the mind into forgetting or ignoring the tragic mementoes of war that lay beneath the pristine whiteness: death, horror, mutilation, destruction, desolation. And with them lay the slow erosion of hope, the mounting despair, the endless pain.

The lines of a poem by the American poet, Carl Sandburg, came to her mind:

> Pile the bodies high at Austerlitz and Waterloo.
> Shovel them under and let me work –
> I am the grass; I cover all.
>
> And pile them high at Gettysburg.
> And pile them high at Ypres and Verdun.
> Shovel them under and let me work.

Now it was the snow. It covered all with its mocking serenity and beauty.

Enough musing, she thought. She had to get home. She looked at Minette.

'Warm enough, *ma chère*?'

The little girl nodded, loosening the long scarf that wound around her head and shoulders, almost covering her face. Alys tucked it back into place.

'I love you.' Alys kissed the tip of Minette's nose.

'I love you,' came the muffled reply.

Alys never ceased to be overwhelmed that this beautiful little girl was her daughter. A precious bit of perfection in this most imperfect world.

Alys began pedaling as fast as she dared along the rutted, icy road toward the village. The once stately trees on the verges between fields and road were now jagged stumps, victims of the German's barbarous onslaught more than four years earlier and the more recent, intense battles as the Americans gradually forced the Germans back toward the Siegfried Line. With their mounds of snow on top, the stumps reminded her of milk bottles in winter with frozen cream pushing up the caps.

When she was a little girl, how she had cried each autumn when the leaves blew off these trees. She had mourned their dying, and had to be reminded there would be new leaves and blooms in the spring. So different from the destructive winds of fall were the gentle breezes of spring. She had not wept aloud when the trees were destroyed, but bitter tears had formed behind her eyelids, and her heart had moaned in sympathy. The weeping must be saved for the people dying in the war. And some of the shattered wood had been garnered to keep warm those who remained alive.

A light snow began falling again, covering the already solidly packed white ground. Alys licked some errant flakes off her lips and brushed others away from her face with a mittened hand. With a faint smile on her lips and her skin glowing in the frosty air, she looked younger than twenty-six. Alys was one of those women whose face never revealed her true age. When she frowned or her features were set in a stern, forbidding pose or if she were depressed or upset, she looked much older than her actual years. On the other hand, when she was smiling or obviously feeling pleased about something or in a gay mood, she appeared much younger. Right now, with her exuberance and feelings of well-being, she looked to be no more than twenty. There were times, however, in the past few years, when anyone seeing and not knowing her would have said she was in her early thirties.

Most of the time her clear, dark green eyes had a merry sparkle that seemed to hint at some secret amusement. Her face was too thin for the prominent cheekbones and generous mouth, but that slight defect was offset by the healthy glow of her clear skin and the touch of pink on the tip of her upturned nose. Thick chestnut hair framed her face in soft, natural waves and curled to a point at the nape of her neck. In the sunlight it glistened with autumnal hues from rich gold to bronze to deep russet. Her slender, five-foot-three body was completely concealed under a long woollen skirt, a thick, hand-knitted sweater, and a well-worn but sturdy loden green coat.

Eager to get to the village before dark, Alys pedaled her bicycle with brisk, sure movements, indicative of the natural energy and sense of immediacy with which she approached everything she did. The frail appearance belied her seemingly inexhaustible, spontaneous energy. It was this energy, a powerful determination to meet and overcome obstacles head-on, and a refusal to lie down and let adversity trample over her that had kept her going during the past four and a half years of German occupation.

But she had endured, and she was now rejoicing in that special kind of exhilarating freedom that one experiences only after months or years of stultifying, smothering oppression.

Alys heard a muffled giggle from the rear seat. A child's laugh, she thought as she turned her head, is the gift of eternity.

'Something tickle your funny bone?' she asked Minette. Her voice was mellow, soothing.

'No, my nose,' the little girl said.

Alys stopped pedaling and turned farther around. The breeze had loosened a bit of red fluff from Minette's scarf, and a wet snowflake had trapped it on the tip of her nose. Alys broke out in peals of crystalline laughter.

'Oh, Minette, you look like a clown.'

'What's a clown?'

What's a clown? How to explain that most fascinating and wonderful of creatures to a child who's never seen one. Or the motley color and exciting vitality of the one-family circuses that had traveled the countryside and captivated Alys as a child. Some of the best had been German, too. What war had done! Circuses. Just one of the many delights of childhood that Minette had to miss.

'A clown is a magic creature who makes you laugh and clap your hands. Part of the reason you laugh is that he's dressed in a funny costume. He has white paint all over his face and maybe a big red nose, or a spot of red on the tip of his nose, like the fluff that's tickling yours. And he does crazy, funny things. It's hard to describe, *ma chère*, but you'll see one someday.'

'Now! Want to see one now,' Minette demanded with all the imperiousness of a two-year-old.

Alys frowned and then smiled. 'Not right this minute, *ma chère*, but just maybe . . .'

The village was giving a party on Christmas Eve for the Allied liberation troops in the area. In fact, Alys had just spent most of the day with Countess Charbonne, widow of a World War I hero and general, who'd long been like a godmother to the entire village. It was she who was making certain all children in the village would find a gift under the Christmas tree at the party.

Maybe the party could provide something else for the children. A clown. Old Raoul, the church sexton, had been a clown when he was a young man. She remembered his tales of traveling all over Europe with a small circus. Surely he'd don his makeup and whatever costume he could concoct in order to amuse the children. And the adults as well. She'd ask him the next day.

'I think, Minette, you might be seeing a clown in a very few days.'

It was almost dusk. The sky had turned opalescent now, a mother-of-pearl range of colors – silver gray to rose, mauve, lavender, and deep purple at the horizon.

Alys pedaled into the village, a town deprived by war of young men and most means of livelihood. The square was dominated by the two-hundred-year-old stone church. Still a bastion of strength and endurance in spite of having its tower demolished and its stained-glass windows broken, the age-darkened structure was the heart of village life. Shell holes from the present war were raw-looking scars amidst those from World War I. It was as if the sturdy old lady were saying to her people: 'See, we have been besieged but not vanquished; we have been damaged, but not destroyed; we have been wounded, but we are not dead. No one can conquer our spirits as long as we have the will to endure.'

Around the square were other battered reminders of the war, remnants of what had once been a few thriving shops and a café. Monsieur LeBrun, the baker, was still converting the first floor of his *pâtisserie* into both home and shop. The top floor had been completely destroyed. The greengrocer's shop was an even worse case, but Monsieur Pollard used the shattered walls of the building to support a makeshift awning of American Army tarpaulins. Under this he sold a meager supply of produce brought in from surrounding farms: sugar beets, turnips, fruit from orchards where a few trees were left standing, and eggs.

The café, however, remained a shell of jagged walls and rubble.

Alys waved to Monsieur LeBrun, standing in the door of the *pâtisserie*. 'Ready for the party?' she asked.

'Thanks to the Americans,' he answered, 'I have the sugar and flour. There will be cakes for all.'

'Wonderful! The children will be so happy.'

Not to be outdone, Monsieur Pollard, the greengrocer, waved

from under his awning. 'I'm saving the last of the apples. It will be a real party, Alys.'

She blew kisses to them, and there was hearty, responsive laughter when two-year-old Minette imitated her.

ii

Just beyond the square, Alys passed the four-room schoolhouse at whose desks she'd indulged in her dreams of becoming a teacher, to inspire children to love books as much as she did. From there she'd gone to Liège. She'd received her teaching degree from the Lycée and had, in addition, studied English for an additional year at the University of Liège. To this four-room school she'd returned. To the younger children she taught English, and to the older ones, she taught French, German, and English literature. As with most Belgians in this section of the country, Alys grew up speaking both French and German. Listening to tourists from England and America, she became adept in English before she started to school.

Alys would never forget her feelings as she prepared for teaching her first classes: her fears that she wouldn't be a good teacher, that she wouldn't be able to motivate her students as she'd been motivated. Most of all she wanted to open the doors to learning for each and every one of her students.

When she did meet her first class on the morning of Friday, September 1, 1939, her stomach was knotted with tension, her hands were clammy, and her mouth so dry she was afraid she wouldn't be able to speak. The fear that day, however, was not that she might fail as a teacher. Her personal feelings paled to insignificance as she greeted the older students in the school and wrote the first lesson on the blackboard: '*L'Allemagne envahit la Pologne.*'

'Will someone volunteer to translate that for me?' she asked.

Georges LaBec, the mayor's son, raised his hand and stood up. He pronounced the English words carefully: 'Germany invades Poland.'

'Well done, Georges. Thank you. As some of you may already know, that was the headline in this morning's paper.'

The next day, the first lesson was '*L'Angleterre déclare la guerre contre l'Allemagne.*' 'England declares war on Germany.'

In spite of the ensuing rape of Poland, in spite of the German blitzkrieg in Norway and Denmark, Alys, like most people in the low countries – Belgium, the Netherlands, and Luxemburg – complacently assumed that Hitler would respect their neutrality; life maintained a fatal normalcy. The days in Ste. Monique and especially at school went on peacefully and routinely. Alys was more concerned during the following months with lesson preparations and the gratification of seeing the excitement in her students' eyes when they conquered a difficult English phrase than with news that the Germans were conquering more land.

At Christmas she took the older children to the woods to find a perfectly shaped tree for the school pageant, and she taught all of them traditional English and American carols. For the younger ones, she translated 'A Visit from St. Nicolaus' while her middle classes, enchanted by the poem, learned it in English and acted it out as part of the entertainment at the annual Christmas fête.

And Gilles was with her then. Gilles, the son of her modern language professor. Wonderful, handsome, happy-go-lucky Gilles. She had been fascinated by him when he strode – uninvited – into his father's modern language seminar and began entertaining the group with some of the more ribald English sea shanties. Within three weeks they were in love. They made plans to be married after her first year of teaching.

Then came May 10, 1940. Hitler attacked Holland and sent an armored thrust through the Ardennes that pierced Luxemburg and cut a brutal swath through Belgium. Alys would never forget the horror of sudden, unexpected artillery and bombing attacks, the fires and devastation, the screaming, the mutilation, and the deaths; the phalanxes of tanks grinding like giant monsters across the land, and the pillaging troops rampaging through the village; the frightened faces of the children who clung to her for reassurance during the cataclysmic upheaval in their young lives.

The Germans advanced so rapidly that the Belgian resistance forces were rendered totally impotent.

On May 28, Alys sat in stunned silence with her parents while they listened to the announcement of King Leopold's ignominious surrender to Germany of his proud and independent little nation. To avoid enforced labor duty under German command, Gilles fled, along with many other men, to France to fight alongside its troops. When Marshal Pétain signed an armistice with Germany on June 22, and the northern half of France became an occupied nation under German control, Gilles joined the French resistance forces, learned their techniques of sabotage, arson, secret communication, rescue, and guerrilla warfare, and returned to Belgium to carry them out.

In spite of the danger, Alys and Gilles managed to meet a few times during the next two years, sometimes in nearby towns, sometimes at a farm on the outskirts of Ste. Monique. Between each meeting, Alys's waking hours were dominated by the fear that Gilles would be captured and executed.

In the spring of 1942, within days after they had spent a few hours together, Gilles was transferred to the coast to ferry escaped prisoners and downed Allied plane crews across the Channel. An occasional assurance from others in the underground that he was still alive was all the comfort she had.

iii

Alys sighed. If only Gilles were with her now, the Christmas party would be a real celebration. She thought about that last night together. They'd spent the hours in a small garret over a tobacco shop. While they made love, they could hear the tramping of boots as German soldiers patrolled the streets, and from the room below them came the voices of men plotting to blow up a munitions dump on the edge of town.

Alys sighed again. Some memories helped ease the longing; others only made it more intense.

Three kilometers beyond the village, Alys turned into the driveway of the three-story inn, *Les Trois Fleurs*, owned by her family for more than four generations. Situated in the valley with a clear, swift-moving river less than fifty meters behind it, and surrounded by the lush, green, forest-covered hills of the Ardennes, the inn had long been a popular hostelry for vacationing travelers from many countries. Being on the Belgian – Luxemburg border, it had also been commandeered during two world wars by both enemy and Allied forces. It had housed German officers with spiked helmets; and twenty-five years later, it was occupied by the dreaded Boches of another generation. In turn, it opened its doors to General Pershing's war-weary veterans, and it was now a command post for the American Army of Liberation.

Like the officers and men who'd stayed there, the inn had its own battle scars. Shelled by enemy and Allied artillery alike, one section, including the bar and the four rooms above it, had been destroyed. On remaining walls, great uneven, jagged chunks of the plaster façade had been ripped off, leaving bare, unhealed wounds of raw brick and mortar.

The remaining interior, however, presented a far different view. Freshly starched and ironed curtains covered windows boarded up or patched with irregular-shaped pieces of glass salvaged from broken panes and held precariously together with tape. Two of the tables in the dining room were spread with fine, carefully darned linen cloths and mismatched crockery, delicate Limoges china, and wooden bowls. There were no complete place settings of silver, but beside each plate was either a fork or spoon, and a few had knives.

Other tables, used now as desks by the American officers, were covered with a hodgepodge of maps, official releases, and field telephones.

Monsieur Émile Prévou continued to preside over the kitchen, where he prepared meals for the Americans from their army rations as expertly and with as much pride as if he were concocting a gourmet dinner. Madame Jolie Prévou, her hair carefully coiffed, her dresses and aprons neatly and many times mended but immaculately clean, was still the gracious hostess as she seated and served her American guests.

During the early months of German occupation, Alys and her family endured, along with the rest of the village, the suffering imposed by meager supplies of food. All fresh baked goods and produce were forbidden them; those went immediately to the Germans. What was left over was quickly snatched up by women who might well have stood in line all day while waiting hopefully for wilting or rotted vegetables, soup bones bereft of meat, and moldy bread.

When there was nothing left over, they subsisted on what the Germans deigned to hand out to them or what could be scavenged from the shell-pitted fields. Alys learned early how to approach the Germans for food – not by choking back her pride but by maintaining and vaunting it. In an eerie sort of way, much of life went on as usual, but like a nightmare from which there is no awaking.

There were constant changes of rules, posted on the church, and one had to check the list daily for fear of breaking a new one. Particularly odious was the almost daily change in hours of curfew, sometimes as early as six o'clock. And always there was the booted tramping of German feet in the streets.

The winters were the worst. If they were fortunate, they could find enough fuel or scraps to burn in the stove for two hours a day. Émile would cook up what food they had, and for two hours they would be gloriously warm. Stones heated on top of the stove would be tucked between the quilts, and if they were lucky, they would fall asleep before the bricks cooled off.

Alys continued to teach, but under strict German regulations, and her salary provided what income the family had.

Then early in 1942, the inn became a German way station for troops returning home on leave and for others being sent to France. At times there were only two or three officers billeted there; at other times, the rooms were crowded with the men and their female companions. But at last there was heat and food.

While in some ways life was easier after the Germans occupied the inn, in other ways it was harder and more brutal. The family's private quarters were summarily commandeered, and the Prévoux returned to the pallets in the basement where they'd slept during the shelling. Not all Belgians were sympathetic to the Allied cause. There were many areas decidedly pro-German, and even in as small a village as Ste. Monique, there were those outspokenly in favor of a German victory. The German officers did not have to look far for women eager to join their dinner parties and share the beds of the heroes of the Fatherland.

More disconcerting than even the army were the scores of German tourists who, once the fighting had ceased, flocked to Belgium and France, and with ruthless condescension flaunted their positions of superiority. If possible, they were ruder and more demanding than the army.

Liberation by the Allies had been purchased dearly with death and destruction, but the price had also bought a long-despaired-of freedom from both fear and want.

iv

'Did Countess Charbonne have something for the Christmas party?' Madame Prévou asked when Alys returned to the kitchen after taking snow-covered coats and scarves to the bedroom.

'Indeed she did.' Alys warmed her hands over the hot coals in the stove. 'A toy for each of the children.'

'They'll have a fine Christmas, then.'

'And the first real one for many.' Alys leaned over and kissed Minette, now ensconced in a high chair and shoveling handfuls of raisins into her mouth. 'Raisins? Where did those come from?'

'Colonel Applegate brought them to me. I don't know whether they're army rations or his wife sent them. At any rate, he asked if I could bake his favorite raisin cupcakes. Fortunately, he was also able to provide the flour and sugar.'

Flour and sugar. How much better things were now than under the Germans! At the thought of the hated Boches, Alys uttered a sound of disgust and spat out a reviling word: '*Merde!*'

Madame Prévou repressed a shudder. 'Careful what you say. The war isn't over yet. Remember which sympathizers would love to see them return.'

'It's over for us. As for the sympathizers, we know who they are. I'm no longer afraid of them. What can they do now?'

'I don't know,' Jolie Prévou said. 'But I won't feel safe until the Germans are beaten all the way back to Berlin.'

'Worry if you want to, *Maman*, but I intend to enjoy the holidays with no thought of the fighting still going on. It's miles away and can't touch us any longer.'

* * *

Still caught up in a heightened sense of elation that everything was going to be all right from now on, Alys began getting Minette ready for bed after supper. She looked at the little girl sitting cross-legged in a loose, bright red woollen nightgown. Minette was grinning at herself in the cheval glass across the room. Alys had a sudden inspiration.

'Want to have some fun, Minette?'

Minette nodded, her eyes shining.

'Want to be a clown?'

'Yes!' The little girl began bouncing up and down on the bed.

'All right, but no peeking until I'm finished.'

Alys hurried into the kitchen and came back with flour that she powdered all over Minette's face. With an old flame-colored lipstick, she made a large, grinning mouth, bright red circles on Minette's cheeks, and inverted *V* eyebrows.

'Now,' Alys said, 'behold! A clown.'

Minette looked in the mirror and giggled. 'Me funny.'

'Shall we go show *Grand-maman* and *Grand-papa*?'

Minette nodded again.

'Wait – one more thing.' Alys slipped into her parents' room and came out with her father's old cloth slippers. 'Think you can walk in these?'

By sliding one foot after the other instead of picking them up, Minette made it to the kitchen.

'*Maman, Papa*,' Alys said in feigned surprise. 'look what I found in the bedroom.'

'Oh, my,' Jolie Prévou exclaimed. 'Who is that?'

'Is it a goblin or a troll?' Émile Prévou drew back in mock fear.

'No, no,' Minette giggled. 'Me a clown.'

'Indeed you are,' her grandmother said, 'and a very good one. I didn't recognize you at all.'

'I scare you,' and she ran to her grandfather.

'A little, precious. Now, kiss me good-night and let *Maman* wash your face.'

'Me a clown, me a clown,' Minette sang all the way back to the bedroom.

Alys washed Minette's face, tucked her into bed, and started reading her a fairy tale. Exhausted from the evening's fun, Minette fell asleep before the story ended. Alys closed the book and folded her hands over it. She looked tenderly at her daughter's face, at the long lashes resting on her cheeks, and her tangled blond hair spread over the pillow. Could there possibly have been a time when Alys didn't want her to be born?

V

The first German officers to stay at the inn were crude, boorish, demanding, and unutterably rude, but they made no physical threats.

Then, early in the spring of 1942, right after Alys learned of Gilles's transfer to the coast, a German colonel and four staff officers arrived at the inn. For the first time, for a haunting, inexplicable reason, Alys felt real fear when around them. It was more than a fear of being brutalized, humiliated, or worked beyond endurance. It was an intense, concentrated vampire fear that consumed every other thought until she forced herself to realize that her natural antipathy to the Germans was being exacerbated by exhaustion and by the unusually imperious and arrogant attitude of this particular group.

While Alys was serving supper a few nights after their arrival, Colonel Subermann put his arm around her waist and suggested she spend the night with him. When she refused, his expression turned surly, but he said nothing more. She was not at all reassured by his grim silence: it could forebode trouble for all of them. She was not wrong. Later that evening, when the other four officers had gone out, the colonel's request became a command. Either she come to his room or he would turn her and her parents over to the dreaded SS to be shot for hiding and aiding escaped prisoners of war. She had no choice. In the early months of the occupation, a number of Allied prisoners and downed plane crews had stayed in the second basement, behind the wine cellar, until they could be spirited by the Underground to the coast and across to England. One of the German sympathizers in Ste. Monique undoubtedly had learned about the Prévoux' work and informed on them.

The hours with the colonel were like an ever-repeating nightmare. He handed her a black lace brassiere, panties, garter belt, and sheer black stockings. The silk against her skin felt slimy and unclean. She had to endure the torment of his gaze while she removed the undergarments, and of his hands when he slowly rolled the stockings down her legs. One vile act followed another. The pain and revulsion were as nothing compared to the shame she felt.

When the colonel left her shortly before dawn, she thought the degrading torture was over. She was wrong. He brought the four other officers in and laughingly told them to enjoy themselves with her. She knew it was not so much for their pleasure as to totally demean and humiliate her. If they expected her to cry out or protest, they would be disappointed. Their actions debased themselves, not her.

Unable to shut out what was happening to her, her mind was awhirl with disjointed, overpowering responses. How could anything that had been so beautiful with Gilles be so filthy and abhorrent? Gilles's tender words of love were now replaced with obscenities that made her feel unclean. The disgusting male bodies exuded a revolting, pungent male stench. How could that monstrous thing, that battering ram that invaded her, be considered a man's pride? It should be his shame that it would lead him to do what was being done to her. These men, with their contemptible behavior, were no better than beasts rutting in the field.

Once the men had left her, she became more acutely aware of the pain they had caused, the burning sensation followed by paralyzing cramps. Never before had she known such physical agony. She began to cry softly from misery and the futility of it all. Her plight was no worse than that of hundreds of women in France, Holland, and Belgium; but this was her own personal agony she was suffering; and it mattered little and helped not at all that she was not suffering alone. She shivered. She felt herself getting colder and colder. She moved only enough to pull the sheet up over her.

The first of the four staff officers had been a young lieutenant. While Alys was trying to escape into a healing semiconscious darkness, she heard a startling sound. Like someone trying to choke back a sob. She opened her eyes and saw the boyish face staring at her. He had come quietly back into the room. His blue eyes, mocking her with their look of childlike innocence, were filled with tears. His pale skin was flushed. He ran one hand through short, blond curls.

'I'm sorry,' he sobbed. 'Please believe me. I had to. You understand? I had to. I didn't want to hurt you. I'm sorry.'

Unmoved by his plea, Alys turned her head to the wall. It made no difference that he was sorry. He had violated her like all the rest. Then she felt him gently covering her with a quilt before he left. Now she was sorry, too. He was as much a victim of the war as she. She should have said something. Assured him she understood.

The colonel and his staff left later in the afternoon. It's over, she thought. Thank God, it's over.

And it was for the time being, but what would happen when another and then another learned that the inn had worked with the Underground?

Anxious and afraid, Alys waited desperately for another German officer to come with his threats. Or the dreaded SS with orders to kill them. The very least would be prison in Belgium or in one of the camps in Germany they were hearing about. As weeks passed safely, Alys decided that whoever had revealed their subversive activities to the German colonel had either left Ste. Monique or else decided there was no point in betraying them again.

Some weeks later, Alys stood examining her image in the mirror. There was no outward change in her appearance. A little more tired perhaps; deeper shadow under the eyes. That was all. The raw places on her body from the buckles and buttons had healed, and the bruises had faded. There should be no evidence remaining of the unspeakable horror of that night. But there was: she was pregnant. There was no longer any doubt. Nor was there any hope that the child was Gilles's. She had not been pregnant when the Germans raped her.

She was facing a decision that, once made, had to be immutable. She could accept what had happened and try to love the child or she could succumb to self-pity and make her life and the child's life completely miserable. 'No,' she said defiantly. 'There's a third choice.' She must be strong enough to make it the right choice and never, never consider either of the alternatives.

Alys found her mother alone in the kitchen.

'*Maman*, I have something to tell you. I'm pregnant.'

Jolie Prévou stood for a moment looking down into the sink where she was peeling potatoes. Alys could see her trying to control the expression of disbelief and disgust on her face. When she spoke, her voice was tight. 'You mean . . .'

'Yes, Gilles and I spent the night – several nights – together. I'm going to have his child.'

There, she'd said it. Now it was true. Now it was real. The child would be considered his, and no one must ever think differently. It would be his, in her mind and to all the world. She would walk a delicate balance between belief and reality.

Madame Prévou started to insist that Gilles be told so he could come to Ste. Monique and marry her.

'He must not know,' Alys said. 'He would come, and it's too dangerous. Time enough to worry about proprieties when the war is over.'

Madame Prévou wrung her hands and turned back to peeling the potatoes with a ferocity that surprised even Alys. 'You have shamed us.'

'The shame isn't ours, *Maman*. It's the war that makes us live the way we do, to do the things we wouldn't do in peacetime.'

As the months passed, Alys continued to teach, and the child within her became more and more a symbol of love for Gilles. It should have been his. It was his. Yet as much as she could face her mother with the lie, could she face herself with it? Would she be able to face Gilles?

In December, 1942, Minette was born. She was a beautiful little girl, with pale blue eyes and soft blond curls that clung tightly to her head and framed her delicate face. Alys finally wrote Gilles that he had a daughter, and his reply was ecstatic. Just as soon as he could find a way to get to Ste. Monique they would be married.

When Minette was less than two months old, Alys received word that Gilles had been captured while preparing to embark for England with several escaped prisoners. He had been summarily executed.

Alys moved through the next months as if in a trance. Instead of being a constant reminder of that hideous night with the Germans, as Alys had feared, Minette became her one reason for wanting to live. She was life and she was beauty and she was all the reasons for continuing to have hope when all other reasons for hope had been obliterated.

vi

Alys left the bedroom and went downstairs. She nodded to Colonel Applegate and Major West, who were drinking coffee and finishing up the last of the raisin cupcakes.

She walked through into the kitchen and looked at the calendar: December 15, 1944. Only ten days until Christmas. The first Christmas in four years free of the Germans. 'Nothing! Nothing,' she swore under her breath, 'will spoil the celebration this year.'

CHAPTER TWO

i

Several miles east of Ste. Monique, the early evening presented a far less placid scene than the one surrounding the small Belgian village.

Dirty gray clouds hung over the fir trees. Shards of sleet and snow dropped steadily from the trees onto the frozen ground on either side of the narrow road that bisected a dismal cluster of small buildings. On the left were two small ecru-plastered, stone houses with stone courtyards fronting each combination house-and-barn. Low walls hid the sight, if not the stench, of manure piles. On the opposite side was a café, *Les Deux Chats*, over which the owner and family lived. Next to it was a large, nondescript building. Earlier a milky sun had thawed the truck-plowed ruts into gray black, sticky mud. A fierce, glacier chilled wind swirled the snow across the ground and patterned it into white patches under trees and against fence posts. The ubiquitous fog billowed and swelled like great clouds of smoke from a hastily dampened fire.

Lieutenant Ryan Middleton stood in the doorway of the large building. Visibility had finally increased from near zero to a few hundred yards. He looked down the road from his platoon command post toward the front some five hundred yards away, near the Our River, the boundary between Luxemburg and Germany.

At first there was nothing for him to see and all was quiet except for the wind soughing in the fir trees. Gradually from within the frozen mist came the sounds of mess kits beating out a repetitive aluminum tune and the hollow, rhythmic, copulative sucking of stiff boots sinking into and pulling out of the heavy mud. Ryan Middleton saw the two infantrymen emerge from the dank, gray fog. They plodded mechanically along, stiff with cold, yet slumped from exhaustion. They were young men with ancient faces and ancient bodies. They walked with rifles in the down position to keep the barrels from rusting.

With a combined sense of objective curiosity and compassion, Ryan continued to watch them. It was the curiosity of a man who wondered just how damn much longer these men could take it without succumbing to battle fatigue – or had they already succumbed and were now merely automatons? – and the compassion of an officer for his men who have given and continued to give their all.

He saw Corporal James Witkowski, head down, reach out with one hand as if to push aside the almost palpable mist, then peer intently, shake his head, and lower it again.

Private First Class Hall Newsome, automatically walking in slow, matched cadence with Witkowski, slapped his mittened hands against his arms in the rough overcoat and pulled his head, like a wary turtle, deep inside the turned-up collar. Ryan knew he was undoubtedly cursing the sleet sliding off the back of his helmet and under his collar.

Like a spectator at a game where he knew the rules but didn't want to play, Ryan continued to watch. Witkowski raised his head at the same time that Ryan heard the grinding double-clutching of a jeep motor as it shifted into second gear. Witkowski must be hoping, as he himself was, Ryan thought, that it would turn onto this road instead of crossing it and heading for division headquarters. The men wanted a ride, even though they'd already walked three hundred of the five hundred yards from the front. They wanted a ride to the command post where a hot meal would be waiting; and Ryan wanted news, especially news about his replacement. He continued to watch as the jeep came alongside the men and slowed down to let them crawl aboard.

In less than three minutes, Marty Goldman, the company clerk, pulled the jeep up to the front of the building and stopped. With a minimum of energy, Witkowski and Newsome slid out and ambled toward the doorway. A nod from each sufficed for a salute. Ryan understood and nodded back.

After six hours on the line, Witkowski and Newsome slouched

toward the containers of hot food and coffee brought up by the cooks. Now some fifteen men, half the platoon, sat slumped cross-legged on the floor or stood braced against the wall.

Ryan waited until the two men had nearly finished eating. With a motion to Platoon Sergeant Karl Svaboda to join him, he walked over to where Witkowski and Newsome were sitting on a bedroll.

'How're things up there?' Ryan asked.

'Quiet, sir. Too damned quiet,' Witkowski said stoically.

'I don't like it, Karl.' Ryan shook his head. 'I don't like it at all. Not the quiet. Nor that German prisoner who couldn't wait to get his ass away from here. We should've questioned him more. Not sent him to the rear so quickly. Hell! Who back there cares what he has to say?'

There'd been no word about his replacement, and Ryan was particularly despondent. He was bitter and furious with the company commander, rear echelon, and all command-grade officers in general. He stalked to the field telephone and put a call through to company headquarters.

Lieutenant Ryan St. Julian Middleton stood just over six feet; his once lean and angular build had been slimmed to near gauntness by months of fighting and more recent days of desperate, annihilating battle in the Hîrtgen Forest. He had the features of a man who took his responsibility as platoon leader with deadly seriousness. His eyes were the eyes of a man who had watched men die quickly from having half their heads shot away, their stomachs ripped open, the lower half of their bodies shattered, or their entire bodies blown sky-high in uncountable fragments of bone and muscle and organs. He'd also watched men die slowly, agonizingly, from insidious mortal wounds that, rather than killing instantly, taunted with painful throbbings the hope that they might live.

'Things are real quiet, Captain,' Ryan said to the voice on the other end of the phone. He waited for another question. 'Several just came in. Report no action.' Another pause. 'No, sir, no noise, no nothing. I don't like it.' He zipped and unzipped his jacket while he listened to the authoritative growlings. 'I understand, sir. No reconnaissance because of the fog.' He hung up the phone and nodded to the private who was silently offering to fill Ryan's mess plate with food.

Sergeant Svaboda got up from the bedroll where he'd been talking with Witkowski and Newsome. He refilled his canteen with coffee, and walked over to Marty Goldman, the clerk. 'What's up back at regiment?'

'Same old scam. Rear echelon living like kings.' He looked over at Ryan. 'Brought up the mail, sir.'

'Pass it out here and give the rest to Svaboda. We're going to check the line when I finish eating. Thought you might bring a passenger, too.'

'Sorry, Lieutenant, nothing green hanging around back there.'

Having been promoted to first lieutenant and company executive officer after the action at Hîrtgen Forest, Ryan had been waiting none too patiently for five days for his replacement.

At times like these he wondered what the hell he was doing on the front line. As manager of one of his family's South Carolina farm implement plants – now manufacturing war materials – he could have been given a permanent deferment. Instead he had chosen to enlist; and with his degree from Yale, he went immediately into OCS. He knew why he'd made that choice. With the home base in Camden, South Carolina, his family had vast land and industrial holdings throughout the South. The first Middletons to come to South Carolina in the seventeenth century had begun the family wealth with indigo and rice plantations on the coast; later generations gradually moved inward with cotton and tobacco. When it became apparent that South Carolina's future lay in diversifying – combining industry with agriculture, textiles, and machine factories – the Middletons diversified their own investments. A Middleton was a founding member of the St. Cecilia Society in Charleston; another, an original sponsor of the Dock Street Theatre there, the oldest in the United States.

More importantly, at least one Middleton had fought in every war since the early skirmishes with the Indians. Thus, instilled in Ryan from childhood had been the belief that the greater the wealth, the greater the responsibility to the community and to the nation. He had no choice but to volunteer.

Nothing green. The words of Marty Goldman invited memories of himself as a green second lieutenant having to lead his platoon of equally untried, un-shot-at, and unbloodied men onto the beach at Normandy. All he'd had to count on was Sergeant Svaboda with his instinctive combat knowledge of how to keep thirty-nine men following orders instead of freezing up while trying to cross a beach under constant artillery fire.

ii

Ryan huddled with his platoon on the landing craft headed toward the area designated Omaha Beach on the Normandy coast. Behind him someone said, 'Forty-two minutes to go.' That meant the first assault wave – due to go in at H hour 0630 – was getting ready to land and, it was to be hoped, would be securing the beach. Ryan's platoon was in the second assault wave, due to land at 0700.

They were surrounded by a deafening cacophony from large guns on destroyers, smaller guns on support craft, rocket launchers, exploding shells, rockets, and distant bombing. But although the noise blasted their eardrums and the concussion rattled their helmets against their heads, it was a comfort to know that so far most of the noise was theirs.

The landing craft moved steadily forward, close enough for Ryan to see the beach, the dunes and cliffs, and the boats of the first assault wave slowing down.

Behind him Sergeant Svaboda grunted, and Ryan found himself swallowing hard. In spite of the chill wind and the cold, leaden morning hour, he was sweating with fear. Fear of facing Germans and of leading a patrol for the first time. To add to his anxiety and discomfort, he was humiliatingly afraid of Karl Svaboda. During their training in England, all other sergeants looked up to Svaboda, waited for him to speak, tried to imitate his way with officers and men, and failed. Svaboda's attitude toward Ryan had been one of barely tolerating this puppy who had no more business leading a platoon than one of the girls at Mabel's whorehouse in Texas.

Ryan wanted to hate Svaboda for the obsequious manner in which the sergeant said 'sir' to his face and then didn't try too hard to hide his disparaging remarks behind Ryan's back. But Ryan couldn't. He respected him. He knew what Svaboda was thinking now; he could put it into words: 'Here we go again. Babying through a green lieutenant. Same as with that other one in Sicily.'

Nearing shore, the waves became more violent with the rising tide. More men were seasick. Another upheaval as the craft hit a trough, the huge wave slapped over the side, and Ryan feared the boat would be swamped.

While steadying himself as the boat lurched and rode with the waves, Ryan was gripped again with the fear that he couldn't carry out his responsibilities of getting his men off the boat and through each objective; objectives he had memorized until he knew them as well as he knew two times two equals four: onto the beach, keep the platoon in order, across the beach, off it immediately, engage the enemy, and move inland toward St. Laurent sur Mer.

It was 0650. The men in the first assault wave had landed. Suddenly the air around them exploded in a volcanic inferno. From concrete fortifications, machine gun emplacements, and sniper nests on the far embankment came a barrage of heavy artillery, mortar, machine-gun, and rifle fire that swept the shoreline. Beach and water alike were showered with flying metal and explosives. Hundreds of small geysers appeared as shells hit the water.

Ryan watched the men in the boat just ahead of him descend the ramp in a crisscross of machine-gun fire, crumple and flop into the water, and float toward shore with the tide.

With the incoming tide, the water was getting deeper, but the boats had already stopped. If they moved ahead in the surf, they would encounter treacherous, many-armed, steel 'hedgehogs,' tank traps, and concrete buffers entangled and connected with steel wire.

Ryan's men were now getting ready to debark as soon as the ramp went down. Each one self-consciously eased the pack on his back. Already the water was waist-deep. Amid the tumult, the men were strangely quiet, so quiet they all jumped when Sergeant Svaboda's voice boomed out, 'Packs off! Now! Get the ammo. To hell with the packs.'

The men looked stunned at the order.

'Dammit! Can't you hear? Packs off!'

Ryan immediately saw the reason for the command. He was watching men drown as the ninety-pound packs pulled them under water. He sweated with fury at himself. Damn! Why the hell hadn't he thought of that? Why did Svaboda have to give the order? He, Ryan Middleton, wasn't fit to be leading men.

The ramp went down. Ryan moved ahead to walk off first.

'Middleton!' Svaboda yelled. 'You dumb-ass second lieutenant. Get in the middle! You wanna make it to the beach?'

Now shaking all over at his stupidity, Ryan remembered that Germans shot officers first, and he cursed himself again.

He was off and in the water. Men weak from seasickness slid down the ramp, many to go under and drown. One after another, others fell off, hit by machine-gun fire. All around him in the inexorably oncoming surf were wounded and dying. His body was washed by the bloodstained water.

Ryan stepped into a hole and went under. He came up swallowing the befouled water, and a moment later threw it back up. He clung desperately to the exposed arms of a hedgehog and breathed rapidly through his mouth to clear his lungs.

The men still able to struggle toward shore were catching hell from the continuous barrage of mortar fire. Worse was the bombardment of noisy confusion, screams, sounds of the dying. One of Ryan's own men was hit as he scrambled in the shallower water covering the rocky shingle of the beach. Ryan veered left to reach him.

'Lieutenant!' Svaboda ordered. 'Get your men on the beach. Leave him. He's dead.'

But we don't leave our dead, Ryan thought over and over. We don't leave our dead behind.

Somehow Ryan reached the beach and collapsed. Tears, sweat, and foul water ran down his face. He thought mechanically of the objectives: keep the platoon in order, get across and off the beach immediately. But they couldn't move. They were pinned down by as effective a mesh of fire as the barbed wire netting eighteen inches over their heads during training. His men were stretched out over several yards in random disorder. He had to get them together and over the dunes to Vierville. He couldn't think what to do. His muscles had frozen with fear when he first fell on this spot. Now they had gone limp and flaccid, too weak to control. He couldn't move or call out orders. He realized without embarrassment he'd been unable to control something else. His trousers were wet with more than saltwater.

When he looked to his left, he clamped his teeth on his knuckles and drew blood. Sergeant Svaboda lay on the sand, a dark red pool spreading under his body.

'What do we do, sir?' It was Sergeant Wilson lying a few feet away. 'We're dying out here.'

Dammit! Dammit to hell, Ryan thought. It's my show now, all mine.

And suddenly he was alone. Totally and completely alone. It was his move, and he had to make it now. His men had not shifted. They were as frozen or limp with fear as he'd been. They lay immobile in awkward positions, like toy soldiers who'd fallen in the last pose they assumed before their batteries ran down.

Still under heavy fire, Ryan crawled from man to man. He kicked, prodded, yelled, and swore at them. 'Get to the dunes! Get to the dunes! The dunes will give you cover. You're alive, Goddammit! Only the dead stay here.'

Once he had them crawling on their bellies, he went back, picked up Sergeant Svaboda under the arms, dragged him to the dunes, and called for the medics. Svaboda'd been hit in the leg, but the medic assured Ryan the brawny Czech would be all right.

Svaboda, trying unsuccessfully to hide the pain, opened his eyes and looked up at Ryan. 'Thanks, Lieutenant. But a damn stupid thing to do, you bastard.' Breathing heavily, he added, 'On your own now.'

Thank God he's all right, Ryan thought. Walking away, he heard Svaboda say to the medic, 'Did damn good job getting them off the beach.'

I feel good, Ryan thought. There would be weeks, many months, ahead of brutal fighting, but he felt good. He'd become a leader. From then on he could do it. He'd lost twelve men – killed and wounded coming in and on the beach, and he was still afraid. He always would be. The voice of Sergeant Svaboda echoed in his ears, 'Not to be afraid is to be dead.'

Every day following brought new terrors, new tests of his leadership, but he learned. He learned about fighting, about protecting his men, and about himself.

In September, Svaboda rejoined the platoon on their march toward the Siegfried Line. Never had Ryan been so glad to see anyone in his life. Svaboda had been a unique mentor, nothing like his instructors at OCS. The sergeant was a pragmatist; the others, theoreticians. The seemingly meaningless drilling acquired meaning under Svaboda. Ryan learned the importance of automatic responses to an order, the necessity for a clean rifle and dry socks, and the obligatory caring for the comfort of one's men before seeing to himself.

iii

Ryan looked at his tray of food: green beans, mashed potatoes, gravy with congealed lumps of fat, a hunk of army bread, something passing for meat loaf, and fruit cocktail, the army's favorite dessert. It had all run together on the tin plate, but that didn't really matter. It all tasted alike anyway. At least it beat the hell out of K rations because it was hot. Sort of. He punched three beans with his fork, knocking the gravy onto his stained pants. He stared at the greasy new spot and then shrugged his shoulders. What the hell!

Low humming conversation and an occasional grunt were all the sounds that intruded into Ryan's thoughts. He looked at the six new replacements sent up that morning and then at the veterans. Out of the fifteen men in the room, only five remained from the original platoon of thirty-nine that had gone ashore six months earlier: himself, Sergeant Svaboda, Corporal Witkowski, Private First Class Newsome, and Private First Class Collins. Even Marty Goldman, the company clerk, hadn't landed on Normandy. The original clerk was killed outside Isigny when his jeep was hit with an eighty-eight.

Four of the men who'd already eaten were preparing to go up on the line to relieve a like number. Ryan hollered to them, 'The weather's wet and cold. Keep your pieces dry. You might need them yet.' He had the feeling of a seasoned fighter that things were too quiet. Not even a mortar shell in three days; and like an old dog, he kept his ears up.

Once he'd finished eating, Ryan got up slowly and reached for his M1. He'd long since discarded his carbine for the M1. He shoved his arms into the sleeves of the heavy enlisted man's infantry overcoat and then sat down to tug the rubber galoshes over his boots. He'd heard that rear echelon had shoe packs, but none had made its way up to the front. The galoshes picked up five pounds of mud with each step and left footprints like those of a primeval monster, but at least they kept the boots dry and helped ward off trench foot.

Ryan called to Svaboda, 'Ready? Let's go see how things look.' He watched the sergeant stick the letters for the men at the front inside his blouse, and he touched the three in his pocket that he was keeping to savor later.

Svaboda picked up his rifle and followed Ryan into the biting air and frozen mist. 'I don't like it one damn bit, Lieutenant.'

'What? The weather?'

'That too. Too damn cold. I meant what's going on. Or not going on. That German prisoner who surrendered. He knew something. You heard him. Build-up of huge tanks and artillery. And troops. He was too damned anxious to get to the rear.'

'I know.' Ryan nodded inside the pulled-up collar and lapels of his coat. 'I asked battalion what they made of Jerry's statement. Said they passed the info on with the prisoner, but no one at regiment and division seemed to take him seriously.'

During this discussion, the two had been walking along the road. They now veered off to the left, entered the woods, and started up a wooded incline.

Svaboda checked a landmark, nodded his head, and continued moving straight ahead. 'It's just too damned quiet. Want to stay on the line tonight? Put the whole platoon out?'

'Too cold, Karl. Let half come in and sleep.'

Once past the woods and on the downward slope of the hill, where the first platoon was dug in, the two men moved from foxhole to foxhole. The brief conversations were limited to the weather, the terrain, and distance – fifty yards – between holes.

'Dammit, Lieutenant,' Svaboda swore, 'we couldn't stop a boy scout troop. I could drive a truck up this hill without getting shot. I'll bet Jerry patrols come through every night. Hell, they could sneak past in the daytime in this fog. We need to double the line.'

Ryan made no acknowledgment of these suggestions but merely asked, 'Did you pass out all the mail?'

'Yeah,' Svaboda answered in a cold voice.

With two privates from the line, Ryan and Svaboda returned to the command post for bazookas, grenades, and more ammunition for

BAR and a machine-gun section which the privates would take back to the front. When the men left with the first load, the command post was deserted except for Ryan and the sergeant.

Some of the men had gone to the café next door to drink what liquor the proprietor had managed to hide from the German invaders. The café larders were empty, but the owner's wife was famous for being able to take Army rations and turn them into something worth sitting down to the table for. What she could do with dried eggs and a few spices was beyond believing. Every hour or hour and a half, three of the men would get up, go behind the café, and shoot off a mortar round just to keep the Germans honest.

The rest of the platoon were in the houses across the street, sleeping or just keeping warm. From one of them came the haunting sounds of 'Story of a Starry Night' being expertly played on a piano. Ryan began thinking about the time he heard the song being played by Charlie Spivak at a dance – the Camellia Debutante Ball back home in Columbia. He took out the three letters from his wife, Janet, and began to read the first one. God, how he missed her!

Janet. Pert, vivacious, petite, spoiled, spontaneous, independent, capricious Janet. Pretty as a kitten with her teasing blue eyes and her blond hair in a soft, shoulder-length pageboy.

Ryan closed his eyes and willed Janet's face to appear. He couldn't believe it. Loving her as much as he did, he couldn't believe that he was forgetting how she looked. Day by day, he was finding it harder and harder to conjure up her face, to bring it in out of the fog. To bring each feature clearly into view. It was like trying to bring a person into proper focus with binoculars. All hazy and blurred. Finally the face in his memory began to clear. First the eyes. Always the eyes first. Then the smile. And finally all of her face and figure.

Strange, too, which memory always appeared. Not the last night they were together. Or their wedding night. Or the afternoon they made love among the sand dunes. But the night he met her.

iv

Ryan arrived late at the Camellia Ball in spite of driving from Camden to Columbia at eighty miles an hour in his '32 Cord convertible. Others might be proud of their LaSalles or even Rolls and Dusenbergs, but nothing could touch his classic beauty with its cream-colored body, white leather upholstery, and its six external superchargers alongside the flat-topped hood, the Cord's unique signature.

He spun into the circular driveway of the country club, handed the keys to the white-coated Negro parking attendant, and sauntered into the Corinthian-pillared building. As one of South Carolina's most eligible bachelors, he'd attended too many of these affairs to be in any hurry. Most bored him, but he'd been reared as a Southern gentleman, duty-bound to fulfill certain social obligations. As he'd expected, the wide center hall and all the rooms he could see into were filled with thousands of camellias in every shade of pink from ones with the merest tinge of pale, delicate color to the deepest rose as well as red, white, and variegated. Mammoth bouquets filled niches, and sat three and four to a table; single blooms with their waxy green leaves rested at regularly spaced intervals on pink ribbons down the center of the dining room tables, where supper would be served at midnight; garlands of them festooned windows, doorways, and arches.

The St. Cecilia Ball in Charleston might be more exclusive, limited as it was to families of St. Cecilia Society members, but the Camellia Ball was the most festive and opulent. Young women in the two Carolinas waited breathlessly for one of the thirty bids to it.

The presentation of the debutantes had already begun, and Ryan was preparing his mind to tune out the sickening strains of 'A Pretty Girl Is Like a Melody.' Instead, he found himself listening to a particularly fine arrangement of 'Deep Purple.'

Well, I'll be damned, Ryan thought. A real, honest-to-goodness band. Not one of the locals.

He stepped farther inside the ballroom to listen to the music if not watch the fathers proudly escorting their daughters through the camellia-covered, latticed archway.

Then, like an almost unseen flash of heat lightning, something attracted his attention. Immediately it was gone. But he had seen it – a pale pink gown among all the white ones. Bouffant white gowns and bouquets of white camellias were *de rigueur* for the debutantes, so he thought perhaps he had seen a sister or other non-debutante guest. No, she appeared again, in pale pink and carrying a bouquet of pink perfections. Then and there, intrigued by someone who dared to flout tradition, he determined to meet her.

That Janet's dance card was filled for the evening was of no importance. He simply whirled her away from each of her prospective partners, and the devil-may-care glint in her eyes told him she was delighted with his high-handed behavior. While they danced to Charlie Spivak's band playing 'The Story of a Starry Night,' Ryan knew he'd fallen in love.

Although Janet's family, the Van Kamerons, had a winter home in Aiken, as well as a summer place on the Hudson in upper New York, he had never met her before. Janet had spent most of each year at a private school in New England. Before the evening was over, Ryan learned also that her life revolved around only two major interests – her thoroughbred jumpers and her champion dogs. Ryan, however, had already determined that he would become a third, and preferably the most important interest for her.

At times, Janet's willful temperament infuriated him; at others, it amused him. In the spring she was one of several debutantes asked to be hostesses during the garden tours of historical homes. As usual, she had been riding all morning and arrived breathless and late.

'What's that smell, Janet?' the senior hostess asked her.

'I don't know – unless . . .' Janet lifted the crinoline skirts under her antebellum dress. Underneath she wore riding pants and boots. The woman was even more shocked when Janet said she'd forgotten to bring underwear and shoes with her.

'But the smell!' the woman repeated.

'Only horse dung,' Janet giggled. 'Maybe the guests will think they've stepped in something.'

Ryan, standing to one side, could barely control his laughter until the other hostess left. 'Forgot your dainties? Am I to assume . . .'

'You're not to assume a damn thing, Ryan Middleton.'

What Ryan found intriguing about Janet was that she carried off her ridiculous actions with an insouciance that made them seem less outrageous than appealing, more clever than scandalous.

The independent spirit that first attracted Ryan to Janet kept him frustrated for months. Yes, she loved him; but no, she was not ready to marry. An only child, she was spoiled and used to getting her way, not so much that she demanded it as she accepted it as due her. She never told Ryan that he must understand she expected him to abide by her decisions. She was not so ingenuous as to make that fatal error. It was merely implicit in her every word and action. Too much in love to argue, he could only wait – if none too patiently – until she wanted to be married.

When America went to war in December, 1941, Ryan agreed to take a deferment because of his position with the family company. But he didn't like it. Surrounded daily by news of how badly the war was going in the Pacific and in Africa, with every able-bodied young man going into service, he felt more and more like a slacker – worse, a pariah. In December of 1942, he applied for and was accepted for OCS. Janet said she was proud of him and she'd wait for him, but made no mention of marrying him.

OCS did more than train Ryan to be an officer. It determined him to take a stronger stand with Janet. No more abiding by her decisions. Some choices would be his. She'd marry him when he finished OCS, or she could forget about him.

In April, 1943, they were married at Trinity Episcopal Church in Columbia. Ostensibly, the Van Kamerons chose Trinity rather than St. Thaddeus in Aiken for their daughter's wedding in order to facilitate travel for guests coming from various parts of the state. Also Vice-President Henry Wallace and Senators Burnett Rhett Maybank and Ellison Smith would be coming directly by train from Washington. Governor Olin D. Johnson and Lieutenant Governor Ransome J. Williams were, of course, already in Columbia.

Ryan knew full well, however, the real reason for their choosing Trinity. All important state and social religious functions were held there regardless of which denomination the participants belonged to. After St. Michaels and St. Phillips in Charleston, the magnificent, dark pink sandstone, antebellum Trinity was *the* church in the state.

In many ways the wedding seemed more of a uniting of two dynasties than a simple marriage between two people in love. It was a merging of the Middleton land and industries with the banking and Wall Street interests of the Van Kamerons.

From the time he stood waiting in the vestry with his best man and listened to the doors on the enclosed pews being unlatched and latched until he walked with Janet to the strains of the recessional, Ryan felt he was participating in a carefully choreographed production rather than a solemn religious sacrament. Janet's fourteen bridesmaids stood posed in front of the groomsmen like so many carefully trained models. Nor was a single priest sufficient to assure they were properly married. The service was conducted by Bishop John Gravatt, assisted by the parish priest from St. Thaddeus and the rector of Trinity.

The only jarring note – if in truth it could be so described – was that not all the groomsmen were in striped trousers and cutaways. It had taken Ryan several hours, over as many days, to explain to Janet that his friends in the service were required to wear their uniforms at all times. She was especially upset that one of the men was not an officer, but a seaman who'd be in Navy bell-bottoms. And why couldn't she and Ryan march out under a canopy of swords?

'Sabers, darling, not swords,' he said. 'Anyway, it's impossible because neither I nor any of my friends owns a saber.'

It wasn't fair, she pouted. It was her one and only wedding and should be perfect. She looked at her engagement ring, a four-carat solitaire, and sighed, 'Just as I've always dreamed about it.'

'I'm sorry,' Ryan said, unmoved by her petulance. 'I thought our being married was the important thing.'

'It is . . . but — ' and then she smiled her beguiling smile, and he had to forgive her for her childishly extravagant ideas.

When Janet finally accepted the situation, her acquiescence implied that it was her wish to combine uniforms and formal dress, to add a patriotic flavor to the ceremony. The bridesmaids, in white, carried bouquets of red, white, and blue-dyed carnations.

A wedding luncheon at a private club for family and one hundred and fifty of the more important guests followed the formal, high-noon wedding. In the evening, the Van Kamerons hosted a gala reception at their estate in Aiken.

In contrast to the rigid decorum of the wedding day, the four-day honeymoon at the Middletons' eighteen-room summer home on a private island off the Carolina coast was idyllic. They swam, sunbathed, made love among the dunes, and Janet appeared to be completely happy as Ryan's wife.

Immediately that Ryan's leave was up and he had to return to Fort Benning, however, the situation changed. Janet didn't think she could join him. It was the same each time he was transferred – from Fort Ord to Camp Carson to Camp Swift. She always had some reason to stay in Aiken: jumping trials, steeplechases, mare foaling, champion dogs having litters.

Damn the war! he thought. Damn what it's doing to marriage, keeping a man away from his wife for months at a time.

He wanted Janet with him. He needed her.

Yet, when he managed to get leave, she was as glad to see him and was as ardent a lover as he could desire. He finally had to accept that Janet, with her mercurial moods, was an enigma he might never understand. And more importantly, horses and dogs would always be his rivals.

His last leave before going overseas in January, 1944, was a memory he'd always cherish. He and Janet had three days completely alone on the island.

Although it was cold, foggy, and damp rather than warm and sunny as on their honeymoon, it was a perfect three days. In slacks and heavy sweaters they walked the beach with arms around each other. With two of Janet's dogs they raced along the sand or played toss and catch. With darkness coming early, they ate by candlelight and then curled up on the fur rug before a blazing fire. They laughed when they had to postpone making love until Ryan went out and brought in more logs. There was the joy of seeking each other's warm body right after crawling between cold sheets when they finally went to bed.

They laughed again over Janet's attempt to cook a 'real meal' that was a complete fiasco, and they ended up eating the last of the hot dogs.

While Ryan had no desire to possess Janet in the sense that one possesses precious objects, he'd never felt, until those three days, that she belonged to him in the way two people deeply in love belong to each other. When he boarded the train for Fort Dix, New Jersey, to go overseas, he at long last felt they were truly married, were truly one.

V

Ryan finished the third letter from Janet. Except for a few remarks about how furious everyone was about having to cope with shortages and rationing, and how she was learning to live, albeit unhappily, with shoe stamps and rayon stockings, she wrote copiously about the latest horse show, the ribbons her jumpers won, and the recent litter from her champion poodles. A P.S. on the second letter said jubilantly that her father had found a black market source for meat and extra shoe ration stamps. She'd bought six pairs of the new open-toed platform style – at different stores, of course – and they were darling.

In the third letter she wrote that there was to be a hunt ball, and she hoped Ryan wouldn't mind if she attended with one of his best friends. First, Ryan got angry and then he became resigned. No one back home would understand; they could never understand. They and he lived in two different worlds.

Beside him were Christmas packages from Janet and his family. The army might be delinquent about getting winter clothes up to the front, but it seldom failed to deliver the mail. Ryan started to open the packages. No, he'd wait. If there had been a threat of action or orders to move, he'd have opened them to save carrying them. But with his replacement sure to come tomorrow or the next day, he'd take them to the rear and wait for Christmas morning. All his life he'd enjoyed the days of anticipation. Let others tear packages open and not take time to look at each gift; he'd always savored the waiting, the wondering, and then the opening slowly and enjoying each one. He slipped the letters from home under the string around one package.

Feeling a sense of frustration and inexplicable anxiety. Ryan decided to check the line one more time. Sergeant Svaboda was getting ready to return and spend the night there, so Ryan accompanied him. For more than an hour he walked up and down the line, talking to the men, reassuring them with the news they should be in Luxemburg City for Christmas.

Back at the post, Ryan could not sleep. One irritating worry after another plagued him. Why the hell hadn't his replacement been sent up to relieve him? He fretted over Janet's statement that she was going to the hunt ball with Dwight, a notorious womanizer of long standing.

The wet snow had seeped through Ryan's boots when he walked the line, and his stockings were still wet and cold. He could get trench foot if he weren't careful. He got up to put on dry socks. Why the hell hadn't they gotten the shoe packs they'd been promised? He thought about Janet's new open-toed shoes and the same pair of wet boots he'd been wearing for months. He lay back down and wrapped the sleeping bag around himself.

He still couldn't get to sleep. He was frightened. In fact, he was scared to death. Like any battle-wise soldier, he'd been scared since the first minute he landed on Normandy.

Then he thought about the men curled up around him or sleeping across the street. They were exhausted, and it was bitterly cold outside. Maybe he should have doubled the line as Svaboda suggested, but these men needed this reprieve. He thought about how he'd brought his men across France and Belgium, the damned hedgerows with Germans behind every one, the door-to-door fighting in the towns, and the men he'd lost.

But he was a good officer; he knew he led his men well. Through the past months he'd learned that his early, carefree years hadn't been wasted ones. His peacetime pursuits, surprisingly, had helped make him a good officer. From polo he'd acquired quick reflexes and instant response to a situation. From hunting, keen eyesight and hearing, an ability to distinguish between slight differences in sounds, an alertness to danger, and an acute sense of direction. Being an executive, he'd been used to giving orders in a way that assumed they'd be followed, and yet he kept the allegiance of the men under him.

Finally, about five in the morning, Ryan walked outside. The atmosphere seemed to be filled with an ominous threat in spite of assurances from headquarters that there was no unusual activity on the German side. He was nagged by fears that all was not right. His men depended on him. Time and again his instincts had saved them when the wrong decision would have meant their deaths.

Behind the café, the mortar sat momentarily abandoned for the warmth and liquor inside. Across the street, the houses were quiet.

In the now clear, cold air, the stars were brilliant against the black sky.

Suddenly something struck Ryan as strange and different. Then he realized there were lights along the German lines. He shook his head in amazement.

The next moment the lights became brighter, brilliant enough to light up the entire area between the line and where he stood.

'What the hell's going on!' he screamed.

For a millisecond the unearthly, blinding glow hovered over the deathly stillness. Then came the sound: it was as if the world were being torn apart by one cataclysmic explosion.

CHAPTER THREE

A few minutes before seven, when Alys came down to start the fire in the huge wood stove, she'd seen the lamps already lighted in the dining room and several officers huddled together around one table. Knowing coffee would be their first request, she'd gone right to the kitchen. Even as she lifted the lid of the fire box and lit the kindling laid the night before, she heard Captain Herlihy on the field telephone. Without catching all of his words, she was immediately aware of the concern and urgency in his voice. Something was wrong. Impatient as she was to hear the latest news, she knew she'd learn when she served them; but she had a discordant, ominous sense of foreboding.

While waiting for the stove to heat up, she measured coffee and water. How good it was to have real coffee again! For so long there had been none. Placing her palm a few inches above the stove, Alys instinctively knew when the temperature was right. Almost as soon as she put the pot on, she began to smell the delicious aroma.

In another few minutes, she carried the coffee and hot croissants into the dining room.

'Thank you, Alys.' Colonel Applegate held his cup up for her to fill. Then he looked over to Captain Herlihy, who was replacing the field telephone, and raised his eyebrows questioningly.

Captain Herlihy shook his head. 'No one at headquarters seems to know anything for sure.'

'Except that the Germans might – or might not – have counter-attacked and broken through someplace along the line. Hell! What're we supposed to do? Wait here for them to march up to the door?'

As if in answer the phone jangled again, and Colonel Applegate almost knocked his coffee over in his eagerness to answer it. The other officers looked up from the confusion of maps spread out over a nearby table and from the lists of supplies they'd been checking. All were trying to keep from revealing the fearful expectancy gnawing at their stomachs.

It continued the same way all morning, nothing but confusion and disturbing reports whenever they could make contact with Intelligence. First the calls elicited the information that something was going on, but no one knew what. Next came word that it was all a rumor; the front lines were still quiet. This was soon contradicted by information that a small German force had started a minor skirmish, but it had been contained.

'There's no such thing as a minor skirmish with the Germans,' Colonel Applegate said, pacing the floor. 'God damn the stupidity of some – some people.'

The phone rang again. Captain Herlihy listened for a moment and then handed it to the colonel. 'Wants to speak to you, sir.'

After Colonel Applegate took the phone, he automatically stiffened in response to the voice on the other end.

'General Carstairs,' Captain Herlihy whispered to the group. Each man was frozen in the position he'd been in when the phone rang. Alys, on her way to the kitchen, turned and waited by the door.

'Yes, sir,' Colonel Applegate said, 'we wait here until there's something more definite.' He started to slam the phone into its case, but got himself under control and replaced it carefully. He saw the men watching him anxiously, waiting for him to relay the word from headquarters.

'Well?' Captain Turner asked.

'Still nothing. Nothing specific, that is. The Germans have definitely begun a strong counterattack, but whether they've broken through at the Losheim Gap, the Schnee Eiffel, or across the Our River has not yet been determined. So – Goddammit – we wait!' He slammed his fist on the table.

Earlier, Lieutenant Colonel Morgan had left the inn to touch base with battalion, nearer the front lines, and word from him was a frightening but succinct 'All hell is breaking loose somewhere along the front.' More ominous still was word that phone wires between battalion headquarters and company command posts at the front had been destroyed, but scouts had already gone up to assess the situation.

'So,' Colonel Applegate stormed, 'from all we can get from one direction it's highly likely there's a real battle raging someplace – God knows where – and from the other direction, word to stand pat and wait.' He began pacing the floor. 'Those are my men up there. And I don't know which ones to worry about more. If the Germans have broken through, can the green troops I just sent up hold?'

'You've got a veteran regiment up there, too, sir,' Captain Turner tried to reassure him.

'Yes – still exhausted from the fighting in the Hîrtgen Forest. Do they have the energy left to go immediately back into battle? Herlihy' – he turned to the captain – 'ring up battalion again. Maybe they have some recent news.' He relit the stub of his cigar while he waited. Alys, still standing by the door, saw the bewildered expression appear on the captain's face.

'Sorry sir,' Herlihy said, 'the line to First Battalion is dead.'

Within twenty-four hours the worst fears were confirmed: what general headquarters had identified as a minor skirmish was recognized as a major battle all along the front. From the Schnee Eiffel in the North to the Our River in the South, the Germans had broken through at the most vulnerable points. They were marching across northeast Belgium and Luxemburg, and it seemed as if no one could stop them.

Several of the officers left the inn to assume new command positions. While she served those that remained, Alys listened and tried to keep her hands from trembling. Clervaux, in Luxemburg, had been taken after bitter fighting, and Ste. Monique was only a few kilometers from the road that ran between Clervaux and Bastogne, obviously a major objective for the Germans. Once Bastogne was taken, the Germans could make a clean sweep through southern Belgium to France.

No matter what she was doing or how she kept herself occupied, Alys thought of nothing but what it had been like – and might be again – when the Germans first attacked Belgium and then later when the Allies were liberating the country, kilometer by kilometer, town by town. Only this time, the shelling, the destruction, the pain, the death would be worse. The guttural throating of Focker bombers; the high, eerie, screaming whistle followed by the brief but interminable waiting for the bomb to hit and explode. Or the sudden explosion from a silent mortar shell that sends out no warning signal. The Germans would be seeking revenge, while gloating over being once again masters of the situation. The thought of their marching in the streets and demanding total and immediate obedience to their commands was unbearable. And even that dread was based on the premise that there would be anything of Ste. Monique still standing and any of the villagers still alive.

In her mind Alys relived the horror of the earlier bombings and shellings. For countless days and nights they had lived like troglodytes in the dank cellar. They had pallets for beds, an old rusted trash burner for heating and cooking when her father dared go up and search for whatever he could find that would burn. Hours without water when he dared not go up to refill the bottles.

And then the night the inn was hit. Alys and her parents had reached for each other and clung together while everything around them shuddered and collapsed as the earth ripped apart. One spasm followed another, and buildings turned into rubble. Gone from the inn were the bar and the rooms above it. Gone, too, was her bedroom. Although scarcely larger than the alcove formed by the bay window, with the window ledge for her bed, the room had been her own little hideaway. Gone with it her few treasures from childhood.

Would they have to endure such fearsome horror again? Could they live through it?

If there had been any hope in Ste. Monique that the Allies could get on the offensive and turn the Germans back before they pierced many miles into Belgium, that hope died by noon of December eighteenth.

The sounds of shelling to the east were no longer distant, muted rumblings beyond the farthest hills. They were now violent explosions that deafened and sent constant tremors of fear along the spine as well as aftershocks beneath the feet.

In midafternoon, Alys stood at the door of the inn and watched as ambulances roared by with the first casualties to reach Ste. Monique. Medical staffs and patients still alive after aid stations and field hospitals had been blown up were being evacuated as far to the rear as possible.

Closing the door, Alys went back to the kitchen and took off her apron. 'I'm going to the school, *Maman*. I think it's going to become a hospital again.'

She bent down and kissed Minette. 'Be good, precious, and help *Grand-maman*. I love you.'

'Love you, too. I be good.'

Alys got on her bicycle and rode as fast as she could toward the school. During the Allied advance, she and many other women in the village had volunteered their help when the school had been used as a temporary hospital, and their aid had been welcomed by the small, overworked medical staff. While she'd spent most of her time with such menial chores as carrying bedpans, bathing patients, and feeding those unable to feed themselves, she'd also learned to change dressings and insert intravenous tubes. From the number of ambulances she saw passing the inn, and still saw coming along the road, she knew her help would be needed.

Nearing the school, she slowed down and then watched, startled and curious, when the ambulances didn't stop but continued on through the village. If not the school, then where? A new fear smote her: maybe the Germans were too close for even Ste. Monique to be far enough in the rear. At least she could follow them for a way and perhaps learn where they were headed.

Soon after, she cycled through the square where three days earlier she'd ridden with all her thoughts on the coming Christmas party and had waved gaily to the baker and the greengrocer. No one had mentioned the party since the morning of December sixteenth.

Past the square, Alys followed the ambulances along the road between the still snow-topped stumps of poplars. She remembered how the leaves of those stately trees once rustled in the summer wind and how these same trees brightened the whole autumn landscape with their golden foliage.

The ambulances continued traveling ahead of her, and she finally saw their destination: the château of Countess Charbonne. Why there? she thought. Why so far from the village?

The answer was soon provided by the number of ambulances winding up the long approach to the château that stood atop a low hill above the valley road. The four-room school was far too small to handle the numbers of wounded being transported.

As she approached the château, Alys saw Countess Charbonne, standing now just outside the door and efficiently but graciously directing the medics where to take the wounded. With all her poise and disarming manner, she might have been welcoming guests to a winter fête. In her long, old-fashioned black dress, relieved by delicate white lace collar and cuffs, and with her mass of white hair piled softly atop her head, she looked like one of her own fragile Dresden figurines. But Alys knew her appearance belied the strong body beneath the silk gown and the determined will behind the clear blue eyes.

Alys parked her bicycle beside the front terrace and walked toward the door. She well knew what onerous tasks awaited her inside.

For the next several hours, Alys worked unceasingly alongside the small staff of doctors and medics. Every one of the twenty rooms in the château was either filled with wounded on pallets and gurney stretchers or being used as operating and postoperative rooms. She moved from emptying waste cans beside operating tables in the former drawing room to preparing surgical trays in the dining room and boiling instruments on the stove in the kitchen.

There was also a soup kettle simmering over one burner of the stove and a coffeepot on another. Occasionally, like the professionals and other volunteers, she stopped just long enough to gulp down a bowl of soup or half a cup of coffee.

Mid-afternoon on December nineteenth, one of the doctors finally ordered Alys to go home and sleep for at least eight hours. More wounded were coming in, but he insisted she'd be no good to them at all if she collapsed from exhaustion.

The main road was now crowded with jeeps, tanks, trucks, artillery, and cars going in both directions. All seemed unorganized, meaningless confusion. To avoid being run over, she had to ride on the verge, where cycling was much harder.

When she reached the village square, it was filled with people standing around in small groups. All looked distraught and were speaking in subdued voices. Numbed with fear, she listened to the latest news from the front.

The day before word had reached Trois Ponts, north of Ste. Monique, that the Germans were coming. In order to keep them from crossing the Amblève River and reaching the town, some of the defenders had blown up the bridge. Retaliation had been swift. Under orders from the German commander, civilians were dragged from homes near the river. Twenty-two men, women, and children were shot.

Murdered! Alys thought. Senselessly, cruelly murdered.

Fear and horror of what the coming days might hold for them if the Allies couldn't stop the Germans in their ruthless advance replaced her earlier exhaustion. Not waiting to hear any more about the war, she sped toward the inn.

With every meter she pedaled, she was haunted by visions of those helpless people in Trois Ponts. She tried to erase from her mind the Germans knocking on the doors, the women and children being forced out of kitchens, bedrooms, and parlors at gun point. Were the women preparing supper? Had children been put down for naps or were they playing by the kitchen stove? As if she were among them, Alys could hear the screams and the pitiful cries of the children who couldn't understand what was happening. She saw little girls carrying favorite dolls, little boys trying to be brave, and mothers pleading to have their children spared. All of them praying desperately that it was a macabre jest until – and even after – they saw the guns raised.

Wiping icy tears from her face, she increased her speed, as if by so doing she could outrun the tormenting picture of those innocent children. No act of defiance deserved such inhuman retribution. The Germans were mistaken if they thought they could massacre at will with impunity, that it would deter other Belgians from fighting force with force, resisting no matter the cost, and dying if necessary to check the German advance. Put fear in their hearts, yes, but also strengthen their will and determination to avenge those deaths. One thing was certain: the heroism displayed at Trois Ponts would not soon be forgotten.

More devastating news greeted her when she finally arrived at the inn. Most of the American forces in Ste. Monique were pulling out to reinforce positions to the east in hopes of making a successful stand and turning the Germans back. Only a single platoon would remain in the village, along with the medical staff at the château. Alys knew what that meant. The small unit would stay in the village; and the inn, three kilometers out in the countryside, would be left vulnerable, alone, and defenseless. If the Allies couldn't hold the Germans back, it would mean a return to the basement, and the days and nights of fear and deprivation. She wouldn't think about it. Most of all she wouldn't think about how much harder it would be on Minette. She, herself, would continue to help at the hospital as long as she could.

Arriving at the château the next day, Alys was immediately assigned to help prepare and carry the breakfast trays. This was something she could do almost automatically. As she moved from kitchen to bedside, she mourned silently. How different the rooms were now from the times she'd been in them as a guest. The priceless Aubusson and Oriental carpets had been shredded by rough German boots when the château had been commandeered. Countess Charbonne's antique furniture – mostly eighteenth-century English and French – had been broken up and used as firewood by the invaders. Count Charbonne's sabers and other war mementoes had been destroyed. Now, as she helped feed a blinded soldier in what had been the count's library, she remembered how proudly those mementoes had been displayed there.

After she returned the last tray to the kitchen, one of the doctors asked her to go into post-op, once the summer parlor, all cool blues and greens against white walls and always filled with a myriad of plants. She was simply to watch the patients for signs of changes in their condition and call if she needed help. Going from patient to patient, Alys felt a desperate inadequacy. Would she know if a change meant the man was recovering or whether he was suffering a dangerous relapse? According to their charts, all had fevers, some higher than others. Some of their dressings were oozing blood.

She was relieved when the doctor returned a few minutes later, carefully checked each patient, and told Alys she was doing a good – and very necessary – job.

'Most of these men, in spite of how they look, are doing fine,' he said. 'These three' – he pointed them out to Alys – 'are not doing so well. I'd like you to watch them more closely.'

Within the next hour there was a resurgence of ambulances coming up the long drive. Both pre-op and the operating rooms were filled. Soon after, two of the three most seriously wounded in post-op died. Alys's immediate reaction, as they were being wheeled out of the room, was gratitude that the beds were free for two of the men now being operated on. Moments later, the horror of that response attacked her. What had the war done to her that she should be glad for death even if it meant comfort, and maybe recovery, for two others? Even if the two who'd died had no hope of recovery.

First she began shaking all over; and when the sobs and then the tears came, she was completely unable to control them. She felt a hand on her shoulder and the calm voice of the doctor speaking to her.

'Go home. You've had enough.' He spoke assertively, albeit gently.

'No, no, I'll be all right in a minute. I'm all right now.' And she determined she would be.

'I insist. You've been here since six this morning, and I was coming in here anyway to tell you to leave. Things have eased up.'

Alys needed no more persuasion. She was not as tired from working as from an intense depression over the men's deaths that had her feeling completely debilitated.

Not until she'd had a steaming bowl of *pot au feu* did Alys think she could function normally again. She joined her mother at the kitchen table where they sorted through a pile of well-worn clothes. While Jolie Prévou picked out torn knitted garments to be unraveled for their yarn, Alys put aside dresses that could be mended or remade. She held up one pale blue wool that she'd been wearing since she first went to Liège. It was badly worn in many places, particularly the back of the skirt, now as thin as voile. At first she frowned and shook her head. Then she brightened up. There was enough good material remaining to make a dress for Minette.

While she was carefully opening the seams, Minette and her grandfather came into the kitchen, both bundled in heavy coats, scarves, and hats. Minette was struggling to get her mittens on the right hands.

'Here, let me,' Alys suggested.

'No! I do.'

'All right, you little minx,' Alys laughed, but she sighed a little, too. Minette was growing up.

'Where're you going?' Jolie asked, her voice filled with genuine alarm. 'Not beyond the inn yard, I trust.'

'A little farther,' Émile answered. 'We're going to find — '

'A twismas twee,' Minette interrupted gleefully.

'Oh no, Papa,' Alys cried in alarm. 'No! You're not taking her as far as the woods.'

'And why not?' he asked stubbornly.

'It's much too dangerous. The shelling and all.'

'*Fait rien!* There're no Germans within fifteen kilometers of here.'

'How do you know? And who knows when a shell might hit near here? No, it's not safe.'

Monsieur Prévou bridled. 'You think – you accuse me – of exposing my granddaughter to danger. *Sacré bleu!* What am I? A monster?'

'Want a twee!' Minette cried. She clung to her grandfather's leg.

'And you'll have your tree, precious,' Alys assured her. 'I think it's wonderful, Papa, that you want to get one for her. God knows we need something to cheer us up and to remind us it *is* Christmas. But – leave her here with me. Come, Minette, we'll look in the cellar. I think the box with the crèche I had as a little girl is still there. And all the beautiful ornaments. And the wooden jumping jack that moves his arms and legs when you pull a string.'

Minette looked at her grandfather and then nodded at her mother. She still hadn't managed to get the mittens on, and the long scarf around her head and shoulders was making her itch.

'All right, *ma petite*, you stay here,' Émile said. 'Grandpapa will bring you the most beautiful tree he can find.' He opened the door, letting in a blast of frigid air.

'I'll make hot chocolate while you're bringing up the boxes from the cellar,' Jolie said. Bless the officers, she thought. They had left a generous supply of powdered chocolate which needed only hot water.

A few minutes later, mother and daughter came up from the cellar. Minette was breathlessly managing to carry the small, dusty box with the crèche figurines, and Alys held the larger one containing the fragile glass and hand-carved wooden ornaments. After putting the boxes down, they carefully unwrapped each ornament or figure. Minette was enthralled with every one, but especially with the hand-painted wooden angels whose arms and wings moved, the little wooden lambs and donkeys whose heads nodded up and down as if bowing to the tiny porcelain babe in the manger. Gently, her eyes wide with wonder, Minette touched the spun glass threads decorating the fragile balls. To Alys, they looked like the spun sugar on cakes in Monsieur LeBrun's *pâtisserie* before the war.

'Now,' Alys said, 'isn't this more fun than taking a long walk in the cold? And tonight, if you take a nap before supper, you can help decorate the tree.'

Minette nodded and asked permission to hold the tiny babe from the crèche. While she cradled it in one palm, Jolie brought the hot chocolate.

Sometime later, Minette having been put down for a nap, the two women returned to sorting the clothes.

Without warning, the kitchen door was thrust open and Émile rushed into the room, stumbling and clutching for support as if drunk or hurt. Fear etched deep lines in his face. Before he could speak or answer the women's barrage of questions, two soldiers burst through the door, looking like something out of Alys's worst nightmares. Their faces had the look of men who hadn't slept in weeks, accentuated by scruffy beards and uniforms encrusted with mud and slime. The men could have been guards at the gates of hell.

CHAPTER FOUR

Between them, the two soldiers half carried, half dragged a third man. Alys and Jolie had instinctively drawn back in fear when they first came through the door. As bloodied and torn as their uniforms were, the men were unidentifiable as either American or German soldiers. Then, almost immediately it became apparent they were too severely wounded to be dangerous. Alys watched with tremulous anxiety as they laid the unconscious man on the floor and then slumped, exhausted, against the wall. Their eyes, however, remained alert, and one of them held tightly to his rifle. It was apparent they were trying to assess the situation before making any kind of move.

Émile had sat down at the table with a cup of coffee in his shaking hands.

'*Boche?*' Jolie asked him under her breath.

Alys looked over toward the soldiers to see what reaction that single word brought, but they had obviously not heard it.

Émile shook his head. Then in stuttered, barely audible French he said, 'At the edge of the woods. A jeep. Overturned.' He could hardly get the words out. 'Two in jeep. One lying in the snow.' He emptied his cup before continuing.

'I thought they were all dead.' The coffee had restored his equilibrium, and he spoke more coherently. 'So I thought if they're dead, there's nothing I can do. I'll get the tree and inform someone when I get back. Then one of them in the jeep moaned. I walked over. The other man was also coming around.

'One of them asked if there was a hospital near. I told them yes and to follow me to the inn. When, in spite of their wounds, they picked the third man up, I thought they were crazy. He was obviously dead, but they insisted not. All I wanted to do was get them on their way to the hospital.'

Alys looked at the man on the floor. He was barely breathing.

'They got this far,' Émile continued, 'and insisted the third one stay here until they could get to the hospital and send back for him.'

'That shouldn't take long, Papa,' Alys said. 'Why are you so upset?'

'No, no! We can't keep him here.' Émile got up from the table and walked over to the soldiers. He began gesturing furiously and demanding they leave. 'Never again in danger like before. Could have been executed.' His speech once more became hesitant, but he continued gesturing and pointing to the door.

Alys knew what fear prompted his emotional behavior. They'd lived for months under the threat of being shot each time they aided an escaped prisoner or a downed flyer. Yet they had never hesitated to hide one in the basement until the Underground could see him safely on his way. And she'd suffered pain and the worst kind of violation at the hands of the Germans to keep from having the SS informed.

These were Allies, too, who needed help. And the Americans still controlled Ste. Monique. Even as seriously wounded as the two soldiers were, one in the head and one in the shoulder, they could make it to the château and send an ambulance back here in less than an hour.

Seemingly in obedience to Émile's gesturing, the two men started toward the door but left the unconscious man lying on the floor. Émile stepped in front of them.

'Uniforms!' He glowered at them. 'I don't trust uniforms,' he said in English. 'What if he dies? Look, he's almost dead.' All eyes looked down at the unconscious man. 'Take him.' Émile began shouting. 'Take him with you.' He went over and opened the door.

At the same time, all of them saw the three jeeps speeding along the road toward them. The soldier with the head wound ran out and waved at it. The second man was right behind him.

The jeep slowed but made no move to stop. The captain seated next to the driver leaned out and yelled, 'Get the hell out of town! Germans coming.' He ordered the jeep to stop. 'Get aboard. Quick!'

'Wait! There's another.' The soldiers turned to reenter the kitchen. The three Prévous immediately went over to help them carry the third man out.

'Leave him,' the captain ordered. 'No room for someone who can't manage himself. German medics will take care of him.'

German medics! Alys thought. If the hospital were being abandoned by the Americans, that meant a general retreat from the village. If so, they would be completely abandoned to the Germans. All those wounded still at the château would become prisoners. Or be left to die if the Germans continued their advance to the west. She couldn't believe there would be no defense of Ste. Monique. The only hope for them here at the inn was for the Germans to march straight through to the next vital point. If not, there would be more shelling and fighting for them to suffer through. What then would be left of Ste. Monique? Or the inn? Or them?

'No!' The word barely penetrated Alys's dazed mind, but she knew it came from one of the wounded soldiers. 'I mean, no, sir. We can't leave our lieutenant.'

'You're crazy, son,' the captain said. 'Climb on or you'll be trapped here.'

The two men made no move to obey, but stood transfixed, as if unable to comprehend what the officer was saying.

The captain shook his head and ordered the jeeps to go on.

'To the hospital, right?' the man with the shoulder wound asked the other.

'Him. Him too,' Émile said, pointing to the man on the floor.

'No, Goddammit!' the other swore. 'He stays right here.'

'No, no!' Émile shouted. 'Not here. I heard them. The Germans are coming. We can't keep him.'

Without taking his eyes from Émile, the soldier raised his rifle and confronted him. Then he spoke slowly, but with a determination that could not be ignored. 'You've got to. I'm Corporal Witkowski and this is Private Newsome. Lieutenant Middleton was wounded two days ago. He led us against a group of tanks and stopped them from getting to you before now. For two days, by car and jeep, by carrying him through the woods, we got him this far.' He raised the rifle a few inches. 'Don't let the Germans get him. Keep him here. Or else!'

'Wait, not that way.' Newsome reached over and lowered the rifle.

'How then? What way?' Witkowski's eyes blazed furiously.

'Please, sir,' Newsome said to Émile. 'We can't take him. We haven't the strength. We'd have to leave him to die on the road or be taken prisoner.' His tone implied that would mean death, too.

'No, no,' Émile kept repeating in a quavering voice.

'Papa!' Alys spoke in a strong defiant tone. She turned to the soldiers. 'Why did you do it? Why the trouble, why submit yourselves to such danger? Couldn't you have left him to be found by medics?'

'There were none.' Witkowski turned from Émile to Alys, as if sensing that she might better understand what had to be done. 'You can't know the confusion. Everyone going in all directions. And the dead. Every town we came to – filled with the dead. No one alive to help. And the woods, littered with the dead and wounded freezing to death. You gotta understand, ma'am, that our lieutenant here led us all the way from Normandy to the German border. He saved our asses – excuse me – our lives a dozen times or more.' His voice got sterner. 'Now, by God, we're gonna save his. We can't take him. He stays here.' He began fingering his rifle again.

Alys looked intently at Witkowski and Newsome. Under the dirt and blood on their faces, she saw their pallid skin. Their wounds needed attending to as soon as possible. If they wasted much more time talking, there would be three unconscious men lying on the floor. The hospital couldn't have been evacuated so quickly that there wasn't at least one ambulance left to send back for the lieutenant. If Witkowski and Newsome left right now, they could make it.

'Leave him here,' Alys said quietly. 'We'll take care of him until you can send help.'

'Alys!' Émile and Jolie said together.

'I said we'd keep him here until an ambulance can get here, and we will.' She turned to the others. 'You'd better go. Go out the back, behind the inn. There's a path, well marked. It will lead you through the woods to a château – now the hospital. You can't miss it. Your friend will be safe with us.'

From the road came sounds of tanks and trucks. Only Alys was close enough to the window to see the large black swastika emblazoned on each one, but she said nothing.

'Go right now,' she said in an amazingly calm voice. 'We'll take care of your lieutenant.' She knew now that no ambulance would arrive. They would be caring for an unconscious officer and keeping him hidden as long as there were Germans in Ste. Monique. Or until he was recovered enough to be helped by the Underground to safety. If the Underground were still in existence.

'Thanks, ma'am.' Witkowski lowered his rifle. 'We'll send someone right back. Come on, Newsome.'

Alys watched them walk out the rear door. No, they wouldn't be sending anyone back. She could only pray they would make it to the château in time to be evacuated with the other wounded if there were a general retreat.

After they left, Émile stood stunned and shaking his head. 'I didn't get the tree.'

Within minutes after Witkowski and Newsome left, there were sounds of gunfire from the village. The Americans had not retreated. They had stayed and were making a stand against the Germans.

Alys looked at her parents, but no word need be said. There was no time to be wasted in getting to the basement again. While Jolie filled bottles with water, Émile carried them down. Alys gathered up enough food for at least forty-eight hours and followed him. Leaving him to get a fire started in the small stove, she ran back up and stripped beds of quilts. With the lieutenant needing one of the pallets, she and Minette would have to share one. In all the desperate confusion, she'd almost forgotten about Minette, who was still napping. Now she ran in and saw that Minette was waking up. She gathered the little girl into her arms and carried her through the kitchen and down the stairs.

The basement was still cold, and Minette started whimpering.

'It's all right, honey,' Alys tried to assure her. 'Bundle up in the quilt and you'll be warm in a minute. I'll be right back. We're going to play a game of hide-and-seek for a little while.'

Minette snuggled down on the pallet and clutched her rag doll. She was trying to smile at the thought of playing a game, but Alys could see the wonder in her eyes at being so hurriedly brought down here.

Not until everything was in place in the abandoned storeroom did they try to move the lieutenant. It took all three of them to carry him down the narrow steps and through the main part of the basement to the small room. Only in these narrow confines could the old stove keep them all warm.

Alys looked at the young man on the pallet. So far neither Émile nor Jolie had indicated in any way that they knew he would be with them throughout the terrible ordeal ahead of them. With Minette sitting in Jolie's lap and listening to a story, Alys could now devote her attention to him. He was so terribly pale and ill. She touched his gray skin. It was clammy and cool. His lips were outlined with a faint tinge of purple. All indications of severe shock that had to be treated immediately. A quick look had shown her that the cuts and abrasions, covered with dried, clotted blood, were less serious and could wait. Time enough for them. But there would be no time for him if he were not brought out of shock. She had no medication, but she could get him warm. It would have to be – it must be – enough.

She wrapped him in quilts and covered him with more quilts. Vigorously she massaged his hands and arms, then his feet and legs, then back to the hands. Her own hands were numb and sore from the effort, but she persisted. She couldn't stop. Not when there was a chance, even the smallest chance, that she could keep him alive. Tired and desperate, her fingers cramping, she was on the verge of tears, but she didn't stop working on him. 'Live,' she whispered, 'please live.'

She paused long enough to look at his face. The skin was still pallid but no longer gray. She looked more closely. The purplish discoloration around the lips had faded. She touched his cheek. It was warm. Barely warm, to be sure, but no longer clammy.

'He's still alive.' She said it loud enough for everyone to hear. 'He's coming out of shock.'

Jolie put Minette down beside Émile, who was warming some stew on the stove, and walked over to Alys. 'What do we do now?'

'Warm water and towels,' Alys said succinctly.

Émile began dishing up the stew, and Jolie put a basin of water on the stove. In a few minutes she and Alys were able to bathe the blood gently off the lieutenant's wounds. As Alys had first surmised, the lacerations were relatively superficial. Thank God they needed nothing more than to be kept clean. Antiseptics and bandages were now only wishful thinking.

Alys was now concerned that during all of their ministrations he'd shown no sign of regaining consciousness. He'd lain there limp and unresponsive as if completely anesthetized. There was no time, however, to worry about that right now.

There was another deadly threat to be seriously considered and averted. One that had to be dealt with immediately.

If the Germans now streaming into Ste. Monique captured it, and if it were discovered there was an American soldier being hidden at the inn, all of them here were liable for execution, or prison at the very least. She thought again of Trois Ponts. Aware of how desperate the situation was, she forced herself to think calmly and make some plans.

All indications that Lieutenant Middleton was a soldier must be destroyed. She removed the tattered remnants of his uniform, shorts, and undershirt. Caked with dirt and blood, the rough, heavy trousers, shirt, and jacket were stiff in her hands, and she thought she would never get them off, even as torn as they were. When it came to the shorts and undershirt, she simply cut them off quickly. For the time being she rewrapped him in a quilt. Later she'd get one of her father's flannel nightshirts for him.

She put the pieces of shorts and undershirt in the stove. While waiting for them to burn, she cut off buttons and zippers from the uniform. Impatiently, she waited for everything flammable to be reduced to ashes. What didn't burn, she'd bury with the metal items.

In her haste to remove the chain from around his neck, it came apart. She held a tag in her hand. 'Middleton,' she read. 'Ryan Middleton.' A pleasant-sounding name.

More than a dozen times she had to open the stove and stir the ashes to make certain everything was burning completely. Finally she was satisfied there was no telltale, suspicious residue. If they were forced to stay in the basement even another twenty-four hours, they'd be burning enough other things to consume what she might have missed. She found a small bag to put the metal items in.

As soon as it was dusk, she started upstairs. Cautiously she looked out the kitchen door. There was no one around. It would be safe now to dig a small hole and bury the bag. Then she remembered something that could have ruined all her careful planning and work. His boots! She hurried back down the stairs.

'Not the boots,' Émile said. 'I can use them.' He held up one foot in a handmade wooden sabot. 'I can hardly walk in these.'

'It's too dangerous, Papa. We can't have anything of his around here.' Surely, after all the precautions they'd taken when working with the Underground he understood that. And after his earlier ferocity about having the officer remain with them, Alys couldn't comprehend what possessed him to want the boots.

'Look at them.' He pointed to the boots. 'They're so shabby, no one will know where they came from.'

'*They* will.' She didn't say 'Germans,' but both knew who she meant. 'They're quick to spot things like that.'

Émile was already putting the boots on. Although some sizes too big, they were obviously more comfortable than the sabots.

'You're an old fool,' Jolie said. 'Give them to Alys to bury.'

'Leave him be, *Maman*. He'll hide them quickly enough when he hears the tramping of other boots outside our door.'

Jolie grunted in disgust; but without another word, she went back to making Minette comfortable for the night.

Going upstairs again, Alys went through the kitchen to a rear service door that was screened from the road by the shattered remains of a wall from the part of the inn destroyed earlier. She continued to listen with horror and dread to the ominous sounds coming from the road: the ponderous rumbling and grinding treads of tanks; the low whine of a command car motor; the tramping of booted feet; and most terrifying of all – because they were the controlling force – the loud, guttural voices shouting commands.

Frantically she started digging in the frozen earth but stopped momentarily when she heard new sounds coming from the village. The firing of rifles, the high, repetitive crescendo of machine guns, the whine of ricocheting, spent bullets. Her hands were covered with sweat. Her stomach churned and then cramped. She needed no imagination to visualize the fierce fighting that was taking place. She'd lived through it before. She tried to dig faster. Finally, she had the hole deep enough to hold the small bag with the metal clues to Middleton's identity. In desperate haste, she filled in the hole, stomped on it to flatten the loose dirt, and covered the spot with a haphazard pile of stones. She ran inside the inn and down to the basement.

Although the fighting was taking place in the village, they were as effectively trapped within the inn as if they were directly under siege. For the present, however, the real apprehension came from being isolated from news of what was taking place in the village.

Throughout the night, Alys lay awake. She knew her parents were awake, too. Her father was not snoring, and her mother turned restlessly on her pallet. Only Minette, held close in Alys's arms, slept. She could sense their fear, even as her own fear held her in a tight grip of physical pain. Every muscle remained taut and her breathing was rapid; she was the mother lion waiting, listening, watching for the first sign that she must leap from her crouched position to protect her cub.

In the darkness, Alys began to distinguish more clearly between the rapid burst of screaming death from a machine gun, the solitary crack of a rifle, and the deep, gut-wrenching growl of the tanks. It was apparent neither side was in control yet, but who was winning? Were the Germans gaining ground or were the Americans steadfastly holding on and getting ready to repel the attack?

Twice during the night she lit a candle and stepped over to the lieutenant's pallet. He was still sleeping soundly and breathing normally. She returned to her pallet, and snuggled up close again to Minette. The little girl was as warm and comforting as a hot water bottle. She'd have to tell her that in the morning. She could already hear Minette's tinkling laughter at the thought of being a hot water bottle.

CHAPTER FIVE

With the coming of dawn, the battle in the village had increased in intensity and confusion of sound. No longer a single rifle shot or machine-gun round exploding. It was now a continuous thudding, shrieking, pounding, exploding cacophony of death.

Émile built up the fire in the stove. Jolie mixed some meal with enough water to make a thick gruel and put it on the stove to cook. Atop this she set a flat pan for warming croissants left from the day before. With picture books to keep her entertained, Minette remained wrapped in quilts on her pallet.

Alys knelt down on the floor beside Middleton. He was still sleeping soundly and had not changed his position.

During the discussion with the soldiers who brought him, she'd paid scant attention to specific words. Nor had she thought about the details of their conversation during the frantic move to the basement and her desperate care of him afterward. Now she began to recall something of what they'd said, and its import made her gasp with a sudden, fearful awareness of what they'd been trying to tell her. They had carried him for two days. He had been unconscious all that time. But from what cause? Not the superficial wounds.

And he was still showing no sign of coming around. He could be in a coma. If he were comatose, his condition was far more serious than she'd first surmised. The care she could give him here was not nearly enough, or the right kind, to keep him alive. She had to get word to the hospital, apprise them of his situation, and hope he could be taken there.

No, be realistic, she told herself. That was impossible now.

Alys's intense concentration on her concern for him was shattered by a gunshot right above them, followed by the slamming of a door. Alys looked at her mother, and both their faces registered their dread apprehension. Émile had gone upstairs a few minutes earlier to search for anything he could find to burn in the stove. Momentarily stunned by the thought that Émile might have been the victim of that shot, neither of them could move. Then, as if jerked up by the single pull of a string, they ran for the stairs.

Before they were halfway up, they heard two voices, Émile's and a stranger's. Alys and Jolie collapsed in each other's arms and then hurried up the rest of the flight.

Émile and an American soldier were standing in the front hall.

'Chasing a sniper,' the young man panted. 'But I got in the last shot.'

'And the village?' Alys asked.

'Still under siege, but holding our own.' He moved toward the door, then turned and offered a halfhearted grin. 'We'll lick 'em yet. Don't worry.'

He was gone before Alys could ask him if the château remained standing, and if the hospital were still there.

If he were to live, Lieutenant Middleton needed to be fed at regular and frequent intervals. He needed the care that only the hospital could give him. There had to be a way to get him to the château. She had to get help.

Alys spent a few minutes reading to Minette. The little girl was understandably restless at being kept cooped up in the small room, and she was too young to understand why she should have to be.

Jolie replaced the pot in which she'd cooked the gruel with one containing a few pieces of meat and the broth from the previous day's stew. Into it she was cutting turnips, potatoes, and cabbage. At least they had sufficient food for several days.

While she was reading, Alys had made up her mind. She would try to reach the château.

'You can't,' Émile and Jolie insisted together. She'd never make it, not through all the fighting.

'I think I can by way of the path through the woods.'

She saw the tears in her mother's eyes, and she knew what Jolie was afraid to say aloud. What if she didn't return?

'I'll be back, *Maman*. If I see I can't get to the château, I'll turn around. I promise.'

'And Lieutenant Middleton?' Jolie looked down at him.

'You can watch him as well as I. He's in a coma, *Maman*, and unless I get help for him, he'll die.' She'd put on her coat and walked over to the stove to warm her hands before putting on her mittens.

'Wait,' Alys said. 'I have an idea.' She picked up a bowl and ladled a bit of the warm broth into it.

'Hold his head up, *Maman*,' she said as they knelt on either side of his pallet. 'Hold it up a little more, and his shoulders too if you can.'

Slowly Alys inserted the spoon with a few drops of liquid as far back in his mouth as she could. Much of it dribbled out between his lips, but she knew he'd automatically swallowed some of it. Thank God there was apparently no paralysis there. Each time, she got a little more down his throat. At the hospital there would be stomach tubes to feed him properly.

'Now,' Alys said, 'if I'm gone very long, you can do this for me. *Papa* can hold his head.' Jolie frowned. 'Please, Maman, it's not that hard. But he'll be so much better off at the hospital.'

'You won't change your mind?' Jolie asked.

'No, I have to go.'

'Then, go with God.' Jolie crossed herself and leaned over to kiss Alys on each cheek. 'And take care. I wish there'd been someone like you when Maurice — ' She stopped in mid-sentence to wipe her eyes.

Holding her mother close for a brief moment, Alys knew Jolie referred to an older brother who'd died during World War I at the battle of Liège. She hugged Minette and told her to be a good girl while she was gone.

Alys made it easily along the path that led part way up the hill and well into the woods. At that point, the path turned and paralleled the road going through the village and west toward the château. When she reached a clearing above the village square, she stopped to look down. German Tiger tanks stood around the square, effectively blocking any mobilized exit from the village. Smoke rose from a disabled American tank. There seemed to be a lull in the fighting, but she could see a number of German soldiers around the tanks and in doorways. From time to time a shot rang out from one of the buildings. Even as she watched, a hand grenade came flying out of a window and exploded at the feet of two soldiers. Their deaths were immediate and horrible.

I'm watching men being killed, she thought. She'd seen men die in the hospital, but this was different. I'm watching and I feel almost no revulsion. Would it be different if they weren't Germans? Do I hate the enemy that much?

She continued on along the path. Having passed the village, she could see ahead and along the road coming from the west. It was filled with a seemingly unending stream of tanks, jeeps, and trucks. And they were American! They were coming to the relief of the troops in the village. They would push the Germans out of Ste. Monique and back toward Germany. With a lighter heart, she hurried toward the château. What she couldn't see was the even larger German task force coming toward Ste. Monique from the east.

When Alys reached the château she was amazed to see no action around it, no one outside. And no sounds from within. What had happened? As far as she could tell, it hadn't been damaged in any way. She hurried across the wide terrace and through the partially opened door, a door that looked as if someone had started to close it but then hurried away before making certain it was shut.

There was no one inside. No doctors, medics, or volunteers. No wounded on pallets or beds. The silence after the usually noisy commotion in the rooms was haunting.

It was immediately apparent what had taken place here. In the face of onrushing German troops, everyone had been evacuated to prevent their being captured. It was also evident that they'd left in a hurry. Trays of instruments still lay, newly sterilized, beside operating tables. A pot of stew sat on the stove. There were more instruments in a water-filled pot beside it. Waste cans filled with bloodied bandages waited to be emptied. A few supplies lay in haphazard disarray on shelves as if left behind when others were hastily removed.

Alys walked slowly from room to room. Viewed in the aftermath of a hasty departure, each room gave her a picture of what was taking place when the order to evacuate had come.

But what was she to do now? How could she keep Ryan alive? She was viscerally alert to how desperate the situation was for both of them.

Then she saw a package lying half off, half on, a table. It was an intravenous pack. She knew now what she had to do. She'd been trained to administer intravenous fluids as well as stomach tubes.

Quickly she looked around for what other supplies had been left behind. To her relief and amazement, she discovered three more unopened intravenous packs. These were worth gold to her. She was able to get them into the large pockets of her coat. The only stomach tubes she found had been used, but these could be boiled and reused again and again. She'd keep Ryan alive in spite of the Germans. She'd begun thinking of him as Ryan. She liked the name. There was strength in it, and strength from any source was what she needed.

In no hurry now, she took time to see if there was anything else she could use. On a shelf she found seven bottles of glucose solution. There was no way she could carry all of them, but she carefully wrapped two in a discarded sheet. She should be able to carry those easily. Into the pocket of her skirt, she put a roll of gauze bandage, some tape, and cotton pads. Slight though Ryan's wounds were, she did need to dress them.

Confident she'd gotten what she needed – and all she could carry – Alys left the château. She had just started along the wooded path when she heard a violent explosion and was thrown to the ground. She lay still where she'd fallen; having been through numerous shellings before, she knew the best move was not to move at all. The continuous reverberations indicated the town was undergoing a steady bombardment. But from which side?

So far, Alys hadn't dared even to raise her head, so she had no idea from which direction the shells were coming. It was absurd. It didn't make sense. Both the Allies and the Germans usually shelled a town they were approaching to take, not one in which their men were already fighting.

Another explosion and then another had Alys clinging to the ground that shuddered beneath her. The shelling was getting closer. She had to decide whether to stay where she was or try to find shelter. She could tell now that the bombardment was coming from the east. From the Germans. That meant an attack, not an effort by the Americans to hold the town.

Alys began crawling along the ground, making her way between the trees. They offered some protection for cover unless they came under a direct hit. To her relief she remembered the one place that might provide a safe refuge: the monastery. The centuries-old, stone monastery was built right into the rock of a bare, vertical escarpment above the village. She'd passed behind it on her way to the château. It was no more than two hundred meters from where she lay.

If she could stop her trembling, she should be there in a few minutes. The thick rock walls would offer real security against even the worst shelling. She forced herself to breathe slowly, but there was no way she could quiet the pounding of her heart or the rapid beat of her pulse.

Having expected to see only the monks when she entered the monastery gates, she was momentarily stunned at the amount of activity going on inside the walls. Monks, doctors, and medics were all working desperately to tend the constant stream of wounded being brought in. Several women volunteers were working with them.

Of course, Alys thought. This is the logical place for a hospital during a bombardment.

A sigh of relief escaped her. Not all the hospital staff had been sent from Ste. Monique.

'Alys,' Regina Essler, one of the women volunteers, called to her. 'Thank heavens you've come.'

But not to stay, Alys thought. She caught herself before saying it aloud. They needed her, but so did Ryan. He needed the supplies she'd so carefully carried from the château. She'd stay as long as the shelling was severe, and until she was calm enough to continue the trip. Then she'd have to leave. Ryan's life depended on her getting back to him. Or maybe getting him here to the monastery.

'What do you need me to do?' she asked.

'The cellar is full of children.'

'Children!' Alys exclaimed.

'Brought here when the shelling started. Some of us have been running up and down between them and the patients up here. No one's been able to stay with them. They're terribly frightened. You'll be perfect with them. You teach many of them, and you can comfort the little ones. Hurry. Some of them have started crying again.'

Without answering Madame Essler, Alys found her way to the

cellar. Floors as well as walls of the monastery were five feet thick, able to withstand the severest of shellings. From that point of view, the cellar was an ideal place for the children. In other ways it was not. Centuries of moisture had covered the walls with luminescent niter, and the huge, pillared, subterranean area was bitterly cold as well as damp. Water oozed through the below-ground-level walls onto the floor. A few thin mattresses and blankets were all that protected the children from the frigid stone floors. Even those lean comforts had been sent down at the expense of the less severely wounded. No more could be asked of them.

Several children recognized Alys immediately and called out her name. One older child had two toddlers trying to share her lap with an infant. Alys reached over and took one of them in her arms as soon as she found a place to sit between two of her students. Curiosity and interest in Alys's unexpected appearance had stilled the crying for the moment. How, she thought, to keep it stopped and keep others from fretting? And try to warm them up. She was already feeling the damp chill through her woollen skirt and heavy coat. Her hands were getting numb.

Looking around the large, open area, she saw there was no need for all of them to be sitting huddled together. She knew they'd done it from fear as much as from hopes of keeping warm. If she could get them moving around, they'd no longer be cold and maybe they'd forget to be afraid.

'How about a game?' she asked, trying her best to put a smile into her voice.

A few heads nodded, but with little enthusiasm.

'A song that we dance to at school?' she suggested.

There were smiles in response to this.

'Good.' She pointed to some of her students and beckoned them to her. When they were standing, she suggested that each take one or two of the others who didn't know the dances and teach them as they went along.

Soon she had the children, except for the ones holding babies, up on their feet and eager to start. For almost an hour, Alys led them in songs that had them dancing around, clapping their hands, and stomping their feet.

'Whew!' she finally said. 'I'm tired. Let's sit down now, and I'll tell you a story.'

Heads nodded in unison, and there were shouts of 'Yes, yes,' and 'Please!'

After three stories, Alys could no longer contain her mingled fears and curiosity. She had to know what was happening above them.

As soon as she opened the heavy door at the head of the stairs, she had her answer. The sounds of shelling were, if anything, worse than before. To them had been added the frequent bursts of machine-gun fire and single shots from rifles. Nearer at hand, mixed with the cries and moans of the wounded, were the shouts from ambulance drivers bringing in more wounded and the staccato orders of the medics.

Alys wanted to weep. It appeared impossible to get back to Ryan even if she could leave the children. She made her way down the stairs.

The hours passed slowly. During this time, one of the women from above came down with bread and hot chocolate. 'It's all we have for them,' she said apologetically. 'We need what other food we have for the wounded and the workers.'

'It's all right,' Alys assured her. 'The children will be glad for this.'

'There's enough for you too,' the volunteer said, 'and you'll need it. It looks as if you'll be here at least all night.'

The meager lunch was followed by an effort to persuade the children to take naps. By curling up several to a blanket or mattress, all were protected in some way from the cold floor and were kept warm by snuggling close together.

After hearing the discouraging news about being in the monastery for many more hours, Alys decided to put her head back against the wall and try to get some sleep herself. She didn't know how long she'd been asleep when she was awakened by voices from overhead. Because of the thick floor, the cellar was soundproof unless the door at the head of the stairs was open.

'What is down there?' The man was speaking German. Alys's heart froze.

'The cellar,' a woman answered, one of the volunteers who, like Alys, spoke German as well as French.

'And? What else?' the German demanded.

'Children. Only children. Protected from the fighting.'

The door was slammed shut. The relief felt when no one came down to harass them was offset by the fear that Germans had taken the village. Were all of them to be held here as prisoners? Surely they wouldn't keep children imprisoned. Then she thought of the children murdered at Trois Ponts. But no one here had defied the Germans. Surely not even they would murder these innocent ones. She tried to keep that positive thought uppermost in her mind.

During the next several hours, Alys alternated between telling stories and leading the children in singing. When they grew tired of the songs they knew, she taught them new ones. After their long naps, they were too restless to go back to sleep but too tired to dance or play games. The night seemed to go on forever. The candles one of the medics had brought down hours earlier were burning low. Some were already sputtering as the flames reached the last of the wax in the holders.

'Hey down there! Is everybody okay?'

Alys sat bolt upright. The man had spoken English. No longer able merely to sit and wait, she dashed up the stairs. At the door was an exhausted soldier in a dirty, sweaty uniform.

'What – what's happened?' She found it hard to get the words out.

'We've retaken the area this side of the village. Hope to have the whole place soon. But you'd better stay below. The fighting's still fierce.'

'We will. Thank God you're here.' Alys's fingertips clutched the stone walls of the stairwell.

'Wish us luck,' he said.

'Oh yes! And God go with you.'

With a much lighter heart, Alys returned to her charges. While she told them the good news, she could see them relaxing, and soon they were asleep. But now Alys was restless. She needed to walk around.

Exploring the cellar, she found several smaller rooms opening off the large, main vault. One was a wine cellar, now denuded of its contents, but most were empty or stored odds and ends of broken, cast-off furniture. She wondered if these cell-like rooms had ever been inhabited by the monks. Maybe those who had taken extreme vows of silence or poverty and abnegation. She shuddered. How horrible to spend all one's life in such dark, cramped quarters. Hurriedly, and grateful she'd soon be leaving, she shut the door.

She started to return to the children when she saw a strip of light under another door. Could there possibly be someone else down here with them? Finding it took all her strength to move the heavy door on its rusted hinges, she knew no one had entered in a long time. Except for a bench and some scattered remains of clothing, the room was empty. The light she saw came from a small barred window up on a wall, just under the ceiling. Through it she saw the pearly gray dawn sky. The long, dreadful night was coming to an end. Maybe with daylight they could all leave and return home.

Ryan had seldom been out of her thoughts during these past hours. She still had the intravenous packets, the stomach tubes, and bandages in her pockets. The two bottles of glucose solution were tucked safely in their wrappings in a protected corner of the cellar. If only she'd be getting home in time for all of those precious supplies to help him. Then when the Americans finally retook the entire village, he could be brought here.

The children woke up and started asking for breakfast. A few were whimpering, but most were trying hard to be brave in what was surely a very frightening situation. Away from home and parents, they'd gone to sleep hungry.

'I'll see what I can find,' Alys said in a more reassuring tone than she felt. There must be something in the kitchen the children could have. With the Allies now in control, there must be food as well as supplies coming to the monastery.

She opened the door to the main floor and then stopped. It was impossible for her to move. The flurried activities of the day before had ceased. Now there were only moans from the wounded and a single commanding voice – a voice speaking German. Stunned, scared, and frantic, Alys backed down a step or two. A single sight had her paralyzed with fear.

All of the monks, from the old, paralytic abbot to the youngest lay brother, were shackled together and being guarded by two rough, unkempt soldiers with drawn rifles. Imprisonment was the price the kindly, peaceful workers for God were to pay for offering sanctuary to the wounded and the helpless.

It couldn't be, Alys thought. The Americans had retaken the area. Had been on their way to retaking all of Ste. Monique.

Going back up the two steps, Alys opened the door a little farther. The uniforms now were all German. The American medical staff was standing silent in a group. A German officer was speaking to them in gutturally accented English. The staff and the wounded were to be transported to prison camps.

The gasp of dismay that Alys tried to hold back came out involuntarily as a choking sob, and all eyes turned in her direction.

'Who! Who are you?' the officer asked in German.

'I'm – I have some children in the cellar. We've been down there during the fighting.'

'Let me see.' The German strode across the room. Pushing Alys to one side he descended the stairway, his boots pounding. Echoing noises bounced defiance off the ancient walls.

Following immediately after him, Alys watched fear and disbelief spread across the faces of the older children when they saw the officer. They remembered, and memory gave birth to apprehension.

'Attention!' he shouted. The word echoed and re-echoed throughout the low-vaulted room. Not a head moved. Not an eye blinked.

'The fighting is over,' he said. 'We are now in command.' Alys could imagine him rubbing his hands together gleefully. 'You are to return immediately – and promptly – to your homes. No loitering, no speaking to anyone. Is that understood?'

Every head nodded in unison.

'Sir,' Alys spoke up, not pausing to wonder how she dared make a request of this stern man. 'The children are hungry. They've had nothing to eat since yesterday noon. Have you anything for them?'

'*Nein.*' He smiled.

CHAPTER SIX

As much as all her thoughts were on getting back to Minette and Ryan, Alys walked down the escarpment with the children to the village. It was worth taking the time to see the grateful arms that welcomed most of them home, even if sometimes it was to homes that were no more than two adjoining, shattered walls that protected them from the wind. Parents and grandparents came up from basements that no longer had even a single wall standing above them. Four of the children lived in farmhouses on the way to the inn, and Alys walked with them. The shelling had done a minimal amount of damage in the countryside, but homes and attached barns were still visible reminders of earlier fighting. Here again open arms and tears greeted the children, who had been trapped in the village with friends when the attack began. '*Mon Dieu! Ils vivent!*' sprang from unbelieving lips.

The sounds of battle had ceased, but other sounds were noticeably absent, too. Here and in the village. There had been no barking dogs to greet the children; no lowing cows waiting to be milked; no scurrying scratching, cackling, honking, or quacking of hens, geese, and ducks. The countryside seemed bereft of life. What few animals might remain were carefully hidden with the families in the homes. Or all of them were living together in barns where homes had been destroyed.

Alys's thoughts raced ahead to the inn. She prayed that it too was still standing. She thought of Minette and tried to run faster. And Ryan. Could he possibly still be alive? There was no way now he could be taken to the hospital. Now she had two challenges – keep him alive and out of German hands.

She finally saw the inn. It appeared untouched. When she got there, she hurried down to the basement. On seeing her, Jolie crossed herself. 'Oh, Holy Mother of God, we never thought to see you again.'

Minette threw herself into her mother's arms, and Alys comforted her as best she could. 'I'm here, *ma chère*, and everything is all right now.'

With Minette still clinging to her, Alys walked over to check on Ryan. He was alive, but barely. At least he hadn't gone into shock again. His skin was still very pale, but there was a tinge of warm color on his lips.

They would have to do what they could for him right here in the basement.

It would take time to prepare the liquid nourishment to feed Ryan through the stomach tubes, but she could start the glucose drip right away. It might even be better for his system to be reintroduced to nourishment gradually. There were a number of hooks in the wall from which they had once hung cured hams and slabs of bacon. She used one of them to hang the bottle of glucose. She had no trouble inserting and securing the needle into a large vein in Ryan's arm, and she adjusted the rate of drip as she'd been taught to do. All was going well so far. She breathed a sigh of relief and realized only then that she'd been holding her breath throughout the whole operation.

She looked at her hands, certain they would be shaking, but they were as steady as when she'd inserted the intravenous needle. With her confidence restored, she no longer worried about feeding Ryan through the stomach tubes. She'd begin that when more broth could be prepared.

For the next several hours, the simple regimen of feeding Ryan small amounts of broth every hour went smoothly. After each time, she cleared the tube with water, and then clamped it off to keep air from entering. He seemed to be having no trouble accepting the food. Soon, she thought, she could give him larger amounts at longer-spaced intervals.

During these hours, between taking care of Ryan and trying to keep Minette from getting too restless, Alys gave almost no thought to what was happening in the village. Then it all hit her at once. Was Ste. Monique totally in the hands of the Germans? Had the Americans been forced to retreat? What would happen to the staff and wounded at the monastery?

The answer came within a few hours. Sounds of guttural commands and feet shuffling hesitantly along the road brought all of them upstairs and to the windows.

In heartbreaking sorrow, tears streaming unchecked down their cheeks, they watched American prisoners being marched past toward trucks waiting to take them to POW camps. There, it was rumored according to a neighbor who'd fled to the inn from the fields when the trucks came up the road, the prisoners were guarded by vicious dogs. They replaced former guards who were needed at the front. Among the prisoners passing the inn were the walking wounded and many of the medics and doctors Alys had worked with. Those unable to walk had already been loaded onto trucks that roared along the road, unmindful of those walking who had to scurry out of their way or be run over.

Quietly Alys prayed that all of them would survive the rigors of imprisonment.

She was frightened. Her body was immobile from fear, a heavy lump of iron was embedded in her stomach. Oh, God, everything was all wrong. The world turned upside down. Not again, oh God, please not again. It was senseless. The Allies had already liberated Belgium. The Germans had no right to be here. They didn't belong here. The Allies had driven them all the way back to the Siegfried Line. Why hadn't they stayed there?

Putting her hands over her face, Alys fought to control the hysteria she could feel beginning to surge through her. It always began the same way. Her legs shaking. The wretched nausea. A light-headedness that had her reeling toward unconsciousness. She closed her eyes and breathed deeply and rapidly.

When she opened her eyes, the trucks were gone, the road was empty. She'd kept the hysteria from getting control of her, she'd be all right now.

Alys thought she had never been – and would never again be – witness to such tragedy as seeing the wounded trying to stumble along in some semblance of military order to show their pride in still being American soldiers. Pride in refusing to be daunted or humiliated by their ignominious position as prisoners.

The pain they endured marked every face, but every single man, even those needing to be helped by companions, walked with head erect, face forward. All followed without hesitation the man who had dared to leave his place in the ranks and walk slightly ahead of the others. Alys recognized him. Captain Allison, one of Colonel Applegate's staff who'd stayed at the inn. He'd never made the impression on her that some of the other officers had. He'd been very quiet, never saying much, but always a polite thank-you when she did some small service for him. Now she saw that behind that gentle façade was a man of great courage.

No, she thought, she'd never witness such tragedy again.

She was wrong.

With the fighting over, the family moved upstairs, but it had been thought wiser to leave Ryan temporarily in the basement. It would not be long before the Germans might begin searching homes or taking up residence at the inn.

On the afternoon of Christmas Eve, they were decorating the tiny tree that Émile had that morning gone out and cut. They stopped when they heard the long-anticipated, imperative knocking at the front door. When Émile opened it, two German soldiers strode menacingly into the hall. The men said nothing at first, but their gaze took in all of the room: the partially decorated tree, the ornaments in Jolie's shaking hands, Minette clinging to her mother's skirts.

This is it, Alys thought. This was the moment she'd been dreading. They'd search the inn, either to find items they could use or to appraise it as a place to house men. Ryan must not be discovered to be an American officer. She'd prepared – she hoped well – for this, and there was nothing more she could do now. Jolie and Émile had agreed to the subterfuge, and she prayed that Minette would remember the one, the most important, word she'd been taught.

'Attention!' the German sergeant snapped. So loud and commanding was his voice, he might have been addressing an entire platoon on a parade ground rather than four frightened people in a small room.

'All civilians to appear in the square promptly at 1600. All late arrivals to be punished severely. *Heil Hitler*!' The stiff salute and the final words hovered over their heads like a curse long after the men left.

At least they hadn't searched the inn. Not yet. That would surely come later, and maybe they could be even better prepared by then.

Less than half an hour to four o'clock and latecomers to be punished. Yet all of them remained frozen, silent, where they stood. Finally Jolie broke the silence. 'Get something warm into Minette first. It's bitter cold outside, and a long walk to the square.'

'You and *Papa* bundle up and go,' Alys said. 'I'll take care of Minette and myself. We'll come on the bicycle.'

By four o'clock the square was crowded. Those who lived in Ste. Monique and others, like the Prévoux from the surrounding countryside, huddled silently together in small groups. Encircling and mingling among them were dozens of German soldiers. They gave no outward appearance of guarding their quarry, but – evidence to the contrary – the Belgians knew they were as much prisoners as those who'd been marched away.

Once before when the Germans first occupied Ste. Monique the people had all been ordered to appear in the square. Most assumed the reason was the same this time: to listen to the new rules and regulations, to be apprised of curfew hours, and to be warned against disobeying any of them. They were silent from natural fear and the bitter frostbiting cold.

Alys held Minette in her arms and tried to keep the little girl warm by unbuttoning and wrapping her own full coat around her.

'Me hot water bottle,' Minette giggled.

'You really are. Sure you're warm enough?'

Minette nodded as best she could against her mother's chest.

Why didn't they start? Alys wondered. How long were they going to keep the people there? The cold made her eyes tear, and then she felt the tears freezing on her cheeks. It was monstrous to get people, children and elderly, too, out into this frigid weather and then keep them standing.

Finally an arrogant voice demanded her attention.

Every head turned in the direction of the church. While the German colonel read from the paper in his hand, there was not a sound from those listening in the biting chill of the late afternoon. But when he finished, a single concerted moan arose from the small groups of villagers. For a moment the eerie wail rose like a prayer above the tense atmosphere, but all too soon it was joined and then overwhelmed by the more pitiful sound of feet marching in slow cadence to the steady, inexorable beat of a drum.

Seven soldiers stood against the stone wall of the church. Their arms were crossed above their heads. One by one they were ordered to step forward, and a guard stripped them of all possessions: watches, money, billfolds, and a rosary. As the last was taken from the prisoner, he said something to the guard, obviously requesting that he be allowed to keep it. With a snarl, the guard tossed it carelessly into the pile of other confiscated items. Alys watched the soldier's valiant attempt to keep from giving way to tears as he backed slowly to his place against the wall.

More booted feet were heard. Seven SS German soldiers with rifles marched to a position opposite the prisoners. The colonel barked an order. The rifles were raised. Another order shattered the heavy stillness, and a single volley ended the lives of seven soldiers unfortunate enough to be trapped in Ste. Monique when the Germans finally surrounded and took over the village.

The irony of it, Alys thought. To prevent being captured as prisoners, which would have offered some hope of being released when the war was over, they had hidden themselves in various homes and buildings.

Alys turned her face away from the seven bodies slumped against the church, and found herself looking at another group surrounded by guards. Men, women, and children, they clung together. Two of the women had fainted and were being held on their feet by men on either side. Faces were drawn in shock and fear.

A truck rumbled up, and the group was forced at gunpoint to clamber aboard, men supporting women, women carrying small children, older children clinging to parents. Among these people sympathy had outweighed caution, and they had hidden the seven soldiers in their basements or attics. Now they were being taken to concentration camps where, with luck, they might survive to return someday to their homes. But not likely, Alys thought.

Slowly, very slowly, and in stunned silence, the small groups left the square.

As Alys had feared, her bicycle was confiscated. She was assured by the nasty, cruel-faced young officer who took it that she would have no more use for it. She knew what was implied. Civilians were to remain at home and not ride around the countryside on errands that might be detrimental to the Nazi cause.

As she trudged along with her parents, the vision of the people being herded into the truck never left her mind. That was what would happen to them if Ryan were discovered. She waited for her father to say something, to bewail their situation and scold her for getting them into it. But he only grumbled about how much his feet hurt. He'd left the boots at home and worn his old sabots to the village.

Alys knew, however, that it was more imperative than ever to keep the Germans from discovering Ryan. Or, she thought, of discovering who he was.

On Christmas Day, Alys, Émile, and Jolie, with Minette on one soft, broad hip, stood at the door of the inn and watched with anxiety and dread and hatred as German troops paraded past and into the village. Like all other villagers, they had been ordered to stand in doorways and along the road to welcome the victors.

When the last of the troops had marched or ridden past, the family went into the kitchen. After all, it was Christmas Day, and there was a Christmas dinner, meager though it might be. How different, how tragically different the holiday had become from the joyous celebration they'd all anticipated with such eager hopes. The party planned for the Allied soldiers had, like an Aeschylean tragedy, been transformed into an execution for seven of them, and prison for many others. Gifts for the children remained untouched, unloved, by the small hands they were intended for. And eight of those children, taken to prison, might never return.

Before they sat down to the table, Alys went to the cellar to check on Ryan. Although still comatose, he continued to breathe normally; and his body was tolerating the liquid nourishment she now gave him every four hours.

'You will live,' Alys said with a fierce determination. 'You will live and you will regain consciousness. I will not let them destroy you too. If I can save even one, they will have lost. They won't have conquered us completely. God! You will live to avenge the ones who died.' Her dark green eyes sparkled with searing hatred and icy resolve.

With Minette at the table, in the pale blue wool dress Alys had made from her old one during the long night hours she sat beside Ryan's pallet, dinner could not be a completely solemn affair. She had refused to sit in her high chair. She was a big girl now. Having been settled comfortably on a pile of books topped with a cushion, she carefully unfolded and spread her napkin across her lap in imitation of her elders. No, she would not let them tuck it under her chin or tie it around her neck.

It was not a traditional Christmas feast, but when Émile said grace, they knew they were truly blessed. They were together in their own home. They were not on a truck or train being transported to God knew where or what kind of existence in a concentration camp. Nor had their home been destroyed. And for today they had enough food to fill their stomachs.

After dinner they gathered around the small tree. There was no piano, but they could still sing Christmas carols and gaze in delight at the ornaments as they caught and reflected the last rays of a cold winter sun.

Minette tried to keep awake, but the soft, lilting strains of 'Silent Night' were too much like a lullaby, and she fell asleep in the middle of the second verse. In her arms she clutched the new rag doll Jolie had made from yarn and scraps of discarded clothing.

'It was a good dinner, *Maman*.' Alys continued to hold Minette, loath to release her one real comfort. Gently she continued to rock in the sturdy old chair.

'And probably the last for a long time,' Émile said. The ham they'd had for dinner was the last of the canned meat left by the American officers. 'Unless . . .' He left the sentence unfinished.

Unless the Germans use the inn again, Alys thought, and she knew her parents were thinking the same thing. It would mean food in the kitchen for them, but it would also mean catering to every trivial whim, following the most ignominious orders, and working past exhaustion. Worse, it would mean exposing Ryan and themselves to the danger of his discovery.

The fierce fighting in all of the Ardennes, the siege of Bastogne, the bombing of German troop concentrations, and the steady march westward of more German divisions kept Ste. Monique in a state of flux. So far, all activity was centered in the town and around the monastery, now used as a German hospital. Although there were as yet no Germans occupying the inn, the Prévous were ordered to prepare the rooms for officers who would be coming in with the occupying troops as soon as conditions stabilized.

'Germans in the town. Germans here at the inn,' Émile mumbled as he paced the floor.

'What are you trying to say, *Papa*?' Alys looked up from the sheet she was darning with thread carefully pulled from another sheet no longer worth mending.

'We can't keep Ryan here any longer.'

Alys's face registered her shocked distress. Surely he could not be suggesting they turn him over to the Germans. 'We can and we must,' she said quietly.

'Good God, child,' he exclaimed in an explosive, projectile outpouring of words, as if his internal railings of fear had finally been uncorked. 'Are you so blind that you can't see what danger your stubborn insistence has put us in? He should have been at the monastery with the other wounded. If we tell the Germans we waited until the fighting was over – or we thought he was dying – maybe they'll believe us. But he must not stay here now.'

'No, *Papa*, I gave my word. He is in no condition to be held prisoner, with heaven knows what lack of care. Even with the right care, think what it's like to be treated by the enemy.'

'He's unconscious, Alys. He doesn't know where he is.'

'But we do, *Papa*.' Shaken by the callousness of his words, she pricked her finger. In her anxiety, the simple prick became an unendurable pain that shot straight to her heart. One by one she licked off the drops of blood until there were no more, but the sweet, metallic taste of them remained on her tongue. 'How can you turn him away when you profess to be a Christian?'

'Always concern for him.' Émile pounded his fist on a table hard enough to shake the lamp and topple it to the floor. Jolie rushed over to pick it up. 'What about all of us with the *Boche* staying here or searching whenever they please? God keep us!' he shouted. 'God help us,' he moaned in despair. 'Have you forgotten Trois Ponts and Malmédy? And our own friends in the village?'

'No,' Alys said. 'Who could forget?' Trois Ponts, where civilians had been executed when the defenders had blown up a bridge to prevent Germans crossing the Amblève River. And Malmédy. Who would ever forget that massacre? The unspeakable violation of the Geneva Convention regarding prisoners of war. After being captured just outside Malmédy by German tank troops, some 120 American soldiers were marched into an open field and herded together. Two tanks were ordered to open fire on the prisoners. Those still alive who dropped to the ground and tried to crawl away were shot by pistols, as were those merely wounded and in pain. A nearby café was fired, and the few Americans who had avoided capture and fled to it were shot as they emerged.

No, Alys thought, no one will ever forget the Malmédy massacre.

Alys was not unsympathetic toward her father's fears. In many ways she shared them. But she had promised Ryan's comrades. Also, she realized, she had developed an emotional attachment to Ryan. The attachment of a nurse to a patient, or a rescuer to the rescued, and she was more determined than ever to keep him out of German hands.

Alys looked to Jolie, who so far had remained silent. 'And you, *Maman*? What do you say?'

'I don't know. I'm afraid. Afraid for all of us. Yet, you gave your word, and we've always prided ourselves on keeping our word.' She shrugged her shoulders, stoically accepting the situation. 'We've been in danger before. We'll survive.'

'You're wrong, both of you.' Émile's voice had the dead, ominous quality of a muffled bell. 'He should be turned over to the Germans now, before it's too late for us.'

'No,' Alys insisted. 'You spoke of Malmédy. They were prisoners, had surrendered. And you learned what happened to them. If you feel so strongly about it, *Papa*, why don't you get the pistol you've buried outside and go in there and shoot him yourself? It would be quicker, and you'd be free of him forever. That's what you want, isn't it?'

'Please, Alys,' Émile said. 'don't use that tone with me. All your thoughts for him. Can't you spare a thought for us? He's probably going to die anyway?'

Alys's concern had turned to fury. 'He's *not* going to die. And stop worrying.' Gradually she calmed down and was able to speak in a more placating, reassuring voice. 'We've agreed to pass Ryan off as my husband who was wounded during the shelling. If we stay with that story, they'll believe us. We'll be all right.'

'Perhaps,' Émile said, his strident anger replaced by reluctant but acquiescent tones. 'We'll see.'

Although no German officers were headquartered at the inn, the family returned to sleeping in the cellar rather than be summarily turned out of their rooms if the Germans needed them. From time to time, officers stayed the night or for a few days. Except for demanding immediate service, they paid scant attention to the Prévoux. The troops who came to occupy Ste. Monique were a different matter. Methodically they made routine checks of the area and searches of the homes.

During the first search, Alys and her parents remained under guard in the dining room while two heavily armed soldiers went slowly through each room. The time they were gone seemed interminable. Alys could see her father sweating. The room was too cold for anyone to sweat. Surely the soldiers would recognize it as fear. Jolie occupied her time by knitting, but Alys noted how often she had to go back several rows to correct mistakes. Alys told Minette fairy tales to keep the child from getting restless and to keep her own nerves under control. They must not – they absolutely must not – lose their self-control, or they would give themselves and their secret away.

Jolie was the first to see the two men returning, and she immediately dropped three stitches. Émile spilled his tobacco pouch while trying to fill his pipe, and his hands were shaking so violently he couldn't strike the match.

It's all right, Alys longed to say. *They expect us to be afraid. It's what they want. They hope to control us with fear, but we must use it instead to strengthen our resistance.* Praying the Germans didn't understand French, she said rapidly, running her words together, 'Let me do the talking.'

'Quiet!' The soldier guarding them prodded Alys with his rifle butt.

Thank God he spoke in German, she thought, instead of answering me in French.

One of the two soldiers who had conducted the search asked her, '*Sprechen sie Deutsch?*'

Alys hesitated. Should she plead ignorance and hope they would leave without asking any questions? She knew without a doubt his inquiries would concern Ryan. No, refusing to answer now would only cast more suspicion on them and bring someone else to interrogate them. It would be doubly suspicious that an innkeeper's family on the Luxemburg border did not speak German.

'*Ja*,' Alys said quietly.

'Who is the man in the cellar? Why is he asleep? He should have been awakened and brought up here while we searched. A very serious violation of orders.' The stony look he gave each of them was enough to immobilize them in their places.

'He is my husband,' Alys said, still speaking slowly and managing by sheerest willpower to keep fear out of her voice. 'He was injured during the shelling, and he has not regained consciousness.'

The soldier brought his heels together and straightened, if possible, to an even stiffer and more erect position. 'Why was he here? Why was he not serving the Fatherland in the army or in a work force? Was he perhaps in the Underground?' His steely blue eyes dared her to lie to him.

Alys looked directly into his eyes as if, in turn, she was refusing to be intimidated, but her words were soft and placating. 'He is – was – a farmer. He was ordered to stay here to provide food for the troops and to help us serve the officers who were billeted here in the inn.'

After being confined so long on her mother's lap, Minette became restless; and at that moment she wriggled free of Alys's grasp, walked over to the soldier, and tugged on his trousers.

My God, Alys thought, what was Minette going to say or do? Yet she didn't dare pull the child back or admonish her against saying the wrong thing.

'Eh?' the man said, looking down at Minette.

'*Pauvre Papa,*' Minette said sadly. Alys hoped her sigh of relief had not been audible. The child had remembered she was to call Ryan 'Papa' in front of Germans.

'What did she say about her father?' The soldier glared at Alys.

'She said 'Poor Papa.' She understands just enough German to know we were talking about him. She is much disturbed at his condition.'

'All right. I believe you. For now.'

With a final '*Heil Hitler*' the soldiers left, but it was several minutes before anyone spoke.

'They believed you,' Jolie said. The knitting dropped from her flaccid arms to the floor; and she let it lie there, as if all her strength had gone with it.

'Yes, they believed me. And they will next time, too.'

'Perhaps,' Émile said. 'We can only wait and see.'

There were more searches, and German officers began staying at the inn for longer periods of time. The story that Ryan was Alys's wounded husband was believed, but often she sensed symptoms of doubt in a single swift glance or a change in tone of voice. How much longer, she wondered, could they continue the charade? Would one of them break, say the wrong thing, or make one false move? Or would an intuitive German find some flaw in their dangerous drama?

Like her father, all she could say in answer to her own questions was, 'We'll see.'

CHAPTER SEVEN

Alys cleared the feeding tube with water and carefully clamped it off. Ryan had been taking, and apparently tolerating, both liquid and puréed food for more than two weeks now. He couldn't possibly be gaining weight, but his face seemed to have filled out a little, and he'd lost much of his gaunt look.

As she'd done so many times before, she stood looking down at him, wondering what kind of man he was, where he was from, what had aroused such admiration in his two companions that they would endanger their own lives to get him to safety. And would he ever regain consciousness? As each day passed, she became more and more concerned about his comatose state. Perhaps *Papa* was right. Perhaps she should have told the American medical staff when she was at the monastery. But, no, there hadn't been time. Then the Germans had captured the hospital, and those too ill to walk had been loaded into trucks and with the walking wounded taken away as prisoners. In German hands he most surely would have died.

She, at least, had kept him alive this long, and she'd continue to care for him until he woke up or until . . . No, she wouldn't think about his dying. He wasn't going to die.

Alys stood up from the pallet when her mother came down to the cellar.

'What is it, *Maman*?' Jolie's face was pale. A sure sign something was wrong.

'Another search. Officers this time.' Her voice shook and her gnarled hands clutched at her apron.

'It'll be all right,' Alys said soothingly. 'Just like the others. Don't worry.' But Alys was worried. Why officers this time? And two days in a row. What had been said or done the day before to make them suspicious?

Alys followed her mother into the dining room where Émile was already being guarded. Alys looked at the German major standing beside her father and at the boots he held. Ryan's boots. She should have destroyed them and not listened to her father's pleading. She looked at her father, now rubbing one stockinged foot over the other. Had he said anything? Oh God, Alys thought, don't let him have said the wrong thing.

'These are handsome boots,' the major said sardonically. 'Where did they come from?'

'An American soldier quartered here gave them to my father. He saw my father had no shoes.'

The major made no comment but simply ordered her to follow him. Nor was Alys surprised when he went directly to the cellar.

He pointed to Ryan. 'Who is he?'

'My husband. Wounded during the shelling.' She'd said it so many times now, she worried that it sounded memorized, a phrase learned by rote, to be repeated like a Pavlovian response to a key question.

'Why was he not taken to hospital?'

'I – I preferred to care for him here. I had the training. I know what to do.'

'You're a nurse?'

Sacré bleu! Why hadn't she stopped after the first sentence? Why had she said she knew how to care for him? Whatever she said now, she knew what the next order would be. Well, no help for it, and maybe better to tell the truth.

'No, I'm not a nurse, but I was a volunteer worker at the hospital here.'

The major glared. 'For the Allies?' His frown gradually evolved into a malicious grin. 'Good. Very good. You will now come to the monastery and help care for our valiant German wounded.'

'But my husband. I can't leave him.' She hoped the tremor in her voice was taken as fear for her husband not of the officer.

'We will take him there, too. As long as you perform the duties assigned to you, he will receive the best of care.'

Alys could not help but sense the tinge of blackmail in the words, the underlying threat that at even a hint of neglect on her part, Ryan would suffer. It was a threat she could handle. There was nothing in the way of nursing duties she would not perform to keep Ryan alive. She'd already done the worst, the most onerous, the most repellent, the most nauseating of tasks at the château. No, the German medics would find her a most competent and willing volunteer. Any idea of sabotage in the form of administering wrong doses or removing tubes or hampering operations would only be foolhardy and gain her nothing.

At the same time, she was tormented by another thought. If Ryan came out of his coma, as she'd been praying he would, it could still be disastrous for them all. For her parents, for herself, and for Ryan. And what of Minette? If taken to a concentration camp, would she and Minette be separated? No, somehow, some way, there must be plans for her parents to flee with Minette if Ryan's identity were discovered. They'd plan for it when she returned to the inn after her first hours on duty.

'How long will I be on duty each day?' she asked the major.

'As long as you are needed. And, of course, you will stay at the monastery. It would not do to have you leave with information that could be valuable to the Allies.'

Alys's heart shrank to a hard, cold mass of despair. Not to get back. Not to be able to make plans. If only there were some way to warn her parents.

'But I have a child, a little girl. She needs me with her. I have to be home sometimes.'

'And she has grandparents,' he answered impatiently. 'Come, we've wasted enough time. Your husband can lie in the back of my staff car. I'm sure the short ride will do him no harm.'

Under the seemingly sincere words, Alys detected a dangerous note of sarcasm.

The major walked to the stairs and called up to the two who'd accompanied him.

'We're taking this man with us,' he said when they entered the room. He looked at the other pallets lying on the floor and ordered the men to take all the quilts. They were needed at the hospital.

Two German soldiers moved to pick Ryan up. Alys could only stand by and watch. Émile and Jolie, with Minette in her arms, had followed the soldiers downstairs. They stood in the doorway of the small room, their faces revealing the one, all-important question: had Ryan's identity been discovered?

'Don't worry,' Alys said to them in French, in words not to alert the major if he understood the language. 'The major has consented to take him to the hospital, and I'm to help care for their wounded.'

'Quiet!' the major ordered. 'They do not need to know where you're going or why.'

So he did understand French. To speak in the Dutch dialect of Flanders, in Northern Belgium, would be to arouse suspicion. There was no way now to warn them. The time had finally come for them to wait for whatever fate decreed for them.

As the soldiers picked up the quilt that had been under Ryan, they moved the pallet a few inches. Alys heard the ominous sound of metal scraping along the cement floor. Others had heard it, too.

The major reached down, lifted up the edge of the pallet, and picked up a metal tag still hanging on its short chain.

Only then, to her horror, did Alys realize what must have happened. In her haste to get rid of Ryan's uniform and all identification, in her struggle to remove the chain from around his neck, she hadn't realized he was wearing two tags. One was safely buried. This one must have remained here, under the pallet, awaiting the opportune moment to reveal its fatal secret.

The major looked at the tag and then down at Ryan. The stern expression on his face was chiseled in stone. He turned his head only enough to look at Alys. 'Your husband?' He smiled. A sardonic smirk.

There was no point in lying. The dissembling was over. Alys had no hope that the truth would absolve them from all guilt in the major's eyes, but she prayed it might in some way ameliorate any punishment meted out to them.

'He was brought here by two of his men,' Alys said, in a tone she hoped would convey that what she was now telling them was exactly what had taken place and why she and her family had been caring for Ryan. 'He was wounded, unconscious, and close to death. They were also wounded and trying to get to the hospital. They simply left him here. They assumed, I suppose, we would take care of him. Or maybe they simply thought he was going to die.'

Until now, Alys had avoided looking at her parents. Her words were putting them in serious jeopardy. She prayed they would understand what she was trying to do. With an uneasy heart, she turned toward them. Their expressions of disbelief castigated her as no words could have done. So now she had to find the right words to save them.

'We had no choice,' she said obsequiously and desperately. The situation demanded humility. 'Do you understand, Major? We had no choice. He was simply left – dumped on us, if you will. As long as he remained alive, we had to take care of him.'

'Very noble, I'm sure.' The sarcasm behind the ostensibly sympathetic words was too obvious to be ignored. There was no semblance of understanding in his stern visage, with its knife-sharp aquiline nose, thin lips, and intense, penetrating gray eyes. 'But you didn't report him.'

That simple statement doomed them all. She'd tried and she'd failed. Alys watched in desperate silence while they carried Ryan out. Behind her, she heard her mother sobbing and Minette crying. Only now was Alys struck by the realization of what she had done, of how her insistence on caring for Ryan had sentenced them to death.

The major spoke rapidly in German to a younger officer. Alys listened, not wanting to believe what she was hearing, yet knowing she must. All hope was lost now.

'You understood what I told him?' The major looked from Alys to her parents. They nodded. 'You will stay here in this room, under guard, until provisions are made for sending you away.'

The major did not say where they were to be sent, nor did he need to. They would follow the others who had dared to aid in any way the Allied cause to the unspeakable horror of a German concentration camp.

Without another word the major left. The younger officer followed him out and locked the door behind him. He or another soldier would be on guard at all times to make certain no one left the room.

It was over, all over. For them there was no more war. There was also no more hope.

CHAPTER EIGHT

i

Ryan tried to wake up, but the swaying motion kept putting him back to sleep. He was being carried somewhere, but in his confused state he couldn't decide whether he was dreaming or whether he was awakening from a dream.

Slowly, very slowly, Ryan was beginning to emerge from his coma, but as yet his mind could not distinguish between past and present. He was no longer a man who had been wounded. He was a boy of eight.

He had fallen from his horse going over the jump. Too high a jump, his father said, for an eight-year-old, but he'd insisted. Reluctantly his father had given in. He'd hit the ground, and the pain in his head was terrible. He was barely conscious of having been driven to the hospital, and his stay there was merely a half memory of aching bones and sore muscles. Of wanting to go home and lie in his own bed. That must be where he was going now. Someone was carrying him out of the hospital.

He felt himself being maneuvered through a car door and laid on a seat. While he waited for the car to start up, he wondered why he hadn't heard the familiar voices of his mother or father. Maybe they were waiting at home.

He was lying in an awkward position, but he didn't seem able to shift to a more comfortable one. He hoped the horse was all right, didn't have to be shot. He'd seen a horse shot once. And men. No, not men. He was wrong about that. Just a horse. The sounds of shots mingled with shouts of men as he drifted back off to sleep.

Amid a circle of silence, bounded around in the distance by the muffled booming of cannon and the heavy tread of vehicles, Ryan drifted again into half wakefulness. He not so much heard the muffled noises as felt the dull reverberations through his body. He was now lying on the ground.

Had he fallen there? He tried to move, and his body responded with a series of quick, sharp pains in his legs and arms. He looked up and saw a single huge tree looming above him. Gradually he remembered. He'd climbed that tree on a dare from his cousin. Forgetting how limber and smaller the branches got the higher he went, he'd vowed he'd go clear to the top. One bent under his weight; and, try as desperately as he would, he could not hold on to the slippery bark. He remembered the falling, the wondering if he would be killed. He hadn't climbed more than a third of the way up, so maybe he'd only broken something or been badly bruised.

Ryan looked around in the early January twilight and wondered where his cousin was. Had he run off, the stinking coward, or had he gone for help? When he again tried moving one leg and then the other, the tingling pain was still there. He looked along the road beside which he lay. Funny. He thought the tree was in the middle of a meadow, not near a road. His brain must have gotten befuddled by the fall. He was too weak to stand, but maybe he should try crawling. He began to get dizzy. Feeling himself blacking out, he lay down and passed out just as his head came to rest on one arm.

ii

In the cellar, Émile stood on a table and peered through a narrow crack between two stones in the outer wall. He looked across the narrow river to the hills and woods of the Ardennes beyond. He had remained silent during all the major's interrogation and the brusque statement that they should stay in the room until taken away.

Jolie sat on a bare pallet. Slowly she rocked back and forth. At first she'd done it to quiet the sobbing Minette. Now with the little girl asleep, she continued to rock, unable to stop.

Alys walked over to her father.

'Why don't you say something, *Papa*?'

'There is nothing to say.' Always a taciturn man, he now seemed to recede further into silence as if seeking its protection.

'Well, at least get down,' Jolie said. 'You make me nervous standing there and staring out.'

'I'm not hurting anyone. Anyway, I don't know how much longer I'll be able to look at those trees and hills, or if I ever will again.' But he clambered awkwardly down from the table.

'*Papa.*' Alys moved closer to him and put her arm around his shoulders. 'Don't say it. Don't even think it. Even if we have to leave, we'll be back. It won't be for long.'

'A week away from here and in – in one of those horrible places is too long.'

Émile didn't have to mention the additional horror of the ride to the camp. On one of her visits to Liège to meet Gilles early in the occupation, she'd seen the masses of people being forced into cattle cars on a railroad siding. Most of them had been Jews, marked with the large yellow Star of David, the stigmata of their belief; but others had been like themselves, persons aiding the Allied cause. And like Gilles, who'd been executed for his part in rescuing downed Allied flyers.

Papa was right, Alys thought. Being taken away didn't mean they were not going to be executed. And Minette. What would become of Minette? She ached to run over to the pallet and take her daughter in her arms, but the little girl was finally asleep, and it would be wrong to wake her.

'It's all your fault, you know,' Émile said, glowering at her. 'Insisting on taking him in. Keeping him here when the Germans came. Look what you've brought us to!'

'I'm sorry, *Papa.*' She walked over to Jolie. 'I'm sorry, *Maman.* It seemed so right. I was sure it was the right thing to do.'

'So did the others we saw climbing into the trucks,' Émile said. 'Will they return? Will any of us return? No, we'll be either starved or tortured to death.'

Alys watched the tears rolling down her father's cheeks. A man who seldom revealed any emotion, he was now weeping. He was frightened; he was really frightened, she thought. And so was she.

'Stop it, Émile.' Jolie's voice remained low to keep from waking Minette, but its very softness penetrated and diffused the gloomy atmosphere. 'Alys did the right thing, and you know it. Don't add guilt to the burden of fear and worry she already carries. We should be proud of what we've done.'

'Thank you, *Maman*. But aren't you frightened, too?'

'Of course I am, but I also have faith. I'm more concerned now about seeing if we can persuade the guard to bring us food and water. When Minette wakes up, she'll be crying for her supper.'

Throughout the last of this conversation, they had been unaware of the continuous undertone coming from outside of shouted orders and vehicles moving at a steady pace along the road. Now these sounds filtered into the room and became part of the ominous silence.

'What do you suppose is going on out there?' Émile strode to the door, and then stopped abruptly, remembering just before he touched the knob that he was a prisoner.

Alys moved over to the door and pressed her ear against it. Something had begun puzzling her, and she turned around.

'What is it?' Jolie asked. 'What did you hear?'

'Nothing,' Alys said. 'That's what's so strange. All of a sudden just silence.'

'Well, makes no difference for us. We're still under guard and can only wait.' And wait they did for more than another hour of prolonged agony.

On Jolie's lap, Minette uncurled herself and slowly opened her eyes.

'Well, little one, you had quite a nice nap.' Alys sat down beside her mother.

'I hungwy,' Minette announced in the matter-of-fact tone that assumed her need would be immediately taken care of.

Alys looked at her mother.

'Ask him, Alys. It can't hurt. Or are you afraid to?'

'No, I'm not afraid of asking, just of his refusing. It will – it will just make things seem so much worse if he does refuse.'

She stood for a moment at the door, her hand on the knob, but not turning it. It wasn't a major decision; and yet, it seemed as if the request were an arrival at a crossroads; and the guard's reply, a guidepost pointing the direction their future would take. Until now, they could only conjecture what was going to happen to them, and they could cling to a scrap of hope, an attitude of optimism. Would she, upon opening the door and asking for food, snuff out that flicker of hope?

Alys turned the knob and waited for some response to the slight metallic sound: there was none. She opened the door: there was no one there. No doubt the guard had gone up to the kitchen in search of food. She hadn't been afraid to confront him here, just outside the room, but leaving the room in defiance of orders was something else. He would have every right to shoot her on the grounds – or pretense – that she was trying to escape.

'There's no one here. I'm going up to the kitchen.' She said it loudly enough so the words would precede her. She was surprised that the guard didn't come to the head of the stairs.

No one challenged her. The kitchen was empty. She walked through the dining room to the front hall. Still no sign of anyone.

He's gone outside, she thought, deserted his post to join the one or two that have surely been left to watch the inn. She was still standing in the hall when the front door began to open slowly. In an instant she froze. Better to be found standing still than running back to the stairs. Then, with cries of genuine surprise, she saw, instead of a German uniform, the worn coat and trousers of Monsieur Gautier, a farmer who lived on his land half a kilometer away.

'Monsieur Gautier, what are you doing here?' Then, remembering her own plight, she warned him, 'You must not stay. It's too dangerous for you. We're under guard – to be taken away for hiding a wounded American soldier. If they see you here, they'll think you collaborated.'

'No,' he said, 'there's no more danger.' Alys found herself surprisingly comforted by his gruff voice. 'They're gone. The Germans have all left the village.'

'Gone! Gone where?' His placid stoicism, his terse, matter-of-fact statements, devoid of all elaboration, had her wanting to scream at him.

'American forces have relieved Bastogne. The siege is lifted, and the Allies are advancing on several fronts. The Germans are being forced to fall back, and many are fleeing.'

'I can't believe it.' Holding tightly to the newel post, Alys collapsed on the bottom step of the stairway. 'We've been saved. We don't have to leave here.' She looked up at Monsieur Gautier. 'You're sure of all this?'

'I stood by the road and watched them retreating. The war isn't over yet, but the end is in sight. The cursed *Boches* are going to lose, and some of them know it already. I saw their faces. They are frightened men.'

'I have to tell the family. They must wonder what's happened to me.' She started toward the kitchen, then turned. 'Why did you stop by here?'

'To see if your father wanted to go to Monsieur Jobert's with me. He sent word by his son. We should be celebrating with a glass of wine. He has two bottles hidden away.' He shook his head sadly. 'The one for Christmas he did not open. The second, of course, is for the end of the war. That is his best bottle. But the second-best is good enough for tonight. So, see if your papa would like to come with me. I think he has much to celebrate, *n'est-ce pas*?'

Alys knew he wanted to keep talking, but nothing must detain her from telling her family the glorious news.

'Eh, Alys, you come, too. You and your *Maman*.' He winked. 'Monsieur Jobert just might have a third bottle tucked away.' His voice followed Alys down the stairs. The invitation to share a bottle of wine was far less urgent than the news that the Germans had left Ste. Monique and they themselves were free.

'*Maman! Papa!*' Alys pushed open the door. 'They're gone. The Germans are gone.'

'Wait, wait,' Jolie said. 'Not so fast.'

'No guards here, *Maman*. And no Germans in the village.' She picked up Minette, hugging and dancing her round and round the room.

'How do you know?' Émile asked. The terrors of two wars and years of occupation had instilled in him a cautious pessimism when it came to dealing with Germans. 'The guard might have just slipped outside. No reason to make such wild statements.'

'But they're true, *Papa*. Monsieur Gautier is upstairs. He saw them retreating. The Allies are on the move again. And Monsieur Gautier says the whole village is celebrating. He stopped by to tell us. To invite us to go with him.'

'Then, it's true? We're not to be transported?' Jolie crossed herself several times and murmured thanks to God, Mary, and all the saints.

'It's true. So – shall we go with Monsieur Gautier? He says Monsieur Jobert has saved a bottle of wine – maybe two – for just such a celebration.'

All the time she was rejoicing with her parents, Alys's mind was filled with concern for Ryan. While the rest were sharing Monsieur Jobert's wine, she'd hurry to the monastery. If Ryan had tolerated the ride in the staff car, then surely he could have endured the few hours since then under German care. Or even no care at all. What was important now was getting him back to the inn. If the Germans had left town in all the haste Monsieur Gautier described, then she doubted they had taken the wounded with them. But they might have taken the medical staff, and that made it all the more imperative for her to find Ryan.

'*Maman, Papa,* Monsieur Gautier is waiting for us.' Her impatience to leave and get on her way to the village was not for the farmer's sake but Ryan's.

'Émile?' Jolie looked to her husband.

'Just thinking about the hills. I do not have to leave them.' He sighed. 'Yes, my dear, certainly we'll go.' Then he smiled. 'Monsieur Jobert's best wine, eh? I wondered if he would ever open those bottles.'

'But first we feed Minette.' She turned to Alys. 'Tell Gautier to join us in the kitchen. We won't be long.'

A somber twilight was settling over the valley when they left the inn and started walking along the road to Ste. Monique. It would snow tomorrow. The wind off the hills was suddenly very cold. Émile hoisted Minette up on his shoulders, and they all began to walk a little faster. Otherwise, they were scarcely aware of the chill penetrating their coats and scarves. The Germans were gone, and pray God they would not return again. Such news brought warmth to the coldest day and brightened the gloomiest of skies.

'I feel like singing,' Jolie cried out, and began humming the first notes of the Belgian national anthem.

'And dancing,' Émile said. Minette squeaked with laughter when her grandfather began hopping up and down, bouncing her on his shoulders.

'More, *Grand-papa,* more,' she cried when he stopped.

'When we get to the square. Your old *Grand-papa* is out of breath now. I expect everyone will be dancing when we get there.'

'Here, let me carry you.' Monsieur Gautier held out his arms to Minette. He grinned at Émile. 'I'm not so old as some people I know.'

Alys had been walking – almost running – ahead of them, more anxious with every passing minute to get to Ryan at the monastery.

Suddenly she stopped short. There was something, a large bundle of some kind, lying beside the road ahead of her. She knew the German practice of booby-trapping innocent-looking objects. Not only might the object explode on contact, but there might be a trip wire hidden alongside or across the road. It was just the sort of dastardly, ingenious ruse the Germans would employ on leaving the village. A macabre joke to play on those who now thought they were safe from enemy guns.

'*Papa,*' Alys called back. 'Monsieur Gautier. There's something up ahead by the road. Do you think it safe to go on?'

'I see it,' Monsieur Gautier said. He handed Minette to Jolie. 'I'll walk along the verge and approach it from there.' He was as aware as Alys about trip wires. 'A quick look should tell us if it's booby-trapped. There wasn't time for them to be too clever about it.'

The rest stood several feet away while Monsieur Gautier approached the object. They saw him bending over and then quickly standing up and waving them on.

'It's a man under a heavy quilt. He seems to be still alive.'

'We ought to help him,' Alys said. 'He could freeze if he stays there all night.' She hurried to stand beside Monsieur Gautier and suggested they try to wake the man up. She leaned over and pulled the heavy quilt away from the man's face.

'Oh God, no! *Papa! Maman!* It's Ryan. Hurry, he's scarcely breathing. Please hurry, we have to get him back to the inn.'

CHAPTER NINE

The celebration in the village and Monsieur Jobert's treasured wine were quickly forgotten. Émile and Monsieur Gautier carried Ryan, now wrapped securely in the quilt, back to the inn. Alarmed at finding Ryan left at the side of the road, they could only surmise that the German order to evacuate the area had been so preemptive and imperative that there'd been no time to take him to the monastery. He'd been merely lifted out of the staff car and laid on the verge. Alys ran ahead to prepare a bed in one of the guest rooms. There was no longer any need to keep him in the cellar. She was still shattered by the terror of the moment when the major pulled up the pallet and found the metal tag. In spite of their seemingly being safe from incarceration or execution, it was a moment she would relive over and over for the rest of her life while re-experiencing those sickening spasms of fear.

By the time the two men carried Ryan up to the room, the bed was ready for him. Within a very few minutes Alys was able to ascertain that he had not suffered too badly from having been moved or exposed to the frigid weather. He was severely chilled, but it should not take too long to warm him. She had a featherbed for him to lie on, and she put several quilts over him.

The stomach tube had been removed by the Germans, and while Jolie warmed up a pot of broth, Alys painstakingly inserted another tube. She placed the open end in a glass of water, watching intently to make certain no air bubbled into the water. It didn't. Air bubbles would have meant the tube was in the lungs instead of the stomach, and she would have to remove it immediately and repeat the insertion process.

After feeding Ryan, Alys collapsed into a chair beside the bed. She wanted nothing so much as to lay her head back and go to sleep right there. To sleep and forget about the dreadful hours they'd all endured. Slowly she got up. Ryan would be all right now for a few hours. With one last smoothing of the quilts and a thankful look at the serene expression on his face, she went in search of Minette. A good meal and a long night's sleep were what they both needed.

Ryan felt a liquid warmth flooding his body. It was almost as if he could actually feel the blood coursing through his veins. He'd been cold, terribly cold, after falling through the ice. Mama and Daddy had warned him. The spell of cold weather – unusually long and cold for South Carolina – had frozen the surface of the duck pond on their farm. But only the surface. 'And it can fool you. It's treacherous.' Daddy had said that over and over. 'Very treacherous. Stay off the ice.'

But how can a seven-year-old boy be expected to resist that glistening surface, that tempting smoothness, just begging him to glide across? He didn't have skates. A frozen pond was a rarity in Camden. But he had on his smooth-soled Sunday shoes.

He tested the ice at the shallow edge. Good and firm, if a bit rough and ridged like corduroy. Daddy was wrong. It was plenty solid enough for him to walk on. His first tentative glide landed him in an ignominious heap with a slightly bruised backside and a more seriously bruised ego. Fortunately no one was around to witness his embarrassment. Farther out, the ice was smoother. Here the gliding was great. He'd seen skaters in movies and been fascinated by their spins and twirls. He stood in one spot and went round and round.

He heard the reverberating crack just before his feet plunged through the ice. The pond wasn't much over his head, and he was a good swimmer for his age. The water was too calm to pull him under the frozen surface. Managing to keep his head barely above water, he tried to hoist himself up onto the ice to walk back to shore, but it kept cracking and breaking apart. At the same time he thought he'd have to break his way clear to land, he began yelling for help. He was getting tired. Near the point of exhaustion, he saw his father and others running toward him. The last thing he remembered, aside from how cold he was, was reaching for the rope they threw to him and getting the noose under his arms.

Now he was warm again. He snuggled under the covers and went back to sleep.

A little later, Ryan awoke to total darkness. It was the sound of frozen rain pinging against and then ricocheting off a windowpane that woke him. He awoke not to a dream of the past – a little boy thrown by a horse, falling out of a tree, or crashing through the ice – but to a frightening, present-day reality. He was in bed, and suffering that miserable grogginess one feels after having slept too long. For a few moments he passed in and out of sleep, like one coming out of etherized slumber. He tried but couldn't get completely awake.

Gradually his eyes became accustomed to the dark, and a soft light from beyond the door filtered into the room. But the light flickered, throwing grotesque shadows on the wall. Now he heard voices, the sound of people talking, but not the words. Just the low mumble of conversation. As he looked and listened, the sounds of rain and voices and the sight of furniture and shadows alternately advanced and receded like waves against a shore. They made him dizzy and then nauseous. He tried to swallow quickly several times, but there was something in his throat, and his throat hurt. He closed his eyes, but that only made his head rather than the room undulate, and he quickly opened them again.

Maybe if he lay on his side or sat up a little. Turning to his side helped some, but the scant movement revealed something startling. It had taken a real effort to shift position. He had no strength to sit up.

With his head turned to the side, he saw the door leading into a hall, from which the light shone with an unsteady glimmer. It was enough, however, for him to see some objects in the room, and he looked from one to another in shocked disbelief. Nothing about them was familiar. Not the room itself nor any of its furnishings.

Where was he and how had he gotten here? Why was he sleeping in a strange bed? He tried painfully to recollect what he'd been doing before going to bed – where he'd been, who he'd been with. Not a name, not a place came to mind. Nothing. A blank nothing. And before that? Still a bleak emptiness. In terror, he reached further back into his mind, searching for the past, but he found only a deep, bottomless void. He could remember nothing past the moment he'd awakened to the sounds of frozen rain. Convulsed with a new horror, he realized he couldn't remember his own name.

'My God!' It was a silent scream. No sound came out. 'Who am I?' No, it was all right, he tried to assure himself. He'd just momentarily blanked out.

Again he tried to sit up, but his arms lacked the strength to raise himself. That was it – he'd been sick. Or hurt. But there was no pain, only a dull, throbbing ache in his head and a general lassitude throughout his body.

I'll be all right. My body's recovered from whatever it was but not my mind. It'll just take time.

As a slow drowsy sleep came over him again, he allowed himself to succumb to it. He felt a strange sense of relief in leaving reality and entering the twilight between sleeping and wakefuless. His tired body was buoyed up by the soft featherbed on which he lay, and his mind floated freely in a dark, quiet wilderness. He felt at peace as he settled into that bodiless, mindless netherworld devoid of pain and memory.

When Ryan awoke again to full consciousness, he had no idea how much time had passed – a moment or several hours. He lay mute and immobile in the opaque silence. There was still a flickering light in the hall, bright enough to show the sizes and shapes of furniture but few details.

Desperately he began to figure out what each piece was – a dresser, a chair, a table – as if by recalling something from memory, all memory would return. If he concentrated on other things, pushed away the fact he couldn't remember his name, it would suddenly come to him in a flash. Like a word on the tip of one's tongue. Forget about trying to remember, channel the mind into other directions, and the word would appear at the most unexpected time. But no word came, no flash of memory from the past.

Ryan allowed the fear that had been lurking on the perimeter of his mind to enter and take over. An amorphous mass of desperation smothered him, threatening to squeeze all sanity out of him. He fought to keep it from closing in completely, but it was like fighting one's way through a dense, ever-thickening fog. Desperation and terror had enisled him and left him surrounded by a fearful unknown world. A world in which he was totally alone. Worst of all, he was alone with a stranger. He felt as if he'd become two people, one lying on the bed and the other looking at him and trying to figure out who this stranger was. Frantically he tossed and turned on the bed, pummeled the pillow, worried over a lump under his back that irritated him. Anything to keep from thinking about what was tormenting him. Who was he?

Filled with loathing for being unable to control his frustration, he finally buried his face in the pillow; and exhausted from his futile efforts at trying to remember anything, he fell asleep.

Sitting at the kitchen table and sorting through Minette's socks to find those that needed mending, Alys listened to the frozen rain chiming against milk buckets waiting on the stoop like empty houses waiting for occupants that never returned. There'd been no milk for weeks. There were no cows.

Usually Alys found the sound of rain soothing, especially on a night like this with all of them sitting around the table, but tonight it only exacerbated a restlessness that had her on edge all day. A mood of waiting and of impatient expectancy had her jumping at the least sound and turning her head quickly when a door opened. At first she attributed her feeling to the dire events of the previous day, the fear that the Germans would return. But this feeling was different. It was not fear: it was anticipation.

When she'd gone to Ryan's room a little earlier, she'd been stunned to see him lying on his side. For weeks he'd lain immobile on his back. She'd moved him several times a day to prevent bed sores, but never before had he moved of his own volition. Could it possibly mean that something was at last stirring in his mind? Was he finally emerging from the deep coma? More important, would his mind take the final step into complete wakefulness?

While she'd stood watching him, yearning to touch him to see if that would awaken him, she saw a very slight movement beneath his eyelids. His eyes were moving as one's do during a dream. Her whole body tensed. Elation vied with caution. She wanted to stay in the room, to watch for even the slightest movement of Ryan's body: a finger, an eyelid, his lips. But the thought of the overwhelming disappointment if nothing happened sent her from the room and looking for something to keep her mind off his condition.

There was plenty for her hands to do, but nothing that occupied her mind enough to keep her from thinking about him. Finally, when she could stand it no longer, she put aside Minette's socks and walked upstairs.

In the confusion of drifting between the neap tide of sleeping and the high tide of wakefulness, Ryan was never quite sure what he was experiencing at any given moment. What were dreams and what reality? He fought to believe that his lack of memory, the not knowing who he was, was a dream. Like running naked in a public place or taking an exam for a course never studied.

I'm dreaming! I'm dreaming! he thought, pounding his pillow. No, dammit, I'm awake.

He'd awakened to an alien world, a world of unknown place and time and circumstance. He was in bed recovering from God only knew what illness or accident, and he didn't know who he was. Damn! That was the worst. Who in hell was he? No name. No past to cling to. To stand on. Like trying to stand without feet. Or entering a room without a floor. Only a vast emptiness beneath him and nothing to hold on to except what he could find ahead of him in an as yet unplumbed future. It was eerie. Ironic: the future is always unknown – one accepted that – but not the past. It should be as familiar, as much a part of him, as his face in the mirror.

Ryan was startled out of his reverie by the movement of a light coming nearer. Now he could see more details in the room. But these were of less interest than who was carrying the light toward the room. One look at the person might provide the clue he needed, might be the ball of string leading him away from the dread monster of forgetfulness. He waited with an expectancy close to mania, as if he sensed this was his last, his one and only chance to escape the bleak, empty, stygian cave.

The light stopped moving, and a shadow preceded a figure into the room. The woman was framed in a corona of light, but her face remained in darkness. *Who are you?* he wanted to shout, but pushed the words and sound back down his throat. She would tell him who she was. She would eventually bring a light into the room and into his mind.

Alys put the lantern on a table in the hall. It would be dark in the room, but it was a quiet darkness she sought. She could sit by the bed and imagine that Ryan was sleeping naturally.

The sounds of the old wooden bed creaking and a quick intake of breath brought her up short. She paused. It could be her imagination or her wish for Ryan to be awake, emerging as sound. She listened. There was the faintest difference in his breathing. Perhaps he'd turned over again. Returning to the hall, she picked up the lantern and hurried back to the room. Then she stopped just inside the door.

Alys had expected she'd shout with joy when she saw Ryan awake at long last. Instead she was paralyzed into immobility and overcome with an absurd attack of shyness. Absurd because she'd never been a reticent person. Instead, she was more apt to plunge full force into a situation, often to her chagrin and embarrassment. Now she stood afraid to approach the bed. What did one say to a young man – a stranger – whom one has kept alive, has nursed, fed, and bathed? Whose most intimate physical needs one has cared for? Only when she saw the confused, questioning expression on Ryan's face did she realize she had to say something to dispel the palpable silence between them.

'Sir? You're awake?' she asked softly. She tried to remain calm, not give in to the heart-bursting, pulse-throbbing emotion that she thought at the time was merely gratitude and thanksgiving. But she found herself rushing toward the bed. 'You're conscious at last. It's been such a very long time.'

Staring at the young woman, so obviously glad to see him awake, Ryan tried to find meaning in her words. She'd spoken with a gentle, easy familiarity, but her face was that of a stranger. Disappointment overcame curiosity. He'd been so certain she'd provide the answers and pull apart the curtains between present and past. He'd deluded himself, and disillusionment is the bitter stepchild of hope.

'Here, let me make you more comfortable.' He felt her hands on either side of his face and then a tube being pulled from his throat. So that was what had been hurting him.

'I'm sorry,' he heard her saying. She was now sitting in a chair beside him, her hands reaching and her upper body leaning toward him. 'I'm sorry if I startled you. You've been here so long I forgot for a moment you don't know me.'

Relief flooded through Ryan. If he were not expected to know her, then maybe he'd never been in this room before. She would explain it all. A long time, she'd said. If he'd been ill, as now seemed likely, then perhaps in time he'd find his way through the maze to where memory was hidden. A few questions might solve the problem, but did he want to reveal his frightening desperation? Maybe it would be wiser to let her do the talking. The answers might come without his having to ask the questions. He continued to look at her with what he hoped was an inquisitive but at the same time somewhat indifferent expression. As if to imply that in the present situation it were her place to do the explaining.

'My name is Alys Prévou.' With all the shocks he'd suffered, he was only now aware of her accent. Where in hell was he? 'You've been hurt,' she continued, 'and I've been taking care of you.'

Ryan could no longer contain his curiosity and despair. His mind formed the words 'Who am I? Where am I?' but somewhere between his brain and his tongue, his damaged nerve cells got the signals confused. The only sounds that came out were the babblings of a still suckling infant, the moronic syllables of an imbecile. He saw the horror spread across Alys's face, and it mirrored the horror swelling like an obscene, cancerous mass in his brain. It was the final ignominy, the ultimate, burning, pincering torture. He turned in the bed and buried his face in the pillow. He'd become an animal. No, worse, a discarded bit of vegetable matter with no memory and no ability to speak. She'd said she'd been caring for him. For a long time. Maybe he'd been near death. Oh God, why hadn't she just let him go ahead and die? He winced under the hand she laid on his shoulder.

'It's all right, sir. It will be all right, I promise. You were seriously hurt. It will just take time.' Desperately she sought for the words to comfort and to reassure him as well as herself. She'd kept him alive, but had it been for this? How could she tell him everything would be all right when she had no way of knowing what damage had been done and whether it was irreversible? Time. Maybe time would do it. Meanwhile, she had to comfort him, subdue his misery, and assuage the terror she knew was overwhelming him.

'Please, please, sir, let me help you.'

He turned over slowly. His eyes spoke what his mouth could not utter. His expression reminded her of a puppy she once had who'd been hit by a car. His eyes had pleaded with her to release him from his agony. There'd been no help for the puppy. The only release for him was a quick, merciful death. For Ryan there must be life, and it must be a life with the ability to speak.

CHAPTER TEN

Ryan lay immobile, beyond thought or will. With both mind and body numb, he no longer had the ability or the desire to react to the stimulus of touch or sound. He felt Alys's hands around his, but they neither soothed nor irritated. He heard her voice, but the words had no meaning. He stared at the ceiling, and his glance never moved from a small, oddly shaped crack in the plaster. As he stared, it grew larger and smaller, as if it had a life of its own. Light magnified it; a shadow crossed it and it became a microcosmic fissure of itself. Then suddenly it broke apart in a skyrocket explosion of tinier, bloodred veins. Ryan closed his eyes and shrank within himself to escape from the nightmare anguish in his mind.

For several minutes Alys pleaded with Ryan, urging him to have faith. To believe that with time he would speak again, just as it had taken time for him to emerge from his somnambulant state. But she knew he wasn't listening. At least, he wasn't hearing what she said. His hands were limp in hers, as if all life had drained from them. She tactfully avoided any show of pity. Finally she released his hands and watched them fall heavily on the bed. When she moved to leave, there was no change of expression on his face.

For the next two days, Alys came frequently to the room, bringing his meals and caring for his needs.

Ryan felt something touch his lips. She was feeding him again. He didn't want to eat. He wasn't hungry, but he opened his mouth and chewed. Swallowing was agony; his throat hurt and he didn't know why. Something hot slid down his throat. He was choking. He needed air. He couldn't breathe. He thought he was gasping, but he heard no sound. Why didn't she slow down? Another spoonful in his mouth now making its painful way down his throat. Followed by something smooth and cool. That was better. There was no pain.

But nothing had any flavor. Just bland lumps of things that had to be chewed or allowed to slide down.

He heard the dishes clatter as she set the tray down, and the din was almost unbearable. Every sound was a blast against his eardrums. He tried to cover his ears, but his hands wouldn't rise from the bed. More sounds. Of water rushing like a torrent. It was bathtime, and she was pouring water from a pitcher into the bowl. Why did she have to be so noisy about it? The wet cloth moved along his arm. It felt as if his skin were being stripped away and the cloth were rasping against raw flesh and sensitive nerve endings. Or open sores. The water flowed over him like hot, heavy, sluggish lava.

Gradually the water became warm and soothing. Hands were massaging his back, absorbing the ache, and he felt his body tingling with life. Life. He was alive. He could hear and feel, see and breathe. All he couldn't do was remember and talk. Four out of six wasn't bad. He could always just lie here and watch time creep along. Or anything else that passed his door. Day to night. Night to day. Gradually, from the minutes and hours, he'd forge a memory. Starting from now. If the blanket doesn't cover your feet, cut some off the top and sew it on the bottom. Imperfect, but better than no blanket at all. Better a memory starting now than none at all.

Alys looked at Ryan's glazed eyes and vapid expression, his limp, flaccid hands. She thought about his lack of response. She was not sure he always heard what she said. He was receding into a different kind of coma, a listless, self-induced coma. Nature's own healing powers had brought him out of the earlier one. What would bring him out of this more malignant, more destructive one? He was slipping away from her as surely as if he'd been fatally wounded. What stimulus could she use to save him from himself? His basic instinct for survival might not be enough. To what could she appeal to motivate him into returning to life? His ego. His natural pride in his own masculinity. She'd done too much for him, made him dependent on her. It was time to force him into becoming independent. No, allow him to be dependent on himself.

'I'm leaving now,' she said. 'There's water here if you get thirsty. Ring this small bell if you need anything. There's a bathroom down the hall. Also a chamber pot under the bed if you feel too weak to walk.'

She started walking out of the room. Her legs were shaking as if she'd been the one who'd spent weeks in bed. 'I'll see you in the morning when I bring up your breakfast. Good night.'

Alys was barely able to hold back her tears until she got into the hall. In her own room she wept with frustration and despair. There seemed no way to reach Ryan, to convince him to let her help him. Even though she was still woefully ignorant of how to help him speak again, there had to be a way. She had vague recollections of studying such problems in the psychology courses she'd taken for her degree. She'd find her textbooks and re-read those chapters. Maybe, too, they'd give her an insight into reaching a person suffering such a handicap.

Damn her! Ryan thought after Alys left. Damn her anyway for assuming to have any understanding of what's happened to me. For sympathizing with what I'm going through now. And damn her for walking out on me like that.

How could she possibly know what he was suffering? Trying to placate him that way with easy words of comfort and soothing assurances that in time he'd speak again. How in hell did she know what was wrong with him? What part of his brain had been damaged, or at best gone into hibernation?

The eating and bathing had him exhausted and he sought the refuge of dreamless sleep, or at least the euphoria of drowsiness, while he floated with Lethe's slow-moving current in his own peculiar purgatory.

Darkness outside and the room was filled with shadows from the lantern by his bed. From the lantern, flames flared up and he was surrounded by light, a blazing light. His eyes burned, but he couldn't close them. The sparks entered his brain and charred his senses, melting them down to liquid nerves that seeped out through his ears and pores and mouth with a foul-tasting sputum. He swallowed again and again until his mouth was dry.

For many hours he moved in wild, spasmodic gyrations. His body was sore and raw; why couldn't he rest? The featherbed was full of nasty little ridges, like skinny fingers, that irritatingly massaged his skin. Gradually some of Alys's words emerged from his subconscious to his conscious mind. He'd been in a coma for a long time. No wonder he couldn't fall asleep now. He'd probably be cursed by wakefulness for an equal number of weeks to make up the deficit, to balance the scales, so to speak. Nature didn't like things to be uneven and out of whack. So many hours of sleep per day were allotted to man, and so many to be awake. They had to come out right, like assets and liabilities.

Oh hell, why was he thinking such stupid thoughts? To keep from facing the truth, he admitted. Not the truth that he couldn't speak, but that Alys wanted to help him. And he'd hurt her by rejecting her offer. She'd been upset with him before she left, but he sensed her casual attitude covered a deep hurt. After all, she'd saved his life by taking care of him. He had no right to remain unmoved or to reject her offer of help, with cold, bitter detachment.

Yet, in his own defense, he argued, she was unaware he had more than one handicap. She didn't know how being a nameless, pastless entity, as well as a voiceless one, could destroy a man's will to live. She didn't know with what enigmatic monster he was struggling. And how could he tell her? There lay the heart-pounding, breath-sucking, mind-tormenting frustration.

Lying there cursing nothing in particular but fate in general, he felt an irritating fullness in his groin. He had to urinate. This need, more than anything else, made him realize how completely dependent he'd become on Alys, without being consciously aware of it. He had no idea how long he'd been unconscious, and she'd taken care of all his needs; but he did know that for the past two days, he'd allowed her to keep on nursing him as if he were an invalid or a helpless child, rather than a man who could take care of himself. He was consumed with fury and shame at himself.

She had said there was a bathroom down the hall and a chamber pot under the bed. It was her way of telling him to get out of bed and stop pitying himself. And she was right.

Ryan managed to raise himself farther up in bed. He'd be damned if he'd use the pot, like a child too afraid to dare a darkened hall. Gradually, shrinking first from the stabbing pains in his feet when he touched the floor but finally forcing himself to endure them, he stood up. With the support of the bedpost and then reaching for a dresser, he made it to the door. He saw a light had been left in the bathroom and the door was open. At least he didn't have to guess which way to go.

By palming his way along the wall, he made it to the bathroom. Although feeling faint and light-headed, he experienced no sickening vertigo; however, there was nothing near the toilet to hold on to. He considered, only momentarily, the idea of sitting down. But his ego derided that thought. He was a man, and even though he was alone, with no one to witness his posture, the very notion of submitting to it was humiliating.

It took longer than he expected to relieve himself, and he felt himself reeling with weakness. He had to make it back to bed quickly before he passed out. Cold sweat already drenched his face, and the nauseous smell of it oozing through his pores made him gag. But he kept going. Once back in bed, he'd be all right. His hands, now slick with sweat, moved along the wall. Suddenly the wall was not there. It had moved away from him. The floor too was moving, but toward him, not away. With both hands he reached for it.

Alys turned out the light and slid in beside Minette. Tomorrow she'd look for the psychology books. In spite of being physically exhausted, she couldn't get to sleep. A thousand disparate thoughts tumbled over and among one another in her mind, like the spinning, whirling colors in a kaleidoscope: the various horrors of the war, the hours with Gilles, the faces of her students, her own days at the university. She felt as if she were living her whole life over again, but in some abstract, hodgepodge, out-of-sequence series of events. Successes vied with and were replaced by failures; tears and laughter, the joyful and the sad intermingled and blended into a huge montage that was her life. So where did the present fit in? And the future? Would she succeed or would she fail with Ryan? Would she, in the years ahead, look back and weep or would she smile? She had healed Ryan's body, or at least given it what it needed to heal itself. To heal itself. That might be the answer. She had to find out what Ryan's damaged mind needed to repair itself. That was the route she would follow.

With that comforting, if not entirely satisfactory, thought, she began immediately feeling more relaxed; and she welcomed the drowsiness suffusing through her.

In Alys's sleep-filled mind, the sound of a soft thud somewhere in the distance engendered a thirty-second dream in which she was lying in an orchard with ripe apples dropping all around. When she woke to consciousness, however, she was fully aware that she'd really heard the sound. She lay for a moment wondering from which direction it had come. Muffled, stumbling, shuffling sounds awoke her still further, and she was instantly alert.

'Ryan!' He'd risen to her challenge and was trying to make it to the bathroom. Hastily she pulled on her robe, made from an old patchwork quilt.

Her first view of Ryan assured her he wasn't hurt. He was on his knees, pounding the floor with one fist. His face betrayed the frustration and humiliation he was suffering. She waited and watched him try to get up, only to fall again. He hadn't the strength yet to walk any distance, and she was ashamed for having taunted him into trying it.

'I'm sorry, m'sieur. I apologize.' She walked up behind him. 'I shouldn't have expected you to be able to walk the distance.'

He swung around, sitting down and crossing his legs. He glared at her, in no way acknowledging her apology. His look implied he'd prefer that she leave him and let him manage for himself. Then suddenly he started laughing. Without knowing what he found amusing, she began laughing, too.

'Do you want me to help you back to your room?' she asked. 'It's more comfortable than this cold floor.'

He nodded.

'Good. Then will you let me talk to you?'

He nodded again, and this time the faintest of smiles appeared.

By using Alys as well as the wall and furniture for support, Ryan made it to the bed. He allowed her to tuck the quilts around him. His face was soaked with sweat, and Alys was aware how much effort it had taken for him to make it to the bathroom.

'I'll be right back,' she said. 'There's something I want to get.'

In a few minutes she returned with paper and pencil.

'Here, this will be a start. You write and I'll talk. I'm not very sleepy. Are you?'

He shook his head and reached for the pencil and paper. She saw him grinning as he wrote, and she wondered again what he found funny about the situation. When he handed the paper back, she expected the usual 'Where am I?' or 'Who are you?' type of questions. Instead, she started laughing herself when she read, *You looked like a small bed walking toward me in that crazy quilt.*

'With a sense of humor like that,' she said, 'you're going to be all right. I thought you were furious with me.'

He grabbed the paper and wrote rapidly, *I was. You made me see how boorish I was being. I'm sorry. I now realize you're trying to help.*

'I am, I really am. I want you well and able to talk. And I think I can help you.'

He began writing again, and when Alys read it this time, she wanted to put her arms around him and comfort him as she would someone bereaved by a tragic loss. How does one cope with the loss of his own past? *Who am I?* he'd written. *I can't remember anything before waking up here. Where am I?*

She could weep or she could sympathize, but neither was what he needed now. He needed as much truth as she could give him.

'Your name is Ryan Middleton. You were injured several weeks ago and have been in a coma since then.'

From then on he wrote almost as quickly as she talked.

She told him he was in Belgium, and then she paused. He obviously had no memory of the war. To tell him the whole truth would involve too many details right now. He'd wonder why he wasn't in a military hospital, and why she didn't send him to one now. With the relief of Bastogne, the Americans had begun their own strong offensive; and the fighting was now taking place along and inside the German border. There was no longer a hospital in Ste. Monique, and traveling to some place like Liège was an impossibility.

Admit it, she told herself. You want to keep him here and be the one who teaches him to speak.

No, he meant more to her than that. Her heart knew, even if her mind wouldn't accept it yet, that she cared very deeply for him. She didn't want him to leave her.

Alys finally told him only that he'd been in an accident and left by strangers at the inn. She didn't know the details. The men who'd left him had mentioned his name and then gone away.

Ryan sensed that she was not telling him everything she knew. For the moment he didn't care. He was alive, and this young woman had saved his life. And she'd made him laugh. With her hair mussed and her cheeks flushed from sleeping and in that ridiculous robe, she'd awakened in him more than just the wish to live. Looking at her now, he saw how really beautiful she was.

'You need to sleep now,' Alys said. 'We'll talk more in the morning.'

After she left, Ryan lay back against the pillows. He was tired. So few questions, and none of the important ones, had been answered. He knew his name, but that was all. Somewhere, there must be someone who knew who he was, where he was from, and why he was here in Belgium. But now he sank into a deep sleep. His dreams were of thunder and lightning, and black monsters with Maltese crosses painted on their hideous iron faces came roaring at him. He awoke in a drenching sweat, and lay awake a long time in a shivering, unnameable agony before going back to sleep.

Nor for another two hours did Alys go to sleep. She hunted through her books until she found the ones she needed. Then she read all the chapters on amnesia and aphasia, the condition that prevented Ryan from speaking. They helped, but she needed much more information if she were to teach him to speak again.

First thing in the morning she wrote to Dr. Barré, her psychology professor in Liège. Then she fixed a breakfast tray for Ryan. When Minette asked if she could accompany her, Alys said she could. The presence of Minette might cheer him up.

'Here we are,' Alys announced when they reached Ryan's room. 'Your nurse and your handmaiden.' She was pleased to see him sitting up amd smiling. She didn't know the smile came from his pleasure at seeing that she really was as beautiful as he'd thought she was last night.

He pointed to Minette and raised his eyebrows questioningly.

'This is Minette, my daughter.' She thought she detected a frown, and she wondered if having the child in the room upset him. But he immediately smiled again when Minette crawled up on the bed and settled herself against the pillow next to him.

'*Bonjour, m'sieur,*' Minette said, snuggling up to him.

'Monsieur doesn't speak French,' Alys said in that language. 'In fact, because he was hurt, he can't speak at all.'

Ryan grimaced as a new terror engulfed him. He was not only trapped in an unknown place and time with all his thoughts and needs locked inside his brain, but now this strange language they were speaking isolated him more than ever. Layer by layer he was being wrapped like a mummy in bindings that threatened to bury him within himself.

Seeing that Ryan was frustrated at being unable to understand. Alys said quickly, 'I was telling her that you don't speak French.'

Relieved at the explanation that released one of the bonds, Ryan nodded as if to say that was all right, and put his arm around Minette. Alys had brought at least a modicum of light into his dark world, but Minette brought something more precious, a special kind of warmth he sorely needed right now. If Alys had a daughter, she also had a husband, and that meant he dared not let himself become too attached, too dependent on her. But there was no reason he couldn't be affectionate toward Minette. For some inexplicable reason he had a desperate need to feel close to someone and have that affection returned.

After he'd eaten, Alys told Ryan about writing to her professor, and she showed him the psychology books. 'There is a way, I know it. Between what's recommended here and what Dr. Barré tells me, we'll find that way.'

He reached for the books and then threw them down on the bed.

'I know,' she said. 'They're in French. But I'll translate the chapters and that will help you understand. Your symptoms resemble those of aphasia. You think in words, and you can make sounds, so there's no paralysis. You know what you want to say, but your mouth and tongue no longer receive the correct impulses from the brain to enable you to articulate them. Do you understand what I'm saying?'

Ryan nodded, intensely interested in what she was describing.

'From what I've read so far, you are going to have to learn specific speech patterns all over again. There are some suggestions for teaching you in the book, and I'm hoping to get more from Dr. Barré. Are you ready to start learning?'

Ryan reached for her hands. He kissed the palms and then placed them on the books.

'Thank you. You do have faith in me and what I'm trying to do. It will work, you'll see.' Dr. Barré had to answer the letter and send really helpful information. The chapters gave her some ideas, but she would need all the help she could get if Ryan were to speak normally again.

CHAPTER ELEVEN

Dr. Barré's answering letter came more quickly than she'd dared hope:

Dear Mademoiselle Prévou,

I received your letter this morning and hasten to answer it because you sounded so desperate. First of all, let me reassure you by saying the young man has many pluses on his side. I think you have diagnosed his condition correctly as aphasia, but it appears to be less serious than many cases. You say that he understands you and can write. Many cannot do either. As you've already read in the text, many recognize objects and their functions – chairs or tables – but cannot remember the name of the object. Others can hear speech, but the words translate in their brains as meaningless syllables. Some, when they try to write, transpose the letters, or even write completely different letters.

Now that you can see all the ways aphasia has *not* affected Monsieur Middleton, we can proceed to work on his problem. Think of him as a child learning to speak for the first time. He must learn specific phonetic patterns of speech. Better still, think of him as a student, one of your students learning a new language. How do you teach them? Flash cards, constant repetition; simple, common words and phrases at first; deal with familiar needs.

Now a word of caution: He is not physically helpless and should be encouraged to do for himself. Any limitations should be accepted with no comment. Because of the additional problem of amnesia, he is already doubly frustrated. Do not be surprised if he angers easily. He will not be angry with you, but with himself, his own lackings and failures.

As to his amnesia. From what you've told me, it appears to be physiological – caused by an injury – although there might be a psychological cause as well. Dread of returning to the war. In either case, everything prior to the moment of injury can be forgotten. Then (and this is something you should know and consider) when memory returns – from another injury, perhaps a shock of some kind – after weeks or even months, the period of amnesia will be completely blotted out. The slate is wiped clean, and he is back to the moment just prior to the original injury and the onset of amnesia. He will have no memory of you or the time spent with you.

Remember, Mademoiselle Prévou, that he will speak again. I've seen many cases reach a successful conclusion. All my best, and don't hesitate to write at any time.

Sincerely,
Georges
Barré

Alys put the letter down. She appreciated the prompt response, but far more worrisome thoughts than teaching Ryan how to talk had been troubling her. She should have notified the American army that he was alive and with her family. Somewhere in the States was a family who loved and mourned for him. Had been told he was missing. Their hopes that he was still alive were shadowed by the fear that he was dead. She remembered her own sleepless nights when she went weeks without hearing from Gilles. And the joy that flooded her when word came that he was still safe and alive. She had no right to deprive Ryan's family of that same joy.

She reread one sentence in Dr. Barré's letter over and over: 'He will have no memory of you or the time spent with you.' When Ryan regained his memory, she would be completely forgotten. She would have no place in his life – worse, no place in his memory. It would be as if she'd never existed. She should let him go now. Each day that passed, each moment of being with him and teaching him to speak, would only make it harder. Rationalize all she would that he needed her now as much as when he was in a coma, she forced herself to admit that her own selfish wish to be the one who taught him to talk had kept her from contacting the authorities.

No, that's not the whole truth, she thought. I love him. I love him and I can't let him go.

She anguished at the thought of sending him away, and yet she knew she must. He would speak again, but it wasn't she who should be teaching him. Now that he could travel, he should be in a military hospital. Until now she had been thinking only of herself and her desire to keep him with her; she must think about him. He must have been terrified to awaken among strangers. The loss of memory itself would put any sane man into a panic. And then to discover he could not talk! Alys tried to put herself in Ryan's place, and then realized no one could possibly know what another suffered under those conditions.

For his sake he must be returned to those who could surround him with love and understanding. She would write to Dr. Barré tonight and ask him to find out whom she should contact at American headquarters in Liège.

With the retreat of the Germans, the village school had reopened. Because the schoolhouse had been badly damaged during the latest shelling, Countess Charbonne had once again volunteered the use of the château. The women of the village had worked long hours to clean the rooms and remove the stench of German occupation and all evidence of its having been a hospital. What furniture, books, and supplies had withstood the shelling were gathered and taken to the château.

Alys had been both dismayed and pleased at the thought of returning to her classes. She didn't feel she could leave Ryan during this crucial time; yet she looked forward to returning to her students. Of great importance was the much-needed salary she'd be receiving again. After anguishing for several hours over what to do, Alys had finally decided she should resume teaching. Both Minette and Ryan would be in Jolie's able hands. She needed to get out of the house, and she needed her lively, inquisitive children.

To help Ryan while away the hours she would be gone, she brought him several books in English.

'Perhaps these will give you something of a past. Not your own, I'm afraid, but at least an insight into the world beyond these four walls and before today. There are two novels here by Somerset Maugham. I think you'll enjoy them. These three are children's brief histories of England and the United States. I use them in my classes. They're very basic and elementary, but they'll give you a quick glimpse into some of the past.'

Ryan wrote a quick thank-you and reached for the books. If nothing else, they'd take his mind off his own problems. He opened one of the novels and immediately became lost in the easy, fascinating flow of words.

While Alys was with her classes, she forced herself to forget about the letter and her decision to notify the American authorities. When school was over, however, and she was preparing to leave for home, all the pain and anguish at the thought of letting Ryan go assailed her again. She opened the front door of the château, and a brutal, January wind whipped across her face. She secured her woollen shawl more tightly around her head and tucked it under the collar of her heavy coat. More furious than ever at the German soldier who'd taken her bicycle, she began the long, frigid walk down the road from the château and through the village.

To keep her mind from the icy blasts that penetrated even the thickness of her sturdy loden coat and blew sprays of snow across her face, she thought about the letter she must write to Dr. Barré. Not for help with teaching Ryan, this time, but for information as to where she should write and what she should tell the American army about Ryan.

On reaching the village, she was tempted to stop in the partially rebuilt café for a cup of hot coffee to revive her sagging spirits as much as to warm her up. Then she saw an American jeep parked in front of the café, a favorite stopping place for the few soldiers passing through Ste. Monique from time to time. An officer sat behind the wheel. It was unusual for an officer to be alone without a driver, but then Alys thought that perhaps he was waiting for someone. As she neared the café, he called to her. She hesitated a moment before remembering that he was an American, not a German, and that she need not be afraid of him.

'Yes, sir? Is there anything I can do to help you?'

From the startled expression on his face, she realized he was amazed to find someone speaking comprehensible English.

'Yes, please.' He pointed to the map in his hand and indicated the road he was trying to find.

'Follow this road,' she explained, 'about eight, maybe ten, kilometers to the fork. Bear right and you will be on the right road.'

Even as she spoke, it occurred to Alys that she could ask this major about where to write and what to say in the letter. Or better still, she could give him the information about Ryan and he could take care of everything. If Ryan had to go, it was better that he go quickly. The days between writing the letter and then finally hearing from the authorities would become more and more unbearable.

'Thank you,' he said after taking another look at the map and putting it on the seat beside him. 'You've been a real help.'

'You're welcome.' Alys swallowed hard to keep down the rising nausea. This was harder than she'd had any idea it would be. She was relinquishing not only Ryan, but the hope that she could love and be loved again, that life could once again be filled with joy and meaning.

She continued to stand by the side of the jeep, and the officer looked at her inquisitively and somewhat impatiently, waiting for her either to say something more or else to leave so he could move on.

'Perhaps,' she began hesitantly, 'perhaps you could do something for me.' Noting his hand ready to turn the key, she explained more rapidly the situation with Ryan: how he'd arrived at the inn, his condition, his regaining consciousness, his amnesia, and his inability to speak.

'And so,' she concluded, 'I wonder if you could contact the right people and apprise them of the situation.' Even as she was talking, she was also writing Ryan's name and the name and location of the inn.

While the major listened to Alys, the expressions on his face vacillated from impatience to amazement to disbelief and then to relief. Seeing the last, Alys assumed he was glad the recital had come to an end.

'Well, I don't know,' the major sputtered, a bit more gruffly than Alys thought necessary. Then almost immediately he changed his mind. 'Yes, yes, of course I can do that for you.'

'Do you – do you need to see Lieutenant Middleton?' Alys prayed silently the man would say no. Some days earlier, soldiers had been inspecting the area in and around Ste. Monique for unexploded mines. Ryan had seen them and begun to shake with violent tremors. At the time, Alys had used his reaction as a reasonable and justifiable excuse not to contact military authorities. Something about the men, their uniforms or their actions, had triggered a momentary flash of memory in Ryan's subconscious and had frightened him. She'd been puzzled. Why that reaction at seeing American soldiers? If they had been Germans, she could have understood. Whatever the reason, she was concerned now that seeing this major would upset him again.

'No, that won't be necessary. I'll report his name and whereabouts when I reach headquarters.' He reached again for the ignition key.

'Should I prepare him in some way? He doesn't know there's a war on. Or that he was in it.'

'No – no, not yet. Wait until you hear from headquarters.'

'You're sure,' Alys insisted, 'you have all the information you need?'

'Fine, fine. All we need.'

'And we'll be hearing from someone? There's nothing more I need do?'

'Nothing more.' He turned on the ignition and then turned it off again. 'But it may be a while before you're contacted. I won't be returning to Liège for several days. Then too, everyone's concentrating on ending the war. But you will hear.'

'And his family?'

'They'll be notified.' He turned on the ignition again and drove away before Alys could thank him.

Well, she thought, it's over. She'd done what had to be done. A few days, a week or so at the most, and Ryan would be gone. Gone from here and from her life. She'd started over before, and she could do it again.

With Ste. Monique well behind him, Private Hector Jamison grinned to himself. Stealing the drunken major's uniform had been the smartest thing he'd done. From being flunky and jeep driver for an insufferable officer, he was on his way to becoming a free man.

And if all continued to go well, he'd enjoy that freedom along the Côte d'Azur. With the war still on, the Belgian and French country people never questioned an American major traveling by himself. If he stayed on back roads, he might not even need the I.D. he'd forged while on headquarters duty and kept in readiness for the opportune moment.

For now his plans took him to Paris. He knew Paris; at least he knew the sections where he could hide out until he could get a new identity. His mercurial brain and educated fingers would pick enough pockets for easy living. Then by the time the wealthy tourists began returning, he'd have worked out a con scheme to keep him living in style.

He breathed a sigh of relief. He'd almost blown it back there with the young Belgian woman. He'd been so anxious to get away, he'd nearly failed to realize that a genuine major would be extremely interested in her story and do everything he could to report a man now probably listed as missing in action. Too bad he wouldn't be doing it. She'd been so relieved to find an American officer to talk to. Well, she'd learn soon enough that the information hadn't been passed on, and she'd contact someone else. At least he'd been smart enough to tell her it would be several days before she heard. That gave him enough time to be far, far away before anyone suspected he was the man she'd talked to.

He whistled gaily when he reached the fork in the road and turned left instead of right as the young woman had suggested. No small detail must be overlooked if he were to avoid capture before reaching Paris.

Evenings now found Ryan joining the family around the cheerfully blazing, rotund stove covered with blue delft tiles. The warmth from the stove vied with the warmth of their welcome, and there was seldom a silent moment. With German retribution no longer a threat, Émile's rancor had long since evaporated. Jolie chatted as volubly and enthusiastically as if Ryan could take an active part in their conversation. Actually, he did in a way, nodding, smiling, grimacing, and gesturing with his arms as expressively as any Frenchman, and when during vociferous discussions on what appeared to be intimate family matters, they lapsed into French, Ryan soon ceased to feel ignored. He could not know that such discussions usually concerned the war or the still annoying problem of food.

Émile and Jolie had agreed with Alys that it would not benefit Ryan to know about the war. It might, in fact, be harmful in trying to help him. If his amnesia had a psychological as well as physiological cause, the truth might be so disturbing as to delay or stop altogether his attempts to speak.

It was plain from the beginning that Minette had adopted Ryan, or 'M'sieur' as she called him, as her very own. While he remained in bed, she could be found sitting next to him with a picture book or curled up in the middle of the bed playing with her dolls. In the evenings, with never a by-your-leave, she crawled into his lap, and ensconced herself there as a queen might on her throne. She seemed blissfully unconcerned that Ryan could neither understand French nor speak to her at all. They had evolved some form of communication, bewildering to the others but clearly satisfactory to them.

Émile often brought out his knife and began whittling on a scrap of wood. One night it was a handle for a fishing pole. By gestures, Ryan indicated he'd like to try. Afraid the knife might slip and hurt Minette, as usual in his lap and intrigued by what he was doing, he lifted her off and onto the floor.

Immediately she set up a wild howling. M'sieur didn't love her anymore.

'No, no, *ma chère*,' Alys said. 'He doesn't want you to get hurt.'

But Minette was adamant. If M'sieur loved her, he wouldn't have put her down.

Ryan didn't need to understand the words to know what Minette was saying. He put up one hand, as if to say 'wait,' and he sat down on the floor beside her. He indicated for her to sit far enough away so she wouldn't be harmed if the knife slipped off the wood. She smiled in understanding, and was now perfectly content to sit a short distance away. As long as he was sitting on the floor with her.

At first Ryan ran the knife idly over the wood. It was merely something to do with his hands. When he saw Minette looking expectantly at him, he sensed she'd be disappointed if he didn't create something for her. It wouldn't do to disappoint this very sensitive, delightful child. He began to shape something, he wasn't sure what, but he knew a figure was beginning to emerge. When it took on the conformation of an animal, he decided it should be a dog, a low, fat dog, with short, stubby legs. The head was rather massive for the body; but when he finished, it would vaguely resemble a bulldog.

Getting the feel now of the knife and wood working together, he was able to carefully hew out some flat ears at the top corners of the head and even incise a mouth. The mouth was a bit higher on the face than he'd intended, with the result that the animal had an underslung jaw that the most regal of English bulldogs would be proud of. With a last lingering appraisal of his definitely amateurish efforts, he handed it to Minette and awaited her judgment.

'*Chien!*' she cried. '*Beau chien!*' She examined it minutely, lovingly, turning it over and over in her hands.

Ryan looked quizzically at Alys, who said, 'She called it a handsome dog, and she loves it. You're very clever with your hands.'

Ryan shook his head deprecatingly. He was surprised that the little animal had turned out as well as it did and that Minette actually recognized it as a dog. This was fun and challenging. He reached for another piece of pine. This time he did a little thinking and planning.

Alys watched with pleasure as Ryan examined the wood. She could almost see his mind working while puzzling over what animal or other figure to carve. Was he picturing it in his mind and imagining what it would look like?

Ryan recrossed his legs, and with a satisfied, introspective, Buddha look on his face began carving short, tentative strokes. His conscious mind was creating a lamb, and he was biting his tongue while he carved the slender, lower half of the legs – thin but not so thin as to snap when Minette played with it. He was completely unaware that his subconscious mind was remembering a time when he had been forced to remain in bed with a fever, and had entertained himself by carving animals from bars of Ivory soap. The memory did not come through, but the interest, enthusiasm, and ability did. With the lamb, he worked in more detail, fashioning ears, a gentle muzzle, and the suggestion of curly fleece.

'*Mouton*,' Minette whispered, setting the lamb down next to the dog. '*Je t'aime. Je t'aime*,' she said to each in turn. She scrambled over to sit closer to Ryan. '*Je vous aime, aussi, M'sieur*.'

'She told each one she loved it, in the intimate form "*t'aime*," ' Alys explained. 'Then she said she loved you, but in the more formal style, used by a child to an adult or to non-intimates.' She saw a frown deepen the furrows between Ryan's brows. 'Because you are an adult, not because you are a stranger. Out of respect, she would always use the "*vous*" form with you.'

Ryan savored her words, the explanation as much as Minette's affection. He committed them all to memory. If his attempt to speak again proved to be an exercise in futility, his time here would not be wasted if he learned to think and write in a second language. If memory never returned, that knowledge might enable him to earn a living as a mute translator of written work. He could not leech on these wonderful people and accept their hospitality like a damned parasite forever.

And so it began. Every night he listened carefully and concentrated on two or three words or occasionally a phrase. Then, when he returned to his room, he quickly wrote them down phonetically. Time enough to learn the proper spelling.

If evenings were pleasantly relaxed for Ryan, afternoons were quite otherwise. Until they heard from the army, Alys saw no reason not to begin helping Ryan speak again. He was restless and desperately needed to be kept occupied. He could read only so many hours a day, and yet it was obvious he craved mental stimulation of some kind. Then, too, she wanted to spend every hour she possibly could with him. They would be hours she would cherish long after he left.

In order to remain undisturbed and to ease Ryan's embarrassment, Alys put a table and two comfortable chairs in an unused guest room on the first floor. She would be the teacher; and he, the student. In this way she could maintain a professional, objective attitude toward him. He must never, in any way, sense how she really felt about him.

Alys began the rehabilitation sessions by having Ryan go through the repertory of sounds he could make. She had to know if there were any that were physically impossible for him, such as those made with the lips, the tongue in various positions, or the back of the throat. To her relief there was no physical impairment. When she asked him to try to speak a short sentence, he hesitated.

'I know,' she said, 'it's hard. You're afraid you'll be embarrassed. But don't be. It's like showing a wound to a nurse. I'm here to teach and to help, not to scoff.'

Her cool, assured voice chilled Ryan at the same time that it eased his chagrin at the thought of the ugly sounds that would issue from his mouth. Ryan had read the chapters in the textbooks that Alys had translated for him, and he understood what she was trying to do. He did not, however, understand the professional, almost distant, attitude she took toward him. From the very first he had been disheartened by her addressing him as 'sir' or 'monsieur' instead of by his name. Gradually, however, he had come to learn that he was in a country where the familiar use of the first name was not casually or quickly adopted. During the evenings, that barrier had come down from between them. So that now, this new professional approach of hers was discouraging.

When Ryan first saw Minette, he had assumed there was also a husband, and he was disappointed. He'd been immediately attracted to Alys. She was pretty and vivacious and had an enchanting accent that delighted him. When, during one of the evenings in the warm kitchen, Alys casually mentioned that Minette's father had been killed during a boating accident, Ryan looked at her with new eyes. He realized he was deeply fond of her. No, dammit, he was more than fond of her. He was in love with her. He'd fallen in love the minute she'd walked into his room. It had nothing to do with her care of him or her keeping him alive. He didn't know then that she'd done all that. He knew only she was the loveliest and the most enchanting woman imaginable. And he'd begun to think she cared for him, too. Then she suddenly became cold and distant. She obviously did not dislike him; she was merely indifferent toward him. Until he found out how to overcome that indifference, he could feign indifference, too.

Ryan clenched his fists under the seclusion of his robe and tried the sentence, 'I will do my best.' It emerged as a garbled series of grunts and hisses. The humiliation was too much. There was no way he could control the warm, despised tears from running down his cheeks or the shaking of his shoulders in this agony of bitter failure.

'No, no.' Alys reached over and put a hand on his arm. 'Just one word at a time. Here, write it down first and then say it.'

Ryan shook his head and turned his face away. Better never to speak at all than to endure another minute of this futility.

'Yes, I insist.' Under the steely cold of her eyes he tried to discern sympathy and understanding, but he seemed to see only determination. 'Write it down and then say it. I need to hear how close to the word the sound is.'

He held the pencil and paper but wrote nothing down, merely stared into space.

'Please. If it seems hard now, I can only assure you that there will be even harder days ahead, days when it seems nothing will be accomplished. I can't lie to you about that. But there will also be days with first one and then another step ahead. I know. I'm a teacher working with children learning English. Think of yourself as a child learning to speak for the first time.'

Ryan lifted the pencil and wrote *room*. When he spoke it, it sounded more like 'groof.'

'Very good,' she said. 'Better than I expected. You spoke one of the consonants and got the vowel sound.'

Ryan snatched up the paper and pencil. *Good?* he wrote. *I sounded like an animal.*

'Yes, you did.' He looked hurt that she agreed with him, and for the moment she had to ignore that pain. 'But now I know where to start.'

For the rest of the afternoon, Alys had Ryan placing his hands on different areas of her throat while she made various sounds. Then she had him watching closely her lips and tongue. She recalled Minette's learning to talk. Three of the easiest sounds for her at first were 'dah,' 'muh,' and 'puh.' She told Ryan to put his tongue against the roof of his mouth, just behind his teeth, and imitate her. Over and over she repeated, 'dah, dah, dah.'

Ryan tried, but his tongue kept slipping, and only an agonized gruffness, like a groan, came from the back of his throat.

Both of them were exhausted and soaked with perspiration when she finally said they should stop.

'We'll try again tomorrow. If this is too hard, we'll shift to a different sound.'

After she left, Ryan fell back against the pillows. For her sake he'd try it for a few days; but then if nothing happened, he'd quit. There was no point in exhausting both of them over something doomed to failure.

When three weeks had passed with no word from the American army, Alys was puzzled but not worried. True, the major had said that with everyone concentrating on winning the war, it might be some time before she would be contacted about Ryan; but she'd never thought it would be this long. She'd thought he meant only a few days.

What puzzled her even more was that Ryan had not received any letters from his family. Surely, even with the army occupied with the war, his family would have been notified that he was alive. Even if they hadn't been given the address in Ste. Monique, letters would be forwarded to him. She had dreaded the coming of these letters because then she would have to explain the entire situation to him. He would know she had lied to him earlier, and he might well hate her for it. Distressed as she was about doing anything to make him dislike her, she was postponing as long as possible telling him the truth. It could well be, of course, that Ryan had no family; or perhaps three weeks was too soon to expect mail from overseas.

Until letters or word came from the army, they would continue with the lessons. If only she could relieve the tension that possessed her, that kept muscles and nerves from completely relaxing at night in bed, and made it almost impossible to breathe at times. It was as if every part of her was taut – waiting and prepared – for the day when Ryan would look at her with eyes that demanded the truth.

Gradually the days developed into a routine that seemed to Ryan to stretch toward an endless eternity. In the mornings he read every book Alys brought to him – novels, poetry, essays, histories – and he devoured their contents like a mole gouging his way through a dark, self-made tunnel toward the light. Every afternoon he and Alys worked with specific patterns of speech. Only in the evenings, sitting with the family near the stove, did he relax. Even then, even as he carved new animals for Minette, he listened and committed to memory French words and phrases.

Finally the day came when Ryan spoke two consecutive syllables. Impulsively, Alys grabbed his shoulders. 'Ryan! You did it!'

It was all Ryan could do to keep from putting his arms around her. He was sorry when she immediately pulled away, as if regretting her momentary lapse from her position as strict teacher.

Even as she pulled away, Alys wished he had put his arms around her. As much as she loved him, though, she had to continue thinking of him as a student. If he had any feelings toward her, they were ones of gratitude, nothing more. And she must read nothing more into them.

Also, she reminded herself, she must remember that they would eventually hear from the American army. Nor must she forget those fateful words in Dr. Barré's letter. When Ryan regained his memory, all memory of her would be gone, buried in the chasm of amnesia at long last spanned by a bridge to the past.

Day after day, Ryan worked patiently on one phonetic sound after another, so Alys was shocked when he had his first temper tantrum. Then she remembered Dr. Barré's second letter. He'd cautioned that just as Ryan was having to learn like a child, he might often behave like one. Ignoring his outburst, she walked out of the room and left him to work himself out of it.

Ryan watched her leave, and he knew she was angry with him. But he'd be damned if he cared. He almost hoped she wouldn't come back with her nagging, persistent, demanding attitude that he repeat one sound after another. And each sound over and over until he thought he'd go mad. It wasn't doing any good. So he made sounds. So could an animal. Or an idiot. He still couldn't form the words that swirled in his brain and taunted him because they had to stay imprisoned there and not leave his mouth. They seemed to pile up, crowd together, and then begin to bang on his brain to be let out. Just as the words were imprisoned in his mind, so he felt incarcerated in his desolate, lonely world.

Furious with himself and what seemed to him her pity and her unassailable tolerance, he stormed out the door. With rapid strides he headed for the riverbank, and then sat hunched over, under a bleak and denuded tree. He'd never learn, not enough to converse easily. Oh, he'd probably be able to make his wants known, to ask directions or purchase something, but so could an idiot. Quite a choice he had: the village idiot or the eccentric recluse that children mocked and adults scorned. He really didn't mind, though, if he were shunned. He had an intense fear of people, an excruciating phobia that he could neither understand nor explain.

Ryan had thought at first, when friends of the Prévous came to the inn, that his fear of meeting them came from his inability to speak. It was a natural reticence, a withdrawal into silent security. When, however, the same cold sweat covered his body at the sight of people walking along the road, he knew the roots of such uncontrollable fears went far deeper than his inability to communicate. They burrowed into that dark, mysterious unknown that might remain forever buried. Whatever the cause or whatever the source of this fear, it was of no importance now. It was part of his past, and all his thoughts must be focused on the future. Until now, he had fled to his room when visitors came to the inn in order to avoid meeting them. He must learn to tolerate people and to feel comfortable among strangers.

Ryan got up and walked briskly along the riverbank, crossed a stone bridge that arched above the water, and headed for the hills. Gradually his frustration receded, .calmed by the serenity of the hills and the dense beauty of the woods.

When he returned, Alys made no reference to his earlier behavior.

As days passed, Ryan continued to alternate between feelings of despondency and despair; devastating frustration, anger, and fear; depression and hatred; physical pain and helplessness. Having to learn to speak all over again and to learn about the world around him was like being a baby in a man's body.

Yet, there were good days, too; days when he finally conquered one, sometimes two, phonetic sounds. Not always did the consonant emerge as the one he started with, but it came out as a specific one, no longer just a gargling noise.

On the day that Ryan was able to reproduce each of the vowel sounds, Alys celebrated by bursting into tears, while Ryan laughed with relief. His feelings of inadequacy and failure were now replaced by hope. He'd finally come to grips with the realization that learning to speak was going to be a long, tedious process. But rather than regretting it, he was glad if it meant being with Alys. Except for brief, impulsive acts like hugging his shoulders or crying over his successes, she continued to keep her distance. But he sensed she had been secluding herself within a shell whose walls were growing thinner and more fragile each day. Someday the shell would be broken, either from within by her or from without by him. He had the patience now to wait. And he had an objective to work toward. The first sentence he wanted to say was 'I love you.'

CHAPTER TWELVE

Alys had been asleep for some time when a scream from Ryan's room awoke her. As she sat up, she heard him screaming again. Having no idea what could be wrong, she grabbed her robe and ran upstairs. Once in the hall, she took from the table the oil lamp that remained lighted all night.

Ryan was sitting up in bed and flailing his arms around. Then he covered his face with his hands as if to protect it or to shut out something he didn't want to see.

Alys sat on the side of the bed. His screams had now become sobs; and he was shuddering so violently, the whole bed was shaking. Her first fear was that his head injury had somehow flared up again and he was tormented by pain.

'Are you in pain?' she asked.

There was no response of any kind from him.

A nightmare, she thought. She herself had had many of those since the beginning of the war, and she knew what agony they caused.

Ryan was still shaking, and he was drenched in sweat. If only she could get some response from him, but he was acting as if he were in some kind of trance. Suddenly he pointed to the lantern and then arched his arms in great sweeping circles.

'Lights?' she asked.

He nodded, but more mechanically than if he were aware of what he was doing. He swept his arms around again.

'A tremendous light? Frightening? A fire?'

He nodded more violently this time. Then he put his hands over his ears and grimaced as if trying to shut out some violent, loud sound.

'Lights and fire and tremendous noise?' He nodded, and relief spread across his face. She had understood.

My God, she thought, he's beginning to remember the war. Something is beginning to come through.

'Do you know what was happening? Why the fire and noise?'

His only response was to begin sobbing and shaking all over again.

Alys moved up beside him. Settling herself against a pillow, she took him into her arms as she often did with Minette.

'It's all right, Ryan. I'm here and nothing is going to hurt you. There's no fire here. It was just a terrible nightmare. I'll stay here until you're asleep.'

Gradually Ryan's sobs and shaking subsided. Several times Alys tried to move his head off her shoulder and free her arm; but with each disturbance, he moaned in his sleep. Alys finally accepted that she'd have to stay the night, and she made herself as comfortable as possible.

In the morning, Alys awoke to find that neither of them had moved from their original positions. Ryan awoke more slowly, but as soon as he realized she was there and he'd been lying on her arm, he sat up as quickly as if something had jabbed him in the spine.

'It's all right,' she laughed when she saw the startled, unbelieving, almost embarrassed look on his face. 'You haven't compromised me. You had a nightmare. You remember?'

He shook his head in bewilderment. He had no recollection of anything unusual happening after he first went to sleep.

'Well, you did. A very bad nightmare that had you terrified. I was trying to help you get over it when you fell asleep. No harm done, except that my arm and shoulder went numb, and now they're prickling with a thousand needles.'

Suddenly aware that their close proximity was proving too disturbing to her, Alys climbed off the bed. Ryan must not in any way think she wanted more than his friendship.

'I'll – get your breakfast.' She hurried out of the room.

It must have been some nightmare, Ryan thought, to have him staying asleep with her lying so temptingly close beside him. And how ironic it was that even those recent memories of the nightmare and of her being with him were being denied him.

It was his memory trying to break through, Alys thought while she dressed and went downstairs. Only a fragment, only a beginning, but it was a beginning. Everything in his past was still there in his subconscious, and someday it would break through to his conscious mind. Against that day she must maintain her distance and not allow herself to hope that there was any place for her in his future. Sighing, she began preparing breakfast and assuring Minette that yes, M'sieur would soon be down to eat with her.

Each night, while preparing for bed, Alys found herself wondering if there would be a repetition of the nightmare. Ryan had been genuinely terrified. Her concern for him was augmented by her dread of revealing how much she loved him. If he needed her to assuage his frustrations, to ease his fears, and to sublimate his sense of failure by immediately having him repeat a success, she would be there. But she would not, she must not, allow him to mistake concern for affection. Night after night, however, went by with both of them sleeping undisturbed until morning.

Coincidentally – there seemed no way for the nightmare to have affected Ryan in that way – he began to improve more rapidly, and most of the guttural sounds were disappearing. The moments of exhilaration were usually followed by plateaux when it seemed as if Ryan would never be able to take the next step upward. His reactions were those Alys had been told to expect, and yet she was never quite prepared. Ryan endured what would frustrate the most patient man, and then got angry at some miniscule impediment. He became obsessively neat about his person and his room. Nothing on his dresser – his French language notes, a hairbrush and comb, and a red glass bead Minette had given him from her collection of Alys's old jewelry – must ever be moved even a fraction of an inch from where he placed it. And his bed must be made without a wrinkle, a near impossibility with featherbeds and old quilts. 'Compulsive neatness is a form of security,' Dr. Barré had written 'and should not be discouraged. Right now it is the one certainty in his very insecure life.' So Alys tolerated his petty complaints and quietly ignored his anger.

When the confines of the inn became unendurable, Ryan continued the habit of going down to the river. There he could look across to the hills and forest, a vista that both relaxed and invigorated him. There was a calmness in the beauty and serenity that broke the steel bands of tenseness that sometimes drew so tightly around his chest he could barely breathe. In the cool air, he took several deep breaths, exhaled them slowly, and felt the strictures of frustration snap. Just as important to his peace of mind was the beauty of the snow-laden trees, their deep green boughs frosted with white. Their tips reached higher and higher up the hills toward the sky, sometimes a clear, cold, crystalline blue, sometimes a mass of billowing white clouds, but often a leaden gray. No matter which, Ryan took pleasure in being part of the scene.

Nearly seven weeks had passed since Alys started working with Ryan and still no word from the army or from the States. She could only assume that he had no family, or at least no one who cared enough about him to write. As for the army, she could only suppose that, now that they knew where he was, they were in no hurry to come and get him. It seemed a strange way for them to respond to her information; but she'd often heard officers and men fuss about the unique way the army had of doing things. At times she thought about writing to Dr. Barré, anyway, and have him tell her whom to write to; but then she thought that maybe a second report to a different person would only confuse things. The major hadn't told her his name, so there was no way she could contact him directly.

So far only friends from the village had come to the inn to chat. Alys had been able to satisfy Ryan's curiosity about lack of patrons by telling him that the inn always closed during the winter and opened only with the beginning of the tourist season. She was aware of his fear of people, and she knew this could be part of the aphasia syndrome. Actually, she was grateful for his fear at this time. It prevented him from meeting someone who spoke English and might make a reference to the war.

With regaining the ability to speak being Ryan's all-consuming concern, he worried less about his amnesia. There was an immediacy about learning to speak that superceded what might have been. It was the here and now that counted. There were times, however, when he gave way to despondency. Usually it was brought on by his dependency on Alys and her parents for his day-to-day needs. He despised being dependent on anyone for what he should be able to do himself. It was all very well to think of himself as a child learning to speak, a child newly come into the world with no past but with a whole brand-new future before him. But he wasn't a child; he was a man. He should be supporting himself, not living off these good people. At times like these, when he sat by the river or climbed among the hills, he despaired over ever knowing what sort of person he was or what his life had been before his accident. He felt deserted and bereft. His past had been stolen from him, and he'd been left to cling helplessly to a frightening present and a nebulous future.

Some relief finally came, surprisingly enough, after his curiosity about the damage to the inn elicited the information that there had been an explosion. Alys had been preparing herself for that question, and she told him a faulty heater in that part of the building had blown up.

With the approach of warmer weather, Émile began rebuilding. From structures in the village too badly damaged to be restored, he brought building materials. Here was something Ryan knew he could do. He began helping Émile erect the stone walls, plaster the surfaces, and tile the roof. Now he felt as if he were contributing toward his keep, and his mood lightened somewhat. He found a new pleasure in the hard, exhausting, physical labor of hauling stones, climbing a ladder with buckets of ecru-colored plaster, and struggling to set tiles evenly on the roof. Although the materials were obviously not new, Ryan assumed their use was simply shrewd economy on Émile's part to rebuild with old stone and slate.

In the afternoons, Alys now had Ryan reading groups of syllables rather than imitating her voice. She printed them on cards, and began by handing them to him one at a time. This technique proved the most frustrating of all. Ryan simply couldn't produce the right phonetic sounds. Worst of all, he began to regress. Nothing he said came out right.

Emotionally exhausted and furious at the way Alys's attempts at encouragement sounded more like pity, Ryan grabbed the cards from her hands. He scattered them on the floor and then proceeded to rip others apart and fling the pieces in her face. All the while, he screamed at her in an ugly, almost obscene, guttural outpouring that was a pathetic attempt to communicate his misery.

'Ryan!' Alys was stunned and then furious. There was no doubt that at this moment he hated her. 'How dare you do that! I spent hours working on those cards.' She lowered her voice and spoke slowly and deliberately, as if to a recalcitrant child. 'Pick them up. Pick every one up and hand them to me.'

Ryan let out a string of syllables that, although unintelligible, were obviously violent oaths. She was grateful she couldn't understand their meaning. She had no trouble, however, interpreting one series: 'I'll be damned if I will!'

'And damn you if you don't.' From the stunned expression on his face, she knew she'd guessed rightly what his mind if not his lips had been saying. He was bitter. He was frustrated. He was angry. But she'd worked so hard, he had no right to turn on her like that.

'All right, leave them on the floor,' she stormed. 'I'll clean them up along with everything else I do for you, you – you ungrateful bastard!' The last came out in a prolonged sob. Before she could help herself she was crying. In another minute she felt Ryan's arms going around her and he was kissing her. First gently, as if to apologize, and then so ardently she could not help but respond.

Clinging to him, she whispered over and over, 'I'm sorry, I'm sorry. I know how miserable you are. I know how hard you've tried.' She finally pulled away from him; and while she wiped her eyes, he bent down and picked up the cards.

He picked them up to let her know he was sorry, too; but he also wanted to keep his face hidden, to keep from letting her know how desperately he wanted to tell her he loved her. But he would wait a little longer. He hadn't given up hope that he'd be able to say it. Let these kisses be ones of apology and his need for her.

As shaken as she was by Ryan's sudden embrace, Alys would not allow herself to believe it was more than one of apology and gratitude. She'd been wrong to respond. She must not let him think she felt more than minimal affection for him. And decidedly, there must not be a repetition of that embrace. Her heart fluttered and her stomach tightened at the mere remembrance of it.

Over and over in his room at night, Ryan struggled with what he felt were the most important words he'd ever say: 'I love you.' But always they sounded more like 'agh braw lau' or something equally abominable. Why was it he could often repeat meaningless syllables after Alys, but could not make his mouth coordinate with his brain on something that made sense. 'Relax,' Alys kept saying, but he couldn't.

He thought about her response to his kisses. The shell was beginning to crack. She might not love him yet; but underneath her cool exterior was an affection she was trying to hide. He thought he knew why now. Someday his memory would return, and she was afraid he would forget all about her. Before then he had to tell her he loved her, that he wanted to marry her and stay right here in Ste. Monique with her. Then, when memory did return, she would be by his side and could fill in all the empty spaces for him. They would be together and that was what was important.

CHAPTER THIRTEEN

In the spring, the usually quiet little river behind the inn swelled with melting snow from the Ardennes hills into a deeper, wider, rushing stream. It tumbled joyfully and exuberantly over colorful rocks and through the mint and thyme along its banks. It occasionally gnawed away at the shore, probing and sending trembling rivulets into the bordering fields.

The snows of 1945 had been particularly heavy, and then the spring rains descended in violent storms and lasted for several days. Cascades of mud and water rushed over the edges of the bank and formed new gullies that, in their turn, eroded the solid ground beneath the topsoil. Into these gullies washed bits of stone, scraps of ragged-edged shards of exploded shells, occasionally a bit of bone from a man killed by one explosion and then buried by the violent upheaval of earth from a second. How old the bones were no one could tell. From the Napoleonic wars, World War I, World War II, or some battle so far in the distant past it remained unrecorded. These artifacts of history, of days of war and days of peace, rested quietly on the gully bottom until another rain stirred up their bed and sent them tumbling into the main current of the river.

At its normal, shallower depth, the river sliced between buried rocks and around larger, lichen-covered boulders. But with the melting snow and heavy spring rains, boulders that had been safe stepping-stones to the other side became hidden beneath the water and the frothy spumes. It was then the mild, pleasant little river became as dangerous as a dragon, breathing not fire but an icy, killing breath. Its greatest danger was its incomparable beauty: the clear, blue green water, the shining stones calling one to follow them across to the fields beyond, their periphery so alive with wild flowers it was as if the whole world had just been born. One forgot to wonder how the fragile plants and delicate seeds had survived through the long ages of continual battle between man and man to kill and between man and the land to live.

The rains had stopped and the sun had shone brilliantly for two days, teasing one into believing that winter was finally over and spring had arrived with its warm days and pleasantly cool evenings. Ryan was fulfilling a promise to Minette to take her for a walk along the river as soon as everything had dried up enough that they wouldn't get their shoes wet. Minette had put on a sturdy pair of boots that Jolie had thriftily saved from Alys's childhood. Her earlier frugality had provided many wearable garments for Minette that otherwise were no longer available for the little girl. Ryan had fitted his feet into a pair of old wooden sabots that were slightly too big but that he could manage with some awkwardness.

Busy in the kitchen, Alys looked out from time to time and took pleasure in watching the two of them together: the little girl so delighted to have Ryan for a companion and the man so patiently stopping each foot of the way to look at something she wanted to show him. Alys noted with glee how carefully Ryan was holding all the wild flowers Minette was picking, no easy task for him since she seldom picked a stem more than an inch long.

Ryan was enjoying the outing as much as Minette. Several rainy days indoors had meant no work with Émile on restoring the inn, and he'd come to look forward to the physical work as a respite from the mentally exhausting hours of repeating syllables over and over, trying to force his mouth to say what was in his brain. Not that he didn't appreciate what Alys was doing for him, and he cherished every moment he had with her. Her nearness was at the same time his greatest pleasure and his most irritating frustration. He couldn't drive from his mind her response when he'd kissed her after throwing the cards to the floor. He wanted to kiss her again and again, to hold her close and tell her how much he loved her. The kiss had meant something to her, too. For one brief moment he'd cracked that cold shell of reserve.

If only . . . No, dammit, he wouldn't wait until he could speak. When they were alone again, he'd let her know how he felt. His stomach tightened at the memory of her response and the thought of holding her close again; of her slim body pressed against his; of her mouth warm and moist and slightly tremulous.

Lost in these thoughts, Ryan wasn't aware that Minette had skipped on several feet ahead of him. Looking up, he saw that she was getting too close to the river. He started to run, but the ill-fitting wooden sabots tripped him up, and he fell. He wasn't hurt, but it took him a minute to locate the wooden shoes. Before he could get up, he saw that Minette had started to cross a bridge over the river. Farther down river was a sturdy stone bridge, but the one she was approaching was wooden, rickety with age, and missing rails in several places. Beneath it were large boulders over and around which the cold water swirled in violent eddies and then plunged to a lower level over more rocks.

As she stepped onto the bridge, Minette began dancing and twirling like a woodland sprite and laughing with elfin glee at having outdistanced Ryan. The old boards beneath her feet rose and fell as she moved, and it was fun to bounce up and down on them the way she did on the bed when *Maman* wasn't looking.

With a gut-wrenching stab of horror, Ryan saw that Minette was bouncing and skipping too close to the edge of the bridge where there were no rails. Forgetting about putting on the shoes, he got up and started to run; but he knew that no matter how fast he ran, he couldn't possibly get to her before she fell off into the dangerous rapids below.

'Minette!' he yelled. '*Arrêtez*! Stop, stop! You'll fall!'

He reached the bridge just as Minette ran off it and flung herself into his arms.

'*M'sieur, oh, M'sieur. Vous parlez! Je t'aime, je t'aime.*'

Only then did Ryan realize that he had spoken, that in his desperation to save her, he had been able to call out to her. He had called her by name and he had kept her from falling into the dangerous waters.

He didn't know which he was more grateful for, having saved her life or being able to speak. He'd wanted his first words to be those of love for Alys. He'd thought those would be the most important ones he could ever say, and yet it was with relief and gratitude he realized that having been given the gift of speech today, having been able to save Minette, was far more important. It had been like a miracle.

Alys had seen Ryan fall and Minette run ahead of him toward the bridge. She'd tried to scream, but no sound would come. Running out the kitchen door, she knew she couldn't possibly reach Minette in time. Her feet were leaden weights slowing her down. Then she heard Ryan call out. In stunned disbelief, she stopped and watched the heartwarming tableau as Ryan picked Minette up in his arms. Then she waited for them to walk toward her.

Safe on solid ground, Minette ran to her mother. '*Il parle, Maman!*'

'I know, *ma chère*, I heard him.'

Minette ran into the kitchen to tell *Grand-maman* how she'd nearly fallen off the bridge and how M'sieur had called to her.

Still weak with the fear that had engulfed her when she saw Minette on the bridge, and yet elated that it was Ryan's being able to call out that had saved her, Alys reached out for him and began sobbing on his shoulder. She felt his strong arms go around her; and as she clung to him, she wished she could stay that close to him forever. When he lifted her face and began kissing her, she responded eagerly. With each kiss, he held her closer, until Alys thought she would faint with joy.

He loved her, she thought. He loved her but could she dare to love him in return? Would he someday remember and be lost to her forever? Looking into his eyes and seeing the adoration in them, she knew the answer. She would love him with all her heart for as long as she could have him. Let the future bring what it would, she'd at least know real happiness for a little while.

Those few words were all that Ryan spoke that day. That he was rendered mute again, overwhelmed by what he'd done, gave him no cause for concern. He was in love, and Alys did not just pity him, she loved him. Before long his speech would return to normal. He'd be a whole person again.

The lessons continued, and each day brought new progress, and soon he was able to express his thoughts. Not always complete sentences, but at least intelligible phrases. Only one sentence remained unuttered. Ryan had still not been able to say 'I love you.' Each time he tried, it stuck in his throat.

* * *

Lying in bed and enjoying the warm spring breeze coming through the window, Alys was startled to hear Ryan again screaming in the room above hers. It had been weeks since the nightmare that had had her running up to his room and then spending the night holding him in her arms.

Putting on her robe while she rushed up the stairs, she paused outside Ryan's door only long enough to see him again flailing his arms about and then covering his face with them, as if to ward off an attack.

Alys sat on the bed and tried to put her arms around him, but he flung them away.

'It's all right, Ryan. I'm right here. There's nothing here to hurt you.'

'Stop them!' he screamed. 'Make them stop. They're coming right at me. My God! There's no stopping them. I can't move and they keep coming. Hundreds of them!' He began screaming and holding his hands out in front of him. 'Will no one stop them? They'll kill us all.'

Then the screaming stopped. He lay down and for a long time sobbed into his pillow. For another long time, he lay very quiet, as if sleeping peacefully. Alys touched him gently, and she saw that he was asleep. He hadn't been awake at all. Through the horror of the nightmare and the convulsive sobbing he'd remained asleep. She was trying to get quickly off the bed when he did wake up, trembling all over.

'What – what are you doing here?' He was obviously startled at seeing her.

'You had another nightmare. You were screaming.'

'I did? Yes, I guess I did. Look at me, I'm shaking all over and I'm covered with sweat.'

'Do you remember any of it?' She sat on the edge of the bed and reached for his hands. She was torn between wanting him, for his sake, to begin remembering his past and the fear that if he did, she would no longer have any place in his life. Just a little longer, she prayed; let him stay here just a little longer.

'No.' He stared as if trying to focus on something a hundred miles away. 'Wait, yes, I do remember something. Nothing very clear. Just a terrible fear of something coming toward me, something bent on killing me. I remember screaming to make them stop, but I don't know who or what was threatening me. There was just the horrible fear of dying. And then I think I was crying.'

'You were. You were sobbing in your sleep.' He was still shaking, and his eyes reflected the fear he'd suffered during the nightmare. 'I think you can sleep now, though. I'll see you in the morning.' She leaned over to kiss him good-night.

'Don't leave.' He reached up and pulled her down beside him. 'I need you right now. Stay for a little while. The way you did before.'

'For a few minutes.' Even as she leaned back against the pillow and let Ryan put his head on her shoulder, Alys sensed this night would be far different from the earlier one.

Ryan reached up and turned her face toward his. 'I love you, Alys.'

He'd said it! The words had come as easily as if he'd uttered them a million times, the thousands and thousands of times he'd thought them. Now he spoke them again and again. 'I love you. *Je vous aime. Je t'aime.* I love you, I love you.'

'I love you, too,' she said softly, startled by the outburst, 'but why –'

'Because,' he interrupted, 'I've tried for weeks to say those words. I've longed to tell you I love you. The words wouldn't come. Now they have. It's like – it's like the very first time I said anything at all.'

'Then say them all you want to. I love hearing them.'

In another moment she was in his arms, and he was kissing her as long and passionately as if the world would stop if he stopped. His hands and then his lips were caressing her, and every part of her body responded to his touch. This was what she'd longed for almost since the night Ryan was brought to the inn. At first it was because she desperately needed to be loved, needed someone to fill the void left by Gilles's death. Then all too soon, it was because she was in love with Ryan himself. She had tried for too long to hide her feelings from him and from herself, but now it was impossible. She loved his smile, the intent, boyish expression on his face when he was carving something for Minette, and even the angry outbursts of frustration. She loved him and he loved her, and she had no thought of not giving herself to him totally and completely.

Long before morning, all their need for each other and their long-suppressed desires to hold each other close, to give and receive love, were fulfilled, reawakened, and fulfilled again.

Just before dawn, Alys reached for her gown and prepared to slip quietly out of bed. Ryan had fallen asleep with one arm across her breast. He stirred at her movement.

'Don't go,' he whispered. 'Not yet.'

'I have to. Minette will be waking up.' She bent over and kissed him. 'I love you.'

'And how I love you! Thank you for bringing me back to life. I mean to real life by loving me.'

Alys was too exhilarated to return to bed. Minette was still sleeping soundly and would not awaken for at least another hour. Alys dressed hurriedly and walked outside. She watched the sun rise over the hills to the east. The new day would be the beginning of a new life for her. She'd forgotten how wonderful it was to be in love.

The days grew longer, the sun shone brighter; and with news from the war front continuing to be optimistic, all the world seemed ready to awaken to a new life.

CHAPTER FOURTEEN

Alys tiptoed into Ryan's room. A shower of morning sunlight fell across the lower half of the bed but had not yet touched his face. She leaned over to kiss him good-morning. It was April 14, two weeks after Easter and three weeks since Alys had first spent the night with Ryan. Since then they had been together almost every night, except for the few times Minette was restless and Alys didn't want to leave her alone. Each time they made love, she fell deeper and more completely in love with him.

When Ryan pulled her down beside him, she offered no objection. Because Minette had a slight cold and kept waking up throughout the night, Alys had been unable to stay with Ryan; and the freshness of the spring morning aroused an urgency in both of them. Alys loved the strength of his arms around her. They were a refuge from the pain and disappointments of the past and an assurance of emotional security for the present. There was only today, this moment to think about, to enjoy, to savor. And the future? Thinking about the future was only for dreamers and idealists. She dared not be either.

As always, Ryan's touch stirred her immediately; and after a night apart, both were ready for a quick consummation.

'It's a beautiful day,' Alys said. Sated with Ryan's love, she felt the euphoric lethargy of satisfaction flooding her. 'I came in to tell you it's a perfect day for a picnic.'

'A picnic,' Ryan said softly. For a moment he looked past Alys as if seeing something very far away, something only vaguely visible that he was trying to bring into focus.

'A memory?' Alys asked. Could something as simple as a picnic be the beginning of restoring his memory?

'Not really. Just a sensation. A pleasant sensation. Something anticipated and a fulfilling of all I'd looked forward to. A rare thing, darling, to have anticipation become reality. Usually it ends in disappointment or disillusionment. No, no real memory, but I think there must have been at least one happy day in my previous life.'

'Do you realize, Ryan, that's the longest speech you've made so far?'

'Then, this is a happy day, too. Come here. I just want to put my arms around you again and tell you how much I love you. Then I promise to dress and meet you downstairs. Minette's going with us, isn't she?'

'Do you think she'd let you out of her sight for that long? She's already supervising the packing of the picnic basket. Bread right out of the oven, cheese, apples, and a bottle of wine.'

'Not more than five minutes, I promise.'

'Coffee and croissants in the kitchen.' Thanks to the American army, more foodstuffs like coffee and flour were becoming available. Real, unadulterated coffee. The sugar beet refineries were operating again after the wintertime hiatus during the German counter-attack, now being referred to as the Battle of the Ardennes or, more popularly, the Battle of the Bulge.

With Minette running a few yards ahead of them, Alys and Ryan headed for the river. They chose a spot under a budding tree to spread a cloth. Leaning against the tree, Alys brought out some sewing from her scrap bag while Ryan lay on his stomach and stared alternately from her to the vista across the river. He puffed on the pipe Émile had persuaded him to try during the cold evenings around the kitchen stove.

Here in the country, away from the village, few ravages of war were evident. The desolation and dormancy of winter were rapidly giving way to freshly plowed fields where the hillocks were sowed with turnips and sugar beets. The framing hills glistened pale gold and dark green as the morning sun touched newly emerged leaves of the hardwoods and the thickly massed needles on firs and pines.

On one corner of the quilt, Minette played with her precious rag doll. She'd had to be dissuaded from bringing all the animals Ryan had carved for her. Now she was happily singing her doll to sleep while promising her some picnic treats.

'It's a beautiful, beautiful day,' Ryan said, turning over onto his back and looking up at an almost cloudless, cerulean sky.

'It's what you dream about all winter,' Alys said. 'A day like this to sit in the sun and be lazy.'

Near them a small clump of dark, amethyst blue hyacinths filled the air with a strong, rich, sweet bouquet. Ryan reached over and picked one. 'Such an odor is almost too dazzling to be real.'

'I know,' Alys said. 'I've always thought of it as the true fragrance of spring.'

'And I'll always think of you and today when I smell one.' Ryan removed a single petal, crushed it between his fingers, and held them up to his face.

I wonder, Alys thought, if you really will. And where will you be?

Growing tired of playing on the quilt, especially since M'sieur seemed less inclined to play with her than to talk to her mother, Minette got up and announced she was taking her doll for a walk.

'All right,' Alys said, 'but only between here and the inn. Not near the river. Remember last time?'

'I 'member.' Minette began walking up and down, her doll baby cradled in her arms.

Alys started cutting the bread and softening the cheese so they could spread it easily. She wanted to ask Ryan to open the bottle of wine, but he seemed to be asleep, and she hated wakening him.

At that very moment he turned over, sat up, and put his hand over hers. 'Marry me, Alys.'

For days now she'd wondered if he'd ask her that. She'd hoped and yet dreaded he would. Her heart was pounding so hard she was afraid she'd have no breath to answer. 'I can't, Ryan.'

He moved closer and put his arms around her. 'Why not? You love me. And God knows I love you so much it hurts.'

'I do love you,' she said. And I can't bear the thought of losing you she thought. 'But we can't think about marriage. You need to know who you are and where you came from. You pretend not to think about it, but I see the need to know eating away at you. I think we should go to Liège, to the consulate.' She still couldn't bring herself to mention the American army; but with the war drawing to a close, they would certainly be contacting her soon. And then . . . And then coming to get Ryan.

'I want to know who I am, yes, but it's still less important than loving you and wanting to marry you. We can find out but we can still be together.'

Alys bent down and kissed him. 'Believe me, *mon cher*, all in the world I want is to be married to you and to have your children.'

'Then why?' He turned with a puzzled look and saw the tears forming in her eyes.

'Because eventually you're going to remember. When that happens, you'll forget all about these months. Nothing that took place, no one you knew, will you remember. I'll lose you, Ryan. I'll lose you as surely as if you were dead. I don't think I could bear that.'

'No! I'd never forget you. Not the way I love you.'

'Don't you understand, Ryan? I'd be a stranger. I'd mean no more to you than someone you passed on the street. You wouldn't believe me, if I tried to tell you. Oh, you might, for the sake of not hurting my feelings, but there'd be no reason for you to still love me.'

As much as he wanted to deny it, Ryan knew she was right. He'd read the books, too. An accident, even something as slight as a fall; the sight of something; a familiar noise: anything could bring his memory back. He'd return to the world he'd left and leave this world behind. It would be as lost to him as his previous one was now. Yet he refused to believe that he wouldn't know Alys or that she wouldn't be as dear to him then as she was now. He must cling to that thought. And he must persuade her that marriage would secure that hope.

'And isn't there a chance I might never recover my memory?' he asked.

'Very slight.' She put her hands over her face to hide her tears. 'Please, Ryan, don't say any more. I love you. I'll love you as long as you're here and – and know this life. Then when – when the time comes, I think I'll be prepared to let you go.'

He pulled her hands away from her face and held them between his. 'And not being married is better than being my wife?'

'I don't know. I'm confused. I can't think right now.' Ryan was still holding her hands, so this time she couldn't cover her face. She had to let the tears run freely.

Ryan started to wipe them off with his fingertips; but when she reached up to remove them, he took her in his arms. 'Darling, marry me and let me think for both of us. We belong together. I want you to be my wife, and I want to be Minette's father.'

Alys caught back a sob and buried her face on Ryan's chest.

'Say "yes," ' he pleaded, 'and we'll be married whenever you feel ready.'

'Yes, Ryan. Oh, yes. Hold me close and promise everything will be all right.' It would be right; it had to be.

'I'll never stop loving you, and I'll do everything I can to make you and Minette happy. Marry me soon.'

'Soon, darling.' She would be happy. She wouldn't let fears for the future intrude on that happiness. She'd live for the present and accept what each day brought. Ryan loved her, and Minette adored him. They'd be a family. At least for a little while.

Alys and Ryan chose May 1 as the date for their wedding. At Ryan's request and with Alys in complete agreement, there were to be no guests. This did not mean, however, the Prévoux were not going to have some kind of celebration. Although Minette had no idea what everyone was continually smiling about, she was excited at the thought of a party and almost beside herself when Ryan told her he was going to be her Papa and stay with her from now on. To make it even more perfect, Alys promised her a new silk dress, made from one Alys had bought during her first year in Liège.

On the day Alys stayed in Ste. Monique after school to talk to the parish priest, and to see if there would be flour and sugar for the wedding cake that Jolie insisted they must have, Alys gave in to an impulse to visit Countess Charbonne. She saw the gentle woman almost every day either before or after school, but only for a brief greeting. She'd missed the long, quiet talks they used to have. Countess Charbonne had grieved with her over Gilles's death, and it would please her to learn that Alys had found a new love.

As she neared the rooms the countess had kept for herself, Alys thought about her first childhood impressions of the château and of the countess herself.

The château was unusual for this section of Belgium, where most were constructed of stone. Four stories high, it was glazed red brick with marble pilasters. From a brick terrace on all four sides, *portes-fenêtres* opened to the rooms within. The exception was in one section at the rear of the château. Here two tall, slender, stained-glass windows indicated the private chapel. They did not depict saints or Biblical scenes or religious symbols, but a variety of flowers in brilliant blues, reds, greens, and yellows.

The original stone château had been destroyed during World War I. Prior to that war, Countess Charbonne had been visiting in England and had fallen in love with the Georgian style of architecture. As soon as peace came in 1918, Count Charbonne began rebuilding the château as an English manor house, although the villagers would always continue to refer to it as 'the château.'

The Charbonnes then traveled throughout Europe and Asia to find the perfect furnishings. From England came an Adams mantelpiece and paneling for the formal drawing room; and to grace the mantel, a pair of Sung dynasty, blue green glazed vases. Tiles from Holland framed the fireplace in the more informal sitting room, and the countess had used English tiles, with chinoiserie figures, around the fireplace in her bedroom.

Priceless antiques filled the rooms, whose floors were covered with Aubusson, Persian, or Chinese carpets. Alys had always loved following Countess Charbonne from room to room and listening to the older woman lovingly describe how and where she had found each precious treasure: the Ming dynasty porcelain jar and matching bowl, the Meissen figurines, the *Capo di Monte* figurines with their soft enamel colors, and the large collection of faience objets d'art. She was particularly proud of the pitcher and delicate cups in a cocoa set of Staffordshire pottery in rare red and white Wedgwood. Alys felt especially honored when the countess used it one afternoon when she came by to call.

It had been apparent to everyone in the village that Count Charbonne adored his wife and would do anything or give her anything to make her happy. His death, following a lengthy illness which kept him confined to the château, saddened everyone. The village was amazed that almost immediately afterward, the countess opened her house and grounds for May Day festivities. Other events at the château also became annual traditions. Each year the village children sang Christmas carols for her, and she invited them in for sweets and small gifts.

It was at this time, also, that she became something of a godmother to everyone in the village. All were welcomed with a smile, whether visiting by invitation or dropping by for advice. She began, too, to come with her cook and chauffeur to the village to shop. In her open touring car she smiled and spoke to everyone. Then she alighted at the café and went inside – or on pleasant days sat at a small table under the awning – for *café au lait* and pastry. While she drank her two cups of *café au lait* – always two – she held court like a queen, giving advice or merely greeting those who stopped to speak to her.

Countess Charbonne did not often laugh aloud, but there was always laughter in her eyes and underlying the sweet, generous smile.

The village waited for the countess to let them know when spring had officially arrived. She herself would fling wide open all the *portes-fenêtres* to air out the rooms. 'Destroy winter with the new winds of spring' was her annual motto.

When the Germans occupied Ste. Monique, the château was commandeered to house officers and men. The countess had been allowed to occupy a small stone building to the rear of the château, all that remained of the original buildings on the estate. She immediately turned the four small rooms into a charming home with the few rugs, pieces of furniture, and household necessities she was permitted to take with her. When Poland had been invaded, she – with more foresight than most optimistic Belgians – had stored the most precious and valuable of her collections in the root cellar beneath the greenhouse.

In her small house she did all her own cooking and cleaning, and into it she welcomed visitors as graciously as she had at the château. There was no stained glass here, but in the winter, the windows were frosted with intricately patterned whorls and swirls and fernlike designs. When touched by the sun, they glowed in strange shades of icy blue. During the Germans' drunken revelries, the crystal chandeliers in the château were broken, but the countess managed to get in and save some of the crystal drops. She hung these at the windows, and the ever-changing colors of the spectrum on the ice patterns were as eerily beautiful as the stained glass.

In the spring, a single fruit tree blossomed outside one window, and she filled the rooms with what wild flowers had lived through interminable shellings and bombings. In her rooms, one could almost forget that a few kilometers away the world was waging a deadly war. Except that, like other women, she was always knitting. From the count's old sweaters, scarves, and socks she unraveled the wool, washed it, and then wound the yarn around a board to smooth it out. The mittens, stockings, vests, and other garments she knitted were not for herself, but for those in dire need.

World War II was the second German invasion she'd lived through. Although she was forced to live in far less comfort than she was accustomed to, nothing could daunt her spirit or humble her imperious attitude toward the interlopers.

After knocking on the countess's door, Alys heard the rapid, spritely footfalls of the older woman crossing the bare floor.

CHAPTER FIFTEEN

Alys looked past the countess to the three rooms of the château she'd kept for herself after offering the others to the school.

'Come in, come in, Alys. This is a lovely surprise.' She led Alys to what had been the small family parlor. It was now furnished with the few precious pieces she'd been able to save during the occupation. The once-graceful crystal chandelier had been replaced by a single bulb, but it shone on the well-polished, fine woods and faded but still beautiful brocade upholstery. As always, there were flowers. Only a few sprigs from an ancient flowering peach tree, but in their small, exquisite, cut-crystal bowl, they added a touch of delicate beauty to the room. There was an intimacy about the small parlor that made Alys feel more welcome than the grandeur of the main hall ever had.

'It's lovely in here,' Alys said after she and the countess sat down.

'Thank you, I've tried to make it as comfortable as I could. This room, the bedroom, and a small anteroom I turned into a kitchen are all I need. When I returned, I realized how foolish I'd been to try to keep up all of the house for myself. The furniture that used to fill those other rooms is all gone, of course.'

'What a pity,' Alys sighed. 'How you must mourn them.'

'No, Alys, I don't. I'm eighty-four years old, and I've had a very good and full life. Perhaps most people my age sit and reflect upon the past. I don't do that, either. I look ahead. The past – thank God, at times – can never be repeated. But the future is a marvelous mystery that is revealed to us day by day. I refuse to let that future, or the present, be marred by useless regrets. Regrets for wrong actions as well as lost people and things. The first cannot be undone and the others cannot be brought back. So I intend to be as happy as I can with what I have.'

'That's a marvelous, healing philosophy,' Alys said.

'No, it's just plain common sense.'

The countess stood up and walked over to the window. For several minutes she remained motionless, staring silently across what had once been the lush green lawn and formal garden to the forested hills beyond. Alys waited patiently but curious as to why the countess had so abruptly ended their conversation. Smiling, the countess finally moved away from the window and returned to her seat. She continued speaking as if there had not been a hiatus of several minutes between sentences.

'Which brings me to something else,' she said, 'and makes me glad you're here. I'm leaving the château in trust to the village. I have no children and no relatives who need it. For the present, while I still live in these rooms, the rest of them serve a very useful function as schoolrooms. Eventually, however, they won't be needed for that. I've suggested that all of the château, including the grounds, be used as a convalescent or rest home. There will be men returning from the war who need such a place, and I can't think of a spot more beautiful. The idea came to me when I heard about the young man you've been helping. We could do so much for other handicapped men. How is he, by the way?'

'He's the reason I stopped by to see you. I wanted you to know we're going to be married. A small wedding, no guests, but I did want you to know.'

The countess reached over and patted Alys's hand. 'I'm happy for you, but' – a frown crossed her face – 'what will happen if his memory returns?'

'It's not an *if*; it's a *when*. But I've accepted that. You don't live in the past; I don't plan for the future. We're not too much different, are we?'

'Good girl. Grab what happiness you can. There's far too little of it in the world. *Carpe diem*: "seize the day." Some disapprove of that philosophy as being too selfish; I happen to think it's a wise one. Now, I was going to ask you to help with the rest home. At least the planning of it so we'll be ready to move ahead when the rooms are available again. But if you're going to be married . . .'

But not leaving, Alys assured her, and for the next few minutes they discussed tentative plans for the rest home.

'When's the wedding?' the countess asked.

'May 1. Next Tuesday.'

Countess Charbonne stood up, and Alys thought her movement a signal to leave. Instead, the older woman said, 'Come. I have something to show you.' She led the way into the bedroom.

With a small gold key she opened the wide doors to a massive linen press. The shelves were layered with colorful quilts. 'You see, those horrid *Boches* didn't get everything I cherish. Some of these were my grandmother's. But what I want is in one of these drawers.' She lifted out a large bundle wrapped in yards of tissue paper. 'This is my second-day dress. My wedding dress was destroyed. Some day I will tell you about that. But this I saved, and I think it will fit you perfectly.'

Alys looked at the dress and longed to try it on. How surprised Ryan would be to see her in something new.

'It should be worn,' the countess said, 'not hidden away like some dreadful family secret.' She spread the dress out on the bed. 'My, but I was a fine figure of a woman then.'

'And you still are.' Alys was still finding it hard to believe that the countess really wanted her to have it for her wedding day.

'Pshaw! I couldn't hook the first hook. But you can. And you should have something special for your wedding day.'

'Thank you. I'll wear it with pride.' Alys felt her eyes tearing when she touched the pale blue silk with ruffled stand-up collar and ruffles down the front of the bodice. The skirt hung straight in front and was gathered back in an apron effect to a small bustle.

Alys saw tears welling also in the countess's eyes. Such happy memories, Alys thought, she must be having now. And so very long ago.

'Be happy.' The countess inclined her head for Alys to kiss her on the cheek.

Two days before the wedding, one of the boys from the village delivered a large package from Countess Charbonne. With nervous fingers, Alys tore away the wrapping. Within was one of the quilts she'd seen in the linen press. Sewn into a double wedding ring pattern were literally hundreds of pieces of silk in almost as many different designs and colors, from fine tissue silk to richly textured brocades and satins. In the center of each ring, the quilting had been done with colored embroidery thread in various floral and bird designs. The whole was backed and bordered with gold satin. It was exquisite.

All the note said was, 'Every bride should sleep under a new quilt on her wedding night.'

Why, Alys wondered, was the countess so generous to her? It was almost as if the elderly woman had adopted her for the daughter she'd never had. Perhaps, in spite of all the activity around her in the school, the woman was lonely in her three rooms. Then and there Alys vowed to see her more often and to take Ryan to meet her.

The parish priest was to arrive a little before eleven. Alys spent most of the morning getting Minette and herself dressed. Together they gathered wild flowers, and Alys braided some of them into crowns for each to wear. She brushed Minette's hair, now reaching below her shoulders, into long curls and carefully fastened the wreath of flowers on top. Alys was remembering the May Day festivals of her childhood when Jolie made such crowns for her to wear. With the other children, she had worn the age-old traditional dress of the area and had danced the traditional folk dances. She wondered if, after these years of despair, those days would ever return.

Then Alys set about dressing herself. Countess Charbonne's blue silk was a perfect fit. She studied herself in the mirror. She looked as beautiful as a bride should look on her wedding day. And she was as happy. She set her own crown on her head and secured it with pins.

In another few minutes the priest would be here and she would be married to Ryan. From the moment she'd said 'yes' to him, she hadn't had a single doubt about wanting to be his wife. She would love him with all the love she had in her for as long as they could be together. There could still be a miracle, and she might not be a stranger to him when his memory returned. She gathered up the remaining flowers that she'd placed in water, wiped off the stems, and fashioned them into bouquets for herself and Minette. She tied the stems with a bit of ribbon. Minette's eyes were glowing with excitement, but they were a pale reflection of the glow in her own heart. She loved Ryan too much to worry about the future.

When Jolie came and told her that Ryan and the priest were waiting, Alys and Minette followed her to the dining room. Ryan's smile when he saw them walking in was all Alys needed to be assured she was doing the right thing. Theirs might be a small wedding, but it was a beautiful one. Jolie had banked the fireplace before which they stood with masses of flowers and greenery. Ryan clutched her hand throughout the ceremony as if he feared she might change her mind. She heard the clear, sure tone of his responses, and with them faded the last of any lingering doubts. She looked at him the whole time she spoke her vows; for her there was no one else in the room.

It had been the quiet wedding they wanted, but afterward the room rang with laughter as they dined on two pheasants Émile had shot the day before and roasted in wine. They cut the small wedding cake and with the remainder of the wine toasted each other and the future.

In spite of its being the first of May, the evening was cool enough for a small fire in the stove. Sitting with Émile and Jolie after Minette had gone to bed, Alys mused that, except for the gold ring on her finger that she looked at every minute or so, the evening seemed much like any other. But it wasn't. She was now married to a man she loved dearly, and it was the first day of a whole new life.

Ryan reached over and took Alys's hand. She gently rubbed her fingers over the rough calluses and toughened skin of his hand. He had obviously fought hard, and now he was working hard. Thank God for his wanting to remain at the inn. There would be tourists before long. Once the war was over, people would travel again. Europeans enjoyed their holidays and would always find the means for them. And Americans might be coming before too long. The inn had always given the Prévoux a comfortable life, and she expected it would again.

When the last bit of wood became embers, they went upstairs. The room was chilly, and they hurriedly undressed and slid under the quilt from Countess Charbonne.

'I love you,' Ryan said, reaching for her and holding her close. 'You were so beautiful this morning. I'll never lose the image of your smile when you said your vows.' He kissed her and then kissed her again and again. Alys felt his hands and then his body seeking her, and for her the day ended as the most perfect one she'd ever known.

Evenings were spent in the familiar setting of the kitchen or parlor with Jolie, Émile, and Minette; but at night Alys and Ryan entered their own private world that only lovers know. They laughed again over some trifling, secret joke; recalled the events of the day; settled small but important differences; made wild, improbable plans for the future; and delighted in a physical intimacy that was the outward gratification of a constantly expanding spiritual intimacy.

Ryan was never a hasty or impetuous lover thinking only of his own immediate pleasure. Alys experienced a sensual exultation in having him caress her body with his eyes before touching her and before they came together with a joyous, mutual, uninhibited passion.

Together they discovered that while physical intimacy was the ultimate act of love, there were a thousand ways of making love: reaching for each other's hands at the same time, laughing spontaneously together at something that amused them, being understanding during a time of stress, sensing the need for a kind word at the right moment, the look in their eyes when seeing each other after being separated awhile, or the gift of an unselfish act.

They seldom went right to sleep. It was as if they couldn't let go of time, couldn't give up a single precious moment of being awake together.

'With you here beside me,' Ryan said one night, 'there'll be no more nightmares.'

'I hope not.' Alys snuggled closer within the curve of his body. 'Yet, at the same time, I hoped they might be telling you something that would offer a clue to the past.'

'I do have one recurring dream,' he said. He settled Alys's head more comfortably on his arm. 'No action. Nothing happening. Just the image of a man – a very tall, husky, strong, domineering man. His face is never clear, but he has a powerful voice. And he always says the same thing: "Ride the wind." That's all. Then he disappears.'

' "Ride the wind." ' Alys repeated the phrase several times. 'I wonder what it means. He must have been someone important to you.'

'I know. I wake up wondering what he's trying to tell me. It seems like he's saying to catch the wind and go full out. Take the challenge.'

'Wind is power,' Alys suggested. 'If you ride the wind, you can use its power.' She remained thoughtful for a minute. 'Interesting the number of connotations from a single phrase, but no clue as to its meaning for you. Someone said it, I'm certain of that, and during some important moment in your life. But who and when? There's so much hidden in our subconscious that emerges when we least expect it to. And dreams are such fantastic, enigmatic things.'

'Strange,' Ryan said. 'I want to know who I am, yet at the same time I don't. Whatever I learn will be a total surprise and mean another readjustment.'

Ryan was no more ambivalent about learning of his past than Alys was. Unlike him, she knew that when they went to Liège, they'd have to go directly to military headquarters. She was certain what one outcome would be: once his records were located, Ryan would be held by the army. It could mean being sent home until everything was cleared up and his status determined. That was what frightened her; and in the dark, she clung more tightly to him.

A promise to Minette that there would be plenty of picnics was fulfilled. Almost every afternoon when Alys returned from school and Ryan finished helping Émile, they took a few treats and spread a quilt out under the trees near the river. They played games and then ate whatever surprise Jolie had prepared for them.

More wild flowers were in bloom. On one such afternoon, Minette brought Ryan a small bunch of violets. Promising to press them and keep them forever, he slipped them into the buttonhole of his jacket. One blossom that kept falling out he put into a pocket of his trousers.

'You keep them forever?' Minette asked with a serious smile.

'Forever, precious. You can help me press them in a book tonight.'

Alys smiled on the two she loved more than anyone else in the world. Tragedy and pain had brought both of them to her; in different ways she had given life to each of them, and she was determined to do all she could to give them happiness as well.

CHAPTER SIXTEEN

i

On May 7, 1945, at 2:41 A.M.., Germany surrendered unconditionally to the Western Allies and the Soviet Union. Although several of the Prévoux's friends stopped by the inn during that day and evening to celebrate, Ryan, confined to bed with a strained back, didn't see them. He'd been fishing the day before and had fallen into the river when he tried to walk across from boulder to boulder. At least the pain and ignominy of losing his balance was offset by the six nice trout he presented to Émile to fix for supper.

Entertained by Minette and smothered with Alys's tender nursing, Ryan remained in bed for four days. Finally he announced, 'Enough of this. I need to get outside.'

'You're sure?' Alys asked. 'There's no pain?'

'Quite sure.' He saw her eyebrow rise suspiciously. 'Well, just a little discomfort from lying down so long. But exercise should help it. I think I'll walk up among the hills again, and maybe a little farther into the woods than I've gone before. Only this time I'll cross by the bridge. No more jumping from rock to rock. Don't worry if I stay for a while. I'll be back in time for dinner.'

Instead of taking the path along the river, Ryan decided to walk by way of the road to the old stone bridge built by the 'God Damns.' According to local legend, Alys had told him, rivers and streams throughout the French and Belgian countryside had hundreds of stone bridges erected over them by the English during the Hundred Years' War in the thirteenth century. The French named the invaders the God Damns because of their constant use of the profanity. The term for the British had remained as intact through the centuries as the bridges they'd built.

Between the inn and the bridge, Ryan passed a small cemetery crowded with mourners. He paused long enough to learn that an old veteran of the Great War was being buried with full military honors. As Ryan started walking on, a six-gun salute was fired. The reverberation was like an explosion in Ryan's head. In agony from the intense pain, and clawing at his face, he stumbled for several feet along the road.

Ryan continued to hear the guns. They were all around him now. He fell to the ground. Where was the command post? He had to get inside. No, there was no building nearby. He was on an open road and the tanks were coming toward him. He had to stop the tanks.

'Set up the guns,' he mumbled, 'we have to stop them. Keep shooting.' There was no sound. 'Shoot, dammit, shoot,' he mumbled again just before the blinding pain returned. Clutching the dirt between his fingers, he passed out.

'Are you all right, m'sieu?'

Ryan looked up to see a boy bending over and speaking to him in French. In spite of feeling dizzy, Ryan shook his head to indicate he didn't understand. The boy spoke again, and Ryan recognized the words as German. He shook his head again.

'Are you hurt?' The boy spoke more slowly and hesitantly in English this time.

'No, no, I'm fine.' Except for being completely confused as to where he was. Where were Witkowski and Newsome? They and he must have escaped from the tanks, but to where? He looked slowly around. Someplace, obviously, where there was no snow. He was not yet aware that the weather was warm and that he was not in uniform.

'Where am I?' he asked.

'Just outside Ste. Monique, sir.' The boy spoke with a heavy French accent.

The name meant nothing to Ryan. 'And where is that?'

The boy looked amazed, as if everyone should know where his village was. 'In Belgium, sir.'

Belgium. Somehow they – or at least he – had gotten miles from the former front. That meant, if memory served, they had retreated all the way back through Luxemburg and across the border. Where in hell were his men? And why had he been left here? Maybe they'd been killed and he'd traveled some distance alone. He had to get to the nearest division.

'Where's the front?' Ryan asked.

'The front? I don't understand, sir.'

Dammit! What was wrong with this boy? 'The fighting, son. The war. Where is the nearest fighting going on?'

The boy stepped back a few feet, both fear and amazement crossing his face. 'Don't you know? The war is over. It's been over for four days.'

'It can't be.' Ryan shook his head to clear his brain, and he again reeled from the piercing, stabbing pain. 'We were retreating, but the Germans can't have beaten us. Not in a few days.'

'Not the Germans,' the boy said, now aware that while something was wrong with Ryan, the man was not dangerous. 'The Allies won. They beat Germany all the way back to Berlin.'

'We won,' Ryan said slowly to himself. Only then did he realize that not only was there no snow, but he was no longer cold. 'What date is it?'

'May 11, 1945.'

'Thank you.' May! Five months couldn't have passed without his knowing it. He had to find out where he'd been and what he'd been doing. Most important of all, he was a soldier; and he had to report to someone. 'Do you happen to know, son, if there are any American forces stationed nearby?'

'I think there are some in Liège. They had headquarters there during the war.'

'How do I get there?' Feeling like a man stranded on a raft floating in the middle of an endless sea, Ryan was getting desperate to be saved by something that was familiar.

'Along this road, sir. But you'll have to walk. The trains aren't running from here yet. But I expect you might get rides on wagons.'

'Thank you. And thank you again for your information.'

'You're welcome, sir.' Ryan watched the boy pick up his fishing pole and head for a small stone bridge.

Ryan started along the road and then stopped. He looked down at himself. Instead of a uniform, he saw faded trousers and shirt. Why wasn't he in uniform? Putting his hands in the pockets, he realized they were empty. No identification. He reached up to his neck to find he no longer wore his dog tags. The mystery was getting more complicated. Each discovery was like getting deeper and deeper into a maze from which he knew no escape.

Without identification of any kind, he wondered just how he could explain his situation to the authorities when he reached Liège. His name and serial number, 0982494. He repeated it over and over to reassure himself he hadn't forgotten that. But what could he tell them about these past months? If he'd been taken prisoner and then released, he'd still have his tags. The same if he'd been wounded. In either case, he would have been returned to a unit, not left to wander the countryside. The one fear he'd been trying to force to the back of his mind finally would not be denied. Had he deserted? Had he been hiding out somewhere all these months?

He needed time. He had to spend some time planning how to present himself to the military authorities to make them understand – and believe – that he remembered nothing of the past five months. Amnesia was such a convenient excuse for someone wanting to avoid prosecution for desertion, but it was the only explanation that made sense. But where had he been? What was he going to say when the questions began?

Ryan looked toward the river where the boy was now fishing. He saw the stone bridge and the forested hills beyond it. They seemed to be beckoning toward him as a place where he might resolve some of his dilemma. One more day would not make any difference after all this time. Ryan turned around, waved to the boy as he walked across the bridge and headed up toward the dim interior of the forest.

He walked, deeper and deeper among the trees. Here a faint light filtered through the branches and spread a soft glow, like the dusk just after sunset. Pine needles rustled beneath his feet. From time to time, Ryan came upon a small glade where the afternoon sun shone more brightly. In one was a narrow, trickling stream, and he bent down to scoop up some of the water. He was tired as well as thirsty, and he sat down with his back against a sturdy fir tree. It was as good a place as any to stop and make some plans.

If he were to present a plausible case to the military authorities, he needed to remember as much as he could of the events leading up to his loss of memory. His mind went back to the predawn artillery barrage by the Germans, the start of their devastating counteroffensive.

ii

Staggering from the shattering blast along the length of the horizon, Ryan hurried back inside the command post. His one thought was to reach Sergeant Svaboda, some five hundred yards farther up front along the line, on the field telephone.

As he crossed the room, ignoring the startled expressions of Corporal Witkowski and Private Newsome, he was thinking, My God! What in hell is breaking loose? What's happening?

After picking up the phone, Ryan heard the familiar, muffled ring. He waited impatiently for a voice to respond. Then suddenly it was like witnessing the end of the world.

Artillery shells screamed in like angry bees. Ryan's combat experience was without value; it was totally negated by what he was hearing and seeing. His benumbed brain watched the entire street blow up in one gut-wrenching, volcanic explosion of fire.

Ryan felt a hand on his shoulder, and he peered toward the other end of the arm. For a moment, he didn't recognize either the face or the voice coming from the tense lips. The words seemed to be echoing from the bottom of a deep pit.

'Lieutenant! Lieutenant, we gotta get the hell outta here.' Ryan shook his head to clear his brain, and he realized it was Witkowski talking to him. 'We gotta get our asses moving, sir.'

'Right. Anybody alive out there?' He asked this of Newsome who was standing near the rubble that had once been the front wall of the building and who was looking out across a scene of total annihilation. The small crossroads was a mass of unbelievable devastation.

'I don't think so, sir.'

'Then let's move out. We'll make a quick check for survivors, do what we can to help them, and send back the first medics we come to.' He looked at the phone still in his hand. Useless to him now. With the first artillery barrage, all lines to the front and to company – and probably regimental – headquarters would have been blown up.

The dust was still settling as they scrambled over the fallen wall and into the street. Looking down the road toward the front, they stopped.

'God damn!' Witkowski said. 'The whole German army is coming up the road. Tiger tanks. Self-propelled guns. Jesus! What we gonna do?'

'Get the hell to the rear,' Ryan said.

'We can't make it, sir. They'll spot us,' Newsome insisted.

'Yes, we can. Thank God for these hills. When they reach that valley between us and them, we'll be hidden from view for about three minutes. If we move fast, we can get away.'

Watching for exactly the right moment to move, the three men hit the road running and scrambling. Each yard of advance was torture on the almost destroyed, shell-pocked road. After traveling about a hundred yards, Ryan realized there was no way they could outdistance the Germans. He was ready to order the others to head for the woods when Witkowski spotted a jeep seventy-five feet or so around a curve. A miraculous bit of luck handed them by the gods of war. It didn't appear as if the jeep were damaged.

'Stay here, Lieutenant, I'll check it out. Our luck can't be that good.'

Ryan and Newsome watched from the protection of some shattered trees. In a matter of seconds, it seemed, Witkowski was back. 'Jeep's okay, sir, but it's Goldman. He's dead.'

The three inched their way forward, still keeping in the shelter of the trees. The company clerk was slumped over the wheel; a sliver of shrapnel buried in his temple marked the mortal wound. Ryan let out a soft moan: 'I'm sorry, Goldman.'

Before ordering Newsome to slide the body carefully off the seat and onto the edge of the road, he took the dead man's M1 rifle and ammunition belt. Then he climbed into the rear seat.

While all three held their breaths, Witkowski turned the key. The engine fired up. He backed the jeep from the bank it had cut into when

Goldman was killed. Spinning it around, he headed for regimental headquarters.

'No damn use to check company headquarters,' Ryan had said. 'They've taken the same god-awful barrage we did.'

Suddenly, a soul-shuddering thought hit Ryan. He was running away and leaving his men, those on the front and those who might still be alive at the crossroads. He'd let panic command his actions; all compassion and all sense of duty had been obliterated. He was deserting his men.

Ryan put a hand on Witkowski's shoulder. 'Pull over,' he ordered, 'and turn around.'

'Impossible, sir. They're hot on our trail.'

Ryan saw Newsome freeze in his seat; the look on his face registered his shock at Witkowski's insubordination.

'Goddammit, Witkowski,' Ryan said, 'stop this jeep.' He lifted Goldman's rifle in his hand, but still kept it aimed away from the corporal. 'I said pull it over, and I mean now.' In spite of the jolting movements of the vehicle, he managed to reach in front and turn off the key.

Witkowski and Newsome remained stone-faced in the front seat.

'Don't you understand?' Ryan asked. 'I have to get back to my men. I can't desert them. An officer takes care of his men before he sees to his own needs.'

'I apologize, sir,' Witkowski said, 'but there's no damn way we can make it. And three of us would be of no use to them now. We gotta get outta here. Let 'em know what's happened. Regimental can send back help.'

His arguments were suddenly reinforced by the clatter and whine of tanks coming toward them.

Slumping in his seat, Ryan knew he was being forced to accept an untenable decision. He must leave his men and go on. He must get to regimental to learn what the overall situation was and explain his own position.

During all this he was continually bombarded with the conscious voice of guilt: Where are your men? Why did you leave them?

Just as Witkowski was cranking up the jeep again, a figure loomed out of the frozen mist, stumbling around the fog-shrouded stumps of what had been dense woods. Newsome aimed his rifle toward the man, but Witkowski knocked it away. 'Goddammit, it's Sergeant Erikson.'

The sergeant was in an almost catatonic state of panic. He obviously didn't recognize them. He had no weapon. He was babbling incoherently while swinging his arms from side to side and backing away.

Ryan leaped out of the jeep. Hearing the tanks approaching dangerously close and unable to get the sergeant to hear him, he struck him unconscious with one well-placed blow. With Newsome's help, he got Erikson into the back seat.

The four men, with two rifles and one jeep, continued along the route toward the rear. They traveled a maze of chopped-up roads, desecrated woods, and mounds of rubble that had once been villages. They managed to outdistance the slower-moving tanks to LeCroix where regimental headquarters had been. There was nothing moving there! They went into the shell of a building. Like the street, it was littered with the dead. Even as they mourned these deaths, they were looking around for anything that might be of value to them. To their inexplicable relief they found rifles, bazookas, ammo, and K rations.

During all this time there was no speech among the men. Ryan knew they were all wondering the same thing: why had just the dead remained? There was no sign of life anywhere, neither human nor animal. It was the same throughout the village. It was a necropolis. An eerie memorial to death. All was complete destruction.

Sergeant Erikson had remained motionless in the jeep. Then, as if awakening from a trance, he stepped out and walked over to Ryan. In stuttered phrases he began to describe what had happened along the line. How the white-caped figures of the enemy emerged through the mist, the artillery buried some men alive, how others who tried to flee were run down under the treads of the tanks. 'All dead, Lieutenant, all dead,' he continued to mutter as Ryan led him back to the jeep.

The words did nothing to ease Ryan's guilt, even as he had to accept there was nothing he could have done to save his men. Nor could his tortured mind believe that Sergeant Svaboda was gone. Svaboda, the war-knowledgeable veteran who had taught a green shavetail how to lead his men and how to fight and stay alive. The realization that this best friend was gone almost destroyed Ryan's will to go on. Then he remembered what that same friend had taught him, and the memory stiffened his resolve to keep going.

They cranked up the jeep and started along the street between shattered buildings. Just beyond the town they came alongside the colonel's jeep. Both the colonel and his driver were dead. They must have been hit, Ryan thought, with a later barrage while trying to get to division headquarters. To Ryan, it seemed as if the whole world had ended, and he wondered why.

'Where do we go from here?' Witkowski asked.

'To division and find out what to do. Turn the jeep and haul ass.'

The jeep pulled about a mile more along the road. There was no abating in the sounds of artillery and tanks behind them. To these sounds was added a new threat. Planes began strafing the road. At the first sound of a plane behind them, Witkowski cut the jeep and hit the brakes, as each of them, with a combat soldier's instinct, threw himself out and toward the woods in one motion. There was a clatter of rapid, automatic firing as the plane put its guns on the jeep. Bullets riddled the engine and the seats.

'Shit!' exclaimed Witkowski.

It was lousy luck, Ryan thought, to lose the jeep; but miraculously it didn't catch fire. As soon as he could, Newsome crawled back to salvage some weapons, ammo, and K rations.

The three divided the supplies and loaded up. Erikson was once more moving like an automaton. Putting him in the middle of the squad formation, they moved out through the woods.

Immediately they were hit with a new artillery bombardment. Ryan, Witkowski, and Newsome flattened out. Erikson panicked at the sound and ran screaming, in spite of Ryan's efforts to call him back. Ryan could only watch with horror as the sergeant was mangled by a shell blast.

Erickson's last words – words that kept repeating themselves in Ryan's brain – were 'Mama, Mama, Mama!'

The artillery pounding increased. The tanks became a deafening roar.

For two more days Ryan, Witkowski, and Newsome, augmented by four others wandering in the woods, managed to stay together. They kept going, struggling through the snow and hoping desperately to find a refuge or command post. At night they kept from being separated by hanging on to each other's cartridge belts. The Germans seemed to be all around them.

They passed dead men in the snow, some killed outright, some apparently only wounded but then frozen because no help had reached them. Beside some were unopened Christmas packages. Poor souls, Ryan thought, they had hoped to make it to safety and a happy Christmas. Ryan gave a silent prayer for them.

At one point they were shaken to see several Germans coming toward them, too many for their small group to knock out without the shots being heard and calling in other Germans who might be nearby. Taking no thought of the cold, they flattened out and covered themselves as best they could with the snow. Ryan raised his head only enough to see two of the Germans going through the pockets of the dead men. One German looked at some letters he'd found, laughed, and kicked snow into a dead soldier's face. They moved on to another; and evidently finding the pickings too lean for their taste, they walked out of sight.

Finally, on the third day, Ryan and his men reached a major road. If they continued traveling westward, Ryan thought, they were bound to reach some post in the rear. Then he heard once again the dread sounds of tanks approaching. During the past days, in spite of leading these men out of danger, in spite of keeping them moving, Ryan's guilt about leaving his other men had increased tenfold. Now he must do something to atone for his failure as an officer and to avenge their deaths.

The men had heard the tanks, too; and, groggy with exhaustion, they looked to Ryan for direction. They needed to get to some safe refuge and rest, but he knew they'd still follow without question any order he gave. Although Ryan was also slumped with fatigue, he once more straightened into a posture of command and defiance. What would Svaboda have done now?

'To hell with running!' he shouted. 'Dammit! Let's fight the bastards here and now.'

The men's first reaction of weary reluctance did not surprise him. He was asking a lot of them. Within seconds, however, they had assumed the determined stance of soldiers ready to fight. Damn, these were good men.

'Witkowski,' Ryan ordered, 'you and the other men set up a roadblock with these fallen trees. Newsome, place bazookas in firing position and load all the rifles.'

With each man working two or three of the guns, they just might manage to stop the tanks and turn them around.

iii

At that point, Ryan's memory failed him, and he returned to the present. Did they stop the tanks? What happened to Witkowski, Newsome, and the others whose names he couldn't remember? They were just soldiers. No, dammit, they were infantrymen who were willing to keep going and keep fighting until all hope, all chance for survival, was gone.

And what about himself? Had he been wounded or had he fled, overcome finally, like Erikson, by a horror he could no longer stand?

Exhausted by reliving those three days, Ryan fell into a fitful slumber. When he woke up, he was still faced with the all-important question: had he been wounded or had he run? Now another question began to torment him: should he turn himself in or find some way to keep hiding out as, presumably, he'd been doing. His thoughts became a dialogue between himself and his conscience.

Why should I report in?

Because you're a soldier and a soldier knows his duty.

I was a soldier, but the war is over.

No, you're still a soldier until honorably discharged.

Discharged! I was probably declared missing in action and now presumed dead.

What about Janet and your family?

They'd be better off thinking of me dead than court-martialed as a deserter. They'd always think I died on the field of honor.

Honor? Or dishonor? You don't care if you become a nonentity? A no one?

I am someone. I'm still Ryan Middleton.

You just said Ryan Middleton was dead.

No! No! Goddammit, I'm alive. Alive and able to make my own decisions. I can start a whole new life here.

So what's that life to be? A coward hiding here in these woods? Or a man with too much pride to cower in fear, to slink away like a timorous rat?

Stop it! Stop it! Don't push me.

How about the men who died? Did they have a choice?

No, but that's the luck of war. My luck was good.

Some of them made a choice. To follow you and then stop, instead of going on, when you wanted glory by slowing down those tanks.

It wasn't glory I wanted. It was revenge. Oh God, oh God, what should I do?

For the next several hours, Ryan slipped in and out of consciousness. Both awake and dreaming, he relived events of the war. Poignant and even humorous moments were interspersed with the more horrifying. The ominous feeling that shrouded him when he saw the old ladies in shawls crossing themselves while he advanced with his men toward the front. Learning during training that the notches on the dog tags were to make it easier to nail them to a coffin. Being shaken to the very foundations of his beliefs when he read *Gott mit uns*, – 'God with us' – on the belt buckle of the first dead German he saw. The hedgerows with Germans skulking behind every one of them. Running for shelter into a doorway and bumping into a German who'd done the same thing. They'd stood there, unmoving and staring at each other, until it was safe to run in opposite directions. And always another damn hedgerow to get across.

He remembered lying for hours in a cemetery while shells hit all around, tearing up the ground and freeing skeletons from their coffins. *And the graves shall be opened and the earth shall give up its dead*, Ryan had thought. It was the same cemetery where he'd lain for hours with his face in a clump of nettles, almost unmindful of the excruciating pain.

And Svaboda. Memories of him intruded into every other memory. Like the time Ryan was humiliated by a chewing out from a superior officer. It had been a training mission. Ryan hadn't gotten his men in attack position. When coming off an LCI, he had his men bunched together rather than spread out. Although he'd followed the battalion colonel's orders, the colonel chewed Ryan's ass in front of the divisional commander, Major General 'Blackdog' Lahoda. The whole division had screwed up, but according to chain of command, the blame came down to Ryan, and he was feeling mighty low. But he'd taken it and then immediately turned and issued a command to his men as if nothing had happened to reduce his standing in their eyes.

'You've got what it takes, sir,' Svaboda had said later. Ryan was prouder of those words than any medal he received. 'Just remember: always ride the wind.' Svaboda had said the same thing several other times. Although Ryan had never been quite sure what Svaboda meant by the words, they clung like a talisman in his mind.

Confused by all these thoughts, Ryan let himself fall asleep again. Sometime later he woke up screaming from a nightmare, and he was still hallucinating. Shells were exploding all around. He was in a foxhole with another man. The sky was lighted up like a carnival. Like the Fourth of July. Like the Christmas morning he received a huge carton of fireworks and he set them off one right after another. Another shell exploded over him. He crouched low and covered his head. He was unharmed, but he watched in sickening horror as the other man was blown into the air in a thousand pieces. Now he was sobbing uncontrollably. Why him? Why was he allowed to live while the other man died?

Ryan sat up. He wasn't to blame for that man's death. But what about the others? The ones he'd left alone on the line when he should have sent up reinforcements. When he should have been with them.

But they were dead now. It was too late to help them. Or if still alive, they were lucky, too. Would turning himself in bring the dead back to life? Would it restore arms and legs and God knew what else that had been taken from the wounded?

Finally, after hours without food or real sleep, Ryan lay slumped against a tree. A swelling, rushing, tumultuous cataract of pain and guilt swept over him. He heard sounds of incessant moaning, like echoes from the hills, of a multitude of wounded and dying. Then he realized it was he who was moaning.

Slowly, with tired but determined steps, Ryan came down out of the hills and headed for Liège.

CHAPTER SEVENTEEN

When Ryan had not returned in time for dinner, Alys went out to call him in. She assumed he'd be at one of his favorite spots along the riverbank. Not finding him immediately, she was surprised but not worried. If he'd decided to go for a walk in the woods, he'd been there often enough to find his way back. If not before dark, there'd be no danger in his spending the night in this warm weather. With daylight, he'd make his way out.

Then again he might have walked toward the village. He'd said he was determined to get over his fear of people. He could easily have reached the village and been invited to have a glass of wine at the local *brasserie*. Alys was about to turn and head in that direction when she saw a boy fishing downriver. She decided to ask him if he'd seen Ryan. As she approached, she recognized him as one of her students.

'Good evening, Mam'selle Prévou.'

'Good evening, Jules,' Alys responded in English and then reverted to French. 'You said that very well. I'm glad you've remembered your English. How's your luck?'

'Fair.' He pointed to the trout in his basket.

'Have you been here long?' After all, it was some time since Ryan left. Perhaps she was being foolish to think Jules had seen him.

'Since Monsieur Cour's funeral. Quite a sight that was. And a six-gun salute.'

Alys remembered hearing the guns soon after Ryan left.

'Then maybe you saw someone I'm looking for. A man. About my age. He might have been heading toward the river. Or this bridge.'

'I met one man I've never seen before. He was stumbling along the road. As if he were ill. He said he wasn't, but he was terribly confused. He didn't know the war was over.'

'Oh, no!' It had happened. Ryan's memory had begun to return. But how much of it? 'What else? Quick! What else did he say?'

'He was surprised to find he was in Belgium. And the date. He kept insisting it must be December, not May. And he complained of a terrible headache.'

'Where – where did he go?' She had to find Ryan. To explain. To tell him who she was and what they meant to each other. 'Do you know? Did he say or did you see?'

'I remember now he asked first where the front was. That was when I told him the war was over. Later he asked if there were any American forces nearby, and I told him I thought there were some in Liège. I gave him directions.'

'And he left for there?' *Bon Dieu!* Ryan had remembered everything – and forgotten all about her and their months together. Or had he? Maybe he thought it necessary to see Army authorities as quickly as possible, straighten his position out, and then return to her to tell her what he had to do. No, he would have to come to her first, to tell her where he was going.

'He started along the road,' Jules said, 'but then he came back. He seemed disturbed. He ran across the bridge and up into the hills. I haven't seen him return.'

Disturbed, Alys thought to herself. *Up into the hills*. Such actions could mean many things. But, oh God, let it mean that he still remembered her, wanted to stay with her, and had to come to a decision about what he should do. What was best for himself and for both of them. That was it. He'd return to her before going to Liège.

'Ryan, don't leave me. Stay or take me with you.' She ran to the bridge. She'd search the woods until she found him. He couldn't have gone too far up into the hills. At the edge of the woods it was dusk, but a few feet inside it was midnight. With her hands protectively in front of her, she moved from tree to tree, all the while calling Ryan's name. Tripping over a root, she fell onto a pile of leaves and sharp twigs. Her hands were dirty and scratched, but she'd managed to keep from hitting her face. It was no use. She couldn't go any farther or she'd lose her way and not be able to return home. Crying uncontrollably, she lay there until she garnered the strength to make her way back to the inn. 'Please, please, Ryan, return to me. I love you. You love me.' I can't, she thought, I can't go on without him.

Numbly she walked slowly across the bridge and alongside the river. There was no way of knowing what had restored Ryan's memory. It could have been the sight of something on the road. Or a sound. The military funeral perhaps. Jules said he'd fallen after stumbling along the road. Maybe he'd hit his head on something.

Alys thought about the other things Jules had said. The man understood neither French nor German. Then Ryan had no memory at all of these past months. But if so, why the retreat to the woods instead of going directly to Liège? There seemed no answer.

Before she reached the inn, Alys managed to bring her emotions enough under control to say what she thought would explain Ryan's absence, at least for tonight. She told them about meeting Jules. The boy was supposed to have come and told them that Ryan thought the evening a perfect one for spending the night in the hills.

Jolie merely raised her brows as if to suggest that was an odd thing for a man only a few days married to do.

How she got through the evening without giving way, Alys never knew. She saw her mother cast surreptitious glances of concern her way from time to time, but Alys pretended not to see them. Nor could she watch Minette playing with her carved animals. She was pretending they'd been locked up in a zoo, and she was letting them go free. How like them Ryan had been, locked in by his amnesia and speech defect. Now he was free to return to where he really belonged. She had provided the first key by helping him to speak again.

'Time for bed, *ma chère*,' she said, picking Minette up and holding her on her lap. 'Would you like me to sleep with you tonight?'

Please say yes, Alys thought. I need you even if you don't need me. I can't sleep alone, not tonight.

'Yes,' Minette said, and she burrowed her head into the softness of Alys's breast. Then she unbuttoned the top buttons of Alys's blouse and laid her cheek against her mother's skin.

'My goodness, baby, you haven't done that for a long time. You like the feel of skin, don't you?' It was a habit Minette had carried over after Alys no longer nursed her, but she thought the child had outgrown it.

'It's soft,' Minette said, 'And it's you, *Maman*.'

How desperately we all need physical closeness for comfort and reassurance, Alys thought. Maybe Minette had missed her these past two weeks more than she wanted to say. Children were far more sensitive to change than adults often gave them credit for.

'Come, then. We'll choose some books, and I'll stay with you.'

Throughout the night, Alys found herself reaching for Ryan but touching the small body of Minette, whom she pulled close to her so as to feel less alone.

In the morning, Alys went across the river and walked for hours through the woods, searching and calling for Ryan. She'd really had little hope of finding him but hope dies slowly. By noon, when she returned to the inn, she knew she had to tell her parents what had probably happened to Ryan. She'd then decide what she should do.

'You should go to Liège,' Jolie said immediately.

'What good would that do if he doesn't remember me?' Alys was fighting to keep back the tears.

'You don't know that for certain.'

'He'd forgotten all his French,' Alys reminded her. 'Wouldn't he have responded or reacted in some way if he hadn't?' She let Jolie take her in her arms. 'I'm not sure I could stand it if he didn't recognize me at all.'

Émile came over and put his arms around Alys. '*Maman* is right. You should go to Liège if only to learn the truth. If Ryan has no memory of his stay here, you need to know.'

'I'll go,' Alys said. 'It would be death to keep hoping.'

'And I'll go into Ste. Monique,' Émile said, 'and see if anyone's going to the city soon. It might have to be a farm wagon, but we'll get you there.'

It was another three days before Alys could leave. The hours of waiting were torment. There was nothing she could do or any place she went that put thoughts of Ryan out of her mind. During mass on Sunday morning, she looked at the priest and remembered her wedding day. On Monday and Tuesday, she went to the school, but the whole time she was remembering the hours of trying to teach Ryan to speak again. She took Minette to the river for a picnic and tried to explain that Papa had to be away for a while. Only when she was alone did she allow herself to cry.

Finally Émile came and said he'd found a ride for her. She would be going the approximately one hundred and twenty kilometers by wagon.

When Alys reached Stavelo, however, luck was with her. A local train to Liège had begun running again once a day. She had to stay in Stavelo overnight, but anything would be better than the jolting wagon. She forced herself to eat a good dinner, and she slept most of the night through. Worry and two days in the wagon had left her exhausted.

From Stavelo it was only a few hours to Liège, even on the slow train that seemed to stop at every junction. Within an hour of her arrival she found her way to American Army Headquarters, housed in one of the ancient city's finest hotels.

Only then did she become frightened. How should she inquire about Ryan, and whom did she ask? But her wants were perceived immediately by a young man in uniform behind a desk marked 'Information.' Alys was directed to a room filled with men who seemed to be trying very hard to look busy.

'Pardon,' she said at the first desk, 'I would like some information about an American officer named Lieutenant Ryan Middleton.'

The sergeant looked her up and down with an appraising eye. 'What do you need to know?'

'Well, I don't know quite how to phrase it. I think he might have come here in the past few days. If so, I would like to know where he is now.'

'Oh,' he said, leering, 'did he skip out? Leave you high and dry?'

'Pardon?' Alys was confused by his words and disturbed by his expression. 'I don't know what you mean.'

'Can it, Mike,' one of the others called across the room. 'See what you can do to help the young lady.' He turned to a soldier at the next desk, and Alys heard him say, 'She doesn't look like one of those we've been getting in here every day since the war ended. God, what promises some men must have made for a few hours of shacking up.'

Alys felt her cheeks redden. Could she be so easily mistaken for the women who gave themselves for food and maybe a promise of marriage after the war?

She thought about Marie, her childhood friend. Soon after the Americans relieved Ste. Monique from the Germans the first time, Alys saw Marie pressed by an American soldier against the broken side wall of a damaged building. Two other soldiers were waiting their turn. Alys should have gone quickly past, but she was too shocked to move.

'Stop staring,' Marie had shouted. The first soldier finished and moved away. While the second approached, Marie screamed at Alys, 'I'm hungry! I've been hungry for five years. At least I didn't serve Germans in order to eat,' she spat at Alys.

That had been the last Alys saw of her. She heard that Marie went to Bastogne where she rented a room with a bed that was surely more comfortable than a broken wall.

Then again, Alys thought, maybe I'm not so different after all. Yes! Yes, she was. She and Ryan really loved each other, and they were married. She was his wife.

'Middleton, Middleton.' The sergeant repeated the name over and over while he looked through a pile of folders on the desk. 'Stevens,' he called to another, 'the name Middleton mean anything to you?'

'I'm not sure. Wait a minute. Isn't he the one who came in claiming to have had amnesia for several months? His is a special case. I think his file is on Captain Richard's desk. I'll get it.'

Alys liked his voice and appreciated his attitude. It was businesslike and seemed to assume that she had a right to be inquiring about Ryan.

'Yes, here it is,' Stevens said. 'What is it you want to know?'

'Where he is now.'

Stevens glanced quickly through the folder, mumbling from time to time. 'Three days ago – no uniform or I.D. – Luxemburg – December to May – amnesia. . .' Then he looked directly at Alys. 'He's being shipped back to the States.'

Alys, finding it hard to understand the various American accents, misunderstood one word. She thought he said, 'He's *been* shipped back to the States.'

'Thank you,' she said softly, and turned to leave.

'Wait,' Stevens said, 'is that all you want to know?' She could hear the sympathy in his voice.

'Yes.' Then something about what he'd said a minute or two earlier struck her as peculiar. Ryan's was a special case because he 'claimed' to have had amnesia. If the major she'd spoken to back in January had turned in a report, that claim would be substantiated or she and her family would have been contacted by now for verification. As unbelievable as it seemed, the only answer was that something had happened to prevent the major from turning the information in. That would account for their never being contacted and for Ryan's never receiving any letters.

Ryan was now in a very precarious situation. For the past several days she'd thought only of herself and her own sorrow. Whether he was remembering her or not, he had had amnesia; and it might be very important for him to have a witness. She didn't know much about military laws, but she did know that any form of desertion was a serious offense.

'There is something you could do,' she said. 'Indicate some way in his file that he did have amnesia. He was with my family for all those months. If more information is needed, I'll leave my name and address.'

'Thank you, Madame. . . Mam'selle. . .'

'Mademoiselle Prévou.' It would only make the situation more complicated if she said they were married. Ryan had a new life now, and it was better for her not to intrude into it. This way would be easier for both of them.

'Mike,' Stevens said to the first man Alys had spoken to, 'you get the information. I'm already late for the meeting.' He turned to Alys. 'He'll take down your statement, along with your name and address.' He picked up the folder. 'I'd better put this back on Captain Richard's desk. Put her deposition in it when you're through.'

Alys gave Sergeant Jenkins a few more details and wrote out her name and address for him. She thanked him and walked out into the large hall, filled with desks and people hurrying into and out of rooms. She wouldn't cry. Not here with all these people. She'd find some place where she could be alone.

* * *

Four flights up in the hotel where he was being held under room arrest until travel could be found for him, Ryan was pacing the floor. Three days of interrogation and they still didn't believe him. The action that aroused the most suspicion was his claiming recovery of his memory just four days after the war in Europe ended. It seemed too convenient, too fortuitous. Nor could he tell them where he'd been when his memory returned. He tried to describe the location: the cemetery, the bridge, the river, the hills. But he could be describing any of more than a dozen places in Eastern Belgium. No, he couldn't remember the name of the village. The boy had told him, but it meant nothing; and he'd immediately forgotten it. Nor did looking at a map help. On foot, in farm wagons, and for one long stretch in a truck, traveling both day and night on dozens of different roads, he'd finally reached Liège. But the map could have been a map of the moon for all the good it did.

'I'm sorry, sir, that's all I remember.' If he'd said that once, he'd repeated it a hundred times.

At least they'd believed enough of his story to give him a uniform this morning. They'd learned that Lieutenant Ryan St. Julian Middleton had been, and was still, listed as missing in action. They seemed ready to believe that much of his story. His fingerprints would prove he was who he said he was. It was good to discard the ill-fitting trousers and shirt. In one pocket he'd found several kitchen matches and shreds of pipe tobacco; and in another, a dried flower. They meant nothing to him, and he threw them away with the clothes.

When his pacing took him to the window, Ryan looked down into the front courtyard of the hotel. He saw a woman emerge slowly into the paved yard. Her face was hidden, but she seemed young, in spite of her shoulders being hunched over as if carrying a heavy burden. He continued watching as she paused by and then leaned against a pillar of the high, wrought-iron fence. He noticed first that she was very pretty and then that she was crying. Maybe she'd come here to ask about someone she knew and had learned he'd been killed. More likely she was probably just disappointed at not finding work. He'd seen many Belgian women during his short stay who'd come to apply for work as secretaries, translators, or even maids.

Whichever, she looked as miserable as he felt. He wished he could go down and comfort her. Maybe take her someplace for a glass of wine, or coffee and pastry.

He opened the window a little. He felt like calling down to her. It would relieve the monotony to talk to her. Just to hear her voice.

No, she'd think he was foolish. What woman would want to stand in a courtyard and talk to a man in a window four floors up? Especially when he couldn't leave the room. Slowly he closed the window. But it might have been an amusing diversion for a few minutes, a momentary hiatus in his gloomy, apprehensive mood.

Alys leaned heavily against the pillar from which swung the heavy, wronght-iron gate. Having managed to make it across the courtyard before starting to cry, she couldn't restrain the tears any longer. She looked back toward the building. She'd come here to learn the truth, and now she knew. Ryan evidently remembered nothing of the months with her. He'd sent no word to her before leaving for home. He could still be somewhere in Belgium, of course, or at some point of embarkation in France; but it would be fruitless to try to get in touch with him. Her name would mean nothing to him now.

Hearing something at a window higher up in the building, she looked up but saw only the fluttering of a curtain. Probably someone closing a window.

At the railroad station she'd learned that a train now ran three days a week between Liège and Bastogne, much closer to Ste. Monique than Stavelo was. The next train was the day after tomorrow, time enough to send a wire to her father to have someone meet her.

The hotels as well as the city were swarming with Allied soldiers. She walked from one hotel to another until every step was agony. At each one she received the same reply: 'I'm sorry, madame, but we have no vacancies.' With each block she traversed, her small suitcase got heavier and heavier. Her arms ached and her feet burned. She was hungry and ready to cry from frustration and exhaustion. In her searching for a place to stay, she hadn't taken time for dinner. The skies were beginning to darken, and the streetlights had come on. Why, oh why, had she ever thought to come to Liège?

She was walking along the Frère Orban; and, seeing that she was near the Parc d'Avroy, she turned onto one of the paths and headed for a slatted wooden bench. Perhaps after a few minutes' rest, she'd be better able to take up her burden of trying to find a place to stay. As she laid her head back and closed her eyes, her mind was beguiled by memory. Liège. The city that had once meant such happiness to her. The hours with Gilles. The planning for their future together. And all to end in bitter, useless tragedy.

Suddenly Alys sat straight up. The Montclairs! Why hadn't she thought about Gilles's parents? They'd be delighted to have her stay with them. She was several blocks from their house; but, weary as she was, the thoughts of a warm welcome, one of Madame Montclair's substantial meals, and a soft bed shortened the distance considerably.

Alys was relieved to see a light in the living room and another shining from the rear of the house, probably the kitchen. She rang the bell and waited. When there was no answer after a minute or two, she rang again. It was most unusual for the Montclairs to be away this time of night. They were homebodies who preferred to spend their evenings with just themselves or a few friends. She could see them now: Professor Montclair leading a stimulating conversation on the values to be found in one of his favorite classics or the emergence of a fine American author like Eugene O'Neill. Madame Montclair would be pouring tea and passing small cakes, quietly so as not to disturb the lively flow of ideas.

When there was still no answer, it occurred to her that perhaps the Montclairs no longer lived here. They might have moved away after Gilles's death, or they might not have survived the war. Far too many had not. No, she refused to think of them as dead. But, for whatever reason, and as far as she was concerned tonight, they had left this house.

The small suitcase seemed heavier than ever when she picked it up and resumed her onerous journey. Finally, in a small cul de sac near the Jardin Botanique she found a room in a boardinghouse for the two nights. Breakfast was included in the price, and she could eat dinner there for an additional fee.

In the morning, Alys began a leisurely walk through some sections of the city that had been particular favorites of hers when she was at the university. Everywhere there was evidence of the bombings the city had withstood.

When she reached the university, she impulsively decided to see if Dr. Barré were in his office. He was, and he sent word that he'd be delighted to see her if she'd wait a few minutes while he finished with another appointment. Alys was glad to wait. She'd been walking most of the morning, and she was ready to sit down and rest.

'Mademoiselle Prévou,' he greeted her, 'how good it is to see you. I want to hear how you're progressing with the young man you wrote about.'

'He's one reason I came to see you, but if you have only a few minutes. . .'

'I've plenty of time for someone who's come all this way. Your very informative letters fascinated me, and I want to know all. He should make an interesting case history for class discussion. How about lunch? The restaurant on Rue de la Regence still has better than average fare.'

Throughout the long luncheon and for an hour more over coffee, Alys related in detail – interspersed with questions from Dr. Barré – all she and Ryan had done, his learning to speak, and their marriage.

Dr. Barré nodded in approval and congratulated her on what was apparently a successful conclusion. 'You said he is one reason you wanted to see me. Is he here in Liège with you?'

'No.' Alys was finding it more and more difficult to talk about Ryan, but she forced herself to keep in mind why she had impulsively gone to Dr. Barré's office. 'That's really why I wanted to see you. I need a good morale booster. Just as you predicted, his memory returned and then he had no memory of the months with me.'

'I'm sorry. I don't mean to sound clinical rather than sympathetic, but what was his exact reaction to you? That's very important in trying to establish a new relationship with him.'

'I don't know.' Alys told him as much as she knew from the moment Ryan left the inn to her visit at American headquarters.

'You need more than a morale booster,' Dr. Barré said quietly. 'You're still in a state of shock, like after a death. It may surprise you that such a condition is almost a manic state. But it's an artificial one, in the sense that the loss has created it. In other words, you're not a person who normally goes through extreme manic-depressive cycles. Knowing that, there are ways we can try to control, or at least help you through, the depression which is bound to follow.'

'If this is manic,' Alys said, 'I dread to think of what the depression will be like.'

'When I say manic,' Dr. Barré explained, 'I mean, for instance, you haven't allowed yourself to mourn. And that is very important for recovery. Accept the fact he's gone. Cry and tear your hair. Let others share your grief. Above all, don't try to hide it or deny it. Then find something to do that will make the best use of your talents and keep you busy.'

This advice brought to Alys's mind Countess Charbonne's plan to turn the château into a rest and rehabilitation home. She and Ryan had talked about working together with the countess; she didn't know if she could carry on alone. 'It's good,' Ryan had said, 'a damn good idea.' He hadn't known, of course, that most of the patients would be victims of the war. No, no, she couldn't do it without him.

'Don't try to think right now about what you're going to do,' Dr. Barré said. 'The right thing will come to you. And remember – whenever you need help from me, let me know.'

Alys returned to the boardinghouse, borrowed a book from the landlady's small library, and tried to read until she fell asleep. Unfortunately, the book was a highly romanticized love story, and every love scene plucked upon her taut nerves. The voice of Dr. Barré telling her to think of Ryan as dead intruded into every description. Weep and tear your hair, he'd said; allow others to share your mourning. No, this was a burden she'd have to carry alone. She'd resume her teaching, help at the inn, spend long hours with Minette, and hope they would fill the aching void.

CHAPTER EIGHTEEN

With Ryan's return to the States, a more insidious type of hell began. Charges of desertion under fire were brought against him, and a date was set for a pretrial hearing at which it would be decided whether he would be court-martialed.

His family and Janet had been notified immediately that he was still alive. There were letters waiting from all of them when his ship docked in New York. Their first questions concerned whether he was recovering from any wounds; and the second was how soon he would be home. There'd been no mention in the official notification of the forthcoming trial.

Ryan anguished a long time over the letters he wrote back. He finally decided to tell them as much of the truth as he could remember. Then he requested them not to try to see him until there'd been a verdict, at least until he'd been declared innocent of desertion or it was decided there was enough evidence against him for a court-martial. He had to go through the initial period alone.

The pretrial hearing was disastrous. He could present no proof to substantiate his statement that he remembered nothing from the time the tanks were bearing down on him and his men to the moment he found himself on a road outside a village in Belgium. A court-martial was ordered.

As he'd promised, Ryan let the family know the outcome of the hearing. Unfortunately, by the time Ryan's letters arrived, the entire country knew that Lieutenant Ryan St. Julian Middleton was being court-martialed for desertion. That the scion of the Middleton family, a name prominent in the nation's business as well as the social milieu, could be guilty of such an offense was far too important a story for news media to ignore.

On hearing the news, Augustus Middleton contacted such powerful men as two Supreme Court justices, several senators, and the highly regarded James F. Byrnes, of South Carolina, recently named Secretary of State by President Truman. All of them assured him that Ryan would receive a fair trial. To improve the odds, however, the senior Middleton, aware that Ryan could have civilian as well as military counsel, brought in a phalanx of attorneys and advisors.

Because desertion under fire is a capital offense, the court ordered that Ryan be given two additional military defense lawyers. Captain Richard Lee Green, graduate of the University of Virginia and Harvard Law School, was the first to meet with Ryan. Every generation in Captain Green's forebears had seen at least one man in uniform fighting for Virginia or his country since the Lees and Greens arrived on this shore in the 1600s. He wore both the Lee and Green names proudly, and his stomach churned at the thought of defending a deserter. A man was never accused of desertion lightly, especially not after the brouhaha following the execution of Private Slovak. So this Ryan St. Julian Middleton had to be guilty. And to make it worse, he was from South Carolina, and no doubt steeped in the southern traditions of military heroism and patriotism.

Yet, after less than an hour with Ryan, he was convinced that Ryan was innocent. Saying only, 'I believe you,' he left; he would be back as soon as he studied Ryan's file. He read every word in it, many of the reports twice, and then returned.

'All right, Ryan, let's settle down to the serious business of preparing your defense. There's not a damn thing in your file to substantiate your claim that you had amnesia.'

'I know.' The captain's belief in his innocence did nothing to relieve the gloom that had entered and metastasized through his body like a malignant tumor. The case would be adjudicated on facts not beliefs.

'So, let's start from the beginning again, and you tell me everything you do remember.' Green sat back in his chair and folded his arms. No pencil and paper. Today he would just listen. To Green, nuances and intonation, facial expressions and body movements, were as important as words.

'I already have, and anyway it's in the file.' Ryan took out a cigarette. Why these questions? Why the postponement of the inevitable?

'No, not everything. I want every minute detail; everything you think is irrelevant and unimportant.'

Sighing heavily, Ryan began speaking in a dull, leaden voice, as if by repeating something he'd learned by rote. Someone else's life he'd learned by memory. To his surprise, Green interrupted almost every sentence.

'Give me names,' Green said. 'I want the name of every man up there on the line, the ones in the jeep, the ones who joined you just before you tried to stop the tanks.'

What good would that do? Ryan thought. Hell, they were probably all dead. But he reached for paper and wrote them down just to placate the captain.

Later: 'What were you wearing when you recovered your memory? Describe the clothes. Was there anything in the pockets?'

Ryan described the work pants and shirt as best he could.

'Underwear?'

'Just plain cotton. Worn, mended and patched. Why?' This was getting ridiculous.

'I suppose they were thrown away. A pity. They sounded like farm clothes. The Germans frequently put prisoners on farms. If we had the clothes, we might be able to tell where they were made, but we'll follow up that line anyway. Could be you were on such a farm and managed to escape.'

Gradually Ryan began to appreciate this intensive questioning. 'There were only two things in the pockets, a wilted flower – a wild flower, I think – and some shreds of pipe tobacco. I don't smoke a pipe.'

'Again a pity. The flower might have led us to a location, and the tobacco – well, maybe.'

The questioning went on: details of the location where he'd recovered his memory, the boy he'd talked to, the people he'd seen and the roads he'd traveled to Liège, and an hour-by-hour recitation of his stay there.

Green leaned forward in his chair. 'You say you were deeply touched by the young woman in the courtyard. And yet no one else attracted you with such intensity or has stayed with you in such detail. Is it possible she was someone you knew during those months?'

'I don't think so,' Ryan said. 'I think I remember her because she was pretty and she was obviously extremely upset about something.'

'Too bad. I'd hoped that in some way she might start jogging your memory about other things. But nothing comes to mind?'

'Nothing. God knows I've tried, and all the doctors can tell me is that maybe – maybe – some day I'll remember. By that time I'll be dead.'

Ryan tilted his chair back and began laughing. 'That's really good. I hope you appreciate the irony of it all. I nearly get my ass shot off landing on Normandy and God knows how many other places, and myself nearly blown up in the Ardennes, and I live through it to stand in front of a firing squad.'

'Dammit, Ryan, you can't think like that. There has to be some proof somewhere. I just have to look in the right place.'

And he looked. Word went out to several headquarters in Europe and the States to search for a misplaced file and to check the files of other men named Middleton. The reports and files of Ryan's commanding officers and of the men who served under him at the time of his disappearance were released to him. The two military attorneys, along with the civilian lawyers, spent days studying every page of these documents. Ryan's ability as an officer was vouched for many times, but nothing to indicate knowledge of amnesia.

Then it was time for the trial to begin.

Ryan's reunion with his father was more businesslike than emotional. Augustus Middleton greeted his son with a warm but reserved, 'Glad to see you alive, son. Janet and Mother will join us in a few days.'

'How are Mother – and Janet?' Ryan asked. He longed to see Janet, but he dreaded the reunion with his mother. An overemotional woman who saw every small problem as a major disaster, she dissolved into tears at the slightest disturbance. If ever there were an anachronism, it was Lucy Middleton. She seemed to carry with her at all times her own ambiance, like an almost visible aura, of nineteenth-century Southern gentility and fragility. In many ways those attributes were as much a façade with her as they had been with her antebellum great-grandmothers. The older women had used them to cover the iron will with which they quietly reigned over the house and ruled their husbands. Ryan's mother used them to hide the person she wanted to be.

Lucy Bull Middleton was born into a family whose ancestors on both sides had seen several generations be born and die in South Carolina before the Revolutionary War. Their names were not merely prominent in the state – they *were* South Carolina. By the time Lucy's birth was recorded in the crowded genealogical pages of the three-hundred-year-old Bible, the names were about all that remained to the family from a once prosperous legacy. But those names assured the Bulls their place in the highest echelons of society in the state as well as in the small low-country town where they lived.

For more than two months, the Bulls ate sparingly to save the money for Lucy's gown when she was presented at the St. Cecilia Ball in Charleston. There she met Augustus Middleton, who immediately fell in love with her. She considered him pompous and boring. Then she thought about the vast Middleton holdings; and when he proposed, she accepted immediately. After all, a good marriage – meaning into a family with as proud a name as those in the Bible, and preferably with money – was the *raison d' être* for a Southern woman of her time.

She brought to her marriage many housewifely talents that she thought would be of inestimable value to her husband as well as a pleasure for herself. Instead, Augustus doted so luxuriously on his young wife, he wanted her every need cared for. She was surrounded by servants, including a housekeeper who planned all the meals and a cook who frowned forbiddingly if Lucy entered the kitchen. They entertained twice a week: a small dinner party on Tuesday night, a large dinner party every Friday night. Her social secretary made out the guest list; the housekeeper chose the menus. As for household accounts, Augustus paid all the bills.

In spite of marrying a man she did not love, Lucy wanted only to be a good wife and homemaker. Instead, she became an actress, playing the part of a spoiled, contented, grateful, petted, helpless, slightly irresponsible woman unable to think or do things for herself. And Augustus delighted in her. Over the years, as with an actress playing in a long-running production, she gradually became the character she'd assumed during her early years of marriage. The only visible sign of her not-quite-dormant frustration was the immediate flow of tears at the slightest provocation.

Yes, Ryan thought, the meeting with his mother would be a difficult one. The reunion with Janet, however, while being more deeply emotional, would be less saccharine. Their real reunion would come when they were alone, and he ached with anticipation.

Ryan was not certain whether he was disappointed or relieved when word reached him that his mother felt unable to make the trip. She had collapsed first on hearing that Ryan was alive and again when she learned of the trial. Janet felt she needed to stay with her mother-in-law. Ryan was not really surprised. His mother had never been able to face up to any misfortune more severe than finding the cat had presented her with a dead mouse on the doorstep to the sun-room. His need for Janet was somewhat offset by his admiration for her staying with his mother during this difficult time. Less than two days into the court-martial, however, he read the detailed account of a horse show in Aiken. Janet Middleton had taken blue ribbons for jumping and dressage. Ryan was at first furious at her failure to see how desperately he needed her with him at this most difficult time. It was not merely her physical presence he longed for, but her assurance of loyalty as well. Then gradually, as he became resigned to her absence, he wondered if it were the first hairline crack in their marriage, the marriage that had sustained him during all the tortuous months of war. He had to be found innocent. He knew for a certainty that only then, only by returning as soon as possible to Camden, could his marriage be saved.

In spite of the intense investigation by the military and civilian lawyers, of advisors and character witnesses, each day of the court-martial found Ryan's defense proving far weaker than the Army's case against him. A neurologist, who studied X rays of Ryan's head, testified that there was evidence of a hairline fracture. With this he could possibly have suffered a subdural hematoma which had gradually been absorbed. It was a distinct possibility that such could in turn cause amnesia for an extended period of time.

On cross-examination, the doctor also admitted that the fracture could have occurred earlier in Ryan's life; and if it was a battle injury, amnesia was only a possible result.

Two witnesses called for his defense were Corporal now Sergeant James Witkowski and former Private Hall Newsome, now returned to civilian life. The reunion with them in the hallway outside the courtroom was subdued but heartfelt.

When each of the men began giving testimony, however, Ryan was hard put to control his tears. He'd had no idea what they had gone through to save his life. They described their movements following the attempt to stop the tanks. The roadblock had turned the tanks around, and their actions had slowed the German advance along that road for several hours. Enough time to allow a company to get safely to a more easily defensible position. For this they had received the Silver Star. They then told how they'd carried the wounded and unconscious Lieutenant Middleton between them in a sling made from branches and two coats taken from dead soldiers. For almost two days they'd walked, fearing he would die at any moment, until they finally came upon a jeep. When a deep pothole in the road forced them to swerve, they hit a tree. Although wounded themselves, they were able to carry Lieutenant Middleton to an inn where they left him after getting directions to a hospital.

They'd intended letting the doctors know where their lieutenant was so the medics could get him to the hospital, too. Instead, they arrived as the patients were being evacuated. They'd thought all this time that Ryan had died. Over and over, both Witkowski and Newsome stressed the tremendous guilt Ryan had suffered because of having left his men behind.

A very touching story, the army prosecutor admitted, but still not proof that Lieutenant Middleton had suffered from amnesia as a result of either his wounds or his feelings of guilt. Nor could either man remember the name of the village – if they'd even known it – where they left Ryan. There was no way to find witnesses there.

A more deeply moving reunion, and one that did bring the tears, was with Sergeant Svaboda.

'Dammit,' Ryan said, after Svaboda released him from a bear hug, 'how in hell did you manage to get away from there alive?'

'Pure luck and my stubborn Czech nature. No damn Kraut was going to take me alive, and I wasn't going to let them kill me either. We lost a hell of a lot of men, Lieutenant. Almost the whole platoon. But some of us were able to dig in, cover ourselves with branches and snow, and let them pass us by. To shoot would have been suicide. Then we headed for the rear, joining up along the way with other stragglers, and fighting and cussing with every step we took.'

'Join me for a beer later?' Ryan asked. 'With encouragement from some of my father's influential friends, they're letting me stay at a nearby motel – under guard of course. Have dinner with my father and me. I want him to meet you.'

'Be a pleasure, Lieutenant. Now let me see how good I am at being a character witness.'

Sergeant Svaboda was good but not quite good enough. What kind of officer Ryan had been or what he'd done prior to the German counterattack was still no proof he hadn't deserted. Even the best of soldiers can crack under pressure.

Two psychiatrists, one for the defense and one for the prosecution, offered similar evidence under examination. Psychological amnesia was possible. Especially in view of Witkowski and Newsome's statements about the tremendous guilt Ryan had suffered because of leaving his men behind. Both of the doctors admitted that traces of that guilt still remained. But again, the evidence was modified by that word 'possible.' He could have lost his memory following the shattering experience on the front and during the succeeding days; but it was also possible that Ryan had decided he couldn't take any more and had chosen to hide out for the remainder of the war. His already-weak defense was further damaged by his having turned himself in within a few days after the war in Europe ended.

The case against Ryan seemed invulnerable to every possible approach. Yet, just as he'd considered himself invulnerable to shells and bullets and refused to believe he could be killed, he would not believe that he could be found guilty. It was impossible – not when he was innocent. Someone had to believe him. Panic overtook him. He clenched his hands under the table so no one could see his desperation. He'd never experienced such helpless fear when he was fighting. This was not a fear of death by execution, but of never being vindicated.

Eating dinner with Ryan and Sergeant Svaboda, Augustus Middleton learned to appreciate his son more than he ever had before. He was also surprised to find himself admiring Karl Svaboda, in spite of an inborn prejudice against rough-hewn, non-Anglo-Saxon, professional soldiers.

Before they finished eating, one of Ryan's attorneys came to the table. He'd just received an unusual phone call. A Sergeant Stevens, recently returned from Belgium, had read about the trial in the newspaper. He had some information he thought would help Ryan's defense. The judge advocate had granted a recess until the man could get to the court-martial.

The name Stevens meant nothing to either Ryan or Svaboda.

'It has to be someone who knew you during those months,' Svaboda said.

'Pray God, he is,' Mr. Middleton echoed.

'Surely he wouldn't have called,' Ryan said, with the first lilt of optimism in his voice since the trial began, 'and be willing to come all this way right after getting home if he hasn't some proof to help me.'

'We'll see,' the attorney said. 'He'll arrive tomorrow afternoon.'

When court reconvened, Ryan looked long and intently at Sergeant Stevens. He didn't know the man, yet there was something vaguely familiar about him. As if he'd seen him on the other side of a large room. Ryan wondered if the sergeant had been among those present when he was held under room-arrest in Liège. If so, he didn't see what the man could offer in the way of proof.

Then the sergeant took the stand and related the incident with the young woman who came looking for Lieutenant Middleton.

'Some of the men thought she was just another pickup, left behind when the war ended. Maybe had come to try to get the lieutenant to make good on some promises. But I thought she was sincere. When I told her that Lieutenant Middleton was being sent back to the States, she merely said "thank you" and didn't ask to see him. Nor did she make any demands.'

'What has this to do with Lieutenant Middleton's defense?' Ryan's lawyer asked.

'At first she hesitated, but then she offered to make a statement for his file to substantiate his claim that he'd had amnesia. I told Sergeant Jenkins to get it all down, have her sign it and leave her name and address in case it was necessary to contact her later. I thought it might be useful since the lieutenant was being held under suspicion of desertion.

'I'm sorry, sir,' Sergeant Stevens continued, directing his attention to Ryan. 'I should have taken the deposition myself and made certain it got into your file.' He turned back to the attorney. 'She'd already told me that Lieutenant Middleton had spent the five months with her family at the inn, had had amnesia, and something called apha – aphy – I can't remember.'

'Aphasia, perhaps?' the attorney prompted.

'Yes, sir, that was it. Sergeant Jenkins took her statement and other pertinent information. But for some reason it did not get into the lieutenant's file. There were piles of papers being shuffled from one desk to another before getting into the files, and it could have been lost in any number of ways.'

'And you don't know her name or where she lives?'

'No, sir. However' – Sergeant Stevens paused dramatically – 'a few days later a Dr. Barré, a psychiatrist and professor at the University of Liège, came by to inquire as to the whereabouts of a Lieutenant Middleton. He said that for personal reasons he wanted to meet him. He had been working with a young woman, a former student of his, who was trying to cure a Lieutenant Middleton of aphasia. During that same period of time he was also a victim of amnesia. He eventually recovered from the aphasia, and when the young woman came to Liège looking for him, she called on Dr. Barré.

'The woman he referred to was no doubt the same who came to our office, so I didn't ask her name. At that point I didn't know her statement had been lost. I learned that after reading about this trial, and I made inquiries.'

'I think,' said Ryan's attorney, 'you have something to show us?'

'Yes, sir.' He handed an envelope to the attorney, who then handed it to the presiding judge.

'This,' said the attorney, 'is a deposition from Dr. Barré containing the information he knows about Lieutenant Middleton, his conditions of amnesia and aphasia. I wired him when Sergeant Stevens informed me about the lost deposition. He wired back immediately.'

The judge raised his eyebrows and began reading silently to himself.

All during Sergeant Stevens' testimony, Ryan sat in stunned amazement. Who were this doctor and the young woman the sergeant kept referring to, and why were they so concerned about what happened to him? They'd evidently helped cure him of aphasia, the inability to speak, a condition he'd never heard of before. And he'd lived with a family at an inn for all those months. Why would they have done all that for him? And why, after all that time, hadn't she wanted to see him once his memory had returned? There seemed to be no answers to these questions; and for the time being, his present situation was of more importance.

While Ryan was lost in these thoughts, the defense psychiatrist was conferring with his legal counsel, who then requested that the doctor be allowed to return to the stand. He testified that there were definite indications in Ryan's speech patterns of having had aphasia. In answer to questions as to why he hadn't mentioned this earlier, he answered that aphasia had not been mentioned nor would it have helped to prove that Ryan had had amnesia at the same time.

The panel of judges conferred for only a few minutes before declaring they found Lieutenant Ryan Middleton not guilty of desertion. They recommended he be released from the army with a medical discharge.

CHAPTER NINETEEN

'He's gone. He's gone.' The words repeated themselves over and over in the echo chamber of Alys's mind. Jesters mocking her: 'He's gone, Alys; he's gone.' In the night the grandfather clock chimed the hours and half hours: 'Gone, gone, gone, gone.' From the fading hours she plucked the fragile minutes: 'He loves me, he loves me not, he will return, he won't return, he will, he won't.'

Through the days that followed her trip to Liège, Alys found herself succumbing more and more to despair. She felt bereft and abandoned, isolated by pain. Loneliness was her only companion, memory her only lover. A somnambulant, she moved in a fugue state. Realities were dimensionless shadows; people were incorporeal phantoms. There was no clearly marked path, no limned destination.

When she lost Gilles, the whole world was suffering its own agony of death throes; death was a part of everyone's life. She had been desolate; but his death also killed what might have been. It was over, a total severance, a finality. She'd mourned for both Gilles and his final, lonely hours before his execution.

The loss of Ryan, however, was a slow eroding of emotion, a deprivation of life-giving sustenance that still existed but was denied her. Hope, like the sight of a distant lake to a weary traveler, had sustained her for a few days and then had mocked her by being only a mirage.

Like the incoming tide, Ryan's return of memory had washed away all memory of her. 'No,' she wailed inwardly, 'he can't have forgotten. Our love was too deep, too strong. We meant everything to each other.' Oh God, maybe he did remember, but he didn't love her enough to remain with her. There was the pain that jabbed her heart with each breath she took. Return of past memory would be such a convenient way to leave without a word. Had he thought that going without saying good-bye would be easier for her? Or just for him? That was it. He'd deserted her. Thought himself well rid of someone he felt beholden to but did not really love. He'd lured her into an affair with those damned nightmares of his. Marrying her was a travesty, a farce, just to appease her sense of morality so he could continue sleeping with her. Maybe memory had already begun to return. How clever of him. Woo her, seduce her, and then leave when he'd had enough of her and it was convenient for him to go.

'I hate him. I hate him for loving me, for letting me love him.'

Cold hatred constricted her muscles; her stomach cramped; her chest tightened until she thought she would suffocate, and then her breath came in short, rapid gasps and shudders. Her throat was paralyzed and when she tried to swallow, she began choking. She hadn't realized she could hate with such bloodcurdling passion.

Shaking with icy fury, she knew what she had to do. Her body aching, her legs so weighted with the oppressive, mordant loathing now swelling within like some monstrous cancer that she could barely move, she walked into Ryan's room. Calmly, deliberately, she searched out everything that had belonged to him. The clothes he'd left behind; his shaving mug, brush, and razor; the little gifts from Minette; the pipe her father had given him; a nearly empty tobacco pouch. Like a ferret seeking its elusive prey, she opened every drawer, searched under the bed, and went through the pages of the books he'd been reading. Finding the notes he'd made while trying to learn French, she added them to the pile on the bed. How clever he'd been to insinuate himself into their lives.

Wrapping everything into a bundle, she twisted the string into a knot and then into another and then another, pulling each one so tightly the string cut into her fingers. If she couldn't bury him, she could bury what had belonged to him. Dig a hole deep enough to make certain he'd never rise up again to haunt her.

With ruthless energy she began digging. She must have been out of her mind to let herself fall in love with him. No, she didn't let herself. You can't control feelings like that. Nor could she have stopped herself. But now that hatred had displaced love, she would be able to forget him. Yes, she would. She'd make herself forget, just as he'd forgotten her. Oh God, if only those months could be wiped out as easily in her mind as memory had been in his.

The shovel struck something and she swore. Why was it when she wanted to get something done in a hurry, something else came along to impede her progress? She moved the shovel a few inches and dug in again. This time it went deep enough; but when she brought it up, it held something besides dirt. A small, cloth bag. A bag filled with a few buttons, a buckle, a chain, a name tag, and a tarnished silver-and-blue medal with a long, old-fashioned rifle engraved on it.

Desperately she clutched the few precious pieces in her hand, the pathetic reminders of that momentous day when Ryan came into her life. 'Oh God, I do love you, Ryan. I love you. I love you.' With a manic urgency, she ran back to his room and carefully replaced everything exactly as it had been earlier. Trousers and shirts were neatly hung in the closet. The mementoes of his love for Minette were replaced on the dresser next to his shaving articles. Not until everything was in exactly the same place where she'd found it was she content to leave the room and close the door. Then she went to her room and cried for what might have been.

'Eat this, Alys.' Her mother's voice came to her from out of her childhood. Always being forced to eat before going to school, to get strong, to recover from an illness, to please *Maman*.

'I'm not hungry.' Everything she tried to swallow, even her own saliva, made her gag; and nausea with its bitter gall rose up and constricted her throat.

'Try. You haven't eaten anything for days.' Yes she had. She'd forced supper down the night before and then immediately lost it all.

'I don't like it.' She looked down at her plate and watched it grow larger and larger while the hated food on it swelled into a monstrous, amorphous mass. 'Clean up your plate,' her mother always said, but that was impossible. With each bite, the plate and its contents doubled in size.

'Let her be, Jolie.' That was *Papa*. He always understood. He never forced her to eat what she didn't like or when she wasn't hungry. 'She'll eat when she's ready.'

Yes, Alys thought, I suppose there will come a time when appetite will return and food will no longer be without flavor. Life will no longer be devoid of meaning.

Right now it seemed as barren of worth and as sterile as an ancient womb. Days were a vapid routine of endless hours through which she wandered like a dead soul waiting for the body to be buried so she could rest in peace.

One morning she walked aimlessly across the bridge and up into the hills. Had Ryan walked between these trees? Touched these leaves? She came upon a stream and, looking down, saw not her reflection but Ryan's smiling face. Then the movement of the water twisted his smile into a mocking laugh. Clutching at a branch overhanging the stream, she stared until the laughing face was expunged by a meandering leaf.

Gradually she resumed her place in the normal routine of the inn, and she found that the day-to-day activities provided the stability and the strong foundations that Ryan's precipitous departure had wrenched out from under her. If she had selfishly catered to her own misery, she must now let it wither and die from lack of the self-pity that had been nourishing it. She helped her mother in the dining room and saw to the needs of the guests who stayed overnight. In the afternoons she romped outside with Minette or sat in the shade of a tree while the little girl played with her dolls. She actually found herself laughing when Émile tried to teach Minette how to cast for trout with the tiny pole he'd made her and Minette imitated her grandfather's intense scowl when snapping the pole. So far, Minette had seemed to accept without question that *Papa* would be away for a while.

Alys suffered relapses from time to time. In spite of the hot, shimmering days in June, she occasionally shivered with cold. Then when it rained, she thought she would suffocate in the muggy heat. Loud noises put her into a nervous frenzy. She vacillated between barely having the strength to get up in the morning and being electrified with such nervous energy that she went from room to room scrubbing the floors, washing the windows, refolding linens, and polishing the furniture until she finally collapsed from exhaustion.

In July, Alys nearly fainted one morning while she was dressing. She attributed the dizziness to standing up too quickly. With her low blood pressure she should know better. There was, however, another symptom she had tried to ignore in May and June; but now, gripping the bedpost to keep from falling and shivering in the cold sweat of nausea, she could no longer deny her condition. She was pregnant. At first she was neither delighted nor distressed. Realizing she was carrying a child meant no more to her than knowing that twelve months from now she'd be a year older. There were certain things one accepted because they could not be changed.

Then quite unexpectedly, she received a letter from Dr. Barré in which he enclosed one he'd received from Ryan. Impatient to read Ryan's letter, she forced herself to look at Dr. Barré's first. Like a child looking at a birthday cake, she could savor the anticipation before enjoying the treat. After a few short, introductory sentences, the doctor wrote, 'As you will see, Ryan asks me to send your address so that he may write to you and your family to express his appreciation for all you did for him. He hopes to visit you before too long. He also suggests doing something for you in a material way. Please let me know if you want me to send him your name and address, and if there is anything you need. I will wait to hear from you before answering his letter.'

Alys wanted to weep silently and to laugh out loud. To hug her joy to herself and to share it with the world. Ryan wanted to know who she was. He wanted to come back over and see her. Would he look at her and know her? Would he hear her voice and remember? Oh, dear God, she thought, let his wanting to know be a beginning of memory.

She would not take time to write Dr. Barré. She would call him. 'Yes, yes,' she would say, 'tell him my name and address.' With all haste. By air mail. By wire. Not by a boat that crawls sluggishly across the water.

Laying Dr. Barré's letter aside, she picked up the one from Ryan. On seeing his handwriting, she wept as she had not wept in weeks. When finally she was able to dry her eyes, she began reading:

Dear Dr. Barré:

My attorney has written you a formal letter of appreciation for your prompt response to his wire, but I want to extend my own personal 'thank you.' Without your testimony, there was a very strong chance I would have been found guilty of desertion.

Interestingly enough, I can now look back on the court-martial and appreciate what I learned about myself and those months of amnesia I would not otherwise have known. The examining doctors said I'd suffered a hairline skull fracture, and I was fortunate to be alive. Until we read your wire, I had never heard of aphasia. Since then, I have read articles on the subject.

In another way, also, the court-martial was a very moving experience. It reunited me with three of my men I thought had been killed. Two of them were the men who helped save my life by carrying me to the people with whom I stayed all those months.

As Alys read those lines, she was grateful to learn that the two who'd brought him to the inn had survived.

For having saved my life and cared for me, I would like in some way to express my ever-lasting gratitude to them and to the young woman who taught me to speak again. I would appreciate your sending me their names and address, so that I can write to them myself. And I hope that in the near future I will be able to return to Belgium to meet all of you and thank you in person. Meanwhile, knowing how conditions are in parts of Europe, if there is any way you think I can help them, please let me know. I can never repay them for all they did for me, but perhaps there is some way I can make life easier for them.

Again, let me express my deepest appreciation for what you did. My parents and my wife have asked me to tell you how very grateful they are, too.

Sincerely,
Ryan St. J. Middleton

Alys began crying again at the thought that to Ryan she was now a nameless young woman for whom he felt only gratitude. At first the word *wife* made no impression on her. Then she read it again. This was the death of their love she'd been unconsciously waiting for; this was her reason for mourning as Dr. Barré told her she must do. This was the finality that was hardest to bear. She understood why the doctor had forwarded the letter to her.

With that death came also the death of any hope that Ryan might eventually return to her. She had nursed in her heart the dream that he would want to know about the months he had amnesia and would someday come back to Belgium to search out the place he'd stayed and learn what his life had been like during those months. She could not believe that if he did he would not remember her. The letter now ended that chapter of both their lives.

If she were never to see recognition or the look of love again in his eyes, it was better that she never see him at all. Or hear from him again. She could not bear to look at something from him and suffer the pain of knowing he was married to someone else. She would call Dr. Barré, but she would ask him to say they had received the letter but wished to remain anonymous. That they had not done any more than another family would have done in the same situation. She would trust Dr. Barré to find the right words.

At night when she could not sleep, she had fantasized about their reunion and Ryan's joy at learning that the child she carried, or who had already been born, was his. From sustaining her through those long, dark hours, the fantasy now tormented her. He'd already had his joyful reunion with a wife who'd waited for him to return. And perhaps there was a child. If not, there probably would be. He had no need for a child he'd fathered on a woman he no longer knew. Nor did she need a child who would be a constant reminder of him.

Alys lay half reclining, half buoyed up by the warm water that reached nearly to the rim of the tub. Lazily she raised and lowered her legs and watched the eddies, like miniature maelstroms, playing around her toes. Tiny wavelets, like lissom fingers, gently caressed her skin and lulled her into an ethereal euphoria. She was a Nereid drifting down Grecian waters to a cobalt sea. A lithesome, graceful swan gliding across a placid lake toward her mate. How delightful it would be to slip beneath the surface and float away like one of those tiny maelstroms, dizzy with the delight of it. Then light-headed and half swooning, without thought or conscious effort, slide into the blissful custody of the dark and quiet womb of the ocean.

The womb. Her womb. She had an unwanted child in her womb.

Death would be like that – a pleasant return to an emotionless, trouble-free, egoless, abstract nothingness devoid of pain and sensory stimuli. Alys had not thought in terms of heaven and hell, or reward for saintliness and punishment for sin, since she was a child. She had experienced both mental and physical hell, and her idea of heaven was a Nirvana-like release. She supposed she believed in God, but she did not see him as the great arbiter of human destiny either during man's life or after death. He did not sit on a great, golden throne and adjudicate between right and wrong, nor did he demand propitiation for man-contrived and man-committed actions. A lone, unhappy woman taking her own life would command no more of his attention than a flower drooping on a hot summer's day or a cloud passing momentarily across the sun.

And yet, she thought, if the death she might seek would be free from sorrow, it would also be devoid of children's laughter. Of sunsets when the sun, like an artist gone mad in his lust for color, had gorged his appetite for riotous, vibrant hues and turned the sky into a wild canvas. Of the tart, succulent, tooth-tingling first bite into an early fall apple. Of odors that delighted and odors that repelled. And – more important than all the tangibles – the intangible of love. Death, it seemed, did not, like life, have its opposites, the yin of shade and the yang of light. It offered only the darkness.

Alys looked with misted eyes at the young woman who was so painfully climbing the steep ascent of indecision. She sighed. The woman looked weary and forlorn. A pity. She had once been so full of life, so responsive to beauty and sensitive to love. A woman who, like the greedy bee, flitted from experience to experience and sucked from each the last drop of nectar it offered. Suddenly Alys felt her body shuddering with horror. It was she herself she was gazing at. She had, for the flash of an instant, left her body and was looking at herself. It was a fearful sensation, and with an all-consuming gratitude she returned to the self lying in the water. At that instant she paused in her ascent. She had reached the lower peak of knowing why a person took his own life, but she was not yet ready to approach the summit.

Not yet. There was something else she could do first. Only if that failed would she resume the climb.

Alys slept easily that night, far more easily than she thought her guilt-rent conscience would let her. It was amazing how once a decision had been made, the agony of indecision vanished like a nightmare with the dawn.

In the morning, with the excuse that she would see if any of the farmers had eggs for sale, she left the inn right after breakfast. After walking nearly a kilometer down the main road to Liège, she turned off onto a rutted dirt byroad that wound around a hill and through a narrow valley. Wild violets, buttercups, and primroses tapestried the hillside. The tall grasses brushed against her legs and left tiny droplets of dew on her skin. The morning sun glazed the road, the fields, and the trees with a golden, shimmering Midas touch.

Another kilometer and Alys arrived at the small stone house set so close against the hill it seemed to be growing out of it. When Alys lifted the latch on the wooden picket gate, she was greeted by an overture of barnyard sounds. Shooing away the quacking ducks and honking geese, she made her way along the path of slate stepping-stones. From the barn came a baaing of sheep, and a cow put her head over the half door and lowed mournfully at her. Near the doorstep a mother cat was teaching her litter of kittens to drink from a flat china saucer, and their awkward antics when they put their feet in the milk made Alys laugh. She had not laughed in so many days, the very joy of it almost made her turn around.

An eagle-beaked, stooped crone, her hair wound in long, tight braids around her head and the loose skin on her face pleated with wrinkles came to the door wiping her hands on a voluminous apron. From the dark interior came the pungent potpourri of spices and dried herbs. The woman squinted against the bright sunlight.

'*Tante* Maria, it's Alys Prévou. I came to see if your chickens have been laying.'

'Six this morning.' The voice was a low, dusky, sibilant whisper. She coughed, clearing her vocal cords, and she spoke a little louder. 'Fresh out of the nest. Did you bring a basket?'

Alys handed her the deep basket lined and covered with clean napkins.

'Come in out of the sun.' *Tante* Maria invited her. 'I'll be only a minute.'

Alys looked around the room. From the smoky rafters hung clusters of drying herbs, many – like thyme, chives, mustard, rosemary, basil, and lavender – that she was familiar with, as well as twice as many she could not identify. On shelves were jars and small packets of spices that mingled their fragrances with those of the herbs to make the atmosphere as redolent with fantasy-inducing odors as an exotic Arabian bazaar.

Tante Maria returned with the eggs tucked protectively among the folds of the napkin. Alys paid for them, and then found her throat paralyzed when she tried to speak of the real reason she'd come here. Like Ryan when he had aphasia, she could form the words in her mind, but her tongue and mouth could not utter them. Ryan. He was the reason she was here, and determination gave her voice. She looked at *Tante* Maria, midwife to the surrounding villages, who officiated at the births of red-faced, squalling, eagerly awaited infants and at the demise of the nameless and unwanted.

'I need your help,' she finally said. 'I understand you know how to. . . that is, if there is something I want to lose. . .'

Alys felt the woman's eyes piercing clear to her soul.

'How far along are you?' *Tante* Maria asked.

'Three. . . maybe almost four months.'

The midwife shook her head. 'You might have waited too long.'

Alys dropped her head into her hands. She should have come as soon as she knew for certain.

'We can try.' *Tante* Maria's placid, emotionless voice insinuated neither condemnation nor approval. She moved to the shelves and began gathering several packets, opening them, meticulously measuring out their contents, and blending them in a wooden bowl with her fingers. She raised the bowl to her face and sniffed, inhaling some of the powdery mixture. She nodded with approval.

Alys watched with catatonic fascination, like a victim hypnotized into immobility by a snake about to strike.

'There will be pain,' *Tante* Maria warned.

'I know. I'm prepared for that.'

'When you are ready, and don't wait too long, make a tisane and drink it all just before you go to bed. Come immediately to me when you awaken. The herbs cannot do it all, but they will make what I have to do much easier and less dangerous.'

Alys handed over the rest of the money she'd brought and, clutching the basket of eggs in one hand and the small packet in her pocket with the other, walked out into the sunlight.

When she was ready. *Tante* Maria must have recognized her slight hesitancy about going through with it. If she were to do it at all, she must do it tonight. No more thinking about it, no more imagining what a child of Ryan's would look like, no more wondering if it were a little boy or a little girl she was carrying.

Alys set the cup of hot herb tea on the table beside her bed. Let it cool a little, she thought. It would be easier to drink then. The idea of pain did not frighten her. It was the emotional aftermath she feared. And yet women aborted naturally all the time from various physical causes – falls, illness, the inability to carry to term. This was no different. She simply was inducing the cause. This was her farewell to Ryan, her severing of their love that had once shone so brilliantly it had blinded her to the truth that someday he would have to remember who he was and forget his brief interlude with her. It was better this way, much, much better.

She lifted the cup and then set it down again. She would also be destroying a part of herself. Could she so casually dispose of what her own flesh had formed? Would she ever, sometime in the far distant future, be able to forget this night? Or would it be seared as deeply into her psyche as were the nights she'd spent with Ryan?

Alys sat on the edge of the bed and gently cradled the cup in her hands.

CHAPTER TWENTY

Ryan looked at the countryside through which they were driving from Columbia to Camden. Now, in mid-October, the low rolling hills were brilliantly alive with color. Set against the dark, rich green pines were the fluttering yellow gold of hickories and sycamores, the majestic crimson of dogwoods, and the more blazing scarlet of the scrub oaks, flaunting their colors like banners in defiance of pending death. For ten months of the year, the scraggly scrub oaks were outcasts among the more stately live oaks, beloved dogwoods, and towering pines. They thrived, where little else could thrive, on the sandhills of the South Carolina midlands. Then for nearly two months in autumn they came into their own.

Ryan rode silently in the backseat of the Lincoln. At Ryan's request, his father had sent the car to meet him at the railroad depot. He wanted no emotional scenes in public. Alton, the family's chauffeur for as long as Ryan could remember, greeted him with 'Glad to see you back, sir.'

'Thank you, Alton. It's good to be back.'

There had been no more conversation as they drove the thirty or so miles to Camden. Ryan was too intent on enjoying this last brief respite between his being discharged and his arrival home. From time to time, the wooded sandhills gave way to flatter fields. Most of the cotton had been picked, and the squat, denuded plants were skeletal silhouettes against the gray earth.

The war, with its nerve-shattering sounds, its indescribable sights, its torturous, pain-filled hours, seemed another world and another generation away. Men called war hell, but not even Satan could contrive the ways to destroy man that man could contrive for himself. The court-martial had severely shaken him, but seeing Witkowski and Newsome still alive was some compensation. Most of all, the reunion with Karl Svaboda, who he'd been so certain was dead, did more to restore his good spirits than anything else could have.

And now he was coming home. He was one of the lucky ones. They'd all dreamed of going home, but so few had made it.

As they turned off U.S. Highway One onto the road that led to Ivywood, the Middleton home just outside Camden, Ryan thought about the house where he'd lived all his life. The formal living room with its grand piano, antique furnishings and *objets d'art* of porcelain, cloisonné, and silver, and its massive, sterling silver chandelier had always intimidated him. From the time he could totter, he'd been forbidden just as harshly to touch anything.

In a different way, he'd been intimidated, or at least made uncomfortable, by his mother's bedroom. Totally feminine in all details, it was an extension of herself – from the ruffled lace canopy on the tester bed to the pink-and-mauve color scheme and the cloyingly sweet, faint scent of her favorite lily-of-the-valley perfume. He never knew whether it was the unrelieved femininity of the room that disturbed him or his memories of always having to go there when he was to be chastised.

His father's room of dark mahogany and maroon leather would have been more to his liking and would perhaps have made him feel more comfortable except that he was seldom invited in. It was his father's refuge; and when Augustus entered it, he shut the door against the intrusion of the world or his family.

Then there was his own room. When he had left for the war, it still contained the sturdy oak double bed and dresser he'd had since he was old enough to leave the crib. Through the years the room had been the fort from which he'd shot at Indians skulking among the azaleas; a castle from whose slit windows he, with Richard the Lion-Hearted, had stared across the bridged 'moat' beyond the rose garden and waited expectantly for the advancing enemy; a laboratory in which, as he dissected frogs and chloroformed beetles, he discovered the cure for the rare, malignant disease known only to him; a secret room hidden somewhere deep in enemy territory from which he spied and sent wireless messages direct to the President in Washington.

All around the bed, on walls and desks and shelves, was a hodgepodge of things he'd collected all his life: books, beetles, butterflies, a copperhead coiled in alcohol, favorite duck decoys, two Ivory-soap animals he'd carved during some childhood illness, a goatskin rug by the bed in place of the bear rug he'd really wanted. Each was a physical symbol of – he had thought – a never-to-be-forgotten memory. But he had forgotten all of it for five months, and now he hoped nothing had been changed or removed. He needed to touch each one, to bring back into clear focus the important moments from the past that had been lost to him for a while.

Thinking about his room, Ryan realized it was still the room of an immature youth, not the man he'd become somewhere between Omaha Beach in Normandy and the front lines of the Ardennes. For those months he had no tangible mementoes to hang on the wall or place on a desk. Only memories so deeply seared into his mind they'd left scars no amount of time could fade.

The limousine slowed down as it entered the long drive bordered with massive pecan trees. Ryan heard with delight the crunching of pine straw on the circular approach to the porte cochère. He was home.

Lucy Middleton opened the door to her son, and Ryan no longer minded feeling her warm tears on his cheek when he held her close. A few feet beyond his mother, Janet smiled and waited, as befitted a proper daughter-in-law, for his mother to greet him first. Then she opened her arms to him, and Ryan felt all the tedious worry and the remnants of tortured days of the court-martial fall away like a desiccated, outgrown skin. In its place were the warmth and love of his family.

In the living room, Alton filled and passed the glasses of champagne along with silver trays of canapés. Ryan sat on one blue brocade couch with his arm around Janet. His mother sat on a matching couch opposite, and his father was poking logs in the fireplace between them.

'It isn't really cold enough for a fire,' Lucy Middleton said, 'but I think it makes such a warm welcome.'

Ryan looked at his mother with a faintly quizzical smile on his face. She was so much more composed than he'd expected her to be. Nor had she fussed at him when her carefully coiffed hair was disarranged by his enthusiastic hug.

'To your return,' Augustus said, when all the champagne had been passed.

'Thank you, Dad.' He squeezed Janet's shoulder a little tighter. 'God! It's good to be back.' Yet even as he spoke, he felt Janet's body shudder and then stiffen under his touch, as if his hand were something loathsome crawling across her skin. Why? Her welcome had been warm and loving and had seemed spontaneous and genuine. Now he began to sense that she was playing the part of a dutiful wife glad to have her husband back home. His stomach tensed and knotted as he wondered which wife she would be when they were finally alone.

For a few minutes there was a lull in the conversation. A silence as deadly and oppressive as a vacuum, as overpowering and concussive as the sounds of battle, coalesced around Ryan. Silence as such had never bothered him. It could be comradely, loving, or warm. But silence juxtaposed with uncomfortable embarrassment was something else. Ryan winced and encapsulated himself deeper and deeper within a protective isolation. One moment he was among his family; the next, he found himself staring at strangers. He was watching them through eyes that had shed the obscurity of youth and saw them with the clear vision of a maturity that had come not only with years but also with devastating experience.

Then suddenly everyone was talking at once, their animated voices and their enthusiastic attitudes expanding in importance events that were really not that important at all. Lucy was to be the hostess for the monthly meeting of the D.A.R. the following week; Janet was thinking about breeding one of her mares; Augustus began quoting the latest production figures of their new plant: it was palpably obvious that all of them were trying too hard but carefully and subtly to avoid mentioning either the war or the court-martial.

Ryan didn't particularly want to talk about them either, but he didn't want them buried in some potter's field of indifference or put into a dusty attic along with family relics that couldn't be thrown out but no one wanted anymore. Those were his years, and their events were as important to him as entertaining was to his mother, horses to Janet, and the business to his father. All his life certain subjects had been considered taboo – unsuitable and improper for dinner table conversations. Now it was apparant that bland, commonplace, non-controversial topics had received the family's official imprimatur but critical, mind-shattering ones had not. Ryan the son was welcome in the bosom of the family, but Ryan the ex-soldier was *persona non grata*.

Well, all right, he wouldn't roil the placid waters right now. He could appreciate their timidity and their overt desire to avoid making him feel uncomfortable. What he could not understand was their ability to behave as if life had remained static, as if the world had not been shattered and nearly destroyed by a devastating war, as if what had been might be again.

But they were his family, and if he were to rejoin them, he must now return with genuine and sincere relinquishment to his prewar status as their devil-may-care, sometimes embarrassingly flamboyant, but always obedient son.

So Ryan cradled the wineglass in his hand and looked at his mother.

'What's hidden behind that secret smile of yours?' she asked.

'I'm wating for your little speech, Mother.' When Lucy Bull married Augustus Middleton, she was given a complete set of gold-banded Waterford crystal in every known size and shape for every conceivable beverage: liqueur, brandy, wine, cocktail, champagne, footed tumblers, and stemmed water goblets. They were a wedding gift from Augustus's grandparents; and every time they were used, she put the fear of God into Ryan by saying, 'In all the years I've been married, not one has been broken.' She repeated the injunction when the table was laid with any of her two-hundred-and-forty-piece Sèvres dinner service.

'What speech?' she asked. 'I never make speeches. They're unfeminine. Remember that, Janet. Ladies never make speeches. They converse.'

Janet nodded obediently, but Ryan burst into gales of laughter. 'If not a speech, Mother,' he said when he was finally able to talk, 'then a clear enunciation: in all your married years, not a single piece of crystal has been broken.'

Lucy Middleton sat up a little straighter on the couch and said somewhat defiantly, 'I can't say that anymore.'

'What! You mean the sacred crystal has been profaned by a chip or crack?' Ryan's second burst of laughter scattered the last of the tension in the atmosphere.

'And I did it myself,' Lucy admitted, joining in the general gaiety now enlivening the room. 'I set a wineglass on an end table. One of the cats jumped over from the couch and sent it crashing to the floor. Would you believe I seemed almost relieved?'

'I would, indeed,' Ryan agreed. 'It's like getting the first dent in a new car. The rest are not nearly so painful.'

'That doesn't mean I want any more broken,' Lucy admonished. 'I cherish every one of them.'

'I promise,' Ryan vowed, holding up his free hand. 'No throwing of champagne glasses into the fire.' He reached over to the coffee table for a toast finger spread with Beluga caviar. 'Any more changes I should know about?'

'There's been one,' Janet said with just a touch of defiance in her voice, as if knowing Ryan would disapprove. 'Your mother and I have redone your room. She thought we'd like to stay here until we find our own place, and I agreed.'

'I hope you don't mind, Ryan,' his mother said, 'but it didn't really seem like a room for Janet. All those bugs and things. I think you'll like it now. Janet insisted there be nothing frilly.'

His old room. The one he'd anticipated returning to. Probably all cleaned out and everything gone. 'And my things?'

'Carefully packed and stored in the attic. I knew better than to throw them away. I had Alton do it. I couldn't abide the sight of some of them.'

After dinner, it seemed to Ryan that Janet kept deliberately postponing the moment when they would go upstairs alone. With almost manic desperation she became absorbed in a detailed description of what she planned to do with her horses and dogs, the horse shows she wanted to participate in, and the exhaustive work involved in grooming and training her championship poodles so they'd be certain to win blue ribbons. Then she involved her mother-in-law in a long, desultory conversation about the massive amount of entertaining they should do before Christmas.

Finally, after looking at his watch several times, Ryan announced that he was tired, and if they would excuse him, he was going up to bed. With an obvious sigh of resignation, Janet said she would come with him.

Ryan followed Janet into the bedroom. The decor, neither obviously masculine nor feminine, was not displeasing; but – like rooms designed and furnished by interior decorators – it lacked any touch of personality. He noted the rust-colored carpet, the dark floral draperies, and the well-framed prints, meticulously spaced on the walls. Then he became aware of the twin beds.

Janet stood between them, as if positioning herself behind a protective barricade.

'All right, Janet, what is it? Tell me now and let's get it over with. I'm in no mood for playing games.'

Janet began nervously to explain that she thought they would both sleep better alone. She'd become used to sleeping alone, and she just wasn't sure she could go back to sharing a bed.

'To hell with the twin beds,' he said. 'That's not what I meant. I want to know what's been eating at you all evening. You welcome me home like a loving wife and then you turn as frigid as an icicle. Something's bothering you, something serious, and I want to know what it is. I don't want lies like the ones you wrote when you didn't come to the court-martial. Saying you needed to stay with my mother when all the time you were planning on attending the horse show.' He began stripping off his coat and tie. 'God, how I needed you then. Just some indication of loyalty and love to show you still believed in me.' He removed his shirt and threw it on a chair. 'And God how I need you now.' He pulled off his trousers, and they followed the shirt into a heap on the chair.

'No Ryan, please, not yet.' She backed up against the farther bed and clung to the headboard. 'I need time. It's been so many months since – since we. . .'

'Time! You're damned right it's been a long time, a hellish long time. But I'm not going to rape you, if that's what you're worried about. You chose twin beds. All right, when I make love to you, it'll be because you come to me, willingly and ardently. But I want to know what the hell's the reason for your acting this way. And I know damn well time has nothing to do with it.'

Janet had already laid a new pair of pajamas on his bed, and he brushed them off onto the floor with one furious sweep of his hand. He hadn't slept in pajamas since he was little enough for his mother to tuck him in.

Janet left her sanctuary between the beds and walked over to the dressing table. For a moment or two she nervously rearranged some perfume bottles. 'You want the truth? I'll tell you. If I've changed it's your fault. Losing your mind in Europe. Being court-martialed for desertion.' Her voice grew higher.

'Have you any idea how humiliating it was to have all that in the papers just before an important horse show? Everyone staring at me as the wife of an officer being tried for desertion. Desertion, of all things! You wonder why I wasn't with you? Did you really expect me to be there, with all those reporters and photographers? Asking embarrassing questions, taking pictures of me beside you. Honestly, Ryan, you must have really been out of your mind.'

'I see it, now,' Ryan said quietly. 'My having to endure a court-martial was of far less importance than your humiliation. I apologize. I should have understood.'

'You don't need to be sarcastic. It was extremely difficult for all of us. The shame, the pitying looks, conversations coming to an abrupt halt when we approached. You don't know how we suffered.'

'So you assumed I was guilty, and it never occurred to you to let people know that you believed me to be innocent.' Ryan lifted the trousers off the chair and reached in the pocket for his cigarettes. With his hands shaking, it took three matches to get one lighted. Damn, he thought, so this is what I come home to, a wife who has destroyed with her own petty, whining concerns the trust that should be implicit in marriage. And not a word about being grieved when I was missing in action or presumed dead.

'Innocent?' She was almost screaming at him now. 'So you say. With all those lawyers and influential people, who would dare to find the son of Augustus Middleton guilty?'

'The army!' He spat the words out. He picked up and put on the robe lying on the bed. 'I'm going downstairs for a drink. I need something to wash this obscene conversation from my brain. Go to bed, if you want to; I won't disturb you when I come back.'

'Wait.' Janet's single word came across to Ryan like a command. 'Don't think you can walk out on me like that. You wanted the whole truth. Well, I'm not through yet.'

Ryan turned around at the door, but he made no move to step farther back into the room. 'What now? In what other way have I bruised your tender ego?'

'I'll accept that you might be innocent of desertion, but what were you doing all those months you claim to have had amnesia? Will we ever know? That is, will I ever know?'

'Probably not. Nor will I. I have no memory of the months between December and May. And, I might ask, in view of your tirade, what were those months like for you? Were you the grieving wife who thought her husband might be dead, or were you consoled by the horse shows and the country club dances?'

'Certainly I was grief stricken. Ask your mother. I fainted when the telegram came. But after a couple of weeks, I realized that life had to go on. This is not the nineteenth century. I hope you didn't expect me to don mourning.'

'I'm rather surprised you didn't. With your blond coloring, you look particularly stunning in black.'

He paused and waited for Janet to respond. When she didn't, he said, 'All right, you've said what you had to say and so have I. I think it would be best if we both simply forgot about those months, forgot about the trial, and try to get back to where we were before I went overseas.'

'Don't you think that's asking a great deal? To forget, I mean. After all, who knows what you might have done that could someday come back to haunt us?'

He moved a little closer to her, and to his surprise, she didn't back away. 'Janet, I love you. I waited like a kid impatient for a birthday party for your letters, and I dreamed of the day I'd be coming home. That's all that carried me through some of the hellish times. But, dammit, if you're going to get bitchy and accusatory about something I couldn't help. . .' He found it impossible to finish the sentence.

‘Don’t use your barracks room language on me, Ryan.’

‘I’ll say what I damn well please in my own room in my own house.’ He saw that she’d begun to unbutton her dress. ‘Now get undressed and into bed. I’ve waited a hell of a long time for this night, and I don’t intend to wait much longer. You’re going to be the loving wife I dreamed about.’

Alarmed at the ominous change in Ryan’s tone, Janet hurried into the bathroom. Ryan soon heard the shower running, and while he waited, he smoked another cigarette. In a very few minutes Janet came out. She wore a sheer gown, and she had not put on her robe.

Looking at her full, softly rounded breasts, her slim waist, and the tantalizing triangle of blond hair between her thighs, Ryan felt an urgent craving to thrust himself upon her immediately. Instead, he patiently walked over to her, took her in his arms, and began caressing her in the ways he knew always delighted and aroused her. Janet could be as wanton and as wildly passionate as he could wish for when she was in the mood. It was this mood he was determined to create. He ran his hands slowly down her back and over her thighs. His lips moved from her mouth to her throat and then down to her breasts and nipples. He knew he had succeeded when, after lifting her gown, caressing her inner thighs, and lightly massaging the soft flesh between her legs, he heard her convulsive gasp and she clutched him closer to her. Already her hips were undulating sensually, and her breathing became more rapid as Ryan guided her to the bed.

Carried on a wave of exultation, they climaxed quickly, and Ryan held her close while she sobbed against his shoulder. He might never know if they were sobs of delight or of regret that she had succumbed to him; but whichever, it was better for both of them that they had not waited. He’d needed her physical love, and she’d needed to learn that he intended her to behave like a wife.

Not until she’d gone to sleep and he was staring into the darkness did it occur to him that some of her more erotic responses were unfamiliar to him. Could it be that those lost months also held secrets for her? If all went well between them from now on, he wouldn’t ask.

* * *

Still attuned to Army regimen, Ryan woke up as soon as the sky began to lighten. He reached over to touch Janet and only then remembered she was in the other twin bed. He had moved to this one when it became evident that neither of them would get a good night's sleep in the narrow bed. And sleep, not more lovemaking or even warm, compatible snuggling together, was what they both wanted after their tempestuous night of recriminations and violent passion.

Ryan picked up and put on the pajamas he'd thrown onto the floor the night before. He found his robe tossed on top of the other clothes he'd discarded so hastily. Hoping to have a word alone with his father, he went downstairs before showering and shaving. Augustus too was an early riser; and 7:30 often found him at his desk in his office. So Ryan was not surprised to find him seated at the dining room table.

'Good morning, son. I thought you might sleep in this morning.' Augustus refolded the newspaper he'd been reading and laid it to one side. a sure indication he would rather talk.

'No, Army habits die slowly. The truth is, I'm glad you're still here. I wanted to talk to you. About getting back to work.'

'Whenever you're ready.' Augustus rang for the maid, and Ryan said he'd have the same as his father: sausage, eggs, grits, juice, biscuits, and coffee. 'No rush,' Augustus continued. 'Thought you and Janet might want to take a little vacation.'

Ryan methodically stirred the cream and sugar into his coffee. At this moment his needs took precedent over any wishes Janet might have. 'Not right now. I'm too restless to enjoy one. Also, to tell the truth, I need to prove myself – to myself, if no one else – capable of handling responsibility again. I have to accept that I'll probably never know what happened during those months I had amnesia, but the experience has left me feeling I have to come to grips with reality. So I'm ready to go to work wherever you need me.'

'Good.' Augustus took time to pile homemade strawberry jam on another hot biscuit. 'My plan has long been to make you a vice-president in charge of expansion. We need more sales outlets, particularly west of the Mississippi. And we've been talking about building a plant somewhere in Europe. We're not quite ready to move on either of those programs yet, but I want you to head up the sales division of farm equipment. We've phased out the armaments, naturally, and we're about ready to go into full production of farm implements. This will be a good position from which to investigate the best locations for new outlets.'

'I gather you wouldn't object to my starting immediately.' Ryan smiled to himself. His father would have been acutely disappointed if he'd said he and Janet were planning a vacation.

'I've called a meeting of the vice-presidents and division managers at ten. I'd like you to be there.'

Even as Ryan nodded, he felt a tightening in his gut. Getting back to work, immersing himself in a routine he was familiar with, was what he needed to dim if not obliterate memories of the war. But could he ever still the nagging voice that would not let him forget he had failed in his responsibility to his men during the first days of the German counter-attack? Objective rationality might remind him that there wasn't a damn thing he could have done, that whole divisions had been overwhelmed from the Schnee Eiffel to the Our River, but none of that mitigated his sense of guilt. Could he now, in good conscience, assume the responsibilities his father was thrusting on him? Or would he fail here, too?

No, dammit, he would not. Before the war, his being named manager of one of the plants had been no more than a sinecure, an accolade bestowed on a son who had surprised his family by graduating from Yale with honors. He had, however, approached his job with the same determination and dedication he gave to winning a polo match or training his hunting dogs. He was not a man who accepted either failure or dilatoriness with equanimity; and his small, but important, parts plant had, before he went into service, led all the others in increased productivity and lowered absentee rate. He was proud that this new position offered him was in no way a sinecure or reward. Although his belief that he had been negligent as an officer would always remain as a stain on his own personal escutcheon, it would also incite him to demand more of himself as a vice-president of the company.

In some ways, the early days with Janet became much like their last days together before he sailed for Europe. They again enjoyed a deeply satisfying sexual relationship, and this now eased them through the first awkward moments after the long months of separation.

With arms around each other's waist, they walked the woods near the house, took long drives sitting close to each other, or held hands while they sat in the library with the family after dinner. It was as if only by close physical proximity could they reassure themselves they were still in love. An almost palpable tension remained between them, but Ryan kept hoping it would fade with time.

One night, as they were leaving for a fortnightly dance at the country club, Janet mentioned a four-day horse show coming up in Aiken. Naturally, she'd have to go down at least a week early to get ready for it.

'Why?' Ryan asked, disgruntled by her casual assumption that he wouldn't object. 'The horses are here. The grounds are ready for George and Alton to set up the jumps.'

'Don't be petulant, Ryan. Of course I have to practice down there.'

'Dammit, Janet, I'm not being petulant. I just think you'd want to stay here, now that I'm home.'

'Well, if you think you can't live without holding my hand every minute, take a few days off and come with me. After all, it is your family business. You won't be docked for the time.'

'I have a responsibility to the company,' Ryan insisted. 'I'm vice-president now, remember? I can't just take off for a personal whim.'

'A personal whim! Well, at least now I know where I stand in your life.' With that, she left to see if her gown and accessories had been laid out for the dance.

Ryan spent most of the evening sitting at their table and drinking too much while Janet danced with one partner after another. Janet returned to the table after dancing with Dwight Truluck, the same Dwight whom Janet had said in her last letter before the German counterattack she was going to the hunt ball with. Ryan didn't like the way they looked at each other while they danced or the close, intimate way Dwight held her. What had they meant to each other while he was gone? He snapped another glass swizzle stick in two. He reached across to the one in Janet's glass and brutally snapped it also. He'd been breaking the sticks all evening.

'Stop it, Ryan,' Janet ordered.

'Why? What's so goddamn earthshakingly wrong with what I'm doing?'

'You're making me nervous, and heads turn every time you break one.'

'Then let's go home,' he said. 'I'm tired.'

'Well, I'm not. This is the first fun I've had since you came home. Anyway, you're not tired; you're drunk.'

'Want to dance?' Maybe he'd feel better if he moved around a little.

'No, you keep stepping on my feet. You're not the dancer you used to be. Anyway, I see Ed coming to ask me for a samba.' She stood up, her hips already swaying provocatively to the Latin rhythms.

No, Ryan thought, he was not the dancer he used to be, the golden-footed Adonis of Ocean Drive and Myrtle Beach who had all the girls clamoring to jitterbug and shag with him. In fact, there were a lot of things he wasn't anymore. Nor was Janet. From the pretty, tantalizing, independent young creature he'd fallen in love with, she'd become stern-lipped and self-sufficient. The pout that he'd loved to kiss away was now a childish, ugly affectation. Yet, he still loved her and very much wanted for theirs to be a good marriage.

Near the end of October, there was a spell of really warm weather such as South Carolina is often blessed with in late fall and during the winter. Ryan suggested they go to the beach over a long weekend.

There was a breeze blowing across the beach, but as long as they lay flat on the warm sand, they could bask in the hot rays of the sun. Two other Camden families had built homes on the private island, and Ryan watched a little boy playing with a shovel and bucket. Then, with the warm sun on his back, Ryan began to doze. The beach here and the beach called Omaha began to merge and fuse in his foggy mind. Why was a little boy playing in the sand when his men were digging in to stay alive? Were there two beaches or only one? Or were both some nebulous never-never land floating in his mind? Past and present. Then and now. Reality and fantasty. Which was real – the past remembered or the present experienced? Lying on the beach at Omaha, he felt he'd been born in a uniform to die in one. All else that he'd thought was life before he entered the war was merely some absurd, teasing trick of his brain cells.

Listening to the monotonous but hypnotic susurrant hiss of water over the shell-covered shingle, Ryan fell asleep. When he awoke, the sun was no longer warm, and the wind had picked up. Now undisturbed by errant, pesky thoughts, he raced with Janet to the house set behind protective dunes.

On their last night, a storm rolled in from the ocean. At first, they'd stood on the porch and watched the heavy black clouds, like a conquering force, control all of the dusky evening sky. Golden spears of lightning jabbed at retreating waves.

Later, while Ryan and Janet were making love, a particularly loud, continuous crescendo of thunder reverberated overhead. Ryan immediately rolled off and under the bed.

'What do you think you're doing?' Janet leaned over the side of the bed.

'Sorry, darling. A natural reflex action. Sounded like we were being shelled.'

'Well, we're not,' she said impatiently. 'So stop acting so childishly and get back into bed.'

Finding his way under the covers, Ryan was still shaking. He could never explain what fears such loud, unexpected sounds brought to the surface of his consciousness from deep within. Buildings exploding. Walls shattering. Men crushed to death by ceilings and roofs falling on them.

'Just like you embarrass me when we're in Columbia.' she continued. 'You cling to the side of a building; and then when the light changes, you dash across the street, giving no thought to leaving me behind. People must think you an idiot.'

'I can't help it,' Ryan said defensively. 'It's how I lived all those months. The buildings offered protection. To be in the open was to make yourself vulnerable to snipers or shell bursts. I can't change habits overnight.'

'The war is over, Ryan. So forget about it.'

'Is it?' I wonder if it ever will be for me, he thought.

When they resumed making love, Ryan found he was impotent. 'I'm sorry, darling. I just can't seem to function.'

'Oh, fine,' she said sarcastically. 'The one part of our marriage that seemed as good as before, and now the war has ruined even that.'

'Not for good, Janet. Just momentary. War does things to a man you can never know. You see things no one not there would believe. Things no man should have to see. You're still alive when by all odds you should be dead. The result is relief but also regrets compounded by guilt. No, you can never know.'

Janet mumbled something about she'd try to understand and turned over on her side with her back to Ryan. He was unable to go to sleep for a long time. He kept seeing Janet dancing with Dwight and Ed and the others, and he couldn't help but wonder if any of them had ever disappointed Janet by becoming impotent at the crucial moment.

What had happened to them while he was gone? Ryan couldn't believe that two people who had loved each other as much as he and Janet had could become two totally different people during a separation of little more than a year. Yet, it seemed as if they had. Or perhaps they'd been playing a game before, pretending to be what the other wanted; and now their true selves were being revealed.

As always, when he thought about the war, Ryan began to dwell on the months of his amnesia. And this brought to mind the letter he'd recently received from Dr. Barré. A strange letter it was. Very brief and almost curt. The family who had taken care of him did not want him to know who they were; and while they appreciated his offer of doing something for them, there was nothing they needed.

'Please believe me,' Dr. Barré had written, 'it is not my wish to keep you ignorant about this matter. But I feel that I must accede to their wishes. It is their feeling that they did no more for you than anyone else would have done in the same situation, and your letter expressed all the thanks and appreciation they want. If you are ever in Liège, I do hope you will come to see me. I would like very much to meet you.'

Ryan toyed with the mystery that he felt certain lay behind Dr. Barré's words. Dr. Barré wanted him to know, even if the family didn't. That was evident in the line inviting him to visit in Liège. There was no point in writing another letter; but of one thing Ryan was certain: he would find a way to get to Liège and learn who his benefactors were and what had transpired during the months he had amnesia.

CHAPTER TWENTY-ONE

Dreaming of Minette's birth, Alys awoke to the excruciating pain of violent, flesh-rending spasms. The pain thrust its way to all parts of her body, cutting a fiery swath through muscles, nerves, and veins. It filled her mouth, and she leaned over the side of the bed to retch.

At the same time she felt gentle hands cushioning her head and wiping her mouth with cool, damp cloths.

Finally, exhausted, she fell back against the pillows. The pain had ebbed into a dull but tolerable aching of muscles recovering from a series of contractions. 'Is there any sign of. . . of. . .?'

'Preparing to lose it? No,' Jolie said softly, 'you've lost only the herbs *Tante* Maria gave you.'

Alys moaned and turned her face away from her mother's pitying, nonaccusatory eyes. With her intolerance for even as mild a drug as aspirin, she should have known the vile concoction would get no farther than her stomach before her body rejected it.

'Why, Alys?' The soft voice was not that of an inquisitor but of a heartsick mother trying to understand why her child would deliberately injure herself.

'I don't know, I don't know.'

'Lie still, and I'll get you a clean gown.'

'Why don't you hate me, *Maman*?'

'Should I hate someone who is too ill to know what she's doing?' Always the sympathetic pragmatist, Alys thought.

She watched Jolie open the drawer, lift out a gown, and then pause. Alys knew her mother was looking at the cache of sleeping pills she'd secreted there against failure, against this day.

Jolie walked back to the bed, the pills on her outstretched hand. 'If the herbs did not work and *Tante* Maria refused to finish the operation? Have you been that unhappy?'

Alys had only enough strength to nod.

'And now?'

God, give me the will Alys thought, to do what must be done.

'Take one,' Jolie said. 'You need to sleep. I'll destroy the rest. That's what you want me to do, isn't it?'

When Alys opened her eyes several hours later, she saw Minette propped up against a pillow next to her and looking at a book.

'Awake, *Maman? Grand-maman* said you were sick. I hope you're feeling better.' She leaned over and kissed Alys on the cheek. 'I love you, *Maman.*'

'Minette, my precious, precious Minette.' She gathered the little girl into her arms.

Oh God, to think what I nearly did. What I was ready to do to myself. I would have lost everything.

Now that this morning was to be a beginning rather than an ending, she found herself comparing her new elation to the times she'd had a bad dream and had awakened to the realization it *was* a dream: she was not going to drown; she was not going to be caught by whatever was chasing her; she was not going to be beheaded by the guillotine.

Ryan was still gone, but life was not over for her. She had Minette and she was going to have his child. She could go on just as she had after Gilles died. If Ryan didn't need her, there were others who did; and she could put her savage energy to work being the best mother to Minette and the best teacher to her students that she possibly could. No, that was negative thinking, an assumption that there were limitations to her abilities. Limitations were nothing more than ghosts of one's feelings of inadequacy and could be exorcised by strengthening her self-concept.

The first thing she had to do was tell Minette that Ryan was not coming back. It was not fair to keep the child waiting for his return.

Minette listened and said nothing at first. It was hard for a little girl not quite three years old to comprehend the meaning of 'forever.'

'Yes he will,' she said with an assurance no one could dispute. 'He come back.'

The child's faith was pure, unfettered by realities. Somehow, from her, Alys absorbed some of that faith. Not that Ryan would return, but that she could make a life – a good and rewarding life – without him.

Autumn that year was wet and chilly. Lying in bed during one of the storms, Alys remembered one of her last nights with Ryan, how they had lain in each other's arms and listened to the sounds of rain all around them. She remembered, too, how the next morning they had gone outside while the ground was still wet. Ryan had lifted Minette up on his shoulders to keep her feet dry. The little girl had clung with both hands to his hair and laughed excitedly, 'Me got nice horsey.' As the rain increased in intensity, the pounding rhythms echoed those of their lovemaking, and Alys cried out in an agony of loneliness and longing.

Finally, after the stormy fortnight, they were blessed with a few days of St. Luke's summer. The sun shone and the breezes were warm and soft. To add to her pleasure, she received a note from Countess Charbonne, who had spent the summer with friends in England, asking her to come for tea. She wanted to discuss with Alys her plans for transforming the château into a rest home. Alys sat holding the note for a long time. Here was something else she could do. At the rest home would be many who needed her talents. Reading the note was like being given a draft of fresh, cool water after days of parching thirst.

As she rode between the hills and through the village on the bicycle she'd recently acquired, Alys thought about the previous December when she and Minette had returned from the château. God! How different life had turned out from what they were planning that day. The Christmas party for the soldiers had literally blown up in their faces. How many of those soldiers were dead now? How many back with their families? And Ryan. He hadn't even existed for her then. Now she was married to him and carrying his child. And he was gone. So much in so few months.

'*Alors*!' Countess Charbonne exclaimed when she opened the door. 'It's good of you to come.' She led Alys to a small garden outside the oriel window in the parlor. It was shady and several plants were blooming.

After they were seated, an old servant tottered down the steps. She set a tray of lemonade and cookies on a low table and returned to the house.

'It's good to see you,' the countess said again, 'but I had hoped you'd bring your husband with you. I've been looking forward to meeting him.'

Alys sipped her lemonade slowly. Having to tell the countess about Ryan's leaving was going to resurrect old pains. 'He's no longer here,' she said at last. 'His memory returned, and he's gone.' Briefly she told the countess everything she knew and described her visit with Dr. Barré.

'I'm sorry, my dear. No need to ask if there's anything I can do. There isn't at a time like this. The most sincere words ring hollow.'

'You're wrong in one respect,' Alys said. 'Some words do help. Your note was what I needed to get me moving again.'

'And you're pregnant?' The countess's keen eyes had been quick to note the subtle change in Alys's figure.

'Yes, and learning I was carrying Ryan's child probably restored my sanity. I was really about to go under.'

'It will be good for Minette to have a little brother or sister.' Alys could hear the regret in the countess's voice at not having any children.

'Yes – my precious Minette. She too once showed me that life need not end with the loss of someone you love.'

'Before Minette was born,' the countess said, 'you confided to me the secret of her birth. I knew why. You had to share it with someone, and you couldn't tell your parents. Now I'm going to confide something to you. Do you know why this house was built and why it once contained all the lovely things you admired so much?'

Alys assumed that the countess had a reason for asking the question. 'Only that you have excellent taste and have been fortunate enough to acquire what pleased you. More importantly, you've opened this house to others and shared its beauty. All of us in the village refer to your estate as "our château." '

'That's very gratifying.' Then she became more serious. 'During most of our long marriage, my husband would do anything to try to keep me happy. But out of guilt more than love. And to make certain I would not leave him or reveal his pernicious secret.'

The countess opened the cameo locket she always wore. 'My daughter, my only child, who died when she was eleven. I was never able to have another child. That was my husband's guilt. He was flagrantly unfaithful to me, and from one of his affairs he contracted a disease that rendered him sterile. His infidelities denied me what I most desired, a houseful of children. So he rebuilt this château in the style of an English manor I had admired. If we couldn't fill it with children, we could with objects. Precious objects to be sure, but not as precious as the children would have been.

'At first I hated him. I had loved him so extravagantly that my hatred was equally all consuming. Gradually, however, it turned to indifference.'

'Yet you stayed with him,' Alys said quietly.

'In a strange sort of way he needed me, to protect him and others from him. Nor was it easy in the early days of my marriage for a woman to leave her husband. So I let him surround me with beauty to hide the ugliness of our life. He continued to have one affair after another, often several at a time. He was obsessed with women, particularly very young women. Nor did he try to hide them from me. I had committed myself to our marriage, and it would have been absurd to leave him once he could no longer arouse any emotion in me.

'I remember his telling me about the supreme delight of deflowering three virgins in one day. Such an exquisite delight, he said, was beyond description.'

Alys shuddered as this tale of masculine depravity unfolded. All this time she'd believed that her experience with the German officers was the worst possible violation a woman could suffer. But it had been over within hours. Countess Charbonne had suffered a far worse violation to her feminine being and she'd had to endure it through many years. Alys said nothing. There seemed to be no appropriate response.

'When the disease began to affect his mind' the countess continued, 'we traveled so no one would know. At the beginning, he had long periods when he was completely rational. Then suddenly, he would become dangerously violent. You must remember that during all this time my husband was an extremely handsome man.'

Alys nodded, remembering the pictures she'd seen of the late count. He would indeed have been attractive to women.

'After one violent attack,' the countess said, 'I knew he would have to be watched continuously and eventually confined. I was in my room reading when I heard the most heartrending screams from his room. I rushed in to find him on the bed with one of the young maids. He had somehow found my wedding dress and given it to her to wear, and in his foul passion, he had ripped it to shreds. Now he was choking her even as he was. . . well, I'm sure you. . . With his valet, who now became a bodyguard, we went on a cruise through the Greek islands. I had thought a sea voyage would have a calming effect. Instead he became steadily worse. The disease was entering the final stages.

'I brought him home, and for more than a year he remained confined to this house. The story we told was that he'd had a series of heart attacks and then a stroke. During all those months, no one but his valet, the doctor, or I saw him.

'I know people wondered why I wasn't filled with sorrow after his death, why I honored none of the traditions associated with a mourning widow. The truth is, I didn't begin to live until he died.'

'I suppose,' Alys said, 'the appropriate response would be to say I'm sorry. But I can't help but wonder why you've told me all this, why you've revealed to me what no one else knows.'

'For several reasons. It is not easy to carry the burden of a dreadful secret that must not be revealed if in some way it could destroy us or someone else. It is, perhaps, one of the most unselfish things we do. That is what we must remember when the pressure of it threatens to become unbearable. Oh, both of us could have received a great deal of comfort and sympathy by unburdening ourselves, but they would have been of momentary, fleeting assistance. And we'd be left not with the victory of unburdening ourselves but the defeat of our own inadequacies.'

'And I could have ruined Minette's life,' Alys said. 'As it is. . .'

'As it is, she will always have the security that she's a child of love and the daughter of a man who died in an honorable way.

'There was another reason for my telling you all this. For a long time my life seemed as sterile as my husband's body. I think you have been feeling the same way. But you must not. As I learned after the count's death, there's a whole life out there to be lived. Please don't misunderstand. I'm not comparing Ryan to my husband, but our situations – yours and mine – are very similar. Remember, I once told you I never look to the past?'

'I've never forgotten it,' Alys said, although she realized even as she said it, that she had been allowing the past to dominate her life to a far greater extent than she would like to admit.

'Then you'll be all right,' the countess said succinctly.

They spent the remainder of the afternoon talking about the rest home, and Alys began to feel more enthusiastic about the project.

In February, Alys had a daughter she named Amalie for Jolie's mother. She was a healthy baby who became the center of all life at the inn of *Les Trois Fleurs*. For Minette, Amalie was a fascinating, living doll. She accepted that Alys had to spend a great deal of time caring for the new baby, but she had a difficult time understanding why she couldn't dress and undress her at will or play with her on the floor.

'In time, *ma chère*,' Alys said, 'she'll be delighted to have you amuse her. But right now she needs to stay quiet between feedings.'

Amalie had Ryan's light brown, softly waving hair and Alys's dark green eyes. Her birth, unlike Minette's, had given her mother no trouble; she had arrived within three hours of the first contraction. From the very beginning she had been cheerful and undemanding except when hungry. She tolerated Minette's waking her up at odd moments, expressed her minor displeasure with a soft gurgling sound, and fell immediately back to sleep.

For Alys, there was no greater joy than to see her two little girls together when Amalie was able to lie on a quilt on the floor and Minette sought to entertain her with the rag dolls or with various antics and mimicry that brought giggles from the baby.

In early spring, the hyacinths Alys had planted in the autumn bloomed. Their rich, dark bluish purple delighted the eyes, and their sweet, evocative fragrance filled the air. Sitting by the river where Ryan had asked her to marry him and surrounded by the flowers, Alys was overcome with a poignant, contemplative sadness, but she was not depressed by them. Partly because they still were the very essence of spring and therefore of a new year. For her, the new year had never begun in midwinter, but with the first sprouting of buds and grasses, the first visual reward of man's hope that life was a continuum. When she had planted the bulbs in the fall, Amalie was little more than an occasional flutter, like a touch of a butterfly's wing, beneath her rib cage. Now she was her precious daughter, the very flesh and bones, the heart and soul of herself and Ryan. She had lighted up Alys's life with an incandescent radiance that scattered sorrow back into the shadows where it belonged. Her pleasure now was to walk to the picnic site with her two girls, Amalie carried on one arm and Minette holding her other hand.

If Minette had any vivid memories of those picnics a year earlier, she never said anything. Not that she had probably forgotten – she had too sharp a mind for that. But that she had hidden her love for and her memories of Ryan, like a special treasure, in some secret cubby-hole of her mind.

By the middle of May, tourists began coming to Ste. Monique. All of the Ardennes had become famous as the great battleground during the Battle of the Bulge. Bastogne was the chief recipient of this influx of wealth, for the stand its survivors had made against the German siege and because of the now-almost-immortal retort of General McAuliffe. When the Germans suggested he surrender, his one-word reply had been 'Nuts!'

American tourists in particular flocked to the various sites where significant actions had taken place: Malmédy, Trois Ponts, Clairvoux in Luxemburg, and Luxemburg City where General George Patton was buried in the American cemetery. Ste. Monique received much of this more-than-welcome traffic. The inn, now roughly restored, was filled with overnight guests most nights, and the dining room catered to many more.

When she could, Alys visited Countess Charbonne and her rest home, now filled with soldiers recuperating from war wounds as well as some elderly patients who needed a minimum of care after surgery or were cast-bound with broken bones.

Alys had wondered how the two disparate age groups would get along together, but an amazing symbiotic relationship grew up between them. Old and young soldiers shared memories of their respective wars; young amputees showed elderly women recovering from leg or hip fractures how to maneuver on crutches or in wheelchairs; one arthritic grandmother insisted on going into the kitchen once a week and baking enough cookies for all the patients.

The most poignant couple was a woman who'd been blinded when she was in her teens and a soldier blinded by an exploding grenade. Whenever Alys took Edmund a meal tray or sat and read to him, she suggested he might like her to get a wheelchair and take him out into the garden or onto the terrace. His only response was to turn over with his face to the wall. He was blind and his life was over. There seemed no way to break through his bitterness. Then one day while she was reading to him, they heard someone singing; and Edmund remarked what a beautiful voice the woman had. At first he refused, as usual, when Alys suggested he might like to meet the singer.

'There's a wheelchair right outside your door. It would do you good to get up for a little while, and I know Madame Duvall would appreciate knowing how much you enjoy her singing.'

Grudgingly Edmund agreed.

'Madamoiselle Prévou, how nice it is to see you,' Madame Duvall said. The elderly woman was sitting up in bed, a pink shawl around her shoulders. She set aside her knitting when they entered.

'I brought Edmund LeClerc to meet you. We've been enjoying your music.'

'Thank you, my dear. It's a pleasure to meet you, Monsieur LeClerc. Isn't it a beautiful day today?'

'I wouldn't know,' he mumbled self-consciously. 'I'm blind.'

'So am I,' Madame Duvall said casually.

'Then how – how do you know what kind of day it is?' He squirmed uneasily in the wheelchair.

'Because I've felt the sun coming in all afternoon. And with the window open I can smell the flowers. Sight is not our only sense, you know.'

'It's the most important one,' he said morosely.

'No, never say that. Why, without a sense of hearing we could never be speaking to each other like this. There are roses outside my window here, and when I smell their fragrance on the evening breeze, the beauty of it is beyond compare.'

Edmund didn't stay long on that visit; and on the way back to his room, Alys explained that Madame Duvall wasn't in the rest home because of her blindness. She had a weak heart. 'I hope you'll visit her even when I'm not here. She loves having people, especially young people, around her. She has a large family, and they see her as often as they can, but she gets lonely.'

'I guess we all do,' Edmund said more to himself than to her.

With the inn as busy as it was, Alys seldom made it to the rest home more than every other week. One of her pleasures each time was to visit part of the afternoon with Edmund and Madame Duvall, who now spent hours together everyday. Madame Duvall was making a quilt top, and she'd taught Edmund to cut out the squares for her by using a cardboard template. She'd been working on the quilt for several months, but now she wanted it finished in time for her granddaughter's wedding.

'I hope you'll feel well enough to attend the wedding,' Alys said, and then wished she hadn't. Madame Duvall's heart was too weak for her to do more than occasionally ride in a wheelchair to the terrace on a warm day.

'No worry about that,' Madame Duvall said. 'The wedding is going to be here in Countess Charbonne's parlor.' Alys thought she detected a hint of laughter in Madame's voice. She was also thinking how thoughtful it was of the bride and groom to have it here so her grandmother could attend. She was not surprised that the countess had offered the use of her parlor. The generous act was typical of her.

She was surprised, however, when Madame Duvall told her that her granddaughter was marrying Edmund. On the girl's many visits to the home, she and Edmund had fallen in love.

'Congratulations, Edmund!' Alys exclaimed. 'I'm really pleased for you.'

'Thank you. And you'll also be pleased to know I have a very fine position waiting for me after we're married. Friends of my family found me work as a translator at the Italian Embassy in Brussels. I speak five languages, and I was about to receive my doctorate when the war began. That's why I was so despondent. What could a blind man do who'd intended to go into the diplomatic corps? Now it seems there is a need for oral translators at all embassies. So my years of study aren't wasted after all.'

The following month, Alys returned to the rest home for the wedding. She was delighted at the happy result of Edmund's stay there, but the wedding affected her in a way she could not explain. Each day found her more depressed, in spite of her joy in the little girls and her busy hours at the inn, which continued to do well.

Although she and Ryan had been married with the blessing of both church and state, she knew that legally and in the eyes of the church she was not married now. Not withstanding Ryan's condition and his being unaware of having a wife at home, he had committed bigamy. Morally, Alys felt they had done nothing wrong, but that did not alter the fact that Amalie was illegitimate. As was Minette. Their futures were what preyed on her mind. They were going to suffer because she had loved two men, one whom she had planned to marry and one whom she had, in all faith, married.

Except for rare occasions, Alys had always appreciated, if not loved, the immediate moment; but at the same time she was ready for the next moment to arrive, with its new surprises, its hints of still more yet to come. Now she found herself facing a future bleak with lack of hope for herself and the girls.

December of 1946, with its birthday celebration for Minette and then Christmas, was a most welcome hiatus in her depression. The birthday fête was small, only a few close friends, but Minette reigned gleefully as queen of the day. For all its frigid weather and snow, the month brought a number of tourists. Most of them were English and American soldiers, some with their wives, who were stationed with occupying forces in West Germany and in France.

Christmas was celebrated with all the joy and gaiety Alys remembered from her younger years. There was a huge tree in the now-restored guest parlor. Many of the patrons staying there the night that Émile put the tree up helped to decorate it. They held Minette and Amalie up so the little girls could place ornaments on the very top.

Jolie prepared hot chocolate and cookies for them all. After the tree was trimmed, they sat around the parlor, singing Christmas carols from the various countries and entertaining by relating the Christmas traditions of their particular family or part of the country.

Two Americans became involved in an amusing re-creation of the war between the North and the South. The Northerner insisted that the Christmas tree should always be put up on Christmas Eve, after the children had gone to bed, so as to delight them in the morning. Then it remained up until Twelfth Night.

The Southerner insisted just as vehemently that it should be up for at least two weeks before Christmas and be taken down before the New Year to avoid bad luck.

'Pure superstition,' the Northerner said, shaking his head in disbelief.

'No, tradition,' the other responded, 'and a damn good one.'

One of the other guests suggested, 'It probably dates back to the use of candles and the danger of fire with a dry tree.'

Both men nodded in way that suggested they would accept the explanation, but each still thought his tradition was the right one.

With that difference of opinion put aside, Alys was fascinated to learn that in some Southern states it was the custom to set off fireworks on Christmas morning.

'Really!' several of the guests exclaimed. 'On Christmas?'

'Yes, indeed,' the Southerner declared. 'I remember one Christmas during the Depression. I think I was ten or eleven. There wasn't going to be much of a Christmas. We were living with my mother's folks, and Daddy had finally found work in another town. He didn't think he could get home; he was deputy sheriff in a small Georgia town, and things can get kind of rough over holidays. But a week before Christmas he sent a huge box of fireworks by a friend who was brakeman on the railroad. I must have opened the box and taken them out half a dozen times a day, but I didn't set off a single one. They were for Christmas morning.

'When I woke up that day, there was still the only box under the tree, but my stocking had two oranges, an apple, and a few pieces of candy in it. And best of all, there at the breakfast table sat Daddy. He could stay only a couple of hours, but, oh, what two hours they were! We lit up the sky with those fireworks.

'Funny,' he mused as he sat back in his chair, 'that's the only childhood Christmas that really sticks in my mind.'

'Does South Carolina have fireworks?' Alys asked.

'I don't know, ma'am. I'm from Alabama, but I think so. Why do you ask?'

'Some of your officers were here at the inn during the war. One was from South Carolina.' Was Ryan setting off fireworks? And was his wife helping him?

More of the guests began to reminisce about early Christmases they remembered – being snowed in in Maine; trimming palm trees in Florida; receiving a doll one had been told was too expensive; decorating with cranberries and popcorn in the North; with holly, pyracantha, and nandina berries in the South. All had been children of the Depression, and most stories concerned a favorite Christmas when they either received something they hadn't expected or there'd been good news of some kind.

When the guests left the next day, they all said the same thing: how very much the evening had meant to them. They had dreaded Christmas away from home and families, but now they felt as if they had spent at least part of it with a new family.

'I come from a big family in Michigan,' one young wife said. 'We've never missed a Christmas of being all together. I didn't think I could get through this one so far away from home. I can't tell you what these two days meant to me.'

Alys had thought that after such a gala evening, Christmas Day would be a letdown. To her surprise, seven new guests arrived that day to spend the night. They were all strangers to one another, but after Émile pushed three tables together and suggested they eat family style, they quickly became friends.

Alys helped them to their seats and began serving the soup while Jolie opened the wine.

'But where are you sitting?' one of them asked.

'We'll be in the kitchen and serving you,' Alys said.

'Nonsense,' a man from Indiana announced brusquely. 'You're eating with us. This is Christmas.'

Refusing any argument, the others pushed their chairs closer together and insisted they bring in all the food and put it on the table.

'That's the way we do at home,' another said.

Room was found for Amalie's high chair, and the man from Indiana insisted that Minette could sit nowhere but next to him. 'Just the age of my granddaughter. I recently came over with the diplomatic corps in Brussels, but Mama stayed until after the birth of a second grandchild. Had plenty of invitations, but Brussels still seemed too lonely. Always found it better to be really alone when feeling that way than with others. So thought I'd explore Belgium a little. Glad I did.' He reached over and wiped some gravy off Minette's chin.

Some two weeks later, a package arrived from Brussels for Minette and Amalie. Inside were two beautifully dressed dolls, gifts from the man from Indiana, and a note that said merely, 'Thank you.'

By the first of February, however, Alys felt the depression returning. At first she thought it was the typical midwinter doldrums. But nothing – not even Amalie's first birthday and her funny, hesitant attempts at walking – could lift Alys's spirits.

'I'm of no use to anyone,' she declared one day when she began crying for no apparent reason.

'I think you should go to Liège and see Dr. Barré,' Jolie suggested.

'Why? What can he do for me?'

'First, I think a few days away would be good for you. Second, he's a good friend as well as psychiatrist. You never know how he might be able to help.'

'How about the girls?' Alys asked.

'Papa and I are not helpless. Go. Go. It will do you good.'

Alys knew better than to argue when her mother had made up her mind about something, and obviously Jolie had decided that only a brief vacation would bring her back to normal.

Alys's afternoon with Dr. Barré was a pleasant visit, but nothing more. He came up with no magic panaceas. Time and keeping busy were all he could offer for advice.

As she'd done on her previous visit, Alys spent hours walking around Liège, noting how the rebuilding and restoration were progressing. She was, to her surprise, beginning to feel more relaxed; she was sleeping better at night. At least the few days away from home were doing something for her.

Later one afternoon while she was walking near the university, she thought again about the Montclairs, as she'd thought about them often since her disappointment at failing to see them before. She had an uncanny need to know whether they were still alive, as if by learning that they were, she would find that the stable foundation of her world had not completely crumbled. Inquiring at the university office, Alys was overjoyed to hear that the professor was still teaching and that they continued to live in the home nearby that she remembered with such affection. So they had merely been away on that bleak and desolate evening.

Alys felt no apprehension about seeing the Montclairs until she was approaching their front door. Then she paused. She had not seen them since before the war, in the summer of 1939. Nearly eight years had gone by. Knowing they still lived here was the important thing, and she wondered what good would come of seeing them. Gilles was no longer alive, so why try to reestablish old ties? Even if the Montclairs were glad to see her, any conversation would be limited to Gilles, to his death, and perhaps to the years before that when she was in Professor Montclair's classes. Too many sorrows might be unleashed for it to be a pleasant visit. It would probably end in frustration.

About to turn and walk away, Alys was startled to see the front door open and Professor Montclair standing there.

'Yes? Who is it?' His nearsighted eyes squinted through the wire-framed glasses that were, as usual, perched halfway down his slender nose.

'Professor Montclair, it's Alys.'

'Alys? Alys Prévou?' he asked hesitantly. She nodded. 'Oh, dear child, do come in. *Maman* said she saw someone coming up the walk, but we didn't hear a knock. I insisted she was mistaken.'

'Who is there, *Papa*?' Alys heard the soft but authoritative voice of Madame Montclair. 'Bring her in here. It's cold near the door.'

'It's Alys, my dear,' the professor said. 'Alys has come to see us.'

All apprehension vanished the minute Madame Montclair

greeted her, and the professor insisted she sit in the most comfortable chair near the fire. They apologized profusely for the very small fire: 'Fuel is so expensive now.'

Only a few minutes were spent talking about Gilles. Like Alys, they had accepted that their only son had died a hero's death. So many men had died in Belgium's cause and so many tears had been shed for them, they had learned to see his execution as one among hundreds of sacrifices.

'He is gone,' Madame Montclair said. 'Weeping will not bring him back, but we do miss him and we have missed you. It has been a long time.'

'Far too long,' Alys said. 'I'm glad I came today.'

'So now,' the professor said, 'tell us about yourself. You, like us, managed to survive the war. I won't ask how. No need to dwell on those difficult times. But since then. Are you teaching?'

Briefly, she told them about the teaching she had done, her work with the rest home, and her activities around the inn. Then she found herself saying, 'You have a granddaughter.'

The words seemed to come out impulsively, without thought or intent, and yet she suddenly knew that this was the reason she had come to see the Montclairs: to tell them she had a child by Gilles. With their son gone, it would ease their sorrow to think he was in some way still alive.

'A granddaughter.' Madame Montclair began weeping, and the professor went over and sat on the arm of her chair so that he could put his arm around her.

For the briefest moment after she had spoken, Alys wondered if she were doing wrong in letting them believe that Minette was Gilles's child. When she saw the expressions of ultimate joy on their faces, she knew she was right.

Then she had to tell them all she could about how she and Gilles had planned to be married, how he'd been sent to the coast the week before he was to bring the priest, when Minette was born, and exactly how the little girl looked.

'She must look like my mother,' Madame Montclair said. 'My mother was blond.'

'And so were you, my dear, when you were a little girl,' the professor added.

'You must bring Minette to see us,' Madame Montclair said, 'Just as soon as you can. A grandchild. I still can't believe it.'

From Minette, Professor Montclair, always the scholar, turned the conversation toward Alys's teaching. He asked if she still considered pursuing her studies at the university with the thought of eventually teaching there. Alys admitted that as much as she would like to, she had not really had time to think about it.

'Then I have a suggestion,' the professor said. 'Come back to Liège and the university. You have too good a mind not to pursue your career. I deplore the waste of a good mind, whether in a man or a woman.'

'Impossible,' Alys said. 'I couldn't afford it. The inn is doing well, but not that well, and *Maman* and *Papa* need me. There is Minette to consider, too.' So far she hadn't mentioned Amalie.

Madame Montclair looked over at her husband and, responding to his wife's silent request, he nodded.

'Come live with us while you are studying,' Madame Montclair urged. 'This is a large house, with so many empty rooms. It would be good to have them filled with your voice and the laughter of a little girl. I'd love caring for her while you're busy.'

'And,' Professor Montclair added, 'there is always plenty of work for good translators. We work with publishing companies, newspapers, and the legations. There would be more than enough to pay your expenses. You need have no thought of having to ask your parents for a single franc.'

'There is one other consideration I haven't told you about,' Alys said. In as few sentences as possible, she described the months with Ryan without mentioning his name, their marriage, and the birth of Amalie.

'He doesn't know about the child?' Professor Montclair asked.

'No, and I think it best that he doesn't. It could cause difficulties with his wife. I'm sure I would find such a situation highly disturbing if I were in her place. Also, I cannot bear the thought of seeing him again, not as a stranger.'

'Bring both the little girls,' Madame Montclair said immediately. 'We will love Amalie as if she were our own.'

'Two would be too much for you,' Alys said.

'We would hire a nurse. Do come back to Liège,' Madame Montclair insisted gently.

'Yes, do,' the professor urged more strongly.

'I'll think about it. That much I promise you,' Alys said. 'All you've suggested sounds very tempting. Yes, I promise. I will think seriously about it.'

On the train returning home, all Alys's thoughts were focused on the Montclairs' plans for her to live with them and continue her studies at the university. It was a very generous offer. From her earliest years she had dreamed of becoming a teacher, but when she was at the university, that dream had been augmented by a desire to become a professor. Not that she didn't love and find satisfaction in teaching younger children. Nor was she particularly impressed with the prestige attached to professorial status. It was the opportunity to continue her own language studies in the great English and German classics. To have for her own use the vast riches contained in the university library. And perhaps to pursue the study of other European languages or even of classical Latin and Greek. Those were the desires that attracted her to Liège.

Leaving Ste. Monique would also mean putting behind her the inn and its constant, painful reminders of the days with Ryan; the room where he lay so long in a coma and where they had first made love, the kitchen where they'd sat around a cheerful fire while Ryan carved the animals and then a funny jumping jack for Minette, and their own special place by the river where they'd picnicked and he'd proposed to her. Leaving would not mean forgetting, but it might ease the turmoil those memories stirred up.

She thought too of how the change would affect Minette and Amalie. The inn was their home. Minette especially might find it difficult to leave all that was familiar, to leave the grandparents she loved and move in with strangers. Nor would it be easy for Jolie and Émile to see them go and to wait weeks between what would have to be very short visits.

Yes, there was much for her to consider.

When Alys told her parents about the Montclairs' suggestion, their offer to have Alys and the children with them, and the availability of translating work to pay her expenses, Alys was not surprised that at first they hesitated. They were proud that she was the first in the family to earn a degree, but they thought she should be satisfied with that. She was a teacher; she could read English fluently; in what way could further studies possibly benefit her?

'You're right, *Maman*. A teacher is a teacher at whatever level, and Professor Montclair will send me books from the library. I'll stay. You need me here.'

Then Jolie saw the yearning in Alys's eyes, heard the dream dying in the long sigh after her daughter spoke. 'No,' she said. '*Papa* and I are wrong. You should go. The Montclairs have made a very generous offer, and you should accept it. At least on a trial basis.'

'Thank you, *Maman*. I'll think about it.'

As cold as it was, Alys bundled the girls up and took them out to play in the snow. They built a snow fort and pummeled each other with snowballs. Alys and Minette laughed when Amalie tried to form a snowball in her tiny mittened hands, but the laugh was on them when she succeeded and put it down her mother's back. Alys showed them how to make snow angels by lying down and then moving their arms up and down and their legs back and forth in an arc.

Thoroughly soaked and frozen, they went indoors for a good rubdown, warm clothes, and hot tea generously laced with milk and sugar.

As Alys sat sipping her tea and looking around her in the kitchen, Liège seemed very far away. Yes, this was a good life, she thought, a fine life for all of them. It might be a real mistake to take the girls away from all of it. But she would do as she'd promised the Montclairs. She would not immediately reject their offer. She'd give it more thought.

CHAPTER TWENTY-TWO

Ryan turned off the main road and headed through the double wrought-iron gate with the name Ivywood entwined among the hand-forged ivy vines and leaves. He was surprised to find the drive leading to the house filled with cars. He'd forgotten that Janet and his mother were giving a formal tea this afternoon for three recent brides. He'd forgotten because of a disturbing experience he'd had while hunting with Joe Wessel. Up hours before dawn, his gear already stowed in the car, he'd dressed and left quietly so as not to disturb anyone and then headed for Joe Wessel's house. With Joe driving his pickup, they hauled a low flatboat along the highway and then down a logging road to the Wateree River. In the boat they made their way through the swamp to their favourite 'duck hole,' an open area in the middle of the swamp.

When they arrived, the sun was barely beginning to light up the sky from below the horizon; but by the time they had the decoys set in place and themselves comfortably situated in the blind, the sky had turned from a dull, leaden gray to a muted ochre, against which the clouds were a pale beige. On this frigid December morning, they sat like figures in the middle of an oil painting of a winter landscape faithfully reproduced in all shades of sepia, ecru, and brown.

Like all intrepid duck hunters, Ryan and Joe had their ears as keenly attuned as their eyes to the first approach of their prey. Soon they heard the whistle of wings as the birds started flying overhead – the high whistle of the wood ducks, the deeper, low whistle of greenheads and black mallards. Then they saw them. Their distinctly shaped bodies and flight patterns silhouetted against the first light of morning, a flight circled above them; the leader pitched in to the pothole, and the others followed.

Ryan had his gun raised, but he found he couldn't pull the trigger.

For the first time since he'd been given a shotgun as a boy, he couldn't shoot. Instead he could only watch them and gaze in wonder at their beauty. They were alive and they were free. They were totally unconcerned that someone waited below to murder them. They were not an enemy that had to be killed before they killed him. Ryan uncocked his gun, took out the shells, and laid it across his lap. For a long time, neither he nor Joe said anything. Joe Wessel, an itinerant handyman from the wrong side of town, would never question anything Ryan did. Instead, he put his gun down, too, and suggested maybe Ryan would like to go back to his house for a few beers.

The few beers became several, along with bologna and cheese sandwiches, a little conversation, and many long silences. Finally Ryan had said he'd probably better get on home.

Knowing better than to go inside the house while a formal tea was in progress, Ryan pulled the car around to the side of his office, as he called the small building on the estate he'd fixed up for himself soon after he came home from Europe. It had originally been the law office of a great-grandfather, and now held his precious possessions relegated from his room to the attic, along with an old, dilapidated but comfortable chair, and a couch in similar condition. Surrounded once more by the objects of his youth, he was content. This was his den, his refuge when he wanted to get away by himself.

Ryan stretched out on the couch and examined with sensuous pleasure the two antique decoys – a greenhead and a Canadian goose – he'd just acquired. He knew too well what was taking place within the confines of the house. One of his mother's 'best' friends would be greeting guests at the door. There would be a receiving line with Janet and his mother, the three brides in their wedding dresses, *sans* veils, the brides' mothers, and perhaps a grandmother or two.

Like diplomats presenting their credentials or actors being presented to the king after a command performance, the guests would walk single file along the receiving line, shaking each hand and making appropriate sounds of 'congratulations' and 'how beautiful everything is.' The last meaning that the silver was all polished to perfection, the crystal sparkled, the china gleamed, and there were the approved number of bouquets of roses or camellias on the dining room table and side tables. On the main table were the requisite chicken salad sandwiches, hot ham biscuits, cheese straws, petits fours, mints, and nuts.

Another 'best' friend and one of Janet's would be serving coffee and Russian tea. In the sunroom, a bride honored at a previous tea sat at the register – the small table covered with a linen cloth and adorned with a single rose in a silver bud vase – to make certain no one left without signing the guest book. Another at the sun-room door bid the guests good-bye. There was a genial undertone of conversation, but no one lingered beyond the appropriate length of time and certainly no one sat down for a real chat. It was all part of a stylized ritual in which each of the participants – guests, honored guests, and hostesses – knew and followed their roles like well-trained seals.

Ryan was fully aware that bridal and other formal teas were gala fêtes, anticipated and thoroughly enjoyed by the women of the community. He had no quarrel with their finding pleasure in such formal occasions, but he was amused at their delight in, and their taking so seriously, such a rigid regimen. At least he wanted no part of it.

Hearing the last of the cars leaving, Ryan thought he might dare to go into the kitchen and see if there were any sandwiches or ham biscuits left. He was hungry. He might smile at the ritualized pattern of a formal tea, but he did not scoff at some of the food served. Mattie, their cook, made tiny ham biscuits, no larger than a silver dollar, with such tender meat and delicate pastry that one savored the taste and texture with every bite. And her chicken sandwiches were worth writing an ode to.

With Mattie's frowning approval, he grabbed up two ham biscuits with one hand and a sandwich with the other and headed for the library where he heard his mother's voice. If they were in there, they were sitting down, and that meant the party was over.

'Good afternoon, ladies,' he said as he strode through the paneled door. Then he stopped. Janet and his mother were not alone. With them were the friends who had served and assisted at the tea – all still in their long, formal dinner gowns, corsages still pinned to their shoulders – and a young woman he'd never seen before.

'Ryan!' his mother said with a scowl. 'Look at your feet. You'll ruin the carpet.'

Chagrined, Ryan realized he'd forgotten to take off his waders, and they were indeed covered with mud that he was transferring to the Oriental rug with each step he took.

'Sorry, Mother. Just forgot.' He sat down on the floor; and as he proceeded to removing the offending boots, his heavy, scruffy, soiled woollen socks came into view.

'Oh, for heaven sakes, Ryan,' Janet said, 'go upstairs and bathe and put something decent on. You look worse than Albert after he's finished working in the garden.'

'Sorry, ladies,' Ryan said with a grin that indicated he wasn't really sorry at all. Two of them got up from their chairs and said something quietly to Janet. 'Oh, please,' Ryan insisted, 'don't leave yet. Janet will never forgive me if I've caused you to go.'

'No apologies needed, Ryan,' Mrs. Charles, the wife of a prominent lawyer, assured him. 'I really intended to leave before this.'

Standing beside her was the young woman Ryan had never seen before.

'Ryan,' Mrs. Charles said, 'I'd like you to meet Louise MacGill, who's staying with us for what I hope will be an extended visit. As you may have guessed, Louise, this is Ryan Middleton, Lucy's son and Janet's husband.'

Polite how-do-you-do's were exchanged. Ryan dashed upstairs while Mrs. Charles and her guest followed Janet to the front door.

'Well!' Janet said when Ryan came down bathed, shaved, and spruced up an hour later. 'I've never been so embarrassed in my life. Walking into the library like that.'

'At least give me credit for not barging into the tea itself.' After all, he thought, Mrs. Charles and the others in the library were long-standing friends of the family and had husbands and sons who duck hunted. It was not as if they'd never seen a man in beat-up corduroys, flannel shirt, and hip boots before. How did he know there was going to be a stranger in the room?

'It's a wonder you didn't,' Janet said, 'considering the company you've been keeping these past months.'

'If you're referring to Joe Wessel. . .' Ryan clenched his teeth against saying what was on his mind.

'And you know I am. Crude, illiterate, vulgar person.'

'Stop right there, Janet, before you say something you shouldn't. He may be only a handyman who's lucky if he makes enough to keep food on the table. But he is also a man who earned three bronze stars for heroism. He and I are brothers in a way you'll never understand.'

' "Never understand." That's always your answer whenever we disagree about something. The war may be over, but you cling to it like a baby to a favorite blanket. No, worse than that, you crawl inside it like returning to the womb. It nourishes your every thought, your every attitude.'

Ryan sighed and walked out of the room. He went back outside to his retreat and opened a book of poems by Robert Frost he'd been reading.

These arguments had become part of their life since Ryan had returned more than a year earlier. At first he had sincerely and actively tried to recapture the past, and at times he thought Janet was just as eager as he to have a good marriage. There could be no thought of ending it. Divorce for any reason was prohibited in South Carolina. Nor were divorces in any other state recognized by South Carolina, except those granted to residents of other states who then moved to South Carolina. So to keep their marriage from being more than one in name only, Ryan had agreed to join Janet in an active social life: golf, tennis, bridge, dancing, polo matches, and always her horse shows. For a while they both tried to pretend that the deeply satisfying communication they'd once shared still existed. Then came the realization on Ryan's part that they were trying too hard to have things and themselves as they had been but were no longer. A life centered around the country club, Saturday morning golf, bridge clubs, and cocktail parties seemed petty to him. He complained about her frivolous life, and she complained about his frequent, morose moods.

One of the first major blowups came when Janet wanted to go to a party where the hostess had a penchant for playing silly games.

'Let's not go,' Ryan had suggested. 'Let's stay here by the fire and read or talk.'

'I've looked forward to this evening for weeks,' Janet said. 'Leslie always has such fun parties.'

'For God's sake, Janet, grow up! We're not teenagers any more. We've outgrown guessing silly riddles with double entendre answers or finding the clue to a phrase by watching someone go through outlandish, embarrassing antics. Those are for tittering juveniles whose emotions are still in their glands. We've grown up. At least I have. Growing up was forced on me by the desperate situation of self-survival. And of trying to keep my men from being killed or mutilated. Of not knowing from moment to moment when the next shell was coming, when I might crawl over a hedgerow and come face to face with the enemy and hope to God he was just a little more stunned than I was so I could shoot first.'

'Stop it, Ryan! Stop it! Can't you ever get it through your head that the war is over?'

'So the headlines have said. The fighting is over. Peace treaties have been signed, I know that. And they're locked away in some vault. But what we, who did the fighting, can never do is sign away those months, those years of our lives that will touch everything we do, every thought we have, for the rest of our lives. I'm alive, and I don't know why. But I do know this: life is not a superficial, casual gift to be taken for granted. It is not a carelessly chosen present to be just as thoughtlessly accepted and then put away somewhere to keep from hurting the giver's feelings. It is something that must be cherished and we should be thankful for every single day. It came to us with meaning and we must constantly replenish it with meaning, or it will have no value.'

They stayed home that night, reading and listening to the radio. In return, Ryan encouraged Janet to tell him about the horse shows coming up and the ones she'd attended while he was gone; he admired her ribbons and cups. He helped her decide on whether to put one of her champion poodles out to stud, and finally persuaded her to take a fee rather than the pick of the litter. She was to use the very generous fee to buy something special for herself.

'Just give me a little time,' Ryan had said. 'Maybe that's all I need to straighten my head out.' In a rare moment of tenderness, Janet agreed, and their lovemaking that night was the most satisfying they'd experienced since he'd returned home.

More and more often, though, Ryan felt as if he were the one doing the compromising in order to keep their marriage together.

Meeting Joe Wessel had been, he often thought, the best thing that had happened to him since his return. He and Joe met in a gun shop where Ryan was having his favorite 'over and under' checked for accuracy, the stock rewaxed, and the barrel reblued. While he waited for the owner to finish with a previous customer, Ryan studied a collection of Parker twenty-six-inch, double-barreled shotguns and then examined with loving and covetous hands an 1890 English double-barreled Purdy with engraved scrollwork that he would give anything to own.

'That's a real beauty, ain't it, sir?' A third man had walked into the small shop that smelled of wax, varnish, leather, and a particular odor peculiar only to hunters and gun shops.

'That it is,' Ryan agreed. 'But damn Wilson's hide, he won't sell it.'

'No, siree,' Wilson said from behind the counter. 'That's my retirement insurance.'

'And even then,' Ryan laughed, 'you'll starve before you part with it.'

One real hunter always recognizes another. They're comrades without ever needing an introduction. Ryan and Joe Wessel immediately started talking about the various qualities of different guns and rifles; and when they left the shop, it was to go to Joe's house for a beer and more good talk.

Before long, Ryan realized there was more satisfaction in hunting and fishing with Joe than in playing polo, tennis, or golf. And that's when the real arguments began. Invariably when Janet made plans, Ryan already had a date with Joe to go to the river, the swamp, on a dove shoot, or a deer drive. Janet would be furious; and he would try to explain that if she would only let him know about the plans ahead of time, they could work out a schedule, and there wouldn't be these recriminations that were driving them further and further apart.

'What you really mean,' Janet said, after Ryan had told her he could not go to an *al fresco* Sunday brunch because he was going fishing, 'is you'd rather spend the day with Joe than with me and my friends.'

'At times, yes. He renews my faith in human nature.'

'That hurt, Ryan. But I guess you meant it to, so I think I'll leave.

I'm filling in at Marie's bridge club tonight. I suppose you'll spend the evening drinking with Joe.'

'That reminds me.' He walked to the liquor cabinet and took out a sealed bottle of Jack Daniels. 'Joe will be glad to see this. It's not a brand he can afford.'

'Well, if you come home drunk, I'd prefer you sleep in the guest room.'

'Be glad to. Oh,' he added as she walked out the door, 'have a good time tonight and at the brunch tomorrow.'

He and Joe never needed to spend the entire evening talking, nor did they drink that much. They could nurse one glass through a long, comradely silence as well as through a heated discussion about the merits of a Browning as opposed to those of a Remington, or an 'over and under' as opposed to a double barrel. Sometimes they talked about the war. Joe had served in Africa and Sicily under Patton and in Italy under Clark. Ryan had known General Patton only by reputation, and he could listen for hours while Joe extolled the virtues of the great, but often misunderstood, general.

'Do you ever think, Joe, that maybe we should forget the war? That maybe we're letting it dominate our lives too much?'

'Might as well forget our childhood, or you your education. What the hell! Our forgetting it ain't gonna change what it did to us. I didn't lose no toes 'cause I fell into a pothole. They were frostbit in Northern Italy. Who the hell ever thought Italy could get that damn cold! You didn't lose your memory in no fistfight.'

'And yet, Joe, that was the most extraordinary, the most stimulating, the most exulting period of my life. Those months of fighting were the most terrible and yet the most alive. Every natural act was accomplished in defiance against an unnatural way of life. There was something about waking up and finding yourself still alive that was more than a miracle. It was a combat against – against what? Not the enemy, not death. It was courage versus fear. It was staying when you wanted to run. It was like a marathon race, reaching the point of endurance of pain, of frozen feet, of tortured muscles, and continuing on. I don't regret those years. More, I wouldn't have missed them for anything.'

'Couldna said it better myself, Ryan.'

Strange, Ryan thought to himself, how many ways war is an enigma. War destroys the tragedy of death. It becomes mundane. Yet, at the same time, each death is a personal defeat.

Then they argued cheerfully as to which was the better part of the river to fish the next day.

Returning home, Ryan remembered Janet's suggestion that he sleep in a guest room. Although he was far from drunk, he did spend the night in what had once been his grandfather's room and decided he'd make it his room from then on.

While his war experiences had certainly changed him and did, in truth, influence his attitudes toward life, what Ryan failed to realize for many months was that the real cancer eating silently away at him was the months during which he suffered from amnesia.

Having been cleared of the desertion charges, he thought he could forget about that period of time as easily as he'd forgotten what had actually taken place. He was wrong. There was an instability to his life because the present rested not on a secure layer of a known past but on a nebulous layer of blankness. His whole life seemed tinged with the dull ache of sadness. It was not an acute pain, but something chronic that he would have to learn to live with, like the loss of an arm or leg that constantly but subtly reminds one of what was once there. He never really felt entirely at peace, as though he were constantly alert to something he might confront right around a corner.

It was not something dangerous he feared; rather it was as if he would at some time come face to face with the clue he needed to recover the memory of those missing months. And if the clue were not to be lost, he must be ready to recognize it and seize it before it disappeared again.

He often thought of his life as having traveled from light to darkness to light, and the darkness was an empty void, a vacuum. Yet given even the smallest, the most infinitesimal of openings, air will rush into a vacuum. It was that opening he found himself looking for. From time to time he thought that the necessary crack was about to occur. Sometimes it was a sound, the ringing of church bells, a child's delightful mispronouncing of a word being spoken for the first time, or a quick, uninhibited laugh. Sometimes it was things seen that tantalized him, particularly certain scenes in war movies. At other times it was the smell of something: fresh, sun-drenched sheets on the bed, acrid medicinal odors of adhesive tape and alcohol, or the sweet, heady fragrance of certain flowers.

From the time he was a little boy, the seasons and their diverse activities had been defined for him by the fragrances blown through his bedroom window from the gardens. Spring – hyacinths and baseball; summer – gardenias and swimming; fall – tea olive and hunting; winter – paper white narcissus and Christmas.

All of these still conjured up scenes from his boyhood and youth, but he found the hyacinths in the spring especially tantalizing. He'd never thought too much about them, except that they were pretty and smelled good, but now he could not get enough of them; and he sensed that in some way they held a key to memory, to something just out of reach in the fathomless depths of his mind.

His visits to the river were not always fishing trips with Joe. Often he took a boat out alone. One afternoon he thought about the small paper boats he'd made as a boy and put into the river. He would watch them race along, then get caught up in the current moving them inexorably downstream toward their fate. He felt like those boats, with no way to find anchorage amid the swirling, rapid eddies of confusion.

One of Ryan's favorite poems was Robert Frost's 'The Road Not Taken.' Unlike Frost's traveler who could not take both roads, fate had allowed him to leave the one road of his life and venture for a ways down the second one. Then fate, not conscious effort, picked him up again and set him down on the original road. Like Frost's traveler, however, he doubted if he ever would or could return to that second road. 'Way leads on to way,' Frost wrote, and since roads usually diverge from their mutual starting point, Ryan knew that the distance between the two roads would get wider and wider as time passed.

Still stretched out on the couch in his retreat after his argument with Janet following the bridal tea, Ryan turned again to that particular poem by Frost. If he were to spend the rest of his life traveling the road to which he'd returned, then he should make that trip as pleasant a one as possible for both himself and Janet. He was old-fashioned enough to consider marriage vows sacred. Marriage was a total commitment. He'd been contributing as much to the dissension between them as Janet had, maybe more. After all, she was only living the life she'd been brought up to expect.

He returned to the house, and that evening they had a long and more satisfying conversation than they'd had since his return. They agreed on a number of compromises. She would always consult him before accepting any engagements or making plans for entertaining at home, and he would keep his excursions with Joe to a minimum. And they would again start planning to build their own home, a project that had been shelved for some time. Ryan accompanied her to as many horse shows as he could, and he stayed up all night when one of the poodles had a difficult time giving birth to a litter of future champions. There were still moments when Ryan's irritability sent him scurrying to his comfortable refuge to keep from saying something that would start the arguments again, but he moved back into their bedroom and realized he'd been missing a great deal of pleasure by sleeping alone.

CHAPTER TWENTY-THREE

Just before Easter, Alys took Minette to Liège so the Montclairs could see and get to know the little girl they thought of as their granddaughter. It was a week filled with the giving and sharing of love. The dignified professor made a most admirable and obedient horse when Minette rode through the house on his back. She laughed with glee when he hoisted her to his shoulders and showed her around his small garden. Madame Montclair took Minette up to the attic, and together they went through an old chest where Gilles's childhood treasures were stored. Minette was to choose whatever she wanted to have for her very own. She came downstairs with picture books and a scruffy, much-washed, and obviously much-loved stuffed lamb.

'Yes,' Madame Montclair said in answer to the question in Alys's eyes, 'it went to bed with him every night until he was twelve or thirteen.'

Alys teared up, remembering the Gilles she had loved, and she smiled at the thought of him as a little boy.

During the visit, they discussed again her returning to the university. Alys finally agreed she would try it for three months. She would stay with the Montclairs, but Minette and Amalie would remain in Ste. Monique until she decided more definitely what she wanted to do. Much would depend on whether there was enough translating work to pay her expenses.

Alys spent Easter at home, walked with the girls along the river, and marveled over the way her hyacinths had doubled their blooms. She could smell them now without wanting to break into tears. Dr. Barré had been right. Thinking of Ryan as dead had helped her to plan her life in terms of the future rather than the past. She would miss Minette and Amalie terribly. She'd also miss the inn, the wooded hills surrounding it, and the river that so often mirrored her moods. But she was consoled by knowing they would be here whenever she wanted to return.

Once settled in with the Montclairs, Alys had little time to be homesick. She was deeply involved in studies of Elizabethan literature, a special seminar on Goethe's *Faust*, and – much to her delight – private tutorial sessions in classical Greek. Professor Montclair had anticipated her request to begin studies in either Latin or Greek by suggesting that Greek would be of inestimable value to her.

In addition, the professor immediately began bringing home English articles, treatises, and letters for her to translate into French. As a result, she had to establish a strict regimen for herself in order to keep up with her studies and get the work out on time. She found that if she divided her locales the same way she did her time, there was little conflict. She left the Montclairs' every morning before 8:00 and didn't return from the university until 5:30. As a graduate student, she had her own carrel at the library. There she could keep her books and notebooks as well as being able to do all her studying when not meeting with her professors. After a leisurely dinner, she retired to her room to work on the translations. Studying remained at the university; translating remained at the house. In that way, although her life was somewhat schizophrenic, the two aspects were never confused.

Alys was particularly fascinated by the articles from American magazines, and she found herself devouring them for every bit of information they contained. The articles ranged from those on food and fashions to more serious ones from business and scientific journals.

Gradually, as the names of magazines from which the articles were being reprinted became familiar to her, she knew from seeing a name what the article would be about. One business journal, from which there were frequent reprints, appeared to be running a series on outstanding American industrial leaders, especially outstanding young men in the business world.

Alys came home one night to find that Professor Montclair had put five articles and six letters on her desk. The letters, to be translated from French to English, were from small businesses in Liège who could not afford to keep someone on their staffs just to answer their few orders from abroad. They were short, and Alys finished them quickly. She rifled through the articles, put aside two that would take an entire evening to complete, and found one that looked short enough to finish before she went to bed.

Halfway through the first paragraph, she put down her pen. Usually she skimmed an article before beginning to write, but tonight she began by writing a rough, literal translation. After reading the third sentence, she could go no further. The article was based on an interview with Ryan St. Julian Middleton, vice-president of the Middleton Industrial Enterprises and the family corporation for its vast land holdings.

Ryan. The name smote her like the shock of an unexpected slap from a friend. Vice-president of a multimillion-dollar company and undoubtedly a millionaire in his own right. And he'd been working like a day laborer when he helped her father rebuild the inn. He had left the inn in the worn cotton trousers and blouse of a poor farmer. How confused he must have been when he regained his memory. He'd come from a wealthy family, been an officer in the American Army, and then woke up to find himself dressed like a peasant.

She thought she remembered seeing some pictures when she first checked the length of the various articles. She turned the pages slowly, and there it was – a portrait of Ryan seated behind a desk, looking very wealthy and very serious. Far too serious. And much older. But still as handsome as ever. The longer she looked at the picture, the more she yearned to see him and the more she realized she would never stop loving him.

Alys finished translating the article, and she continued to be amazed at what she was learning about the extent of the business and Ryan's life in South Carolina. How right she'd been to stay out of his present life and how wrong it would have been for him to remain in Belgium, even if he had wanted to, after he regained his memory.

For a long time she was tempted to cut the picture from the article and keep it. Then she thought better of it. Having the picture would do nothing to alleviate her loneliness, and it would be more likely to keep her from becoming independent of the past.

The next morning, Alys woke up feeling depressed and exhausted after a restless, sleep-denying night. 'I'm tired. I'm so damned tired,' she said to the small clock on her bedside table. She snuggled deeper under the covers. It was too much of an effort even to think about getting up and dressing. The day ahead of her seemed more than she could handle; the meetings with her tutors that she wasn't adequately prepared for; the pages and pages of reading to do at the library; and then another evening of translating. She tried to look ahead to the following day, Saturday, and to concentrate on twenty-four hours from now when this day would be over and she could sleep until noon if she felt like it. 'Just get through today. That's all you have to do. You made the schedule to help you, now stick to it. Think in terms of hour by hour, not the whole day. Each hour will ease the tension and bring you closer to the end of the day.'

She lay there questioning whether what she was doing was worthwhile. Did it give a really vital meaning to her life? She had come to Liège to fill a void and fulfill a promise to herself. But how could it be succeeding if she found it a chore? It wasn't the difficulty of it; it was the tedium. Each aspect taken separately seemed good: the reading in fine literature, the stimulating discussions with her tutors, and the translating; but it was the routine that was debilitating.

Maybe she should break the routine. Allow herself a luxury of some kind, a luxury of either time or something she wanted for herself. She hadn't any money, so it had to be time. Time to herself to do something frivolous, but it would be of no benefit if she worried about what she should be doing instead. She'd think about it during the day.

After a few weeks, Alys settled more easily into her routine, and she found she was no longer feeling breathless and apprehensive about being able to keep up with both studies and work. After debating with herself about a number of things she might do to relieve the monotony, she'd finally chosen to devote a part of each Saturday to a relaxing beauty regimen and then spend a few hours in a museum, at the park, or one of the historial places of interest.

The challenge of the studies was offset by the increasing ease with which she accomplished the translating. Best of all, there were finally no worries about money. She was beginning to consider bringing Minette and Amalie to Liège. The Montclairs had fallen in love with Minette during her brief visit, and Madame Montclair mentioned so often that they would love Amalie just as much. Alys knew there was certainly room enough for them, and she could now help with the expenses of a nurse. Best of all, she would have the weekends to spend with them.

Before she could talk to Madame Montclair about it, the professor made a startling announcement. The English consulate was expecting a large influx of visitors over the coming weekend, groups from Liverpool and Manchester as well as London. They needed an extra interpreter to accompany one of the groups.

'So I want to give them your name,' he said to Alys. 'Translating for the consulate pays exceptionally well,' the professor said. 'Besides, I think you'd have a good time.'

'Yes,' Madame Montclair interposed. 'You've been working so very hard since you've been here. Studying all day. In your room working every night. You need some relaxation, and you'll enjoy meeting the people.'

'How long will they be here?' Alys was intrigued.

'They'll arrive Friday noon and leave sometime Sunday afternoon. The itinerary has all been planned – meals, transportation, places to visit, the people they have appointments with. Your only responsibility will be interpreting and answering questions.'

Alys wished she could take a few days to think about the offer. Even a few hours would be a help, but Professor Montclair was leaning across the table as if expecting an immediate answer. It might be novel to spend a weekend with a group from England, and it would certainly improve her own fluency in the language. She could put the money away toward an apartment of her own. As kind and generous as the Montclairs were, she still thought she was imposing on them.

'Submit my name, Professor.' She wouldn't refuse to let him do that, but she was doubtful they would want her. 'They might think I don't have the necessary experience.'

Professor Montclair smiled to himself. Alys didn't know that whoever he suggested was automatically hired.

'If you enjoy the experience,' he said, 'there will be more opportunities in the coming months. Sometimes there are groups who want to tour other sections of Belgium. We could always arrange your university studies to accommodate the schedules.'

'I'd be away during the week?'

'Probably.'

With that went all thought of having Minette and Amalie with her. There would be no point in taking them away from Ste. Monique and bringing them to Liège if she were not going to be here every day. But the money would mean a great deal; there were so many things she could do with it. More help for her parents; education for Minette and Amalie; and before that, the pretty clothes she wanted to buy for them.

In spite of a few problems, the weekend went far more smoothly than Alys had hoped. One of the cars wouldn't start when they were ready to leave St. Paul's Cathedral, and the restaurant where reservations had supposedly been made for lunch had the dates confused. However, a new car was quickly dispatched to pick them up, and the restaurant manager was able to ready a private room.

The people were interesting, and Alys told Professor Montclair she'd be happy to go with another group any time.

During her third tour, which included a two-day visit to Antwerp, she met Kenneth Winston, a member of the English consulate staff. He had organized the tour and was accompanying it to make certain everything went as planned. Although he spoke French, he wasn't fluent enough to keep up with ten bankers all at once. He was, however, extremely efficient in managing the details of the tour.

Equally as important, as far as Alys was concerned, Kenneth was a charming companion with a delightful, casually understated sense of humor. Alys returned to the Montclairs feeling more alive than she had in a long time.

The next day came the phone call that Alys didn't realize she'd been hoping for until she heard the phone ring.

'Alys? *Ici* Kenneth. Kenneth Winston.'

'Yes, I know.' She tried to stifle a laugh. 'How could I forget that atrocious accent?'

'Atrocious?' he asked in English. 'I thought I'd really improved during the last four days.'

'Improved, yes. Forgettable, no.'

'Then maybe you would tutor me.' He paused. 'With the finest dinner in all of Liège as payment.'

'I'd be willing to tutor you for nothing,' she answered, 'but the finest dinner in the city is an offer I cannot refuse.'

'Tonight then? Seven o'clock?'

'I'm sorry, Kenneth, but I have my own tutorial session to attend. I'm days behind on my Greek.'

'Greek? My God, you can't mean it.' He gave a smothered exclamation of dismay.

'I do. It's fascinating.'

'Can you tell me all about betas and gammas over dinner tomorrow night?'

'From alpha to omega. I'll be ready at seven.'

Alys ran up the stairs and glided down the hall to her room. She liked Kenneth, but more than that she liked the idea of going out again with a man as charming and as fun to be with as he was. If she weren't the mother of two little girls, she could almost imagine herself as an undergraduate student again. The next day she used some of her precious translating money to buy a new dress and shoes. As she was trying them on, she realized these were the first pretty, party-type clothes she'd bought since before the war. She'd purchased a few, very practical dresses and one suit when she came to Liège, but nothing that was sheer luxury. Life was going to be fun again.

The first dinner led to one and then two or three a week. Somehow, Kenneth usually managed also to find a reason to be with whatever group she was interpreting for. In order to keep up with her studies, Alys asked that she be assigned no more than four a month. Sometimes she was asked merely to accompany an English wife for an afternoon of shopping while her husband was involved with business affairs. These excursions she particularly enjoyed. Frequently, after such afternoons, the couple asked her to have dinner or attend a play or the opera with them. Alys's world was expanding; becoming more cosmopolitan and less provincial was an exhilarating experience.

Each time she had dinner with Kenneth, he brought her some small surprise – a single flower, a book she had mentioned, a funny cartoon he'd cut from an English magazine. Then one night, when she'd known him for nearly three months, he handed her a small, oblong box. Inside was a blue and white Wedgwood brooch with an intaglio-carved image of Athene. He had brought it back on his recent return from London.

'For my favorite student of Greek,' he said.

'No, Kenneth, I can't accept it. It's much too expensive a gift.' She looked intently at him as she spoke. His blond hair was neatly brushed with no strand out of place. His blue eyes were set widely apart in his cherubic face, always closely shaved and with a hint of talcum powder clinging to his cheeks and upper lip. His hands, lying on the table, were smooth, and his nails were meticulously, if not professionally, manicured. He was totally unlike Ryan. Maybe that was for the best. It would hurt too much to be with someone who constantly reminded her of him.

'Please,' he said, 'I want you to have it. If you don't take it, the trip will have been a total loss. Consider it my way of saying 'thank you' for some very wonderful evenings. Evenings with a special friend.'

'As a friend, I'll accept it then. It's very beautiful.' Not only was it exquisite, it was probably one of the loveliest pieces she would ever own. If only she could feel about Kenneth as she knew he was beginning to feel about her. When he asked if he could see her again the next night, she was relieved she could tell him she was going to be busy. Two nights in a row might lead him to think she was beginning to care for him more than she did and was encouraging his attentions.

'An evening with the Greeks, I presume,' he said.

'With the professor, yes, but not a tutorial session. We're going to the opera.' It might have been kinder of her to lie, but she had to disillusion Kenneth of any idea that theirs was growing into a permanent relationship.

'Oh.' A long pause. 'I see.'

'Yes, I've been seeing Alex for some time now.' She smiled. 'As a friend, too. Please try to understand, Kenneth. I have loved two men very dearly, and I lost them in the war. I'm ready to return to life, to enjoy it, to have a good time. You've done that for me, and so has Alex. I love being with you, and I love you both in a special way that's very important to me. But I am not in love with either of you. I would miss you terribly if I couldn't see you often, but I hope you will understand I'm not ready for any serious relationship.'

'Thank you for being honest.' Alys sensed the undertone of despair and wished she hadn't heard it. She was fond of Kenneth, but it would be a long time before she would want to think about spending her life with him or with any other man. There were still wounds to be healed and memories to dim. 'If I hope it can someday be more than friendship,' she heard him saying, 'I won't press you, I promise.'

When Kenneth suggested they spend Saturday having a picnic in the Bois du val Benoit and then a boat ride on the river, she agreed enthusiastically. She'd meant it when she said she would be sorry if she couldn't see him often.

Alys continued seeing both Kenneth and Alex. With Kenneth it was cozy dinners for two, long walks, more picnics, and he was often with her when there were tours for the English visitors. So far most of these were businessmen who were establishing companies or branches in Belgium or helping to reestablish the Belgian economy. Often their wives were with them, and Alys particularly enjoyed such groups. There were also diplomatic visitors who needed to be shown the city or wanted to see something of the countryside.

With Alex, the evening was more likely to be spent at the theater, the opera, or the ballet; and Alys felt her cultural world expanding as much as her social one. In some ways when she was with Alex she was more relaxed. She was well aware that she was only one of several women he escorted around town, and she found the fact amusing. He wasn't exactly an artificial person, but he projected a predesigned image of a *bon vivant*, man-about-town, eligible bachelor and then worked hard at living up to it. With his crisply curled black hair, and almost swarthy complexion, she often thought how much more appropriately he would fit the picture of a sheikh galloping across the desert than that of a serious professor of Greek.

Her relationship with Alex was one she could not possibly have envisioned or anticipated when, after a tutorial session, he had asked her to go with him to the theater that evening to see a production of Racine's *Phèdre*. She'd been longing to enjoy some of the fine dramatic and musical events the city offered, but there was no possible way she could afford them on her meager budget. The hours at the theater were pure classical delight.

When Alex had suggested they go to his apartment afterward for a light supper, she didn't hesitate to accept his invitation. After all, she'd been there before when he wanted to lend her some books, and they'd walked over together from the university.

'A toast,' he'd said after they'd eaten and he was refilling her wineglass. 'To Dionysus, god of drama, god of wine, and god of inestimable pleasure. There's only one fitting, Dionysian ending to a perfect evening like this.'

Whether affected by the erotic and tragic passion of the play or the reawakening of her own dormant sensuality, Alys knew only she could no more have said no to Alex than she could have refused his invitation to the play. The pleasure they found with each other that night and the succeeding evenings they spent together could in no way be called making love. It was a simple satisfying of an appetite like indulging a craving for dessert and coffee after dinner.

Alys was both relieved and grateful that Alex did not pretend to be in love with her and did not wait expectantly for her to fall in love with him. She could give herself wholly to the pleasure of whatever musical or dramatic performance they attended and then enjoy an intimate hour with Alex, free from any binding commitments. With him she could live for the moment, unhampered by unwanted intrusions of the future.

Undressing in her room after one evening with Alex, Alys began thinking about their rather unconventional arrangement. She knew her moral sensibilities should be affronted, but they weren't. Probing to try to discover if she still had a conscience, she found only a pleasantly satisfied ego.

She stood in front of the mirror and tried to see herself through

Alex's eyes as they made ready to bring their evenings to a close. She unfastened her skirt, lowered it to the floor with one hand, and stepped out of it. She nodded approvingly to the image in the mirror. The movements were graceful and natural. Unbuttoning her blouse, she slowly removed it one arm at a time. Alex had never so much as touched one of her buttons; preferring, he said, to find pleasure in watching her disrobe. Her brassiere was next. At this point, Alex usually reached out and touched her breasts with his fingertips before leaning down to kiss each one as dispassionately as one would kiss a friend on the cheek. Not until they were on the bed did he begin the gentle caresses that gradually became more violently passionate as she felt herself becoming more aroused.

Garter belt, panties, and hose were removed in a few slow, easy movements. Now she stood nude in front of the mirror. This was the Alys that Alex craved, and this was the body that found delight with his. Staring at herself, Alys felt as if she'd stripped her psyche as naked as her body. Lying open and exposed before her, it revealed something she'd been unaware of until now: she had become totally devoid of normal, feminine emotion.

The fount that had been the source of that emotion had dried up; the vessels that carried it to heart and mind had atrophied with the realization that although Ryan would always remain a part of her life, she was no longer a part of his.

Perhaps that lack of emotion was the reason she could not love Kenneth. She was incapable now of loving anyone. The capacity for love and the need to be loved had been replaced by chilling indifference and an invincible self-sufficiency. Alys shivered. She'd become a cold, emotionally – if not physically – frigid woman. Frigidity was a form of emasculation she'd always thought particularly despicable and abhorrent. In short, she'd become anathema to herself.

Several times throughout the summer and early fall, Kenneth mentioned that he'd like to go to Ste. Monique with Alys and meet her parents. Yet always she found a reason to postpone the visit. They would like Kenneth, and the outcome would be inevitable. He would ask her to marry him, and she would either have to say yes or stop seeing him. She could never love him as she had Gilles and Ryan; but at her age and with the future of the girls to think about, maybe love should no longer be a serious consideration. Maybe security and a comfortable home were more important.

It was strange, Alys often thought, how she could give herself with such total abandon to Alex and at the same time appreciate Kenneth's gentlemanlike quality of restraint that would not allow him to sleep with the woman he wanted to marry. Thinking of her as a widow, he had no illusions about her being a virgin; but Alys sensed that he would look on her as his virgin if they were to marry.

They were dining out on a pleasant evening in late September when Kenneth again brought up the subject of meeting her parents.

Alys looked across the table at Kenneth and tried to imagine that she was viewing him across the breakfast table. Maybe unshaven and in a bathrobe. No, he'd never come down without shaving first. And probably never in anything more informal than a smoking jacket. She hoped he wouldn't care if she appeared in a robe. For her, who had always had to be ready for the day's work immediately after waking up, a height of luxury would be eating a leisurely breakfast before having to think about getting dressed.

Strange, she thought, that after knowing Gilles for several years and having been married to Ryan, she had not yet been through a situation that required compromise. With Gilles in Liège, they had remained on that ethereal lovers' plane of wanting to do only what the other wished. The war years had, very simply, been unnatural and antithetic to any kind of normal life-style. It was much the same with Ryan. They had not been married long enough to reach an impasse solvable only by compromise.

Yes, she could visualize Kenneth across their own table, but the thought of seeing him there every day for the rest of her life gave her pause.

She wanted a home and security, with a husband who would adopt Minette and Amalie. Kenneth had more than once indicated that he wanted to adopt them. And she herself was lonely. She dreaded being alone and unloved once she passed through her present period of emotional isolation. She knew herself too well to think that she could remain cool, indifferent, and independent for the rest of her life. She would soon again be craving affection and tenderness, a warm body in bed with her on cold nights, and someone to help her make important decisions.

She thought about her parents, and she realized that was always the way she thought of them. Not individually, but as two halves of an indivisible unit. Through all the tragedies and calamities they'd suffered, through the insignificant as well as the bitterest disagreements, there had been no diminution of their love for each other. That was still evident in the secret glances that passed between them, the way their hands touched when they were working together or relaxing in the evening. That was what Alys yearned for.

Alys could think of nothing about Kenneth she vehemently disliked. He was perhaps a little too much of a perfectionist, and neatness was almost an obsession with him. But at least she wouldn't have to pick up after him or put his clothes away. He had a few petty idiosyncrasies that bothered her, but certainly not reasons justifying her refusal to marry him. Most women would find him easy to love and be delighted that he was in love with them.

That was the problem, however. She didn't love him. Try as she would, she was finding it hard to convince herself that love no longer mattered; that the security and comfort of a home were more important.

After all, for hundreds of years marriages had been arranged by parents and still were in many places. Love was not even a consideration, and yet not all of them could have been unhappy.

She sensed that Kenneth was waiting none too patiently for an answer.

'I'd already planned to go down in about three weeks,' she said, 'after I complete two very important tours. Would you like to go then?'

'Very much. I've been looking forward to it for a long time. I'll borrow a car from the consulate, and we'll drive down. I think that would be more pleasant than going by train.'

'Yes, yes it would.' But why, she wondered, was she already thinking of the next three weeks as a reprieve or a stay of execution?

CHAPTER TWENTY-FOUR

Ryan took the house plans down from the shelf in the library and dusted them off. They'd been rolled up so long, he had to place a heavy book on each end of the large blueprint sheets to keep them spread open on the table. These were the plans Janet and he had received from the architect more than a year ago when they were talking enthusiastically about building a home. Then the plans, like his dream of raising a family in his own house, were shelved.

As vice-president of the vast Middleton holdings, Ryan found himself traveling at least three weeks out of every month. There were district offices in Charleston and Atlanta, a purchasing and sales office in New York, and there were plans to open a West Coast office in either Los Angeles or San Francisco. Often the days he was at home, Janet was involved with one of her many interests. As Ryan had promised, he attended at least one weekend social function with her.

The result was not only much less time for them to look for a lot on which to build the house, but also equally less time for him to spend with Joe Wessel. Although, as he told Janet, the duck hunting season was sacrosanct. The deer drives and the dove shoots he could forego, but nothing and no one would interfere with his duck hunting.

Ryan hadn't shot often since the day he'd laid down his gun, overcome with the beauty and vulnerability of the ducks as they flew overhead. What he did kill he gave to Joe to eat. There was a difference between killing for the pure pleasure and satisfaction of being an expert shot and killing for food. But he really preferred sitting for hours and watching the birds come in, their grace and symmetry silhouetted against the opaque sunrise.

Although the tension between Ryan and Janet had been alleviated considerably by their willingness to compromise, there continued to be an underlying instability that kept Ryan feeling he was teetering on the edge of a precipice that could give way at the slightest jarring incident between them.

Such an incident had almost occurred the night before. Ryan had casually mentioned that he would be home all week and there would be plenty of time for them to look for a lot to build on. He'd already seen several he liked, and all he needed was Janet's approval for him to consult a contractor. With a home of their own, they could begin to have the children they wanted. After all, he was nearly thirty, and he didn't want to wait much longer to be a father.

Janet had hesitated just a little too long before responding to his suggestion. Then she said she too had been thinking about having their own house and decided it would be foolish. His parents' house was plenty large enough for a second couple; they liked having Janet and Ryan with them; and, after all, it would be theirs someday. Building another house seemed an unnecessary waste of money.

'Waste of money!' Ryan couldn't believe what he was hearing. 'And how much of our money goes for your horses and dogs and charge accounts for the new boots and riding habits you need for every horse show?'

'No more than for your guns and heaven knows what hunting and fishing gear you're always buying,' she retorted.

'And what do you mean by the house will be ours eventually? That 'eventually' is a long way off. Mother isn't fifty yet and Dad's not much older. You want to live in someone else's home for at least another thirty years? My ancestors were very long-lived people.'

'I like living here, Ryan. I like having this beautiful home and all it contains for entertaining. Our plans don't call for anything as gracious and large as the living room and dining room here, to say nothing of the library and sun-room. And not a lot you've looked at has the grounds for a large garden or kennels or stables and a riding ring.'

'Ah,' Ryan said, 'I think I see what you're really trying to say. You not only enjoy the house, you enjoy having someone else take all the responsibility for running it. You like it that Mattie does all the planning and cooking of meals, while George and Albert are here at your beck and call to help with the stables. You are lazy, Janet. You want all the accoutrements of being wife to a Middleton but none of the day-to-day living that provides them.'

'That's not fair,' Janet said. 'I do my part. I help plan meals; I assist your mother. And I do a great deal of work in the community, especially charity work.'

'Oh, I can't fault you for that,' Ryan said. 'But have you forgotten that you are also a wife, and I would like you to be a mother to my children as well?'

'I – I've been meaning to talk to you about that, Ryan.' She turned her back and began brushing her hair.

'Good. But I'd like to do more than talk about it.' He went over and put his arms around her waist. He moved her long hair aside and tried to kiss her on the neck.

'Please, Ryan,' she said, pulling away. 'I said I wanted to talk about it. I don't want . . . that is, I don't think I can have children.'

'What do you mean you can't have them?' He was genuinely concerned to hear this. 'Is there something wrong? Something I don't know about?'

'The doctor thinks it would be too dangerous for me. I would probably miscarry easily.'

'I don't understand.' He stepped back and sat on the velvet chaise longue. 'You're young and healthy. You've never had any problems I've been aware of. Why does he say that?'

'Oh, I really don't know,' Janet said hastily. 'It was just an opinion when I talked to him during a routine physical.'

'Then I'm going to talk to him,' Ryan said. 'I want to know what kind of danger and why you might miscarry. There have to be reasons.' For the moment he'd forgotten all about the house he wanted. Right now his only concern was for Janet and the children they might not be able to have. 'I've known of women who had to stay in bed for the first few months. If that's the only problem it's one easily taken care of. I'll call him in the morning.'

'No, Ryan, please. It would be too embarrassing. The thought of your talking about my intimate personal problems with anyone.'

'With the doctor? Don't be silly.'

Janet had said nothing more, aware there was nothing she could do to keep Ryan from calling Dr. Reynalds. But when Ryan began the first overtures toward making love, she said she didn't feel well. In fact, she hadn't been sleeping well for several weeks. Ryan didn't argue with her, but he wondered just what did lie at the base of her refusal to have children, and refusal, more than inability, was what it seemed like.

When Ryan went to Dr. Reynalds's office in the morning, he was not surprised to hear what the doctor told him. Pregnancy itself would not be dangerous for Janet, but she would have to give up steeplechase riding and jumping. She could continue to ride for several months, as long as she limited herself to the more gentle paces; but the others, along with hunts over the countryside that involved jumping fences and hedges, were out of the question.

'I know Janet is a good rider,' Dr. Reynalds said, 'but there is always the danger of falling. What I told her was that if she insisted on continuing with the hunts and the shows as in the past, the possibility of miscarrying was perfectly evident.'

'But otherwise, there would be no danger to her or the baby?' Ryan asked.

'None whatsoever. She should carry children easily, and she's built to have them with a minimum of trouble. By that, I mean no more than most women, who certainly find labor and delivery a somewhat painful and uncomfortable few hours.'

Ryan left the doctor's office with his mind made up. They would build the house even if choosing the lot and attending to all the details were left entirely up to him. He was not staying with his parents any longer than he had to, and they were going to have children.

He continued to study the house plans, sketching in with pencil a few changes he'd like to see made. From the doctor's office he'd gone to that of a realtor, chosen the lot he wanted in a wooden section less than two miles from DeKalb Street in downtown Camden and within walking distance of a small park. Tomorrow he would have the architect redraw the plans to include the changes – one of which was a large, country-style kitchen that he envisioned as the center of household activity – and then he'd submit them to contractors for bids.

Janet could have a cook, and they'd eat their large midday dinner in the formal dining room, but by damn, he was going to have breakfast and supper at a big, old, round table in the kitchen. A kitchen with a fireplace and copper pots hanging from the ceiling. Janet could sleep late in the morning; he knew how to fix his own breakfast, but she was going to learn to cook and preside over supper, or at least warm up what the cook had prepared during the afternoon. Even leftovers in his own kitchen would be preferable to another formal meal in the near-empty dining room. But it wouldn't be empty long. There were going to be children.

When Janet returned from a charity tea for refugees in Europe, he told her about his plans. His mother and father had gone out to dinner, and they had the house to themselves. Ryan had told Mattie she could go home early, and he casually announced that they were eating supper in the kitchen.

'The kitchen!' Janet exclaimed.

'Yes, I found an old checkered cloth and put it on the worktable in the center of the room. I even have it all set.'

'How *gauche*,' Janet said. 'Tell Mattie I'll have my supper on a tray in my room.'

Ryan ignored her sneer and her request. 'Mattie has gone home. She has left some things for you to warm up. A meat loaf and scalloped potatoes, I believe. While you do that, I'll make the salad. I've been rummaging in the refrigerator and found everything I'll need. Think how cozy and domestic we'll be.'

'Don't be ridiculous, Ryan. I do not intend to warm up supper or eat in the kitchen. If it's what you want, go ahead. Mary Ann asked me to come to her house for the evening; Richard is away. I'll see you later.' She reached for her coat and started for the front hall. Ryan blocked her way.

'You will stay here,' he said, 'and eat with me. If necessary I will prepare all of the supper, but it will be for the first and last time. Then we will talk. Do you understand what I'm saying?'

'I understand you're being crude and boorish, but I'll stay. I'm going upstairs. Call me when supper is ready.'

During most of the meal, Janet remained moodily quiet while Ryan did all the talking. He told her about buying the lot, working over the house plans, and his wish they start their family right away.

'That way,' he said, 'we can move into the house about three months before the baby is born.'

'Babies!' Janet said. 'That's all you can talk about. Didn't I tell you what Dr. Reynalds said?'

'And I talked to Dr. Reynalds today.' Ryan lowered his head and concentrated on his plate. He didn't want to see the expression on Janet's face.

'Oh,' she said quietly.

'Look, honey, it will mean giving up all jumping events for only a few months.'

'A few months! At least seven months, depending on how soon I know I'm pregnant, and then heaven knows how long afterward. You're asking me to give up what I love most for at least a year each time.'

'I'm sorry, Janet, I thought you loved me. But I see what comes first in your life.'

'I do love you, Ryan, but why can't it be just the two of us? We'll build the house, and I'll play housewife, if that's what you want. But, please, let's wait a bit longer for children. I assume I can still keep the stables and riding ring here.'

'You can, and there's something else. If you did have to curtail your riding to have children, I thought you might like more stables and a larger spread where you could raise thoroughbreds. Would you like that?'

'Oh, Ryan, I'd love it. Raising thoroughbreds, having my own stable and own silks. I'll do whatever you want if I can have that.' She got up and ran around the small table to kiss him.

Well, give a little and you sometimes get a lot in return, Ryan thought, when they went upstairs early after poring over the house plans and making a few more changes that she wanted.

The building of the house went faster and more smoothly than Ryan had anticipated, but somewhere between Janet's frequent trips to Columbia to confer with the interior decorator and furniture stores and her continued involvement with her horses and dogs, the thought about her becoming pregnant went astray.

Several times during that spring of 1947, Ryan was in Charleston on business. As was his custom, he stayed at the Fort Sumter Hotel where the company maintained a suite of rooms overlooking Charleston Harbor and the Battery. After a tiring day of making decisions and dealing with district problems, Ryan enjoyed sitting in a comfortable chair by the windows in the livingroom of the suite and savoring one or two predinner drinks while he watched the activity in Battery Park or in the harbor.

There were often families enjoying a warm spring evening under the huge old trees. The children climbed on the cannons from which the Citadel cadets had sent the opening shots of the War between the States arching over to Fort Sumter on its island in the middle of the harbor. With the azaleas in full bloom, the tourist season had begun; and Ryan was usually able to distinguish the visitors from native Charlestonians by the way they took pictures of everything and frequently raised binoculars to look out over the harbor.

The harbor itself was filled with life, too. From time to time, naval vessels from submarines and Coast Guard cutters to carriers, destroyers, and battleships entered the harbor and proceeded up the Cooper River to the Navy Base north of Charleston. On these balmy spring evenings, there always seemed to be a flotilla of sailboats, their sails catching the wind and sparkling in the brilliant reddish glow of sunset. He watched, fascinated, one evening while two small sailboats tried to outmaneuver each other. It was obvious the sailors were tyros. The wind freshened and shifted suddenly and both the boats tipped over. There was a great scrambling among the crews to right the boats and get back on board. Finally they succeeded and headed back in the direction of a marina on the Ashley River side of the peninsula.

Citadel cadets, Ryan thought to himself. It was Thursday, and some of them would do anything, even to drowning, to get out of Friday afternoon parade.

Often Ryan called room service and ate his dinner without moving from his comfortable chair. Tonight, however, he felt like eating in the dining room. After showering and changing into sport coat and slacks, he went down and was greeted by the maître d'.

'Good evening, Mr. Middleton. A table by the window?'

'Please, Edward. The deviled crab good tonight?'

'As always, sir,' the maître d' said, a bit miffed that Mr. Middleton would think whatever they served wouldn't be.

Ryan ordered another Manhattan and began perusing the menu to see what he wanted in addition to the deviled crab. While the rest of South Carolina might be dry, Charleston was a law unto itself. No one was going to tell Charlestonians they could not have cocktails before or wine with their meals in public dining rooms. Some places kept up a pretense of mixing or serving the drinks from the patron's own bottles kept behind the bar, but most simply kept their own stock.

After deciding what he wanted for dinner, Ryan looked up to see a young woman being seated by herself at another table for two. In a moment he realized it was Louise MacGill, who was still visiting the Charleses in Camden. He waited to see who joined her; and when it became obvious that she too was alone, he went over to ask her if she wouldn't like to share his table.

'Thank you, Ryan, I'd be delighted to. I really hate eating alone. See? I brought a book along to read so I wouldn't appear quite so forlorn.'

While Louise was selecting from the menu, Ryan looked at her. Over the past months, he had seen her at a few social functions. From their first meeting, he had thought of her as fairly attractive, if rather shy and unprepossessing. Gradually he had found her much more self-assured and yet imbued with a gentle femininity that gave her an aura of sexuality he hadn't been aware of before.

Watching her now, Ryan was struck again with what a very desirable woman she was. There was some ellusive trait about her he couldn't put his finger on. Something quite different from other women he knew. He wished he could learn what it was that drew him to her in a way he could not explain. Like any man, he'd always been attracted by pretty women, but not enough to want to know everything about them. Nor was Louise oustandingly beautiful.

Her warm brown hair was cut short and worn close to her head like a cap. A few strands curled softly around her face. She had large, dark brown eyes, a very small upturned nose that gave an elfin quality to her face, an average-sized mouth, but with just enough of an overbite to give it a sensual quality.

At the beginning of the meal, they talked about Charleston. It was her first trip to the port city. Then he turned the conversation toward her. She was from Quebec. In fact, she had met the Charleses there while they were all touring the Gaspé Peninsula.

'Ah,' Ryan said, 'That accounts for the slight accent. I knew you were from Canada, but I couldn't place the accent.'

'Yes, I spoke French all my life, but English as well. So I do not have as much of an accent as so many who speak French most of the time.'

For some strange reason, learning that the accent was French, rather than simply Canadian or New England – her mother had been born in Maine – made her even more attractive to him.

She had married a flyer in the Royal Air Force who was training in Canada. 'Training actually in Ontario. But he came to Quebec often on leave and I met him there. He was from Scotland, as you may have guessed from my name.'

Her husband had been killed – shot down – some months after her little girl was born. She was thinking about going over to Scotland to meet his family and let them get to know their granddaughter. Louise had studied to be a teacher, but instead she'd opened a small book store with money left her when her parents died.

'I enjoyed the store tremendously, especially the people I met, but when Mrs. Charles invited me to visit them here, I thought it would be a good time to close it and then leave from here for Scotland. I hadn't really planned to sell the store, but I received a very good offer from a retiring professor whose lifetime dream it was to own such a store, and I couldn't turn it down.'

'I'm glad you didn't,' Ryan said, 'and I'm glad you came down here.' Looking at her and listening to her, he was overpowered by such a strangely haunting sensation, he wondered whether he were falling in love with her or becoming enchanted by her. 'How old is your little girl?'

'Emily is four. She's a pretty little thing. I'd be lost without her. She loves it in Camden. In fact, that's why I've extended the visit far longer than I'd intended to. I've rented a small house. Mrs. Charles wanted me, urged me, to stay with them, but a month is long enough to be a guest.'

'So Scotland is not in the immediate future?'

'No, not the immediate future.'

Ryan wondered why he felt so relieved and elated at that news. He wouldn't be seeing any more of Louise when they returned to Camden than he had in the past. He and Janet were about ready to move into the new house, and they could get back to the serious business of having children. He and Louise were sharing a pleasant dinner and that would be the end of it.

When Ryan suggested a liqueur with their coffee, the waiter shook his head. Two men from liquor control were in the dining room. Charleston might make its own laws, but there were times when it didn't flaunt them, when it was wiser to obey the state laws.

'All right,' Ryan said. 'But' – he turned to Louise – 'I have a generously stocked cabinet in the living room of my suite. We can have coffee sent up. Agreed?'

'In your suite? With a living room?' Louise asked hesitantly.

'Yes. I'm not trying to lure you to an assignation. I offer merely a brandy, or other liqueur of your choice, and coffee. In comfortable chairs before a window with a delightful view of the harbor.'

It became an evening Ryan would long remember. While she sipped her crème de menthe, and he his Napoleon brandy, he told her some of the history of Charleston. They had stood looking out of the window for a short time, and then settled in the chairs and put their feet up on a large, soft leather ottoman. They could see the lights in the homes along South Battery and those of the ships coming into the harbor. Louise kept the conversation going by asking dozens of questions about the city.

'Do you like to walk?' Ryan finally asked her.

'I love to. What do you have in mind?'

'A walking tour of the city tomorrow. It's really the only way to see it. And with someone who knows every fascinating little alley and which churchyards to visit. I have some other surprises up my sleeve, too. How about it?'

'Sounds like what I really wanted when I came down here. A bus tour is fine, but . . .'

It was finally agreed they would meet in the dining room at nine for breakfast, and then Louise said she really had to get to her room.

She'd promised Emily, who was staying with the Charleses, to call; and it was already past her bedtime. But she doubted if the little girl had gone to sleep without the call.

Ryan started to suggest she call from his room, and then changed his mind. So far the evening had been perfect. Just the right atmosphere of close friendship between them without any underlying hint of his wishing they could mean more to each other. No need to spoil it.

Together they took the elevator to a lower floor and walked to her room. He bid her good-night with no more expression of his feelings than saying that he was looking forward to seeing her at breakfast.

Louise walked into the dining room promptly at nine. Ryan was already outlining their walking tour on a small city map. He'd noted with satisfaction not only her prompt arrival, but her neat navy blue suit, fresh white blouse with scarf, and her comfortable but smart-looking shoes.

'We'll start with a brief stroll around the Battery,' he suggested, 'and if I begin to sound too much like a history professor, just stop me. Then up King Street, with detours into a few antique shops and colorful little alleys. Then to the famous corners of Meeting and Broad streets, known as the four corners of Law. No tour, of course, would be complete without stops at St. Michaels and St. Phillips for their cemeteries with tombstones of both the famous and the infamous as well as their interiors. Then we'll finish up the morning with a brief stop at the Market. There is a continuing controversy as to whether it ever was used as a slave market or merely sold fruits, vegetables, and flowers. Across from the Market is Henry's, probably Charleston's most famous restaurant and well worth the reputation it has. Their she-crab soup is unbeatable. Early in the afternoon we'll take an excursion boat to Fort Sumter and be back in time to watch the Friday afternoon parade of cadets at the Citadel.'

'Whew! Do you think I can hold up for all of that?'

'This tour guide promises plenty of rest stops for sitting down and catching your breath. I had hoped we could get over to Fort Moultrie as well, but maybe another time.'

As often as Ryan had been to Charleston, the city was too familiar for him to see it through the eyes of a tourist. Now he enjoyed watching Louise's reaction to the various sights and answering her incisive questions. She loved the history he bombarded her with as well as the places they saw. Just before lunch he bought her a bouquet from one of the Negro flower ladies who plied their trade at most of the corners.

'How fascinating and almost European it is to buy flowers on the street,' Louise said when they were seated in Henry's and Ryan had given their order. 'I love their faces. I wish I could paint.'

'Someday, if we do go across the river to Fort Moultrie, we'll go on up Highway Seventeen a ways and you can see the basket weavers. That's another interesting group. They cut and prepare their own reeds and then weave them into baskets and trays. Mostly old women though. It's an art handed down through generations, but I'm afraid it's dying out. Not many of the younger ones want to continue with it.'

When they arrived at the Citadel, after the boat trip to Fort Sumter and stopping to get Ryan's car, they found room on the bleachers to sit down.

'Thank heavens,' Louise sighed. 'I don't think I could have stayed on my feet another minute. How much I saw today! Except that it's level rather than on a hill, Charleston reminds me so much of Quebec,' she continued. 'Very old, very European. It could be transported to England or France and not be out of place.'

'I love the way you pronounce it: "ké-beck," ' Ryan said.

'My French heritage coming out.'

From the moment he'd met her, Louise's accent had fascinated him, but why he should find it even more intriguing since learning it was French piqued his curiosity. With certain words and phrases she used, he had the feeling he was listening to an echo rather than her voice, and he seemed to hear another voice in the background. Then just as quickly the sensation disappeared, and he wondered if he were having some sort of hallucination.

While he was at Yale, Ryan had occasionally visited friends of his attending the Citadel. He'd never watched a formal Friday afternoon parade without being moved by the precision marching of the cadets in their gray-and-white dress uniforms, black leather shakos, and the officers with their scarlet sashes. As each company walked past in step with the stirring cadence of Sousa's 'Stars and Stripes Forever,' the guidon corporal dipped his guidon in salute to those on the reviewing stand.

For no apparent reason, Ryan now found himself laughing inwardly over one particular incident. He'd attended a final parade before most of the senior cadets, having been given commissions, were leaving to go to war. Among them was a cousin, Randolph DuPre MacDonald, who was a cadet colonel of a battalion of senior privates. He and his battalion, like many of the other seniors, had spent the previous twenty-four hours getting skunk drunk.

While Randolph was standing at attention, the only way he could remain erect was by sticking his saber in the ground and supporting himself on it. The time came for the cadets to march before the reviewing stand, which held not only the president of the school and the faculty of commissioned officers but also a number of visiting officers and dignitaries. In his almost asphyxiated state, he jerked the thin blade of his saber from the ground and broke it off less than a foot from the hilt.

With his inebriated battalion weaving behind him like the stripes on the windblown flag atop the flagpole at one end of the parade ground, he managed to keep in step with the battalion ahead of him. When it came time to present arms, he whipped out his ignominious, ridiculous-looking, fore-shortened saber and held it stiffly in front of his face. The nonmilitary visitors in the stands howled with laughter, but the president of the school and the commanding officer of the corps were not amused. Randolph was not immediately dismissed from school only because there was less than a week to go before graduation.

Lieutenant Randolph DuPre MacDonald was killed on Iwo Jima within minutes after raising the Confederate Battle Flag that his great-grandfather had carried throughout the Civil War and his father had worn inside his blouse through all of World War I.

When the cannon was fired, Ryan involuntarily ducked and closed his eyes. As he opened them, he saw for the most minute fraction of a second not a parade ground with young cadets, but a cemetery with crosses, flowers, and a group of mourners. Just as quickly the cemetery disappeared, replaced again by the familiar quadrangle and the gray-and-white uniforms.

It had not been a military cemetery, but a small country graveyard.

Try as he would, his conscious mind could not recall ever having seen it before, and yet he had the feeling it was of momentous importance in his life. Could it be possible that the pall over those lost months was beginning to disintegrate even slightly? Was a light beginning to dispel the shadows? Even so, he now realized, it was going to take more than the haunting glimpse of a cemetery to restore that memory. Perhaps in time, the pieces would begin to fit together, but to worry about it would be to lose his mind. Better to concentrate on the present.

Yet the sight of that cemetery had disturbed him in another way. He thought again about Randolph and friends in the class of 1939, and those in the classes that followed, who'd marched on this field to the stirring music of Sousa and then had marched away to war and more ominous but no less heart-throbbing sounds of artillery and strafing planes. How many others had not returned, or had returned so badly wounded their lives might just as well have ended? They would have been young officers like himself, the most vulnerable, the most expendable of those who held commissions. Once again he wondered how in hell he'd managed to make it back.

While they drove to the hotel, Louise laid her head back against the seat. She closed her eyes and Ryan thought she'd fallen asleep. Maybe then they had done too much. If having dinner together was more than she wanted to do and she had agreed only to thank him for entertaining her all day, he wished she had said no.

'Wake up,' he said when he pulled into the hotel parking lot. 'We're here.'

'I wasn't asleep. I was reliving it all, the whole day. What time tonight?'

'Eight o'clock? I'll come by your room.'

When Louise answered his knock just after eight, he was pleased to see her wearing a white dinner gown with a colorful brocade jacket. He too had dressed with more than ordinary care.

During the meal they talked about nothing but what they'd seen during the day. Louise wanted to hear more about the pirates that had once been the scourge of the Atlantic coast and all the stories surrounding the churches and other important buildings. Her avid interest was obviously sincere, and Ryan found himself talking with her more easily than he had with anyone else – except maybe Joe – for a long time.

He had known Louise, really known her, for only twenty-four hours; yet he felt more and more as if he'd known her before. It was an eerie feeling. He'd never believed in reincarnation; yet if anyone asked him about it now, he'd swear he'd been with Louise in another life or another setting. It was probably what people referred to as *déjà vu* – the uncanny sensation one gets on being someplace for the first time that he's been there before. Something about the subconscious entering a place a fraction of a second before the conscious mind and body do.

When he suggested they have liqueurs and coffee in his suite again, she agreed with a smile; and when the waiter arrived, they were already seated by the window with their shoes off and their feet up on the leather footstool.

'I hope you don't mind,' Louise said when she removed her pumps, 'but I am feeling the effects of all that walking.'

'I'll join you. Ah, that feels good,' he said, wriggling his toes.

They discussed plans for seeing the gardens the next day. Then Louise put down her cup and walked to the window. She stood looking out for a long time and not saying anything. Finally she spoke, as if to herself rather than for Ryan's benefit. 'I'll be sorry to see these days come to an end.'

Ryan got up and walked slowly over to her. He put his hands on her waist and turned her around so that she was in his arms. As he kissed her he could feel her body as well as her lips responding to his.

'I love you,' he whispered.

Louise put her fingers on his lips. 'Don't say that. It's enough that you find me desirable.'

'I want to make love to you.'

She stepped back out of his arms, and he thought he had upset her. Instead she took off her jacket and unfastened the halter top of her dress. As it fell below her waist, he looked at her full, soft breasts. In another moment she was in his arms again, and he was caressing those breasts and feeling the nipples harden under his touch.

They made love, passionately and ecstatically. Every part of her body responded with pulsating urgency to the touch of his hands and lips and then welcomed him breathlessly and eagerly with his first hard thrust. Even after they climaxed, they clung together, as if loath to become again two separate entities. When at last they lay side by side, Louise was so quiet that Ryan thought she'd fallen asleep. Instead, much to his surprise, she slipped quietly out of bed a few minutes later and began to dress. Rising up on one elbow, Ryan looked at her in the pale light from the streetlamps below the window. Her face was shadowed like a faded daguerreotype.

'You're leaving?' He was afraid his words sounded more accusing than plaintive, and he was sorry.

'Yes. I'm going back to my room.' Her voice was a monotone, and he couldn't tell if she were feeling guilty, regretful, or merely tired.

'Why? There's no reason for you not to spend the night.'

Now fully dressed, she turned on the lamp by her side of the bed. Ryan's eyes teared at the bright light, and he blinked them two or three times to clear his vision.

'I needed you tonight,' she said, 'and I think you needed me.'

'I did, and I still do. That wasn't just physical lust that propelled us together. It was a much more deep-seated longing for something missing in our lives.'

'You're wrong, Ryan.' She sat on the edge of the bed, her body profiled against the light. 'It was a satisfying of a purely physical hunger. But we needn't apologize to each other. I've been a widow for over four years, and my husband had returned to active duty several months before that. I've had to sublimate my sexual desires for far too long. More importantly, for my ego's sake, I haven't had a man find me desirable for many years.'

'Louise' – he was almost pleading now – 'you're much more than merely desirable. You're a warm, loving person. We could mean so much . . . be so much to each other.'

'Yes, I think I am, and so are you. We could probably have a wonderful affair, very satisfying to both of us. But it would still be an affair, and I could not live with anything sordid. If you think I merely used you, you're wrong. I'm leaving because I could very easily fall in love with you. I'm not going to let that happen because I don't want to be hurt.'

Ryan put on his robe and walked around the bed to where she was now standing. He tried to take her in his arms.

'No, Ryan.' She walked toward the door to the living room. 'That part is over.'

'We can still visit the gardens tomorrow?'

'I don't think so. I'm going back to Camden in the morning.'

'I'd like to see you again.' He couldn't let her slip out of his life as easily as she seemed to be slipping away from him now. He'd meant it when he told her his need for her was more than physical. Just to be with her, just to see her and be able to talk to her would be almost enough.

'It would be pleasant to see you, too. I'd like you to meet Emily.' She walked back a few steps toward him, and then impulsively put her arms around him and kissed him goodbye. 'We needn't be ashamed of tonight, Ryan, but there would be shame in continuing. I'll – I'll look forward to having you come by the house.' She turned and hurried out into the hall.

Ryan watched Louise go and decided there was no point in his staying in Charleston either. He phoned the desk and left a call for seven in the morning. Unable to sleep, he packed everything except his shaving kit, and then picked up a book he'd bought the last time he was there. But he found he was automatically turning the pages without knowing what he was reading. He didn't know whether he was in love with Louise or merely enchanted by her. She was a warm and loving as well as fascinating person. Admit it, he said to himself, she is everything Janet is not. He'd said he loved her, but she'd been right to say it was too soon to know that. The words had come automatically because he'd wanted to make love to her. He'd never before thought of himself as a man who could be unfaithful to his wife. He'd always hated and tried to ignore the locker-room braggadocio of the men who compared their scores of conquests as casually as they would their golf scores.

What had happened to his marriage, where it had begun to fail, he could not say. But it was now like a house with dry rot. It appeared externally to others to be in good condition, but it was disintegrating faster than he could repair it. Each thing he did, each compromise he made with Janet by showing an interest in her interests, merely shored it up temporarily to keep it from falling apart around them.

He couldn't go on like that. He had no thought of ending his marriage, but it was evident that Janet was perfectly willing to follow her own pursuits, and so it was time he followed a few of his own. He would go to see Louise after he returned to Camden.

The hours in Charleston with Louise had been a euphoric idyll, but idylls are ephemeral and vincible and can exist only as long as they are not touched by reality. The return to Camden was reality.

Throughout the rest of April and the month of May, Ryan saw Louise whenever he could, but he was also occupied more and more by his work. At first Ryan was disappointed and his masculine ego bruised when Louise remained adamant about not having an affair. Then, to his amazement, he discovered there was real pleasure in spending a few hours of an evening with her and Emily. These hours were a fulfillment of a new need.

Before going overseas, before having amnesia, in fact, Ryan had never considered himself an intellectual. Intelligent, yes, but with no great passion for expanding his knowledge of the world. Yet on his return, he found himself delving hungrily into books he would have ignored before, and Louise both stimulated and appeased that yearning.

In answer to her question one night about why he continued wanting to see her in spite of her refusal to have an affair, he said, 'You're intelligent and you don't hide it. We have stimulating conversations about history, politics, books, education, philosophy. You listen with interest and you express opinions. Thank God you're not a twitter-brain.'

'A what!' She sat up in the chair and started to laugh.

'That's my term for people with more than a modicum of intelligence who are really stupid because they're intellectually lazy.'

'I know what you mean,' she said. 'I call it a chaise-lounge mentality. Like people who should know better than to call a *chaise longue* a chaise lounge. But I never thought you were a snob.'

He walked over to the mantel and started to pick up the pipe that had belonged to Louise's husband and was one of the few things of his she'd kept. Ryan wondered where his pipe was, and then shook his head in stunned disbelief. He'd never smoked a pipe. Why had he thought he did? Another irritating gadfly sting from the past? Rather than dwell on it, he responded to Louise's accusation.

'About some things I am, yes. Not my money or family. I had nothing to do with those. But about exercising my intelligence and intellectual curiosity I am.'

'Yet you admire Joe Wessel.'

'Joe is not a stupid man. Very little education but keenly intelligent in his own surroundings. As is Willie at the garage. Quit school after the third grade, but he can repair any car that drives in. Yes, I'm a snob, but I don't think I confuse education with intelligence. And, like you, I mean people "who should know better." '

On a particularly hot, humid, enervating evening in early June, Ryan suggested to Louise they take Emily and go for a swim in a secluded spot he knew along the Wateree River.

'I'd love to. It sounds delightful, and Emily would enjoy it. But' – she hesitated – 'we're busy packing. We're leaving for Scotland tomorrow.'

'But I thought . . . you said you were staying until fall.' He felt as if everything he'd been clinging to these past weeks was suddenly pulling free of his grasp.

'It's time to go now, and I think you know why. I said once I would not allow myself to fall in love with you. If I stay any longer I will.'

'And that would be wrong?' He looked at her face and knew the answer. 'I'll miss you terribly. You've given me something I've been searching for since I returned from Europe. With you I've found tranquility. An old-fashioned word, perhaps, but it encompasses so many needs – peace, contentment, solitude without loneliness, and a gentle smattering of love. I haven't known tranquility since one memory emerged and the other became buried.'

'Thank you, Ryan.' She reached over to his chair and took his hand. 'That means more than if you said you were in love with me.'

'And if I said I did love you?'

'No, you love what I've been to you for a very brief time.' She picked up a small, crudely carved wooden horse from the table beside her. 'You remember this?'

'Yes, someone brought it back to you from Sweden. It's one of Emily's favorite things.'

'And do you remember the evening you asked her where the other animals in her collection were, and you seemed terribly confused when she said there were no others?'

'I don't know what I was thinking of,' Ryan said. 'Something I had as a child, I suppose.'

'I don't think so. That evening I became acutely aware of something that had been bothering me almost from the time we met. You say you love me, but you're wrong. I remind you of someone you once loved, and perhaps in your subconscious still do. You've never loved me; you love the person I remind you of.'

There it was again, Ryan thought, a hint of something from his buried past. A glint of perception flashed through his mind, but as he reached for it, like quicksilver it was gone. His head was reeling from the effort to recapture it, to bring to life the picture that taunted for less than a second and then just as quickly disappeared. Had he loved someone while he was in Belgium? Was it that love that haunted him, that was in some way affecting his marriage to Janet and had attracted him to Louise? No, a ridiculous thought. Louise was either being an imaginative romantic or else was trying to find some kind way to end their relationship.

'I'm longing to tell you to stay,' he said, 'but I'm not going to. I hope your visit to Scotland is everything you want it to be.'

He bent over to kiss her good-bye. He saw the tears glinting in her eyes, but he knew she would never let him see her cry.

If Joe Wessel wondered why Ryan suddenly had more time to go fishing or Janet was surprised at the almost unnatural enthusiasm Ryan displayed over her interests, neither of them said anything. In his own way, Ryan was sincerely trying to live a life so circumscribed by routine that his actions would require no more volition than those of a machine on an assembly line in one of his factories.

Almost every other week, Ryan was traveling to Chicago, San Francisco, New Orleans, and back to San Francisco, with the idea of opening branch offices for the company. Each time, he asked Janet to go with him. Each time she had something to keep her home.

It seemed to him that their differences were forming an ever-widening chasm, and his attempts to build a bridge across it, to reach out and touch Janet, were met only with rebuffs. Or would it make any difference now? Even if one did build a bridge across an abyss, the abyss was still there. Or like a piece of china that is broken and then mended, even so carefully that the mending doesn't show, the break is still there beneath the surface. Nothing once damaged can ever be restored to its original perfection.

Then, much to Ryan's surprise, Janet said she would like to go with him on his next trip. She came to him while he was siting at his desk and looking over the itinerary.

'Were you planning to ask me this time, Ryan?' She put her arms around his shoulders and nestled her head against his.

'No. Not because I wouldn't like you with me, but I think you'd be bored. It will be all business.' He shrugged off her question. She was teasing him, and he didn't find it amusing.

'You're wrong,' she said. 'I think I'd enjoy it.'

From then on Janet accompanied him frequently. Whatever her reasons for changing her mind, he was delighted to have her with him; and he began to think he'd been wrong to feel their marriage was foundering too seriously to be saved.

CHAPTER TWENTY-FIVE

Alys stared at the clothes spread across the bed, and was aghast at the amount of money she'd spent. There was a beige suit, with an additional brown tweed skirt she could wear with the Chanel jacket; a softly flowered silk afternoon dress and another in black crepe that would be suitable for evening as well; and the pale blue dinner gown with full bishop sleeves. In addition, there were blouses for the suit, flat-heeled shoes for walking, two pairs of high-heeled pumps for dressier occasions, and such accessories as jewelry and scarves. She picked up the double strand of pearls; they were not real; they were not even cultured, but they were good costume jewelry and would look quietly elegant with the dresses.

She'd not had one qualm while she was selecting everything or while she was paying the bills, but now she was quite sure she'd been much too extravagant.

Professor Montclair had received a letter from the American Embassy in Brussels. Three American senators and their wives were coming over on a fact-finding mission to see how best the United States could aid the Belgians in restoring their economy to prewar levels. They would be touring several cities as well as visiting farms throughout the country. The embassy had learned that a Mademoiselle Prévou was an excellent interpreter, and they wanted the best for this group. Would Professor Montclair recommend her?

He had, and Alys had received the assignment. This was the first of the two interpreting tours that Alys had told Kenneth would keep her busy for the three weeks before she could think about going to Ste. Monique for a visit. This longer tour had come at a most felicitous time for two reasons. Alex had announced he'd been offered a position at the University of Paris and was leaving Liège within the month. Forced to reevaluate her relationship with him,

Alys came to the painful realization that he was becoming too important in her life; she could not have been the one to initiate the break. And yet at the same time, she felt an overwhelming sense of relief that she was free of her physical dependency on him. Being away from Liège on the tour would obviate any lingering, emotional farewells.

With Alex gone, she was sure Kenneth would no longer be the patient suitor willing to play the waiting game. Between now and their visit to Ste. Monique she must make up her mind one way or the other; but for now she could put all those worries aside and concentrate on the tour with the American senators.

Tomorrow a car would drive her to Brussels to meet the group from the States. To relieve all her various tensions she had gone on an extravagant shopping spree. She'd read enough in the articles she'd translated to know that American women, especially those married to important men like senators, were always beautifully and fashionably dressed. She was not going to be among them for several days looking like a poor relation. Although not aware of it, Alys had the same style consciousness of French women who can look elegantly and superbly dressed in almost anything they wear. She did know, however, that simplicity was the keynote of style; and even as she shuddered at the amount of money she'd spent, she was pleased with what she had bought.

When she asked Professor Montclair if he thought the fact-finding tour would really mean substantial aid for Belgium, he shrugged his shoulders. 'I've heard that American congressmen will leap at any opportunity for an all-expense-paid trip abroad. It's one of the prequisites of the position. So how much genuine interest they have in conditions over here is a moot question. On the other hand, the Americans began giving us some real help even before the war was over. You'll learn soon enough which type of group you're with.'

Belgium needed so much help, Alys thought, to rebuild the cities and restore the farms. Maybe, in her own way, she could send the senators back home with the kind of information needed to convince America that Belgium would be grateful for whatever their country could provide. It was that, as much as the needing to get away from

Liège and the excitement of meeting such important people, that had her looking forward to the tour.

Alys found herself feeling alternately relaxed and apprehensive on the ride to Brussels. She had now interpreted often enough not to be worried about that. Such groups usually asked the same questions and were interested in seeing the same sights. Having learned which were the best shops for buying the world-famous Belgian laces, materials, and diamonds, she knew where to take the wives for shopping while their husbands were involved with the business end of the trip. She could handle all of those aspects of the tour with ease.

The apprehension came when she wondered if the itinerary were going to include sections of the cities and the countryside where the people were in desperate need of aid. It was all very well to browse through the fine stores and eat in the best restaurants, but what about the small shops that were still struggling to recover what the war had taken from them or the farms that had not yet earned enough money to replace seeds and implements? Well, as Professor Montclair had said, she would know soon enough.

At the embassy, Alys was greeted warmly by the *chargé d' affaire*. In a few words he expressed his appreciation for her coming to translate for the group and said he hoped she would enjoy the tour and find the accommodations at each stop pleasant and comfortable. He introduced her to his aide, who would in turn introduce her to the senators and their wives. Following the aide through a richly carpeted hall, she found herself hurrying to keep up with his long, rapid strides. The way he turned his head from time to time to make certain she was still behind him, she wondered if she had arrived later than expected and her delay was causing problems, or if the aide had another appointment he had to keep as soon as he fulfilled his function of getting her and the senators together. Alys stifled a laugh when she realized he reminded her of the white rabbit in *Alice in Wonderland*. She kept expecting him to pull out a large watch and mumble, 'I'm late, I'm late.'

Alys was unable to do more than glance into each room they passed, but she was impressed. Not awed, but impressed. She'd long since become accustomed to the grandeur of many buildings in

Liège. Nor could any furnishings surpass in magnificence and beauty those in Countess Charbonne's home before the war.

At the open double doorway leading to a reception room, Alys paused. Only momentarily did she allow her apprehension to overtake her professional poise. The room was filled with more than thirty people, laughing and talking together as if they'd known one another for years. She'd thought she was to meet only the three senators and their wives. She felt not so much a stranger; after all, she was accustomed to meeting new people every day at the inn and on previous tours. Becoming comfortably acquainted with them was as natural as greeting her classes at school each morning. No, she felt more as if she'd come to the wrong party, a party she'd thought was to be a masquerade and she'd arrived in a costume only to find everyone else in their everyday clothes. The people in the room were undoubtedly too preoccupied with their own interests even to be aware she was standing in the doorway, but she expected that at the next moment they would all turn and stare at her.

The women in their stunning, ultra-fashionable cocktail dresses of rustling taffeta, shimmering moiré, and soft crepe could have been posing for the pages of a haute couture magazine like *Vogue* or *Elle*. Their gowns shrieked Schiaparelli, Worth, Chanel, Patou, and Mainbocher, and probably some American designers she was not familiar with. She wished she'd been told there was a reception and given enough time to change before attending. Then she remembered that rather than being wife to either a senator or an embassy dignitary, she was one of the hired personnel, like the aide who was worriedly trying to locate the senators so he could bring them over and introduce them to her. At his fussy, unctuous, almost effeminate airs, Alys wanted to laugh again, and she felt better. In her new beige suit and beige silk blouse, splashed with red in an indeterminate, surrealistic design, she was appropriately dressed for her position with the group. Her hair might not have been meticulously coiffed for the occasion, but it was clean and well brushed into a soft style that framed her face. She smiled, not at any person in particular but for the benefit of anyone who might be looking her way, and she was ready to meet them all.

While she was waiting for the aide to return with the senators, she looked around. Straight gilt chairs with brocade seats stood against three of the walls, all equidistant from the wainscoting and from each other. They reminded Alys of sentries standing stiffly on duty, guarding the room and forbidding anyone to touch the alternating paintings and gilt-framed mirrors on the antique-white walls. Their positioning announced they were not there to be sat on, and Alys wished she dared to.

In the center of the room a long table was laden with silver trays containing a variety of cold hors d'oeuvres, all of them arranged in intricate patterns and embellished with greenery and hothouse flowers. At each end were chafing dishes containing tiny meatballs, stuffed mushrooms, and fondues into which the guests dipped toasted croûtons. For the first time since she walked into the embassy, Alys was truly awed. She hadn't seen such a prodigal display of food since before the war. The family inn had been famous for its excellent cuisine for over three generations, and the sight of the richly laden table brought back memories of the multicourse dinners they had once served and the munificent receptions her father had catered for gentry that came long distances because of his reputation as a chef. Would they ever, she wondered, return to those days?

The aide, now sweating beneath his stiffly starched, button-down collar, had finally located his quarry. Alys had time enough to appraise the three senators as they approached. Two were middle-aged, she thought, as she noted their graying hair and protruding paunches not quite hidden beneath tightly buttoned vests and coats. The third was a more stately-looking man whose slim face and chiseled features were framed by an almost startling mane of white hair cut longer than that of the others and billowing around his head as if no comb or brush could bring it under control. A rugged individualist Alys thought.

As she was introduced, she found herself chatting easily with the men. They were friendly but not so hearty as to embarrass or make her feel uncomfortable. When they left, one of them said something about being glad she was aboard, which did confuse her. He sounded as if they were about to embark on a cruise. Then she decided the expression must be one of those fascinating American colloquialisms that were always confounding her when she was translating articles. The wives were mechanically polite, shook her hand, and then moved away to resume their conversations.

The aide, his duties now performed, wandered off to speak to a member of the embassy staff that he'd earlier pointed out to her. A waiter came by with a silver tray of filled glasses, and Alys saw no reason why she couldn't now sample some of the delicacies on the table. She selected a tulip-shaped glass of wine from the salver and moved casually over to the buffet. Slipping a lace-edged linen napkin under a small crystal plate, she moved slowly around the table. The size of the plate and her own innate sensibilities forbade her sampling everything spread before her, but she would have loved to. When she'd finally made her selection, she retreated to a *porte-fenêtre* that led to a terrace. Heavy draperies on each side hid her partially from the activities in the room and allowed her to look out at a carefully tended garden while she ate. Some of the trees were already changing color, and a few were dropping their leaves; but a bevy of asters and chrysanthemums in shades of blue, yellow, gold, and bronze highlighted the borders and edged the walks.

Alys was now completely enjoying herself. The tiny meatballs were hot and spicy; the tangy mushrooms were stuffed with a mouth-melting cheese. They were also very hot; and after popping one into her mouth, Alys found herself reaching quickly for the wine she'd placed on a small table beside her. She looked around quickly, but no one had noticed her embarrassment. She was taking a small bite from a cracker covered with salty Beluga caviar when the aide approached her to say there was someone else he wanted her to meet. A later addition to the group. Another senator, Alys thought. Finishing off the rest of the caviar, she hoped she would have it all swallowed before she had to speak to him.

Alys followed the aide's glance to a door on the opposite side of the room. Her immediate reaction was to open the *porte-fenêtre* and flee into the garden as quickly as possible. But she was too stunned to move. Nauseated and afraid she would faint, she clutched the back of a fragile gilt chair. She could feel the color draining from her face; rivulets of cold, clammy sweat trickled between her breasts. She was certain everyone in the room must see how tense and nervous she was, but no conversations came to an abrupt halt. The room was not swirling around them; their complacent world was not spinning toward a disastrous end. They were not about to see a dream dissolve into a nightmare. Alys took another sip of wine to force the burning gall back down her throat, and then set the glass on the table. Her hand was shaking too hard to hold it.

She watched with a catatonic stare as Ryan crossed the room. No longer the gaunt, painfully thin man who had left the inn, never to return from his walk up into the hills, he now had the athletic build of one who prides himself on keeping fit and trim. His face was deeply tanned, and tiny wrinkles radiated from the corners of his eyes, as if he'd been squinting at the sun over a long period of time. He'd grown a mustache since posing for the picture accompanying the magazine article she'd translated, and it gave him a more mature appearance, as did the touches of gray at his temples, in spite of his having only recently passed his thirtieth birthday. The only discordant and disturbing feature was a tautness about his mouth that had not been there even when he was most frustrated at his inability to speak.

He strode through the room, speaking to some, nodding to others, and every aspect of his demeanor bespoke a man of position and authority. Others might see him as vice-president of a large, national corporation; she saw him as her husband, the father of Amalie, and the man she loved. She knew as surely as she looked at him that she could never love anyone else. She dreaded trying to acknowledge the introduction as if meeting a stranger for the first time. Would there be any recognition on his part? Would he acknowledge it if there were?

The answers came when the aide introduced them. Alys was amazed when she was able to remain as poised as she had been with the senators. Her hands had stopped shaking, and if they were still damp with perspiration, she could only hope Ryan would attribute it to a natural nervousness at meeting so many people.

'How do you do, Mademoiselle Prévou,' she heard him say. 'We're delighted you're going to be with us on the tour.' There was no recognition in his eyes or voice. His ingratiating smile completely unnerved her, and she found herself able to mumble only a few words in response. While Ryan said something to the aide, she began to regain her composure; and when he asked questions about some of the places they would be seeing, she was able to answer quite calmly.

A young woman joined them; and Alys knew immediately, when Ryan put his arm around her waist, that she was his wife. Her cocktail dress, with its bouffant, shirred taffeta skirt, was a shade of purple designated as aubergine. On most women the color would have been drab; on Mrs. Middleton it was stunning. She wore her long blond hair in a softly curled pageboy. Parted low on one side, it was drawn across her forehead and held in place with a single diamond clip. Her only other jewelry was a watch, its face rimmed and its band encrusted with diamonds, and a diamond solitaire engagement ring of at least three carats. Alys reluctantly admired her taste for daring to wear a neckline cut nearly to her waist without ruining the lines by filling it in with a necklace. Her skin was flawless, and her eyes were exceptionally large without dominating her face. Her smile did that. But it was a cold smile, a smile that warned everyone not to get too close to her. She acknowledged the introduction with the air of one admitting a new lackey to her retinue of servants.

But of course, Alys thought, that's exactly what I must seem to her. I am the interpreter hired to make the tour more pleasant and comfortable.

Ryan asked another question, and Alys responded by describing the countryside through which they'd be traveling.

'What a delightful accent you have, mam'selle,' Mrs. Middleton said. 'Doesn't she have a charming accent, Ryan?'

Alys would have accepted the words as either a compliment or an impulsive statement if she hadn't sensed an undercurrent of sarcasm and irritation in the tone. Perhaps in the days ahead she would learn what there was about her accent that would so set the woman's teeth on edge.

'Yes, yes, it is,' Ryan said. He added something more about again being pleased Alys would be with them and left to join one of the small groups.

Ryan's response to Janet about the young woman's accent had been automatic. He did find it charming, yet there was something disturbing about it, almost like a pleasurable irritant. She continued to haunt him throughout the evening.

He hadn't known her, Alys thought. He had no idea, as he stood there calmly talking to her and being as pleasantly charming as he would to anyone he met for the first time, that they had been married after falling deeply and totally in love with each other. He didn't remember that she had kept him alive all the weeks he was in a coma and then had taught him to speak again. Of those months that were so dear to her he remembered nothing.

Of one thing Alys was certain; she could not accompany the group on this tour. She would have to make her apologies and find some excuse to return to Liège. There was no way she could spend every day in the company of Ryan as he was to her now. To listen to him speak and watch him with his wife during those interminable hours would be torture beyond bearing.

Still deep in her thoughts about Ryan, Alys jumped involuntarily when the aide spoke to her: 'Mr. Middleton is vice-president of a large firm that manufactures farm machinery.'

I know, I know! Alys wanted to scream. I know all about him. Where he's from, what he does. And I know more than you do. How much he loved me and I still love him.

'He's joined the group as an expert consultant,' the aide continued in a particularly grating, supercilious way.

Pompous ass, Alys thought, but once again she felt more like a servant than an intelligent, well-educated teacher.

'His function is to help recommend how the United States can best aid Belgium,' the aide said. Then he softened his voice as if realizing he should conciliate Alys in some way for having implied by his tone that she was one of the unfortunate needy. 'We really appreciate your coming on such short notice. Several of our embassy staff are on leave. Although the Belgian drivers speak passable English, they are not proficient enough for the translating that will be needed. I know the senators will be most grateful for your assistance.'

Well, that ended any thought she had of making her excuses and asking to be driven back to Liège. If she had only herself to consider, she would still have done it; but she would be letting Professor Montclair down, and she couldn't disappoint him that way. No, she would have to act the stranger, one of the hired personnel needed to make the tour group function efficiently and pleasantly.

She declined the invitation to join the group for dinner – an invitation she was pleasantly surprised to receive – by saying she was tired after the drive from Liège, and asked if she might have a light supper on a tray in her room. The aide said he would arrange it and then directed her to the guest house in the embassy compound.

Once in her room she took off her suit, blouse, and shoes. Along with them she shed the smiling, self-controlled façade that she'd somehow prevented from dissolving while she was still in the same room with Ryan.

Alys lay on the bed a long time, staring at the ceiling and trying to compose her emotions. It became dusk and then dark, and she still didn't turn on a light. She lay as if in a trance and tried to reconcile what she knew was her duty with an instinctive feeling that if she remained with the group for the several days of the tour, there was trouble ahead. Someone was going to be hurt, and that someone would be she. She could sense she'd already made an enemy in Janet Middleton, although she had yet to determine why, except that her accent displeased the American woman. No, more than displeasure had initiated that sarcasm in her voice. Alys would probably never know why, but she'd been cautioned to keep out of Janet Middleton's way, and maybe away from her handsome husband as well. No fear, Alys thought; she intended to stay as far away from him as she could the whole time.

Before coming to the guest house, she'd been informed that because there were nine in the group, they would be traveling in three embassy cars. She would simply make it a point never to ride in the same car with Ryan. During the various stops, she would be working with the entire group, and she would divide her attention equally among them. She could do it if she put her mind to it, but it was not going to be easy.

Think rationally she kept reminding herself. Don't let your emotions gain control. Ryan is here as an expert consultant. You are a hired interpreter. Continue to think that way and you'll be all right.

No one could hurt her but herself, and that would be only if she responded irrationally to any particular situation. Ryan, though maintaining a distance commensurate with his position, would always be considerate and polite. She must never try to imagine that his attitude implied anything more personal. In turn, she would be unfailingly polite toward, yet keep her distance from, Janet Middleton. She suspected the woman was inordinately jealous of Ryan when he was around other attractive women, and Alys had no intention of causing any ruptures between husband and wife.

A waiter finally came with the light supper she'd ordered. It was exactly what and all she wanted. Her tongue was still tender from the hot mushroom she'd popped whole into her mouth in her eagerness to taste it.

She'd brought along one of Somerset Maugham's novels, *The Razor's Edge*, to read in whatever spare moments she had, and she began it while she ate. She continued reading it after putting on her gown and getting into bed. Fascinated by the story, she could forget momentarily her personal concerns, although her misery hovered constantly on the edge of her consciousness.

When she turned out the light, however, she was unable to sleep in spite of the fact she'd hardly been able to keep her eyes open for the last few pages of one chapter. The memory of Ryan as she'd seen him tonight mingled with earlier, more poignant memories, and all of them intruded and swirled in her brain like some unwanted dream from which one hopes to awaken. But she was awake. It was as if sleep were a curtain she was trying to pull across the window of her mind in order to block out reality. But Ryan kept holding it open, demanding that she look at him and recognize that the reality of the past and the reality of the present could never be separated. She must live and accept them both.

All right, she said to herself, I have endured worse than this, and I have survived.

But it was not going to be easy. She would always be conscious of Ryan's presence; and she knew that no matter whom she was talking with, she would unconsciously be speaking to him, listening for his approval, and watching for that smile she loved.

Finally, after shifting position more than a dozen times, changing one pillow for another, opening and closing and then opening the window again, she fell asleep.

* * *

At 8:00 the next morning, Alys went down to the guest house dining room. She had hoped to breakfast unobtrusively at a small table by herself; but when two of the senators, sitting at a table for four, asked her to join them, she could not very well refuse without appearing rude.

Their wives and the third senator were breakfasting in their rooms. Ryan's name was not mentioned. Actually she was glad to have the opportunity to become more closely acquainted with a few of the group at a time. One of them, Senator Delgardo, was the rugged-looking older man with the handsome white hair. She was not surprised when he said he was from the Southwest. Somehow, she'd rather expected him to be. The other, Senator Henderson, was from the Midwest; and with his unassuming, fatherly attitude, he reminded her of the man from Indiana who had spent part of his Christmas vacation with them at the inn and sent the gifts to Minette and Amalie. Already she felt at ease with both of them. Their mood was lighthearted and yet became serious when they began questioning her about where they were going and what they were going to see. It was evident they were genuinely interested in the needs of the country, particularly in agricultural areas.

'All of us,' said Senator Henderson, 'are from rural rather than industrial sections of our state, and we want to see the farms and talk to landowners and farmers. We want to determine what kind of financial aid and what specific farm machinery the United States can provide to help your country recover from the war.'

'That pleases me,' Alys said. 'I live in Liège now, but my home is a small village on the Luxemburg border. Farming is very important to our community as it is to hundreds of communities in the country. Some cities, like Brussels and Antwerp and Liège, are business and industrial centers, but farming is a very vital part of our economy. I'll enjoy showing it all to you. I'll also enjoy showing you how beautiful the Belgian countryside is in early autumn.'

She had just finished speaking when she saw Ryan coming to join them. Alys's back was to the door, and she hadn't seen him come into the dining room, but he'd obviously been there long enough to get coffee, which he brought to the table with him.

Actually he had nodded to the senators when he entered and then chosen to sit by himself in order to read the Paris edition of the *New York Times*, undisturbed. Instead of concentrating on the news, he'd found himself listening to Mademoiselle Prévou. He found every nuance and inflection of her accent disturbing as well as enchanting. Now that he was sitting across from her, he saw that her face was as ingenuously expressive as a child's, and the way she used her hands to emphasize what she was saying was delightful.

It hadn't taken him long, of course, to realize who she reminded him of: Louise MacGill. Yet, at the same time, there was something unique about this young woman. She was not a copy of anybody else. He had met her only last night and had decided she was pretty in a gaminesque sort of way; but he had been more aware of her accent than her physical appearance. He'd then given little thought to her during the rest of the evening. He'd drunk too much at the cocktail party and later after overeating at the banquet. He was trying to soothe a vicious headache and upset stomach with aspirin and Alka Seltzer when Janet began berating him for flirting with the date of some dignitary whose name he didn't even remember – the woman's not the dignitary's. As usual, they went to bed without speaking to each other.

Now, more aware of Mademoiselle Prévou, he noticed that even when she was speaking seriously, she had a piquant charm that with its very naiveté was tantalizing. If he were not certain that she was reminding him of Louise, he would swear he had met her before.

He had, of course, been across Belgium during the war, fighting all the way from France to Luxemburg. And she'd said her home was on the border of the two countries. That could only be it. He'd seen her or someone like her then. Maybe in one of the villages during the advance. This morning she was smiling, and yet he kept visualizing her with head bowed and fighting to keep back the tears.

'Mam'selle,' he asked, 'did you ever visit American Army headquarters in Liège? Right after the war was over?'

Alys nearly said yes, before she caught herself. She remembered her despondency during the days after she learned that Ryan had been there under room-arrest when she thought he'd already left to return to the States. She remembered too the slight disturbance she'd heard at an upper window, but when she'd looked, all she had seen was a curtain blowing in the wind. Could it possibly be that Ryan had looked out that morning and seen her in the courtyard? If she said yes, there would be questions, and some of them she was not prepared to answer. Not here, not now. Dr. Barré had cautioned her – not once but many times – that once Ryan recovered from his amnesia, it would mean nothing to him just to tell him what had taken place during those months. It might help him feel less lost, but it would not help him to recover that memory. Only time or a traumatic incident of some kind could do that. Ryan was married and leading a life far different from what he'd known at the inn. It would not benefit either of them to refer to the past.

'I've been by the American headquarters many times,' she said. 'But I didn't move to Liège until more than a year after the war.' Maybe a half truth, but better than the whole. 'Why do you ask?'

'It's not important. You just remind me of someone I saw while I was there.'

'I've heard that everyone has a twin somewhere in the world. Maybe it was she you saw.'

By this time all of the group had gathered, and they went outside to where the three long, black Cadillac limousines were waiting. Never had Alys seen such plush interiors, and she thought how tempting it was going to be to fall asleep during the long drives between stops. She noted the small embassy flags on the front fenders and hoped the simple farmers they were going to talk to would not be too intimidated to answer questions. It would be her job to assure the country people that these men were sincerely interested in farming conditions and in their particular needs.

Alys stood to one side while it was decided who should ride in which car. She would wait to see which car Ryan got into, and she would choose another. But her plan to remain as far away from him as possible was once more sundered by the women's opting to stay together. 'We've had quite enough of senate business on this trip already,' one of them said. 'We have more interesting things to talk about.'

An aide who was accompanying them for part of the trip guided two of the senators to a second car. That left Ryan, Senator Henderson, and Alys in the third war. At least her position determined that she should sit in the front seat with the driver. She assumed that Ryan and the senator would concentrate on talking to each other.

Instead, as they drove through Brussels and out into the countryside, she was distressed to have Ryan directing most of his questions toward her. With each question, she became more miserable. Rather than enjoying the ride in the luxurious car, she felt with each kilometer they traveled more cramped and closed in. She was confined within a prison from which there was no escape, and smothered by the ever-increasing, uncontrollable suspense of wondering how long she could keep up the charade of not knowing him. She was certain now the tour was going to be even more difficult for her than she'd first feared. It could be a real fiasco.

CHAPTER TWENTY-SIX

For both Alys and Ryan, the tour was a haunting, eerie reliving of the war years. The towns and villages they drove through were many of them unfamiliar to Alys, but conditions in them and in the countryside were the same as in Ste. Monique and its environs. She could be traveling over and over the road between the inn and her village, seeing the same devastation and the futile attempts to rebuild homes and barns and restore the land. Like her father, men all over Belgium had become scavengers of stone, wood, tiles, and glass, in order to replace, even temporarily, walls and roofs. The past seemed to echo around her – she could still hear shells screaming in the distance and see the explosions that had gouged huge holes in the ground, cut down trees like a scythe mowing wheat, and crumbled the sides of buildings. The scenes were a poignant reminder that, like the men they saw working in the fields and the women in the courtyards and on the village streets, she was a survivor. They had endured the onslaught; they had been the recipients of the cruel ravages of war, and they were still alive.

If Alys thought of herself as a recipient of the pain, the rapine, the destructive forces, and the fearful hordes, Ryan relived the war as a participant. He had been the purveyor of death. Whose shells, theirs or the Germans had destroyed these particular homes and made unplantable these fields didn't matter. Or whether American or German planes had bombed this village they were driving through. People had been deprived of homes, barns, shops, churches, land, their very livelihood, and their lives. Could he, in all conscience, now speak to these people as an advocate of the United States, the great savior from across the seas that would now restore to them what had been lost? He felt more like humbly asking their pardon for the misery that had been wreaked upon them, that had catapulted them from a placid, albeit difficult, hard-grubbing-from-soil life to one of daily struggling to remain alive. Whatever malevolence these people might, in turn, feel for him was justified. He felt like a parent who had without cause punished a child and was now trying to atone for his thoughtless actions with offers of sweetmeats. Not the candy yet, only the offers, unless the donees proved truly worthy or in need of them. A sop to the conscience.

Now that he was over here, he truly wanted to help these people. He would do all he could to encourage the senators to return to the States with enough verbal ammunition to begin a program of genuine and practical aid. Such ideas, however, had not been the original motivation for coming on this trip. It was a way to get to Liège and to Dr. Barré. And he still would. Just as soon as he had impressed the group with the need for positive action, he would leave them and go to Liège. Not a week had gone by without his yearning to know about the months he'd had amnesia and wanting to meet the family he'd been with. He was certain that if he accepted Dr. Barré's invitation to visit with him, the man would reveal what had been kept secret all this time: the name and address of his benefactors. Ryan was haunted by the feeling that there was more of a mystery there than just his having had amnesia, and he would not be content until it was revealed to him.

The senator's responses to the varied situations they saw differed markedly among themselves and from those of Alys and Ryan. There were both cautious assurances that all would be considered and immediate promises that all damages would be rectified. Restitution would be immediate. Such differences prompted lively discussions among the four men most concerned. They had not been given *carte blanche*. They were an investigative team only. Reports must be taken back to the States, submitted, passed from committee to committee; eventually perhaps there would be tangible results.

If ever Alys had wondered whether the tour would show the committee just how desperate the situation was in Belgium, her concern was laid more and more quietly to rest as they proceeded through the countryside.

The number of stone houses and attached barns that had been damaged or destroyed was uncountable. When they came upon one house whose barn had, miraculously, remained standing, some of the Americans were horrified to see that the family was now living with the farm animals. Alys had already had to explain to the Americans, who were accustomed to large barns built at some remove from the houses, that in Belgium, one low, stone building, divided by a wall, sufficed as living quarters for both family and animals. Nor was it unusual to see goats and chickens wandering in and out of both doors. As vital as the animals were to the farmer's livelihood, they were really considered members of the family. In bitter cold weather, animals and family shared the heat from the single fireplace or stove, and shared their own body warmth with one another.

At first the senators were much like tourists enjoying a pleasant ride through the countryside. Then Alys saw they began taking notes after they passed a farm so decimated with huge shell craters that there seemed no possible way for it ever to serve a useful function again. There were more notes taken after they talked to several farmers who were having to pull their dilapidated, many times mended wooden plows while their wives or children dug the furrows. Their animals had been killed or in some cases slaughtered for food – sometimes by the family, sometimes by foraging troops.

Once-paved side roads were now merely two parallel ruts, impossible for the embassy cars to navigate. Alys and the committee frequently had to walk a half mile or more to visit some of the farms. Unexploded shells lay along the edges of the fields, placed there after being removed from the fields themselves. Nor had all the damage been done to the fields. The senators did not remain unmoved when they heard stories of bodies being shattered while trying to remove the shells or when plows dug them up. The large craters left by the shells that had exploded immediately after falling were booby traps for unwary children and animals that fell into them and drowned after a heavy rain.

To Ryan it was like revisiting a hell he'd once managed to escape from. He'd watched those shells explode; he'd heard the cries of children as they fled from or crawled out from beneath fallen stone walls. He'd seen the stately poplar trees that had once bordered the roads and were now jagged stumps.

They came to one particular field where a number of people were working. It was on the edge of a village, and to one side was a small building with the roof missing and most of the four walls destroyed. It could be distinguished as a church by the bell that lay on its side in the rubble next to a splintered wooden cross. The people were not plowing the field; they were trying to restore a cemetery. Around them lay piles of rocks, bones, shell fragments, shards of casket wood, nails, and splintered crosses. All the detritus of war.

Ryan's thoughts reverted to another cemetery. His platoon had run across a road much like the one he was now standing on. They had never walked in those days. Both shells and aircraft began hitting at them from all directions. Artillery spewing a fatal vomitous; planes defecating their deadly offal. He'd fallen to the ground, then rolled several feet toward a hole that one shell ironically and fortuitously opened up for him. He had lain there, unthinking, unfeeling, merely existing. When he could react and realized he was still whole and untouched, his mind dwelt on only one thing: he was still alive.

He had instinctively fallen on his face and covered his head with his arms; and as long as the shelling continued, he remained in that cramped position: his face in the dirt, one leg being scratched, almost pierced, by the sharp point of what felt like a stone, and his diaphragm resting on a hard, round object that made it difficult to breathe. When at last he felt it was safe enough to change position and get more comfortable, he realized with horror and shock that he was in a grave. The casket had been blown open. A shattered armbone had been irritating his leg, and his chest had been lying on a skull.

Ryan glanced at the cemetery the people were working so diligently to clean up. One large section had already been restored, with mounds delineating where their dead were once more laid to rest. Crosses and stone slabs identified who lay there. Rest in peace, Ryan thought. There'd been no more peace for them than for the living. Nor had the grave he'd fallen into been a sanctuary for only the man or woman who'd lain there undisturbed for many years. It had provided sanctuary for the living. If politics made strange bedfellows, Ryan said to himself, so did wars. He'd stayed in the grave from noon until darkness brought a respite in the fighting.

While they rode along, Alys too was aware of the blasted trees on either side, but she saw among them the brilliant profusion of wild flowers and the new shoots coming up from the roots of the trees. There was death all around them, but there was also rebirth. Farmers were plowing, even if they had no draft animals, and nature was exclaiming to all who would listen that she was indomitable and immortal.

'You've been very quiet the last few hours,' Senator Delgardo said to Ryan as the group made their way slowly along a dirt road to the cars.

'I've been remembering.' He'd wanted to come on this trip, and yet he was wondering now if it had been wise. Some painful memories were best laid to rest. But there were also the months for which he had no memory, and those were the ones that had him looking at each village, each forest-covered hill, and each river for something that would awaken that period lost to him. He thought the actual place where he'd lived during those months was farther east of where the tour was. He'd always had a good sense of direction, and he was certain he'd traveled somewhat northwest on his way to Liège that day. But then, he could have been anywhere during the previous months and merely regained his memory of that place. While all around him seemed familiar – the partially destroyed villages, torn-up roads, pitted fields, and ravaged countryside – it was a familiarity from the days he'd fought in areas such as these.

'That's right,' Senator Henderson said. 'You were in the war. Near here?'

'Farther to the north and then to the east. In the Ardennes.'

Yes, Ryan thought, these roads could be the same ones. He would never forget each time they advanced toward the front. The gut-wrenching fear. The silence of the men. There was never any talking when they were going into battle. They were only thinking and dreading their own thoughts. And the endlessness of it. No matter how many yards they advanced, how many towns they took, there was always another field and another village ahead of them.

He looked at the women working in the cemetery, and he remembered the women along the roads. Long dresses, shawls, and kerchiefs on their heads.All in black or gray. As dismal and forboding as the skies. It was always a gray, dank day when they were getting ready to fight. The sun must have shone sometimes, but he didn't remember when. The women would fall to their knees, bring out their rosaries, and begin to pray. He'd found himself seeing the men through eyes that had seen husbands, brothers, and sons killed. The women didn't see men walking. They saw the ghosts of the dead who'd be brought back laid out in a truck. It was more unnerving than the sounds of shells or the silence of his men.

'You don't like to talk about it, do you?' Senator Delgardo said.

'No, because as genuinely sincere as people are, they can never know or understand. I don't mind telling you one thing, though. Soon after I landed on Normandy, I discovered I had a secret weapon. His name was Andy. That's all I ever knew him by. An elderly Negro. At least I thought he was old. He taught me to hunt when I was still a boy. You'd call him illiterate, but he was wise in the way hunters have been wise throughout the ages. He taught me that if I wanted to catch a fish or kill a duck or flush a quail, I had to learn to think like the fish and the duck and the quail. Many's the time I was saved because I learned to think like the Germans and then to outthink them. It wasn't hard once I'd studied and understood their behavior. Then luck or happenstance – call it what you will – brought me the rest of the way.'

Alys listened with searing but spellbinding interest. She'd known nothing of Ryan's months of fighting. What had he experienced that made him look so somber now and yet unable to talk about it? She thought about the nightmares he'd had. Certain devastating experiences must have so branded themselves into his mind that even loss of conscious memory could not negate them. Each word he said now tore at her and shredded away more and more of the protective cocoon she'd wrapped around herself – like Chinese weavers unwinding the gossamer threads so carefully and meticulously entwined around a silkworm. Alys did not, however, dare to reveal her feelings by either word or facial expression. This was the third day of the tour. Ryan was making a point of staying too near her all the time for either her peace of mind or Janet Middleton's preference. Ryan's wife had come dangerously close to losing her studied poise and composure a number of times when Ryan obviously sought Alys out with questions or made it a point to sit beside her during meals.

Although Ryan was attracted to Mam'selle Prévou, he was naively unaware that he'd become the focus of titillating gossip among the senators' wives and the cause for the discomfiture of both his wife and Alys. He had so many questions to ask the farmers and landowners, it seemed only natural for him to stand near her so she could translate. The answers he received stimulated more questions, and it was these he posed to her whenever the group stopped for lunch or dined together at night. As for Janet's morose and brooding manner, he'd become so used to it over the past two years, he didn't realize she had a new reason for her indignant behavior.

While talking to a landowner about replanting his orchard, Ryan stepped backward, tripped over an uprooted stump, fell, and hit his head on the hard ground. He was only momentarily dazed, but when he finally got up, slowly and unsteadily, he was dizzy and unsure of himself. He leaned against another shattered tree and looked around, trying to get his bearings. The people near him appeared frozen in place, and he waited for someone to speak. He felt as if he and the others had remained motionless for a long time, although it was actually for only a second or two.

Seeing the stunned and bewildered look on Ryan's face, Alys's first reaction was one of concern that he'd seriously hurt himself. This was followed immediately by such an overwhelming fear, that she hurriedly moved to stand behind one of the cars so that no one could see how upset and shaken she was. She found herself trying as desperately to bring her emotions under control as she had the night he had walked into the embassy reception room. As much as she had longed for him to recover his memory of those months together, this was neither the time nor the place for it to happen. The confusion and the questions would be more than she could bear. What explanations could they give to these people and most of all to Janet? For the first time since Ryan left her, she found herself praying that memory would not return to him right now.

'Careful, darling,' Janet finally said sarcastically, 'you don't want another concussion. Or do you?'

This was the first overt hint to Ryan that Janet was more than a little angry about either something he'd done or the trip itself. Still somewhat bewildered, Ryan looked around and saw the curiosity and dismay on the faces of the others. 'Sorry, folks,' he said trying to laugh. 'A little family joke. She thinks I might lose my memory – or is it my mind, Janet?'

'Neither, darling,' she said in a saccharine tone for the benefit of the others. 'I would just hate to have an accident spoil this trip and force you to return home before it's over.'

When Alys heard Ryan speak, she collapsed against the side of the car. Thank heavens this interview was nearly over. Hardly knowing what she was saying, she stepped forward to speak to the landowner for the group and assure him, as she had so many others, that his needs had been recorded and would be considered in the report the men would make.

Then she climbed into the front seat of the car, grateful that they had a ride of nearly an hour before she would have to begin interpreting again.

Ryan and Janet went to their room immediately after dinner.

'I don't know,' Ryan said, 'why you had to make that remark about a concussion. At least they took it as a joke. There could have been all sorts of unnecessary questions. My amnesia is no one's business but ours.'

'Ah, yes, the questions. Like just what you really did during those months. You seem to forget there are unanswered questions that bother me too.' She saw the tense look on his face that always foreshadowed an angry outburst, and stopped short of the comment she started to make about his attraction to pretty Belgian women. It would only irritate him further, and she didn't need him irritated right now. Now when she wanted a favor from him. 'I'm sorry, darling.' She went over and put her arms around him. 'It's just that I'm so damned bored. All we see is one farm after another and a few decrepit villages. Nothing of any real interest.'

'It is to me, Janet. It's what I came along for.'

'Is it really?' She started to pout and then remembered that it no longer charmed him. 'I think your walk down memory lane has gone on long enough. It's time to return to the present.' She snuggled against his chest. 'Don't forget your promise to me: to take a few days off and go to Paris. Couldn't we go tomorrow?'

'I said we'd go after the tour is over. There's no way I can leave the group now.' Why couldn't Janet understand that this was a government-sponsored trip? True, the company was paying his way as a contribution to this study on foreign aid, but that still didn't justify his taking off whenever he wanted to. And, dammit, he didn't want to. 'The information we're getting is vitally important to the recommendations I make. Only a few more days and then we'll stay in Paris as long as you like. Will that satisfy you?'

It wasn't the answer Janet wanted. She wanted to get him away from Alys Prévou. She had not been unaware that Ryan had been seeing Louise MacGill before the young woman left for Scotland; and she'd assumed, as had many others, that they were having an affair. Her own affair with Dwight precluded her making an issue over Ryan's relationship with Louise. Ryan might begin to get curious about her own activities when she was ostensibly visiting her family in Aiken or attending horse and dog shows. She did go to those functions, but they were an ideal subterfuge for her rendezvous with Dwight.

The affair had begun the night of the Hunt Ball. While they were dancing, Dwight held her so close she felt him get a hard-on, and the stimulation nearly drove her crazy. Between that and having too much to drink, she found herself being laid in, of all places, the backseat of Dwight's car. In spite of being in an excruciatingly uncomfortable position, she also found it the most exciting, shatteringly erotic, and sexually gratifying experience she'd ever known. She'd intended it to remain a one-night fling. Then Ryan was reported missing in action, and Dwight was on hand to comfort her. The real affair had started then and continued even after Ryan's return.

It wasn't so much that she still needed Dwight as it was the fun in outwitting her staid and oh-so-righteous husband. It was another matter, however, having him flaunt his affairs. The situation with Louise had been one of the reasons Janet decided she'd better begin accompanying Ryan on some of his business trips. And now his paying so much attention to Alys did not suit her at all. Not only was

Alys very like Louise in many ways, she was rather pretty in her own way. It was not a way that Janet found particularly attractive, but then she saw Alys through a woman's eyes, not a man's. The young woman lacked any type of sophistication; she was, in fact, so unworldly as to be almost childlike. And there was something so distastefully foreign about her. Janet didn't think anything serious would come from Ryan's attentions to Alys, but it was humiliating to know that everyone in the group was amused by the way he was flirting with her and ignoring his wife. Janet did not like being made a fool of.

'Please, darling,' she begged. 'Just for a day or two. The others can get the information, and you can go over the reports when you meet them back in Brussels.'

'I'm sorry, Janet. I cannot leave. Cheer up, darling, when all the work is over, we can relax and play tourist to your heart's content. I'll even give you *carte blanche* with those fashion designers you always talk about.'

Janet forced a smile and put up no argument when Ryan indicated he wanted to make love. At least she had one strong point in her favor: she had him in bed with her and she knew how to please him.

At breakfast the next morning, Janet was greeted with loud exclamations from the other wives: 'Janet! We're going to Paris today.'

'What!' Too startled by their outburst to say anything more, she barely heard their words as they explained they would be taking a train in a few hours, spend three days in Paris, and return to Brussels to meet the men.

'There you are, Janet,' Ryan said. 'Your wish has been granted. You didn't need me to take you after all.'

'But it's you I want to be with,' she whispered, maddened by this scuttling of all her well-made plans.

'We'll go later, too,' he said, trying to placate whatever was upsetting her. He was too puzzled at her reaction, after her pleading of the night before, to say anything more.

Dammit, she thought. She didn't want to go now, not with all those silly women. And leave Ryan here with *her*. That was why he was looking so pleased. He'd have four whole days with Alys while she was gone.

'It sounds like fun,' Janet said with strained enthusiasm. There was no way she could stay behind after telling Ryan how bored she was with the tour and how much she wanted to see Paris. 'How soon do we leave?'

In order to keep to their schedule, the men had to resume their tour before the train left for Paris. It was with some relief that Janet saw Ryan get in one car with only a driver while Alys rode with one of the senators. She was also somewhat appeased by the generous letter of credit Ryan gave her when he kissed her good-bye. 'Have a good time,' he said, 'and I'll see you in four days.'

As was her custom when she was with one of these tours, Alys had left her itinerary with Professor Montclair in case there were any need to contact her. There were often letters from her family waiting for her at the various hotels where they stayed. When they arrived at Namur late in the afternoon, she found one note in Minette's childish printing, and a message that she should call the professor immediately.

Ryan was standing by the desk in the hotel when Alys made her call to Liège. He saw her go white; fearing she was going to faint, he walked over to her. He waited until she hung up and then reached out to support her.

'What is it? What's wrong?' He heard her trying to control a sob and felt her body shaking under his touch. 'You've had bad news of some kind, haven't you?'

'It's Amalie. My daughter.' Alys had to swallow a few times before she could go on. As full of sympathy as the professor's voice had been, his words had been more heart-breaking than consoling. She didn't see how she could speak, but she had to let Ryan know wha was wrong. 'She's been rushed to the hospital in Liège. The pro fessor wasn't sure what it is, but if our doctor drove her all the way to Liège, it's serious.'

'Then you have to be there with her,' Ryan said. He led her awa from the desk and to a chair in the lobby.

'How – how can I?' The thought of her precious little Amali dangerously ill in a hospital had Alys struggling for every breath an palsied with fear. She had to get to her, but there seemed no possibl way. She couldn't leave the tour; and even if she could, she had no idea if there were a train from Namur. She began sobbing in spite of her valiant efforts not to.

'You can and you must,' Ryan insisted. 'You need to be with her.' He hurried over to one of the senators and in a moment rushed back to her.

'First I'm getting you a drink. Then we're taking one of the cars, and I'm going with you to Liège. They're going to contact the embassy for another interpreter.'

Alys said nothing while he led her to the bar and she finished the brandy he handed her. 'Thank you. I'll accept the car, but there's no need for you to go with me.'

'Yes there is. I insist. You can't make the trip with just the driver. You may need me in Liège, too.'

Alys was too weary and distraught to argue with him. The professor had said that because of having to stay with Minette and being busy with the inn, neither of her parents had been able to accompany Amalie and Dr. Lavolie.

Not until she was in the car did Alys allow herself to break down and cry. Nor did she resist when Ryan put his arms around her and tried to comfort her.

Oh, God, Ryan, she thought. You don't know how it feels to be in your arms again. This is where I belong. And it's going to have to end in a few days. Just like before. I'll lose you for a second time.

Then all her thoughts turned to Amalie. So tiny. So precious. So young to be suffering, and from what? That was what terrified her now. If only Professor Montclair had been able to tell her what was wrong. In spite of her worry and fears, her crying gradually became a quiet sobbing; and exhausted, she fell asleep in Ryan's arms.

Liège, Ryan thought, I'm finally getting to Liège.

But how different this trip was from the way he'd earlier imagined it. Poor Alys, worn out with worry and exhaustion. But at least she'd finally fallen asleep. Her needs were his first concern now. After all this time, he could wait a few more days before contacting Dr. Barré. Ryan felt himself shaking with excitement and anticipation at the thought, and he braced himself against the back of the seat for fear the tremors might disturb Alys. But nothing could control his soaring spirits at the realization that he would at long last have those lost months revealed to him.

CHAPTER TWENTY-SEVEN

Alys and Ryan were met at the hospital by Dr. Lavolie from Ste. Monique and Dr. Boyer, a surgeon on the hospital staff.

Amalie was being treated for peritonitis following a ruptured appendix. If it hadn't been for Ryan's supporting arm around her shoulder, Alys would have fainted. All during the two doctors' explanations of how Amalie had seemed to have only a slight, typical childhood fever the night before and Dr. Lavolie's treating her for a minor infection, Alys kept hearing the dread word 'peritonitis' over and over again. Not until Amalie began screaming in pain during the night had anyone been alerted to the idea of appendicitis. By the time Dr. Lavolie arrived at the hospital in Liège, the appendix had ruptured and peritonitis had set in.

'We're treating her now with drugs,' Dr. Boyer assured her. 'But I won't burden you with false hopes. She's not out of danger yet.'

Alys gave no thought to the tears streaming down her face. She felt rather than saw Ryan wiping them off with his handkerchief.

'May I see her?'

'Of course,' Dr. Boyer said. 'She's resting now, under sedation, but you can stay with her.'

Alys followed the doctors into the semidarkness of Amalie's room. She looked down onto the bed where the little girl lay asleep. A long, slim tube ran from under the sheet, and Alys had to turn her face away. She knew it was draining the poisonous infection which must be completely eliminated before the surgeon could operate. Only a small incision had been needed for the tube, but the thought of even a minute cut on that tiny body brought Alys close to hysteria. Beneath the feverish flush on Amalie's face, she saw the deathly pale skin. She listened fearfully to the labored breathing. Amalie was fighting to live, and Alys was well aware how tough a fight it would be.

You can't die, little one, Alys prayed. *You're much, much too precious to me.*

Once again she felt Ryan's arm go around her shoulders, and she was grateful for his strength.

Amalie remained asleep, but now and then Alys heard little mewings of pain followed by soft sobs and shuddering sighs. There were tears coming from under the little girl's eyelids. Each time Alys leaned over the crib, but all she could do was hold Amalie's hand and sob, 'My baby, my baby,' and feel the hurt deep inside.

She remembered the pain of giving birth to Amalie. But a mother's pain for a child in pain is a much greater agony. Birth pangs can be endured because they are bringing life. But Amalie's pain might end in death. Her fears for Amalie – and the thought of losing her – completely vitiated whatever ability she'd had up to now to remain calm. Only Ryan's hands holding her shaking ones kept her from giving way completely.

How ironic, she thought, that he should be there trying to comfort her, while being completely unaware that Amalie was his daughter, too. How ironic and how tragic that he didn't realize it was his own child who was struggling with the insidious infection that threatened her life. The temptation to tell him was overwhelming, but she resisted giving in to it.

In a few minutes, Dr. Lavolie returned and suggested she might like to rest a bit. There was an empty bed down the hall she could use. She begged to stay with Amalie, but Dr. Boyer said a little more strongly that she would have to leave soon while he examined Amalie.

Alys couldn't decide whether it was his way of seeing to it that she did go and rest or whether there was some treatment for Amalie he didn't want her to see. Despite the many disagreeable and difficult and painful tasks that Alys had done for the wounded, she could never watch her own daughter being treated without becoming emotional.

During all this time, Ryan had watched the changing expressions on Alys's face and wondered what she was thinking. She was frightened for her daughter, but he couldn't help thinking that something more was worrying her. If only she felt close enough to tell him. But then, he was merely an acquaintance, and one she'd known for a very short time. He bent down and said quietly, 'I'll be back by the time you have to leave the room.'

Ten minutes later, when Alys walked into the small waiting room at the end of the hall, she saw Ryan sitting in a large, overstuffed chair. He motioned for her to sit in a similar chair on the other side of the other table beside him.

With no preamble, he said, 'You need something to eat. We never did get dinner.'

He began emptying paper bags on the table and spreading the bags themselves for plates.

'Thank you,' Alys said, 'but I couldn't swallow anything right now. I'm choking clear up to here.' She put her hand under her chin.

'You must. We may have a long wait before there's any real change in Amalie's condition.'

Alys heard the 'we,' and it brought tears to her eyes. Again she came dangerously close to telling him the truth. Perhaps it was his right to know that he'd fathered a child. Perhaps if she didn't tell him they'd been married, the trauma would be less severe for both him and Janet. She had to remember that Ryan was married, and been married before coming overseas, and it was imperative she do nothing to endanger or rupture that marriage. She thought about Janet Middleton and her possessive attitude toward Ryan. No, she couldn't tell him. He'd leave in a few days, and she'd never see him again. Better for Amalie to remain her secret.

All the while that Ryan was laying out the slices of bread, cold ham, and cheese, he wondered if he should be feeling guilty about being here with Alys when he'd refused to go to Paris with Janet. No, the circumstances were completely different. Janet's request had been a selfish whim. With Alys he was fulfilling a real need. He tried to suppress the feeling that, in truth, he really wanted to be with Alys. He opened the bottle of wine and filled the two glasses.

Alys looked at the freshly baked, crusty bread, with a warm yeasty aroma still clinging to it, the thin sliced ham, and the smooth cheese. She wasn't really hungry, but Ryan was right in saying she should eat. Maybe the wine would stimulate her appetite.

'If only Dr. Lavolie would bring us some word,' she said fearfully.

'He will when he can.'

Alys closed her eyes and found herself assailed by all the pungent, antiseptic and sickly sweet odors typical of a hospital. The very sterility of the place seemed to imbue it more with the quality of death than life. A nurse walked past with a vase of faded flowers, and the rotten smell of stems long immersed in water was nauseating. Alys took another sip of wine, and she held the glass to her lips long enough to inhale the tangy bouquet and clear the odors from her nostrils. She followed the first glass with a second and a third. Usually wine perked her up, but tonight she was beginning to feel drowsy.

Seeing Alys nodding, Ryan leaned toward her. 'Why don't you lie down on the couch for a little while? You'll feel much better.'

'No, I might fall asleep. I want to be awake if Amalie wakes up or Dr. Lavolie has some word.'

'Just close your eyes and rest. If you do fall asleep, I'll wake you if there's a reason. I know how badly you want to be with Amalie when she's awake.'

Determined to do no more than rest, Alys lay down on the couch. For Ryan's sake, she pretended to be asleep. She heard him ask a nurse for a blanket, and she felt him gently laying it over her. But her mind was in a turmoil. Memories of the first night she and Ryan made love, the afternoon he proposed, and her wedding day swirled through her brain too rapidly for her to catch hold of them and keep them with her. She lived again through the realization of being pregnant and the moment of Amalie's birth. Then she was smote by an overpowering sense of guilt. She should never have come to Liège and left the little girls at home. It had been pure selfishness on her part to abdicate her role as mother and pursue her studies at the university. Especially since she was devoting more time to earning money than she was to those studies.

So she had been unhappy and depressed. She'd received no written guarantee when she was born that life would be all joy and delight. It wasn't written on her birth certificate that she'd never know unhappiness. She had the little girls, and they should have been enough for her. And they would be enough, if only Amalie would live. Oh God, let her live!

Scarcely realizing it, her memories became dreams, and then she fell into a deep sleep.

Dr. Lavolie came out one time, but only to say that Amalie was still sedated and there'd been no appreciable change in her condition. On the positive side, it did mean she was holding her own. On the negative side, it meant they were still fighting the infection. He nodded approvingly at Alys asleep on the couch.

'The nights are always the worst,' Dr. Lavolie said as he lit up a cigarette. 'I don't know why, but fevers go up, pain increases, and fears multiply. I seldom have emergencies during the day. Always at night.'

'Man's basic fear of the dark?' Ryan suggested.

'But would the body know that? Perhaps. Anyway, there should be a change in a few hours. With the dawn, the crisis, whichever way it goes, will be past. So, I'm going back to our patient. Maybe I'll have good news in the morning, or even before then.'

'I'll be right here,' Ryan said.

'You try to rest, too.'

Ryan nodded. The doctor didn't have to tell him that Alys might need his even stronger support the next day if Amalie didn't respond to treatment and pass through the crisis successfully. He put his head against the back of the soft chair. Memories of having to stand watch during the war flooded over him. Two hours on, two hours off. He'd learned to wake up automatically after exactly two hours of sleep. He could do it again. He allowed himself to doze off. Two hours later, by the clock on the opposite wall, he woke up. Alys was still sleeping. There'd been no word from the doctor. He stayed awake for little less than an hour, then set his mental alarm clock again. He continued this routine throughout the night. Twice he started to go to Amalie's room and then thought better of it. If there were any important word, the doctor would bring it.

At a few minutes before seven, Ryan woke up completely refreshed. Coffee would find him fully awake. He looked over at Alys. As heartbreaking as the situation was, he envied her the little girl in the hospital bed. His longing for a child had taunted him when he watched her sitting by the bed, holding Amalie's hand, and wishing for her to wake up. The room had been so flooded by love, it was almost palpable. The love for a woman was important in a man's life, but the love for one's own child must be something very special. And the love one received in return. It wasn't fair that such a longing wasn't being gratified, that he was being deprived of what should be a most important part of his life.

He saw Alys stirring. Hurriedly he put on his coat and slipped quietly out of the waiting room. When he returned a few minutes later with coffee and hot rolls, she was no longer there, and he felt a sense of panic. Had Amalie passed through the crisis or had she been lost to it? Why in hell had he left just at the moment Alys might need him the most? He put the coffee and rolls on the table and ran as quietly as he could down the hall.

Without entering, he looked into the room. All he saw was Alys weeping in Dr. Lavolie's arms. Ryan retreated a few paces along the hall. As much as he'd wanted to be the one comforting Alys during her sorrow, he knew he didn't really belong in the room. He meant no more to her than a kind, recently met friend who had brought her here. Dr. Lavolie was a longtime friend from her childhood, as well as her doctor. He'd stay in the waiting room only in case Alys needed something and then he'd leave. He was heading toward the waiting room when Dr. Boyer came out and hurried to walk beside him.

'Wouldn't you like to go back to the room?' the surgeon asked him. 'Amalie is awake. I'm sure Madame Prévou would like you to be with her.'

'Awake!' Ryan had not at first grasped what the surgeon was saying.

'Yes, thanks be to God. She passed the crisis about six this morning, and her fever has been coming steadily down ever since.'

'Thank you, doctor. Thank you!' He turned and sped back to the room.

Alys was sitting in a leather wing chair and cradling Amalie in her arms. The white blanket around Amalie fell in soft folds over Alys's lap. Ryan wished he were a painter able to capture that moment on canvas. Tears were still streaming down Alys's face, but they could in no way diminish the brilliant smile and beatific expression. The scene was one of love and joy and tenderness incarnate.

Alys looked up and saw Ryan standing in the doorway. 'Look, Ryan, she's smiling. Come in and see what a beautiful little girl I have.'

He walked in and pulled up a smaller chair so he could sit beside them. 'She is, Alys. She's very beautiful.' When he looked at Alys again, he saw an expression that puzzled him. Beneath the joy of having Amalie out of danger was a hint of pathos. The expression was not there when her glance rested on Amalie, only when she looked up at him. It was almost as if she'd seen inside his heart and was feeling sorry for him. No, he was imagining things. It was his own frustration infecting his imagination.

She could never let him know, Alys was thinking. He'd comforted her the day before when she was in despair and now he was sharing her happiness, but she had to let him return to the States without ever knowing that Amalie was his child. If there were some way, she continued thinking, without causing trouble and complications, she would; but she knew there wasn't. Janet would never accept any explanation she offered. If Janet were a warm, loving person, she might have reconsidered, but she'd seen the woman's jealousy. Janet might be vindictive enough never to allow Ryan to see his daughter. That would be a greater tragedy than his not knowing.

'They're operating this afternoon,' she said. 'The infection is gone and they need to remove the damaged appendix.'

'I'll be right here with you,' he assured her.

Strange, she thought, how ambivalent she'd gradually been able to make her feelings toward him. She was able to speak to Ryan as someone she'd only recently met. Yet at the same time he was the man she loved and would always love. The words she would say to a lover and husband must remain inside of her while she conversed with the friend.

The surgery began on Amalie at five o'clock. Alys watched the clock in the waiting room tick off the seconds, each one seeming several minutes long. The delicate surgery could not be hurried, but surely it should be over by now. Then she looked at the clock again and saw that only fifteen minutes had passed. Finally another fifteen went by and then another. Ryan tried to occupy her with light conversation, but she only shook her head. Nothing must take her mind off Amalie in the operating room. When this was over, she would never be separated from Amalie and Minette again.

After little more than an hour, Dr. Lavolie came in to tell them the surgery was successful. Dr. Boyer was scrubbing for another operation, but he would see them later in the evening. Amalie was in the recovery room and would be there for several hours. There was no cause for alarm, however; such close observation was routine with children as young as she.

Ryan waited while Alys followed the doctor to the door of the recovery room.

Alys peered through the window. Amalie looked so much smaller and more fragile on the large recovery bed than she had in the hospital crib. The sides were up so she wouldn't fall off, and she reminded Alys of the premmies she'd seen in the maternity ward. Amalie's skin was still very pale, and her eyelids fluttered from time to time as if she were trying to return to the world.

'She's fine,' Dr. Lavolie reassured Alys again. 'She's doing very well. She'll probably be back in her room by eleven. I'll leave orders for you to be allowed in. And bring your nice young man with you. I like him.'

So do I, Alys thought. *Oh, how much I like him.*

Now that Amalie was recovering, Ryan insisted that Alys have dinner with him. He'd already selected the restaurant. Instead of one large dining room, the Maison Havart consisted of several small rooms with only a few tables in each. Ryan had immediately liked the intimacy and privacy these afforded. In each was a fireplace, with glowing fires now that autumn evenings were getting cooler. The fireplace in the dining room to which they were led was faced with blue delft tiles.

After looking at the menu, Alys said she wanted only soup and an entrée, but Ryan ignored her wishes. Studying the wine list along with the menu, he told the waitress that with onion soup they would have Moët and Chandon Brut Imperial champagne, 1928; with broiled trout, a Château Olivier 1943; with beef roulade, a Château Margaux 1934; and with chocolate mousse for dessert, a Chateau d'Yquem 1921. Then he looked up at Alys and grinned as if daring her to say a word about his selections.

Alys couldn't help but smile back at the high-handed way he'd taken over. She sat back and let Ryan light a cigarette for her.

He looked across the table at her, and she appeared to be relaxing at last. She was far prettier than he'd thought at first. She had changed at the hospital from her beige suit into a softly flowered silk he hadn't seen before. Other evenings on the tour she'd worn a very smart but rather austere-looking black crepe. He knew it was sophisticated, but somehow it wasn't Alys. The rose-hued flowers put color into her cheeks, and the large ruffled collar framing the V-neck softened the lines of strain in her face. The double strand of pearls glowed against her skin.

In order to take her mind off Amalie, Ryan searched around in his mind for something else to talk about. The work of the group they'd been with seemed like an obvious subject. It was soon apparent, however, that Alys's mind was totally involved with her concern for Amalie. Maybe he'd been wrong to insist she come out for dinner.

Alys knew she was being rude not to be more responsive when Ryan had taken such pains with the dinner and was trying to keep her from worrying about Amalie. She couldn't tell him it was he, not Amalie, on whom her thoughts were concentrated. She was thinking about the last time they'd had dinner together. In the kitchen at the inn. Not a splendid dinner, but a bowl of *pot au feu* and some hot, crusty bread. How happy they'd been then. The whole future before them. No thoughts of his leaving. Afterward they'd walked to the river, basking in the glow of a brilliant sunset and their own love for each other. Minette had given him a flower she'd picked, and he'd said he would cherish it forever. Like the flower, all her hopes and dreams had been allowed to wither and become lost.

Ryan finally broke through the silence by saying, 'I have another reason for wanting to spend some time over here. I fought from one end of Belgium to the other. Now I'd like to see it without being shot at.'

Alys found herself waiting with total concentration to hear what he would tell her about his experiences. This could be getting into dangerous territory, and yet it was what she'd been anticipating since he walked into the embassy reception room.

'Were you wounded?' This seemed like a normal question for someone to ask.

'I was wounded in Luxemburg, but I actually ended up in Belgium.'

Alys found her breath coming faster and her heart beating more rapidly. She couldn't help but wonder if there were a chance, even the slightest chance, he was beginning to remember.

'It's a confusing story,' Ryan continued. 'One minute I was being shelled and nearly run over by tanks, and the next thing I knew, I was standing on a road near a river. But that was several months later. I had no memory of how I'd gotten to Belgium or what went on during those intervening months. I don't know whether I was more bewildered or frightened. But I do know this: those lost months have continued to haunt me. I'd like to know where I was and who I was with.'

So, Alys thought, he was still concerned enough about that period to talk about it. And he wanted to know. This might be the moment Dr. Barré had told her about. Yet, what was it exactly the doctor had said? Not just that he would want to know, but that it would be important for a place or a person or an event to bring it back to him. But no one could do it for him. Telling him would not be enough. It could also be extremely traumatic and dangerous for him to be suddenly faced with someone from his past. No, it was not quite the right time yet.

'As much as I want to know what happened during those months,' Ryan continued, 'I have more of a need to recapture something that is missing in my life right now.' He paused and seemed to be reaching into his mind for something. 'A sense of peace and belonging. I think if I can find that, I'll be content to return home. Perhaps it will be a hopeless search, but I have to try.'

And if he found it, Alys thought, he would be content to return home. She had to remember that, as well as the fact he was married.

'Maybe,' she finally said, 'you'll find that past you're looking for, but I hope you won't be sorry if you do. Maybe it's hidden because it should stay hidden. Your subconscious might be wiser than you are.'

Ryan was startled by her odd response. 'You sound as if you're telling me I shouldn't look.'

'Sometimes it's better for the past to remain buried. I've told you about my two daughters. I lost their father near the end of the war. It took me a long time to convince myself it's better to focus on the future. The past is over; it can't be brought back.'

'Yes,' Ryan said. 'We have an American writer, Thomas Wolfe, who said much the same thing: "You can't go home again." '

'I know, I've heard of him. Some feel it's a gloomy, pessimistic thought. I don't. I think it's a very positive belief. It's better to look ahead. Dante had one group in Hades walking with their heads looking backward. The fortune tellers. He had his particular reasons for punishing them in that way; but I've often thought that if we spend our time looking backward, we're punishing ourselves. And we're denying ourselves the excitement of waiting to see what each day is going to bring.'

Ryan nodded. 'It's something to think about. But,' he added, smiling, 'I shall continue to look.'

The dessert had been set before them, and Alys indulged herself with hedonistic delight in the chocolate mousse and the sauterne. Ryan had done what he'd set out to do; take her mind off Amalie. Unknowingly, however, he'd replaced those worries with a more acute awareness of how desperately lonely she would be when he returned to the States. Not merely lonely and distraught; but, having been made aware again of how much she loved him, depleted of all hope that they would ever be together as they once were. It would be better for both of them if his search proved fruitless, if he never learned the truth. She was certain now that only tragedy for both of them would result if he did.

They walked quietly back to the hospital where a bed had been put in Amalie's room for her. Both would have been surprised to learn that the thoughts of each were concentrated on the other. Alys was disconsolate at the thought of saying good-bye on Ryan and losing him for a second time. Nor was she any more prepared than she had been the first time. She thought about Amalie. The little girl could be the means of forging a lifelong bond between Ryan and herself, and again she was tempted to tell him, with the argument that it was his right to know. She fought with her conscience all the way to the hospital, and decided finally, once and for all, that it would be better to disappear from his life completely. This time she would accept that she'd never see him again.

Ryan glanced down at Alys, who seemed absorbed in her own silence. Once again he was puzzled by her resemblance to the young woman he'd seen from the window when he was being held on house-arrest. Several times in the past few days he had noted the similarity of their features. Today, he was more than puzzled; he was convinced Alys was the woman he'd seen crying. Her reasons for denying it when he'd asked her the first morning were her own and not for him to tamper with; nevertheless, the mystery tantalized him. Mysteries intrigued him, but only if he could eventually solve them, or have them solved for him.

Just before they reached the hospital, Alys looked up and smiled at him. Another picture, with the speed of a camera shutter, flashed through his mind: the picture of a young woman seated on the grass with a wreath of flowers in her hair. Just as quickly the image was gone. Louise had insisted that she reminded him of someone he'd once loved, and now Alys seemed to be doing the same thing; at least reminding him of someone he'd known, and probably during those lost months. He had to stay in Belgium; he had to clear up the mystery of those months before he could settle down to a normal life in Camden and to a better marriage with Janet. If flashes of memory were the elusive fruit of Tantalus, there must be a way to pluck them and keep them from disappearing out of reach again. He would put his mind to discovering a way to extend his stay in Belgium.

Telling Alys he'd see her in the morning before he left for Brussels, Ryan left her at the hospital and spent the night in a nearby hotel.

CHAPTER TWENTY-EIGHT

When Ryan arrived at the hospital in the morning, he saw Alys standing in the hallway with an elderly couple and another man. It was with obvious affection that Alys introduced Professor and Madame Montclair. Ryan recognized immediately that they were the couple with whom she was living and that the professor was her much-loved mentor. Although she introduced Kenneth Winston as a friend from the English legation, it was immediately apparent to Ryan, from the casual and familiar way the young man put his arm around Alys's waist, that Mr. Winston considered himself something more than a friend. Acknowledging the introduction Ryan winced at Kenneth's cavalier attitude while explaining that unfortunately he'd been in England when Amalie became ill and how very much he appreciated Ryan's being there with Alys.

Ryan had lain awake most of the night before, beguiled by haunting images of Alys: Alys holding Amalie in the hospital, Alys smiling at him across the table in the restaurant, Alys clinging to him when Amalie was so desperately ill. When he did sleep, he dreamed of her, sitting alone by a river, surrounded by flowers, and looking wistfully toward the hills beyond as if waiting for someone.

Standing with Alys now in the hospital corridor, he realized that any hopes of seeing her again were as ephemeral as his dreams of her. When she impulsively hugged him while thanking him for all he'd done, he had to force back a momentary desire to stay at least another day. Instead, he made some inane remarks about hoping all would go well for her in the future and how much he'd enjoyed meeting her. Then he fled like a schoolboy too embarrassed to ask the prettiest girl in class for a date.

Dispirited by his rather awkward and ignominious leavetaking, Ryan walked along the street with his head down. It was an unusual posture for Ryan, who usually strode along, head high, self-assured, and ready to take on the world. He would probably never see Alys again. There was no reason why he should, except that he was attracted to her by a strange and inexplicable magnetism.

While he was shaving that morning, he had decided to see her at the hospital, make certain everything was all right with Amalie, ask Alys to have dinner with him again that night, and then go look up Dr. Barré at the university. Well, part of that plan had been shot down, but he could still pursue the reason he'd wanted to come to Liège in the first place.

Ryan consulted his map of the city and found he was only a few blocks from the university. After starting off at a brisk pace, he gradually slowed his steps. He remembered Alys's words from the night before; 'Maybe your subconscious is wiser than you are.' As much as he wanted to know, he'd often been disturbed by similar thoughts. To make such a journey back in time might take him into areas best left unexplored. He was not afraid of the physical or emotional pain such an odyssey might reveal, but he hesitated about meeting the Ryan Middleton who'd lived those five months in another guise. Anonymity itself often anesthetized inhibitions and allowed man's baser nature to emerge. How much more potent could be the anonymity of amnesia? What dark forces in his own nature might he have revealed?

He passed a small *brasserie*, paused, and retraced his steps. Once inside he sat at a small round table and ordered a cognac. While he sipped the smooth liqueur, he tried to recall what little he had learned about those five months. To his surprise, he knew more than he'd realized, and he could surmise a good bit more. He'd been wounded, and the amnesia had resulted from either a severe concussion or emotional stress or both. He'd had aphasia and been unable to speak. The family who'd taken him in had known he was a soldier. That much he knew from evidence presented at the court-martial.

But then came the questions that had so long puzzled him. When he'd regained his memory on the road to Liège, he was no longer in uniform and he had no identification of any kind. The being in strange pants and shirt was less disturbing than the missing dog tags. When and why had they been removed?

Ryan ordered another cognac and began recalling all he'd read about those months in Europe before the war ended. Having had almost a fanatic compulsion to learn what had occurred, he'd read every publication he could find and seen every movie that appeared about those last desperate months before the Allies finally defeated Germany. Now certain incidents began coming to mind. During the thrust of the German counterattack, prisoners and wounded soldiers as well as innocent civilians had been massacred at places like Trois Ponts, Malmédy, and other Belgian towns. Ryan now tried to recreate the situation of the people who'd taken him in. What had they already suffered and what fears beset them while they had in their home a wounded American officer?

They must have kept him hidden somehow and destroyed all evidence of his being with them. That would account for the disappearance of the uniform and identification. He'd spent enough nights himself in French and Belgian basements, sometimes with the families, to be able to visualize all of them huddled together for safety while fighting went on in the streets above them and shells exploded all around. He also knew how Germans searched the houses in the towns they captured.

An overwhelming sense of gratitude engulfed Ryan. Now it was less important that he learn about himself than that he find those people and thank them for saving his life.

One point, though, continued to disturb him: why hadn't they wanted him to know who they were? He thought about the young woman who had traveled to Liège and what Sergeant Stevens had told him about her. She had been concerned enough to want the authorities to know where he'd been and what his condition was during all those months. She had also made an attempt to contact the military authorities earlier by way of a major, who for some inexplicable reason had failed to enter a report. She had cared enough to do those things and yet had made no attempt to see him while he was under room-arrest.

Ryan shook his head. It could well be exactly what Dr. Barré had indicated in his letter. They were proud, caring people who didn't want to be overwhelmed by effusions of gratitude nor be repaid for what they had done. Remembering that Dr. Barré had invited him to call if ever Ryan were in Liège, any fears he'd had about coming face to face with the Ryan of those months seemed unfounded. If his benefactors still wished to remain anonymous, Ryan would accede to their wishes. Perhaps Dr. Barré could tell him much of what he wanted to know. He had to learn as much as he could. It had been his memory he'd lost, not an arm or leg, but he would still be less than a whole person until some part of that memory was restored.

Having paid for the cognac, he once again headed for the university. At the main office he walked resolutely in and asked where Dr. Barré's office was and if it would be possible to see him at this time. It was then, however, that he received another devastating shock. Dr. Barré had died a few months earlier from a massive coronary. The young woman behind the desk was sorry, but was there another professor Ryan would like to see?

'No, no thank you. I – that is – he is the only one who could give me the information I want.'

He turned and strode out of the building. A heavy chilling rain was falling, and it had turned the pleasantly brisk autumn day into a dank, blustery precursor of winter. The sky was gray and weighted with ponderous black clouds. Ryan was reminded of similar days when he'd slogged along country roads during the war; and the thick, gray, clinging mud had turned army boots into leaden hobbles.

He thought again about Dr. Barré's wire and the court-martial. The sergeant who had recalled Dr. Barré's visit – and was thus the catalyst for bringing about his acquittal – had said that the young woman's deposition had been lost. Now Dr. Barré was dead. All Ryan's contacts with his past were gone. He sighed despondently. He now had to accept that fate did not intend for him to find those five lost months. Or did he? Ryan had never been one to give up. He had not given up when he was determined to head his class at Yale. In spite of a near fatal bout with flu and then pneumonia that had kept him bedridden for weeks, he had defied the rules and studied when he was supposed to be sleeping. And he had been graduated number one. He had not given up on the beach at Normandy or after the German counterattack on the Our River. He would not give up on this. Somewhere, someday, he would find what he sought. It might be the result of his patient looking, or it might be a fortuitous word or happenstance, but it was there waiting for him.

* * *

Alys watched Ryan walk away, and she wanted to weep. It had been too cruel of fate to torment her by bringing him back into her life for only a few days only to immediately snatch him away. If she hadn't seen him again, she might have been satisfied to marry Kenneth and live a comfortable if unexciting life moving from one legation or embassy to another. Now, if she did accept him, it would be from desperation, not any hope of real happiness. Minette and Amalie needed a home with someone who would be like a father to them, and Kenneth could provide both. She herself needed security, if not from a man she loved, then from someone who loved her and would be good to her.

Marriage, however, would have to wait at least a year. She was quite determined to finish her studies. At the moment, however, neither studies nor marriage occupied her mind for long. Having said good-bye to the Montclairs and telling Kenneth she would see him in the evening, she returned to Amalie's room to keep her vigil by the little girl, who had gone back to sleep after a light breakfast.

Here before her, Alys thought, was one of the two real reasons for living. Their happiness was far more important than hers and must always come first. She was more determined than ever to have them with her in Liège. As soon as Amalie was recovered enough to travel, they'd go to Ste. Monique for a few days' visit and then return together. Nor would there be any more tours with visiting Americans and English. Professor Montclair had said he could get her a position as his graduate assistant. With that and her translating at night, she would be able to have a small apartment. Most important of all, she could have the girls with her. Madame Montclair had given her the name of an elderly woman, a retired nurse, who would be willing to stay with the children during the day for a minimal amount. All Madame LeClerc wanted was enough to add to her pension for a few small luxuries.

Amalie woke up and smiled at her mother with the smile that always turned Alys's heart upside down. At least this precious reminder of her love for Ryan had not been lost to her. There was already a little color in Amalie's cheeks and a devilish glint in her eyes that said she would soon be impatient to get out of bed.

Both Minette and Amalie were sensitive children, easily hurt and quickly responsive to love and affection. Whereas Minette was the more serious of the two – a real little sobersides sometimes – Amalie was the comedienne. If Minette misbehaved, she would wait fearfully for the reprimand she knew was coming. Amalie, on the other hand, would grin and put the stolen cookie or the torn sweater behind her back and dare anyone to say she'd done something wrong. When Minette did have to be chastised, she would accept it stoically and then retreat to someplace where she could be by herself until she could return to the others with no indication that she'd suffered from the punishment. Amalie would simply scream loud and long for a minute or two and then laugh and return to her play.

The separation from them while she'd been in Liège had probably been hardest on Minette. She'd had her mother all to herself for three years before Amalie came along. From the beginning she'd adored her baby sister, and she'd never seemed jealous of her in any way. There had been signs, however, that she'd resented her mother's coming to Liège and leaving her behind. With Amalie there would be perhaps the need to wean her away from her grandparents on whom she'd depended all these past months. Kenneth would have to understand that she needed to be with both of them as much as possible. She would not be able to see him every night, and the girls must come to accept him before she would consider marrying him.

Now that she had those thoughts settled in her mind. Alys picked up the book of fairy tales the Montclairs had brought and began reading to Amalie. Amalie was content to listen for a short while and then she wanted to hold the book herself and look at the pictures. She much perferred to pretend she was reading to herself than to have someone read to her.

During the ride from Liège to Brussels, Ryan let the driver concentrate on the road. He himself was far too busy formulating plans in his mind to pay much attention to the scenery they passed. If his proposals were to be accepted, he had a great deal to do before the senators arrived and the women returned from Paris.

Accepting that Dr. Barré's death meant that he would now have to search out his past by himself, Ryan had begun mulling over a number of alternative proposals for remaining in Belgium. Try as he could to concentrate on them logically, to weigh the pros and cons from a rational point of view, he found his thoughts dominated as much by Alys as by his need to learn about his months of amnesia. At first he saw her as one of many Belgian women he'd seen: the husbands dead, left to rear children alone, forced to earn their own living, still suffering from the traumas of the war in a way American women had not had to suffer. These women, as well as all the men he'd talked to, were the reasons he felt a desperate need to find some way to atone for what the war had done to their country.

Almost from the beginning, two cogent and irrefutably plausible projects had emerged. The Middleton company had long been considering building a farm implement factory in Europe. What better place for it than Belgium? The building of it and then the employing of Belgian workers would aid the economy tremendously; and in turn would be the foreign investment the Middleton accountants had been advising. Looking for the right location for the plant would justify his staying in Europe for several months. Surely by that time he would either have learned something about the lost months or would have to be satisfied to return home.

The second project held much more appeal for him, but it rested precariously on two vital contingencies: the office's approval of his decision to oversee the building of the Belgian plant and American willingness to send aid. He wanted very much to see that such aid was distributed with judicious planning, not political expediency.

Either or both projects would require his traveling extensively throughout Belgium; and it was his idea to explore every village, every foot of the countryside in hopes of finding the places that as of now were merely brief, kaleidoscopic images in his brain. In spite of rational arguments to the contrary, he had an almost mystical feeling that Alys might provide an important clue to the mystery of those lost months. A fleeting expression on her face when he didn't appear to be looking at her, a hesitation about answering certain questions; and, most important of all, her strange insistence that perhaps it would be wiser for him not to try to return to the past had him both mystified and expectant. He wanted to believe that even if she hadn't known him before, she at least knew something about him that she didn't want to reveal. If that were so, the mystery now had the added intricacy of an enigma: what was it she knew and why was she unwilling to reveal it?

For most of the next day, he was on the transatlantic phone to his father in Camden and closeted with a number of embassy officials. Augustus Middleton's response was a conservative suggestion that Ryan investigate possible sites for the plant. When he had a number to report on, they could discuss further the feasibility of building the plant. Meanwhile, they would also need to consider the availability of raw materials as well as the outlook for European markets and methods of distribution.

Ryan concurred, saying he could be considering those at the same time he was exploring locations. With a sigh of relief and a heightened sense of exultation, Ryan placed the receiver in its cradle. He felt like a wild animal must who's been freed from the cage in which it's been pacing back and forth with no hope of release from confinement. Time, that most valuable of incorporeal commodities, had been gifted him not on a silver salver but by way of a thin wire that stretched from his hand to that of his father. Time to seek out five months that most people had now allowed to slip unmemorably into history; months that had been discarded as one discards an out-of-date calendar; but months that haunted him like an unrepented act that must be atoned for. If only there were one other person for whom those months had some special meaning. If there were, he had the uncanny feeling some inexplicable, ethereal magnetism would draw them together.

With the one project approved, Ryan now waited with exquisite anticipation to talk to the senators. Embassy officials had listened to his request to help supervise any distribution of aid granted by Congress and had enthusiastically agreed to do what they could to have him appointed to such a position. When the senators did return, they assured Ryan that they were going to recommend aid for Belgium and would certainly submit his name as one to be considered. The fact of his being in Belgium for the family company would weigh heavily in his favor.

The response from Janet when he told her he was remaining in Belgium for several months was something quite different.

'Don't try to tell me,' she raged, 'that you're staying over here for a year in order to establish a new plant. Or supervise assistance to the farmers. It's that woman. You want to be with her. I knew you couldn't wait to get your hands on her as soon as I was out of the way.'

'Careful, Janet,' Ryan warned. 'Don't say anything you'll be sorry for.'

'Sorry! There's nothing I could say I'd be sorry for.'

'Then will you at least listen to me?' At last she quieted down, and he was able to explain that in the first place his office would be in Brussels, not Liège. And in the second place, Alys Prévou was not interested in him; she was seeing a member of the English legation. 'So you see, my dear, you have completely misjudged both of us. I did not have an affair with her while you were in Paris. We spent most of the time sitting in a hospital waiting room.'

Janet was somewhat mollified as regards Alys, but less so about remaining with Ryan in Belgium.

'All right,' she said, 'you stay. This is where you've wanted to be since you came home. As if the years here were the only important ones in your life.'

'Not the most important ones,' but he wondered even as he denied her accusation if maybe she were right. Was it because during those years he had learned not only the value of life itself but also of making that life have meaning? Not so much of being thankful for having been given life; not so much of having to repay a debt to whatever creator had endowed him with a body, a mind, and a soul, of exchanging value for value, but of never mistaking the dross of pettiness and greed for the pure gold of selflessness and generosity.

'No, not the most important ones,' he repeated, 'but ones that gave me an insight into aspects of the world I didn't like very much. I recognized I had finally left my secure, sheltered world and would have to learn to accept that knowledge. I watched a sixteen-year-old boy die on the beach, and he'd never fired a shot. He was a scapegoat to a world gone mad. I ate K rations while people at home gorged on black-market beef. I had socks and shoes freeze to my feet because there weren't shoe packs for us, and then I read about all the new, illegal shoes you were buying. Have you ever gone months without brushing your teeth? Or craved a Coca-Cola on a blistering hot afternoon while lying facedown in a patch of stinging nettles to keep from being shot? I did. But then I realized there are probably millions of people who, for other reasons, never brush their teeth, and it no longer seems so terrible. And there are people who are dying from thirst for lack of water, and I felt sorry for myself because I couldn't have the soft drink I'd always taken for granted would be in the refrigerator.

'So,' he continued, 'I do feel the need to be doing something of value. Supervising whatever aid is sent over here will be that. Then, too, what I'll be doing for the company is vital. I wouldn't be staying if I didn't think I was needed here.'

'You are? Or does your ego need it? You'll be the big-shot supervisor, the generous hand of America doling out to pitifully grateful people just enough to salve your conscience and that of the omnipotent Congress. Why, don't you know, any of a thousand men could do it? As for the new plant for the company, one of your industrial managers could locate a site.'

Janet turned around and began hanging up the gowns she'd bought in Paris. Ryan had winced at the thought of what they probably cost; but he still hoped that if he didn't disapprove, she'd more readily try to understand why the projects meant so much to him.

'All right,' he said, 'any of a thousand other men could do it, but it so happens I want to be the man who does it. It's that important to me. It's also important that you be here with me.'

His need for Janet had ceased to be the desperate, aching longing of a soldier dreaming of the day he'd return home; but it had evolved into a natural conjugal wish to have her beside him as companion and helpmate, hostess and lover, the other half of the whole they had created when they were married.

Janet listened with resigned boredom while he described how pleasant their life could be in Brussels. His saying that she could choose wherever she wanted to live – either a luxurious apartment in the city or a château in the environs – did not placate her for a year away from her horses and dogs. She brightened up a little at the thought that, because they would be part of Belgium's diplomatic circle, they would automatically be in the forefront of international society. She began to visualize balls in London, soirees in Paris, and long weekends at Cannes and Monte Carlo.

It was finally decided that Janet would return to the States just long enough to see to closing their house for a year, find a permanent trainer for the stables, and sell all but two of her dogs. The last she would bring back with her. She was already planning to choose a house in the country, as well as an apartment in Brussels, and would immediately see about acquiring a second stable of horses.

'A month, no longer,' she promised when Ryan kissed her good-bye on the train that was taking her and the Congressional committee to Le Havre to board the Cunard liner taking them home.

A month, Ryan thought, as he made his way back to his temporary headquarters in the hotel that would serve as both home and office for the time being. A permanent home could wait until Janet returned, although he would spend some of his leisure time exploring the surrounding countryside and looking into apartments in the city. The office could also wait. With a rental car he planned to begin touring more of Belgium for the factory site. He already had an appointment with a Belgian architect. He had immediately decided that, with the exception of a few advisors, there should be no Americans either building the plant or working in it when it was finished.

There was more than enough for him to do to occupy his days; but in the evening, when he was lingering over a brandy with his coffee, he dwelt on the real reason he'd wanted to remain in Belgium: hills, cemetery, and a river. Someday he would stand again on the spot where he'd regained his memory. He did not expect an instant revelation; but like a treasure hunt, one clue after another would reveal itself. Liège. He had traveled by foot and by wagon probably some one hundred miles to Liège, but along so many byways and country roads, he had no idea of the actual distance. But he had to get to Liège. He had to start there. His mistake so far had been exploring other areas for a plant site. He must now concentrate within a hundred-mile radius of Liège.

Liège immediately brought Alys into his mind. He wondered if she were now in the apartment she'd mentioned wanting to find and if her daughters were with her. He found himself trying to visualize the three of them in the evenings. Or walking in the park on Saturday afternoons. The temptation to see her again if he went to Liège was overpowering. No rational argument could dissuade him from thinking, from being convinced, that she was in some way a link with his past; that in the treasure hunt for the lost months, she was an important if enigmatic clue. That she was also an extremely attractive young woman did not escape his thoughts, but he tried to hold onto the obvious fact that he meant no more to her than someone who had been there during a time of great need.

The days turned colder. In the mornings there was frost on the ground and, in spite of the sun shining, a biting chill in the afternoons. Hunting season. Gradually his frustration at not being able to get to Liège because of previous commitments was replaced by an even greater longing to be watching the ducks that would be flying into his favorite potholes. He should be spending his evenings with Joe while they planned how many decoys to take out in the morning and whether to take the boat downriver or through the swamp.

Ryan sighed. He'd just finished reading one of Janet's short infrequent letters. More than the promised month had already gone by, and she was still having difficulty finding just the right person to manage the stables. As long as she was still at home, she hoped Ryan wouldn't mind if she stayed until after a steeplechase in Virginia. An additional three weeks, she promised, and she'd be over. He felt something vulnerable, like a taut violin string, snap inside his chest. There was no pain; there was no accompanying agony, but he knew he had been present at a death, at the severing of a golden cord that should have grown stronger, not more fragile, through the years with Janet. The death of love was more tragic and more grievous than the death of a loved one. The first severance is abstract and nontactile, a widening gap from unspoken communion to silent sundering. The physical was the last to die. Was physical the least or most important part of love? At the same time, he was overcome with an indifference that shrouded him like a carapace against any unwelcome, intrusive emotional reaction.

Alys found exactly the apartment she wanted on the rue d'Archis. It had only one bedroom, but that was large enough to accommodate a double bed for her and Minette and a crib for Amalie. The best thing about the apartment, aside from a rental she could afford, was its location – an easy walk to the university and within two blocks of the Parc

D'Avroy where she could take the girls on Saturday and Sunday afternoons. The kitchen was barely large enough for her to turn around in, but Minette and Amalie always managed to squeeze in with her while she was cooking. Madame LeClerc proved to be a gem. Not only did the girls take to her immediately, but she insisted she had plenty of time while the little ones were napping in the afternoon to prepare supper and keep it warm until Alys returned home.

Weekend afternoons found them not only in the parks but often walking along the boulevard Frère Orban or the quai de Rome that ran along the Meuse River. The little girls were enchanted with the barges that plied their way up and down the river and especially with the idea that families lived on them.

'I'd like to live on a boat,' Minette announced one afternoon. 'I think I shall when I get a little older.'

'Me too,' Amalie said in staunch support of her sister. Whatever Minette suggested, Amalie was agreeable to.

'Fine, when you're older,' Alys said. 'Now, home and into something pretty. Dinner tonight with the Montclairs.'

The girls adored them both, the professor for the amusing and sometimes scary stories he told and *Tante* Yvonne for the wonderful surprises she always had for dessert.

The one person Minette and Amalie had not taken to in their new surroundings was Kenneth Winston. Amalie paid him scant attention when he came to the apartment and Minette actually seemed to avoid him. Alys tried to rationalize that, being a bachelor, he was ill at ease with them and the children could sense this. She still hoped that time would bring them closer together and that the children would eventually learn to love him as a father. If they had shown any overt signs of actual dislike for Kenneth, she would have stopped seeing him immediately; instead, their attitude was one of apathy and indifference.

Although Alys had not told Kenneth in so many words that she would marry him, she knew he was assuming they would be married as soon as she finished her studies. Nor did she make any effort to dispell that notion. She prayed that by then the girls would feel closer to him, would have come to really like him if not love him. If only she could look forward to being his wife with some glimmer of excitement, some feeling of joy at the thought of belonging to someone who loved her. Instead, she saw marriage to Kenneth as only a practical step she would be a fool not to take.

In January, Alys received a letter with a Brussels postmark. On the back was Ryan's name and a Brussels address. In spite of her curiosity as to what he was doing back in Belgium after – she assumed – returning to the States with the tour, she held the letter unopened for a long time. The handwriting conjured up memories that lay constantly on the verge of her consciousness, not deeply hidden as they should be. The first writing he did the night he was finally willing to accept her help; his bitter, desperate frustration at being unable to talk; the agonizing humiliation of trying to sound out syllables. She remembered the day he had gotten furious at himself – and at her – for his failures and had thrown the cards onto the floor. How she'd longed to tell him she loved him when he held her close in what she thought was a gesture of apology, not knowing he loved her, too. And the day he had saved Minette's life by calling out to her before she fell off the old bridge. She stopped there. Other memories were too bittersweet to recall right now. Memories that flooded her nights when she lay awake and ached to feel his touch, to hear him telling her over and over again that he loved her when he was finally able to say it.

She was overcome with a temptation to tear the letter up without reading it. How dare he come back into her life, into it and then out of it again, as if her life were some continuous play that he could attend or not attend at his pleasure? She didn't need him; no, she most definitely didn't need him right now. She finally had her priorities assembled in a nice, neat row and lined up in the proper order. Now came this letter that threatened to scatter them like a set of tenpins.

She should, she supposed, at least read it. She could always refuse to answer it. She would't know why he was writing to her unless she did read it.

The note was almost insultingly brief. But what had she expected? A long epistle detailing what he'd been doing in the past months, a heartrending confession that he was in love with her and couldn't live without her? No, simply that he would be in Liège soon and he hoped he could see her. He asked about Amalie, said he would be waiting for her reply, and signed it 'Sincerely.'

Reason told Alys that the wisest thing would be to find some excuse for not seeing him. She took the letter into the bedroom, intending to put it away and think about answering it later. When she opened her top dresser drawer, she saw something that had her choking back the tears. She picked up the slender silver-and-blue enamel medal. On its face was a long-barreled rifle, and backing the oblong was a silver wreath of laurel leaves, the classical, universal symbol of a champion. She had no idea what the medal was for, some act of bravery she supposed, but that was less important than its being his. She clenched her hand around it. Its four corners dug into her flesh, but she continued to clutch it ever tighter, hoping that somehow the physical pain would negate the pain she felt in her heart.

In a frenzy, she found a sheet of paper and hastily, frantically, replied to his letter before she could change her mind. Leaving a bewildered Madame LeClerc, who agreed to stay a few more minutes, Alys ran down the apartment steps and the two blocks to the mailbox. Breathlessly, she noted that she was posting it in time for the last evening pickup. She leaned exhausted against the box. Her short, fitful gasps finally became longer, deeper, more normal breaths. She had done it. Let happen what would. She had to see Ryan again.

While Alys was waiting for Ryan to arrive at the apartment, a thought occurred to her that she should have considered earlier. Minette might very well recognize Ryan. As honest and straightforward as children were, Minette would reveal it if she did. What to do if she called him Papa or asked where he'd been? It wouldn't do to lie. Children could recognize dissembling for what it was. For a brief moment, Alys panicked at the thought of the tragicomedy that might very well take place. Then she forced herself to think about it more calmly. Minette had not yet been two and a half when Ryan left and she was now five; the chances of her remembering him were really quite slim. Yet Ryan might do or say something to awaken Minette's memory. Children could remember so much more than adults often thought, especially people or events that were important to them.

She'd told the girls that a Mr. Middleton was taking her out to dinner. Minette had never known Ryan by that name. His mustache and slightly graying hair had altered his appearance enough that now she could only pray that Minette didn't recognize him.

Ryan arrived promptly at seven, his arms laden with packages. The long florist box was filled with a massed array of colors and intermingling fragrances.

'I told them to put in two of every kind they had,' Ryan said with a grin. Her smile when she let him in had already lighted up the whole room for him, and now the pleasure of seeing the delight on her face suffused him with a warmth that made him wonder why he had waited so long to come to Liège.

Finding a vase and arranging the flowers helped Alys over the first few moments of confusion and brought under control the joy and the pain at seeing him again.

The other boxes were presents for Minette and Amalie, two dolls and two funny-looking jumping jacks worked with strings. Ryan had had no problem about selecting the dolls. He knew little girls liked them and could never have too many. But then he had seen the amusing, hand-painted marionette clowns. What had attracted him to them, aside from their bright colors, he couldn't fathom. He only knew he couldn't leave the store without them.

He shouldn't have brought the jumping jacks, Alys thought. Minette will surely connect hers with the one Ryan made for her after he carved the wooden animals. She watched Minette carefully to see what her reaction would be.

Amalie immediately began cuddling her doll. Minette picked up the jumping jack and looked quizzically at Ryan. But all she did was ask him to show her how it worked.

Both girls had hugged Ryan enthusiastically when they thanked him before settling down to play with their new toys. They'd never done that with Kenneth. When he brought them something, they smiled and thanked him politely, but their smiles were cool and their thanks much more reserved. Was it possible that at their age they could detect their mother's hesitation in accepting Kenneth for herself, her inability to love him? Were their attitudes an outward reflection of her own inward confusion and compromise? Were they that sensitive to emotional atmosphere? There seemed no other explanation for their impulsively embracing Ryan. They had only done what she wished she could do. They were stand-ins for the actress who could not, who dared not, walk onto the stage.

When Alys returned to the living room from getting her coat and checking some things with Madame LeClerc, she found Ryan sitting on the floor. He and the girls were deeply involved in a puppet show with the dolls, the jumping jacks, and other assorted toys that had been persuaded to take part in the play.

Amalie set up a wail when she saw her mother was ready to leave.

'There, there,' Ryan said, 'we'll finish the play. Your mother won't mind waiting a few minutes.' He turned to Alys. 'You won't, will you?'

Alys shook her head. If she'd tried to say anything, she would have broken out in laughter at the sight of him sprawled there, or in tears at the memory of the many nights he'd played on the floor with Minette at the inn.

After giving the waiter their order, Ryan was all questions about the girls and Alys's studies. He was acutely aware of her alternately twisting her wedding ring, consciously putting one hand in her lap to avoid doing it, and then unconsciously beginning to twist it again. He could think of no reason why she would be nervous or uncomfortable with him. He didn't think he'd said anything to upset or displease her. If he had inadvertently mentioned something that disturbed her, perhaps he should change the subject from her to himself.

Alys forced one hand back down in her lap. She would be glad when the food arrived so she would have something to do with her hands and be forced to keep her fingers away from her wedding ring – the ring he had given her with such love and adoration. With such sincerity and strength in his voice when he said his vows. Dear God, how could someone forget a moment like that? She was also nervously impatient to learn why he wanted to see her again. She should never have agreed to this dinner. She should have written and said she was leaving Liège, that she was engaged to Kenneth – anything to have avoided this meeting. She'd answered his questions: she'd conversed casually in a surprisingly calm and pleasant voice. But why had he asked to see her again?

There was a pause in the conversation while the waiter placed soup in front of them. Then Ryan began enthusiastically detailing his plans for building a company plant in Belgium as well as overseeing some of the aid being sent from the States. At least, she thought, we're now on more impersonal grounds. No more straining to talk about Minette and Amalie without aching to remind him of the picnics he'd shared with Minette or the desperate longing to tell him that Amalie was his daughter.

Alys finally found herself listening with increasing interest as he explained that he'd opened his first office in Brussels because it was the capital and the American Embassy was there. Now he was going to open a branch office in Liège because the site for the plant would be chosen from one of several in this vicinity.

That much was true. The best sites for the new plant were nearer Liège than Brussels. What he did not tell her was that at first he'd wanted to see her again because of his being so certain she held a clue to the lost months, but that now, after being with her tonight, he wanted to see her for herself. The only letters he received now from Janet were blatantly concocted explanations of why she was postponing her return. But he no longer cared. That love had died a whimpering death. Whether from atrophy, attrition, or a quick break didn't matter. He wasn't in love with Alys, not yet, but that was just as well. He wasn't ready to be in love yet, but he was lonely for the company of an attractive woman.

Earlier remarks had already apprised him that she was still seeing Kenneth Winston, but was not formally engaged. The one impediment that deterred his hopes for seeing her socially was Janet. Alys was a woman with strong and well-defined principles. She might have scruples about dating a married man. He wouldn't take the chance of never seeing her again by suggesting it. He would return to his original plan.

'So,' he said, 'that's why I wanted to see you tonight. I need an executive assistant. Someone to manage the office when I'm not here and to be my right hand when I am.' He saw the startled look on her face, but hurried on before she could say anything. 'I can't think of anyone more perfect for the position than you. You're extremely intelligent and capable. You proved that on the tour. It's important that I have someone who can translate the correspondence and interpret for the people I'll be talking to about the plant and the aid.' Then he stopped. He was suddenly afraid that instead of complimenting her as he'd intended, he'd somehow offended and insulted her by his unintentionally cavalier manner.

'I'm sorry,' he said. 'Perhaps I've put all this too bluntly.'

Alys's first inclination had been to laugh at herself for thinking Ryan wanted more than a business relationship between them. But what else should she think after he'd brought all those flowers tonight? His offer of a position had disturbed her. A wish to see her socially could easily have been discouraged by saying she was going to marry Kenneth. A business offer could not be turned aside so easily, but she had to find a logical excuse for refusing it. She did not want to see Ryan again. For her peace of mind, she wanted everything to end tonight, right now.

Ryan looked at Alys while waiting for her answer. He could sense from her hesitation that she was having difficulty making up her mind; but he could not understand why. From the expression on her face, she seemed almost frightened about accepting.

'No, no, you haven't been blunt at all. I'm very flattered you would think of me for the position. But I really don't feel qualified. Then, too, I have my studies and the translating I do every night, I couldn't give up the university. I waited and dreamed too long to give it up now.'

Ryan knew from something she'd said earlier that she was working all day for Professor Montclair and pursuing her studies on an independent study basis with her tutors. She must certainly be aware she could do the same while working for him. Something else was preventing her from accepting his offer, and he wished he knew what it was.

'Please,' he said, 'just say that you'll consider it.' He mentioned the salary he would pay, and he saw the expression of disbelief on her face.

'I really don't think I'll change my mind.' Her cool, impersonal tone shattered what little hope Ryan had of seeing her again. 'But I will give it serious consideration.'

'I'll be back next week. Perhaps we could have dinner again.' Maybe he'd been wrong to renew their acquaintance on a business level; perhaps he should have simply asked her to go out with him again. If so, he hoped the dinner invitation would negate that faux pas.

'I'd prefer to give you my answer in a letter. Then, if I do accept, you can let me know when you wish me to come to the office.' There must be no more dinners, no more coming to the apartment. If she did accept – and the temptation of that salary was too strong to be denied – their relationship must remain on a business level. He was married; she was going to marry Kenneth. Above all, she must remember her own advice: let the past remain buried. Nothing but pain results from disinterring what was once alive but is now no more than a handful of dusty memories.

They returned to Alys's apartment in a silence that was deafening with what each wanted to say to the other but felt forced not to utter. Alys was miserable at the thought that Ryan would be here in Liège, constantly in her thoughts whether she accepted the position or not. Ryan was still bewildered as to why she had developed such a sudden chill toward him. In the entryway she thanked him again for the flowers and the gifts for the children. She would write him within a few days with her answer. She shook his hand and ran upstairs as if afraid he would try to follow.

As soon as she bid Madame LeClerc good-night and closed the door behind her, she fell on the couch and cried until there was no tear left to be shed.

Ryan slammed the outer door to the entryway and then looked back to see if in his violence he had shattered any of the glass. He hadn't. He drove to the nearest bar, and for the first time in as long as he could remember, he drank until he was almost senseless and had to call a cab to take him back to the hotel.

CHAPTER TWENTY-NINE

Indecisiveness was not normally Alys's nature. She was not one who fretted an hour over which dress to buy, whether to have fish or stew for dinner, or how best to present a new lesson to her class. Even with more serious decisions, she relied on her own judgment as being as sound and sagacious as anyone else's. Nor was she guilty of snap judgments that she then regretted later. All experiences in her life, whether frivolous or momentous, had been shelved like a library of reference books, and when the time came to make a decision, she reached into her mind and pulled out the relevant one. She used the information to make her choice. Nor did she ever feel insecure once a decision was made.

Now, however, as she thought about working for Ryan she struggled with the ambivalent, polarized desires to continue seeing him or to expunge him completely from her life. Loving him as she did, she longed to be with him as much as possible, yet there would be the pain of knowing they could never be more than associates or, at best, friends. When she thought about it rationally, she knew she should refuse the offer and continue at the university with the hope of eventually teaching there. It was what she'd dreamed of for so many years and the reason Professor Montclair had gone to such trouble to help her. Yet her heart told her she'd never be happy after turning down the opportunity to be close to Ryan.

Then, too, there were her finances to consider. Even with being the professor's graduate assistant and the translating work, she found it more and more difficult to meet expenses. Several times when her purse contained only enough to pay Madame LeClerc and buy food for one more day, she'd thought she'd have to take Minette and Amalie back to Ste. Monique and find a single room for herself. Then there'd been a generous influx of translating for her to do. But she wondered how much longer she could count on that happening. With the salary Ryan offered, there would be no question about her being able to maintain the apartment and keep Minette and Amalie with her.

Alys turned from the stove where she was heating up the dinner Madame LeClerc had prepared earlier in the afternoon, and she looked at Minette and Amalie playing school with their books. Minette, naturally, was the teacher; and Amalie was trying very hard to sit still as she'd been told, but her little bottom kept wriggling on the rug. So that's what wore out all her panties. She had to keep them with her. She had no heart to send them back to their grandparents. These weeks with them had been pure delight, and she'd miss their tantrums and naughtiness as much as their laughter and their exuberant welcomes when she returned home each evening. And they needed her more now than ever. To send them back would appear to them as rejection, and that could affect them for the rest of their lives. She might never regain their confidence or their assurance of her love. Just as she would probably marry Kenneth eventually to assure their future, so now she must take the position with Ryan in order to keep them all together. She would write the letter tonight before she lost her courage again.

On the morning she was to meet Ryan at his office and begin working for him, she was furious with herself for taking so long to dress. Twice she rehung the green silk blouse that deepened the green in her eyes in favor of a plain white shirt. In the end she wore the green silk. Then she fussed over her hair and makeup. Keeping their relationship on a business, impersonal level didn't mean she couldn't look her prettiest when she saw him.

Ryan's office was very much what she had expected it to be. It was small but pleasingly decorated and furnished. It was immediately obvious that no expense had been spared. As soon as she entered the reception area, Ryan rose from behind a desk in another room and came forward to greet her. She'd only had time to see that the reception room contained several comfortable chairs, attractive reading lamps, and tables with magazines in both French and English. He led her immediately into the larger of two other rooms, and it appeared that although there was furniture in the third room, it was unoccupied.

'Coffee?' he asked after she sat down across the desk from him. 'I'm not much of a hand at domestic things, but I can brew a passable pot of coffee.'

'Thank you, I'd like some. It's very cold outside.' That's it, she thought; talk about the weather. There certainly was no more innocuous subject. Nor a more stupid one!

'Yes, it is. I'm beginning to realize that winters in Belgium are far different from what I'm used to in South Carolina.' Damn! Couldn't he think of a more interesting conversation than the weather? Next thing he'd be telling her how hot it got in Camden in the summer.

Alys nestled the cup in her hand. She was here to begin working for him, not to indulge in an hour of cozy conversation. She wished he would tell her what her responsibilities would be. 'When you asked me to come here this morning, I gathered you wanted me to begin work. I've made arrangements to be here all day.'

'Good. I had hoped you would.' So she intended keeping it on an impersonal, businesslike plane. That was probably just as well. He'd had no right to assume there was even a scant possibility of their relationship becoming anything else.

Within an hour, she was seated at her desk in the smaller, third room and Ryan had explained what she would be doing. On the days he was in the office, she would be mainly translating letters, a pile of which had greeted her when she sat down, and being available to interpret for any non-English-speaking callers. There would undoubtedly be many of those when he began accepting applications for American aid.

The more important functions would be hers when he was away from the office. Then she would be in complete charge of all activities – whether concerned with the aid or with the building of the plant – that came to this office rather than to Brussels. His announcement that he would be leaving in the middle of the afternoon and not returning until the end of the week had left her giddy with apprehension. But after a few minutes of evaluating the correspondence, checking appointments, and organizing her desk, she felt quite confident about the amount of responsibility the position entailed.

Ryan was seldom in the Liège office more than two days a week, and Alys found it less difficult than she'd thought to work by his side. The hours were filled with appointments, often with people she had to interpret for; correspondence to be sorted as to what had to be taken care of while he was there and what she could handle after he was gone; and a myriad of projects for her to assist him with.

On the days he was coming in, Alys arrived earlier in order to have his coffee made, his desk straightened, and everything he would need right at hand. When she learned there was a *pâtisserie* that baked the kind of croissants he liked, she stopped on her way to work to buy some and kept them warm for him. Sometimes a florist had a special on flowers in full bloom, and she would buy a small bouquet. Although they'd last no more than a day or two, that would be enough time for Ryan to enjoy them. She took genuine pleasure in doing everything she could to make the office comfortable and pleasant.

The days he was not there were even busier, if possible, but she missed him dreadfully. She'd thought she would be relieved not to hear his voice or to spend hours in the same room; instead she found herself counting the days and hours until he would be back. Although she knew she should forget she had been his wife for a few brief days, she could not. His reemergence into her life had awakened in her a wife's normal concerns for the husband she loved: where he was and what he was doing, if he were well or ill, if he were worried about something. For too long she had tried to deny those feelings; now they refused to remain dormant. Of only one thing was she certain: she must never in any way reveal those feelings to Ryan. While working for him, she would remain the cool, professional assistant he had hired.

If she could no longer consider herself married to Ryan, she could still do for him the things a wife would. He kept extra shirts and suits at the office in case he needed to change before an evening appointment, and she made certain these were always freshly laundered or cleaned and pressed before he returned. She knew his favorite brands of cigarettes, mints to suck on when he was deeply absorbed in a problem and aspirin for his frequent headaches. She kept a good supply of all of them in appropriate containers on his desk.

On the mornings she was expecting him, she listened with nervous anticipation for his footfalls in the hall. When something unexpected kept him in Brussels or on the road, he always called. Somehow, after she put the receiver down, the sun went behind a cloud, and the day was gloomy and dour.

Alys was not the only one who missed Ryan. Minette and Amalie were constantly asking when Mr. Middleton was coming back. They had made up new puppet shows, and they needed him for some of the parts. Alys explained that he was away most of the time, and when he was in town, he was very busy; but it didn't satisfy them. She tried to placate them by having Kenneth come to the apartment the two or three evenings a week she saw him rather than go out. She was still hoping that in time the girls would begin to feel some affection for him, but they either ignored him and went on playing by themselves or listened politely but impatiently when he read from a new book he'd brought them.

Minette and Amalie never told Alys they didn't like Kenneth, but she knew they considered him an interloper. They were always particularly naughty when they knew she was going out with him and leaving them in the care of Madame LeClerc. They adored the former nurse and greeted her jubilantly when she arrived each morning; but let them learn that she was keeping them during the evening because Alys was going somewhere with Kenneth, and they immediately began to misbehave.

One night they put Alys's lipstick and eye makeup down the toilet, and the concierge had to take all the pipes apart. Another time they crumbled their cake all over the table, crawled up on the table, and pretended they were horses having to eat with their mouths. As might be expected, Kenneth looked horrified when he arrived before Alys could finish cleaning up the mess. How could she expect a bachelor to understand, she thought while brushing the thousands of crumbs into the dustbin.

One of the worst times was the night Kenneth was taking her to the opera. They were dining afterward with other members of the consulate, and she'd bought an expensive evening gown for the occasion. When she and Kenneth were ready to leave, Amalie ran across the room to hug her good-bye and spilled an entire glass of water down the front of the gown. The impish grin on Amalie's face patently announced that it was no accident. The dress was not ruined, but the evening was. Alys changed dispiritedly to the blue dinner gown she'd bought for the senators' tour and which she'd already worn several times.

Suffice to say the girls were severely punished each time, but like little stoics, they accepted the spankings or the denial of something they really wanted. Nor was there any such misbehavior if Alys were going to the Montclairs for dinner or to the theater with friends from the university. Only Kenneth was anathema in their eyes. Alys was forced to conclude that they feared he was going to displace them in their mother's affection, and they would have none of him. Fortunately, Kenneth was not pressuring her about setting a wedding date. He seemed perfectly content to see her as often as he could while still assuming they would be married eventually. Perhaps, set in his ways as he was, 'eventually' suited him as much as it did her.

Winter in Liège that year lasted well into March and was unusually miserable. It snowed almost every day; and by evening, the streets and sidewalks were covered with a dun-colored slush that soaked through the sturdiest boots. Then the snow and slush froze, and there was danger of each step ending in an ignominious and painful fall. Curbs disappeared under mounded layers of ice; however cautious one was, crossing a street became an exercise in timidity and fear. The damp cold seeped into the bones and stayed there until one began to wonder if he were ever going to be warm again. Smoke hung low over the roofs, encircled the barges on the river, and rested in a billowing, yellow gray haze just atop the surface of the water.

Ryan swore as he stepped off the curb and up to his ankles in a pile of wet snow. Damn! He'd be sure to come down with a cold now. He'd awakened sneezing; his throat was raw and scratchy, and there was that irritating tickle in his nose that presaged a cold. He was in a miserable mood when he finally arrived at the office. Mumbling a gruff, curt good-morning to Alys, he stormed past her toward his desk. He was somewhat placated when he saw waiting for him the steaming pot of coffee and the warm rolls wrapped in a linen napkin. By noon he was sneezing every five minutes. Not even the portable electric heater he'd bought as an adjunct to the central heat or a pot of strong, hot tea laced with brandy could keep him warm.

Alys listened to him sneezing and blowing until early afternoon, and then she could subdue her maternal instincts no longer.

'You're going home,' she announced in her no-nonsense, don't-argue-with-me tone of voice.

'I can't. I have –' and he started sneezing again.

'You have four appointments this afternoon that can be rescheduled with no problem. None of them is urgent. Back to the hotel with you.'

Ryan lacked both the will and the strength to debate with her. His eyes were already burning and running; he knew from the clammy feeling of his shirt against his skin that he had a fever. Alys helped him on with his coat, tied his muffler around his throat, and handed him his gloves, all the while she was scolding him for not wearing galoshes.

'I hate them,' he croaked. 'Remind me of the war.'

The next few days, as tedious and miserably uncomfortable as they were for Ryan, were blissful for Alys. She spent her lunch hours and at least two hours after work feeding him homemade soup and hot lemonade toddies; covering his chest with warm flannel compresses; replacing his sweat-dampened pajamas with clean ones washed at the apartment. She was a child playing house. She was a wife who could no longer be a wife. She fluffed his pillows, and she stood over him while he took his bitter, evil-tasting medicine.

If what she saw in his eyes were merely gratitude, not love, it would have to suffice. So what if caring for him like this were a travesty of what her life with him should be, it was senseless to blame the fate that had catapulted him back into her life. She was no longer the little girl permitted to cry because she'd been given a book of paper dolls and someone else had received the life-sized baby doll she'd wanted at Countess Charbonne's annual Christmas party for the village children. She must not weep because circumstances denied her what she had no right to.

Ryan's fever remained high, and at times he was too delirious to know more than that someone was putting something warm on his chest and cool cloths on his forehead. His throat had been painfully sore and constricted, but the pain had begun to ease. Probably because she'd removed the tube. No, that wasn't it. He hadn't had a tube in his throat; just an excruciating pain like that from hundreds of ulcers. Why had he thought there'd been a tube?

He saw Alys coming with a bowl of soup. He hoped it wasn't too hot to swallow comfortably. With his feverish eyes he saw two of her, and he tried to blink away the double vision. It had been an odd kind of dual sight, though, because one of her was in the suit and blouse she wore to the office and the other had on a heavy woollen skirt and sweater. He blinked again, and they blended together into the Alys he was familiar with. Odd, though, he could distinctly remember that while she held the hotel's white china bowl, the other figure had carried a blue patterned one. There was surely a rational explanation. Perhaps during his more feverish days she'd worn a skirt and sweater and brought a bowl from home. That memory was what was confusing him now.

Under Alys's comforting assurance that all was going well at the office, he stopped counting the days he was sick. He slept most of the time, awaking only when he heard her unlock the door with the spare key he'd given her so she wouldn't have to ask the concierge to let her in. Not a man who enjoyed being coddled and fussed over, he apathetically tolerated the food she brought and her insistence on his taking the medicine. It tasted like the quinine he'd had to take as a child during recurring bouts of the malaria so prevalent then in South Carolina. Even the soup tasted like quinine. He would have preferred drinking nothing but the whiskey-and-hot lemonade toddies she fixed.

As the restless fever became an impatient urge to get out of bed, he realized how much her being there meant to him. Now that he was awake most of the day, he counted the hours between each visit. Four hours from her morning visit at 8:00 to lunchtime at noon. Then another four and a half hours from 1:00 to 5:30. Still lethargic from the fever, he'd lie back and enjoy watching her put away the clean pajamas she'd brought, fold up the soiled ones he'd changed before she arrived, arrange a mixed bouquet of flowers and then go into the small kitchenette to prepare his toddy.

Today she'd fixed two, and she came to sit down beside him while she drank hers. He scarcely listened while she went through the list of calls he'd had that day, the letters she'd answered and the ones that could wait until he returned, and the appointments she'd tentatively scheduled for the following week if he thought he would be there. She had on a new blouse, all dusty rose and feminine with ruffles at the throat and cuffs.

He stared at her until she looked up in embarrassment, and he watched with pleasure as her cheeks flushed a pale pink. Since she'd come to work for him, he'd concentrated on keeping their relationship as impersonal as she had obviously indicated she wanted it to be. He had tried to deny to himself that he was falling in love with her, and he had stayed in Brussels and traveled from there far more than he wanted to – or that was convenient – so as not to be around her every day.

Although longing to tell her how he felt, he had to remember he was still married. He'd heard there was the chance of a bill legalizing divorce in South Carolina for a few specific grounds, like desertion and adultery, being passed within a year or two. But by that time, Alys would no doubt be married to Kenneth Winston and he would have returned to the States. Even if there had been no Kenneth Winston, the thought of suggesting an affair with Alys repelled him. There was a fine and delicate quality about her that aroused the protective spirit in him. With her it would have to be marriage or nothing.

'I really appreciate your taking care of me this way,' he said. 'Nothing in our agreement required you to do it.'

'I didn't do it for that reason.' *I did it for the same reason any wife would, because I love you and I worry when you're ill.* 'I've enjoyed it. It's been a break in my routine. And I need you back at the office. The work is piling up and threatening to overflow your desk.'

I doubt that, he thought. He'd probably find it all cleaned off and neatly segregated into appropriate piles. Or she'd have taken care of the less consequential matters herself. A break in her routine. That's all he meant to her. That and a boss who needed to be in the office.

Throughout the conversation he kept inhaling a heady, tantalizing fragrance that haunted him with trying to remember where he'd smelled it before. Instead of a bouquet today, Alys had brought in a variety of spring bulbs just beginning to bloom. In a blue china bowl, the bulbs were nestled among small, shiny, myriad-colored stones; and the daffodils, narcissus, and hyacinths stood at varying heights on their sturdy stalks, each vying for his attention. The paper white narcissus immediately reminded him of Christmas at home when they bloomed just in time for the holidays. The others blossomed profusely in his mother's garden at Eastertime. It wasn't the sight of them that tantalized him, but the aroma. He had smelled that odor of hyacinths someplace other than in that garden, and he knew it was his chained memory trying to free itself again. He reached up and plucked a single petal from a hyacinth, crushed it between his fingers, and held it to his face. In spite of willing as hard as he could, nothing emerged from the deep cavern of his mind. He'd been too busy the past weeks to continue his treasure hunt; but he knew he held a clue between his fingers, and he would resume his search as soon as he was out of this bed.

Alys had gotten up to return the toddy glasses to the kitchenette and didn't see Ryan fondling the hyacinth petal. She'd bought the bulbs on impulse, partly because she loved them and partly because they would always remind her of the day Ryan had proposed. She'd intended taking them back to the apartment; but he seemed so delighted with them, she'd let him keep them.

'I'll be back in the office on Monday,' he said. 'No need to come here over the weekend. I'll manage fine.'

'It will be good to have you back. It's lonely when you're not there,' she said and then wished she hadn't added that. He might misunderstand her meaning, or understand it too well.

'You might come to renege on that statement. I plan to stay here in Liège most of the time from now on. More and more of the work is being centered here, especially now that the site has been approved and we'll be starting construction in a few weeks.'

When Alys walked out of the hotel, the sky had cleared and the sun was shining with such brightness it seemed to be trying to atone for all the dull, drab, gloomy days of the past two months. There was even a semblance of spring in the air, and she could swear she caught a fragrant hint of flowers about ready to burst open in a profusion of color.

On Monday Alys was finishing up some work that needed to be done before leaving at 5:30 when the phone rang. It was a transatlantic call for Ryan. The Camden office often called at this time; but while she was waiting to make certain the connection was clear, she heard Janet's voice. She had no wish to overhear even one end of the conversation, but there was no way she could be rendered momentarily deaf. She heard him exclaim, 'Janet, I'm glad you called. You've gotten my letter then?' There was a pause while Janet was talking. Then, 'Yes, I think we can agree on that. I see no problems over here.'

There was no denying the elation in Ryan's voice. Hurriedly, Alys put on her coat, indicated to Ryan that she was leaving, and waited for his approving nod.

Benumbed with a lethargic melancholy, Alys walked for a long time along the boulevard de Frère Orban beside the river and then through the Parc d'Avroy. She once thought she had used up all her capacity for suffering during the dread days of the war and occupation, the night with the German soldiers, and the loss of Ryan. But like the unplumbed depths of a spring-fed well or the ocean into which all the rivers pour, there was always room for more pain.

She should never have allowed herself to think there could be some happiness in seeing Ryan in a professional relationship. She should have put an end to their association long before this: refused to allow him to come to Liège with her when Amalie was ill, found some excuse not to have dinner with him, and never answered the letter that resulted in her working for him. If Janet finally came to Belgium to live, as it now seemed likely, she would have to resign. She'd been playing at being a wife and that must end. She felt herself becoming emotionally and physically exhausted. All her energy had liquefied, flowed into frigid pools beneath her skin, and was now seeping out through her pores.

Remembering suddenly that Kenneth was coming for dinner, she neither looked forward to nor dreaded the evening with him. It would be like so many they'd spent in the past and would undoubtedly spend in the future. She panicked at the thought that she'd told Madame LeClerc not to cook anything in the afternoon; she'd prepare it herself when she got home. Kenneth wouldn't be angry – he never let himself get angry – but he would be annoyed. He liked to eat promptly at seven. Something about his digestive system and regular hours. Damn his digestive system! She'd set out some cheese and crackers, and he could have more than his usual two martinis. In spite of wishing that Kenneth were across the channel in England right now, she realized it was probably better to have company for the evening than to sit brooding and trying to read after Minette and Amalie had gone to bed.

The evening passed more pleasantly than she'd expected. Kenneth was gracious about the delay and then suggested that since she had not yet started dinner, they go out to eat. The girls were not only civil to him but kept him amused while she changed to a silk dress, by allowing him to help them color in the *Alice in Wonderland* coloring books he brought them. It must have been the new crayons he also brought. A separate box of twenty-four for each of them. They'd never known such riches before.

Kenneth had given her a portable record player for Christmas; and after returning to the apartment, they listened to her albums of Chopin. But she could tell by the way he alternately paced the floor and returned to sit on the edge of the couch that he had something momentous on his mind. Kenneth was never one to pace.

'I'm being transferred,' he finally said. 'To the embassy in Stockholm.'

'Oh, Kenneth, I'm pleased for you. You've been wanting it for a long time.'

'Yes, I've wondered when the home office would recognize that Scandinavia is my specialty.' He looked away from Alys and stared out into the night where the streetlamps were blurred into concentric circles by the misty evening rain. 'I'll be sorry though to leave Liège. I'll miss it. It will always hold many happy memories.'

There was something about the tone of his voice that sounded as if he were saying good-bye. Had he given up on her? Or, perhaps, having been a bachelor for so long, he was really no more eager to be married than she. Janet was coming to Belgium. Kenneth was transferring to Stockholm. Where did that leave her? In the doldrums. In limbo. Beyond the pale. Trite expressions, but all too apropos. The future spread before her like a vast wasteland, Eliot's Wasteland, bereft of love and hope. The empty thunder with no reviving rain.

'How soon will you go there?' She could at least profess an interest.

'In six weeks. Two more weeks here and then a month in London.' He adjusted his tie and recreased the knife-edged press in his trousers. 'Will you come with me?' His voice took on an urgency rare for him. 'I've loved you since we first met, and I'll do all I can to make you and the girls happy. I think you know that. If you need more time . . .'

'No, I don't need time, Kenneth.' This would be for the best; it had to be. There'd be a permanent home for Minette and Amalie; Kenneth would adopt them, and they'd no longer bear the stigma of illegitimacy; and she would have the security she needed. Without realizing it, Kenneth had chosen exactly the most propitious time to propose. A week, even a day, earlier and she would have said no. But now she accepted him and prayed she was doing the right thing.

After Kenneth left, Alys lay awake a long time trying to visualize her future as his wife. It could be an exciting life, moving from one embassy to another, seeing more of the world than she'd ever dreamed she would. They'd be married before he went to England; she'd have a whole month in London and in Canterbury with his family before going to Sweden. She'd always wanted to see England.

Then she thought about having to submit her resignation to Ryan. He'd be sorry to see her leave, but he could easily find a replacement. More easily than Kenneth would be a replacement for him in her life. She'd ask if she could have tomorrow and Friday off for a long weekend, then she'd submit her resignation on Monday. She suddenly felt a desperate longing to go home.

CHAPTER THIRTY

Having said good-bye to Janet and assured the transatlantic operator that the call was completed. Ryan sat and simply stared at the phone for several minutes. Janet wanted a divorce. After the agonizing months of wondering how to approach her about dissolving their marriage, she had very neatly and succinctly brought the issue to a head. She wanted to marry a man who raised thoroughbred horses on a farm in Virginia, thereby negating any conflict with South Carolina divorce laws. For him, it meant remaining single if he returned to Camden or staying in Belgium if he chose to remarry.

He was free. He found he had to repeat it over and over in order to believe it. He was free! Janet was leaving almost immediately to establish residence in Reno. Surprisingly for her, she had agreed to let their lawyer in Camden work out all the financial details while she was gone. She would, of course, have to have a Nevada lawyer for the actual divorce proceedings; but with a settlement already agreed upon, that should be only a matter of a few minutes.

Ryan went over to the liquor cabinet and fixed himself a drink. He should be elated, and he was. But it was an elation muted by poignant memories. Love had long since died, but he felt as if he were only now entering a period of mourning. Not for the loss of Janet, but for what might have been. He couldn't blame the war, as convenient a scapegoat as that would be. Other marriages had survived the trauma of that separation. The years had simply shown that while he and Janet had started out at the same point, somewhere along the way they had taken two separate paths leading to two disparate destinations.

Too restless to go straight home to the apartment, Ryan left his car at the office and began walking in the opposite direction. He walked along the river for a while. A few lights at a time were turned on in the barges, and he found himself almost hypnotized by their shimmering reflections in the water. Now, like these boats, he was free to go where he wished, to chart the course he wanted; he was no longer moored to an unhappy marriage.

Soon he found himself near the Parc d'Avroy. He sat on a bench and watched the young couples walking by hand in hand and the families with children who ran around their parents' feet or tugged at their hands. He was free, but he was alone. He knew why he was restless and what kept him from returning to his lonely apartment. He wanted to see Alys. To take her in his arms and tell her how much he loved her. He almost laughed out loud at the thought of how shocked she would be. He couldn't tell her that yet, but he could go to see her.

He started toward her apartment, just two blocks from the park, and then realized he'd better call first. He wondered what he would say. May I come up for a little while? Will you have dinner with me? No, she'd probably already eaten with the children. Will you go for a walk with me? She'd think he was crazy. He was. He was crazy in love with her.

After finding a telephone kiosk, he searched in his wallet for her phone number. Not until the fourth ring did he hear someone answer it, and then it was an older woman who said she was sorry but Madame Prévou was out for the evening.

Ryan slumped against the side of the kiosk, disappointment suddenly making him feel old and tired. He signaled a passing taxi to drive him to the office and his car. Throughout the long, dull evening he consoled himself with the thought that he'd see Alys in the morning, and the first thing he'd do was ask her to have dinner with him. The second was to let her know that he intended to compete with that Englishman Kenneth for her affections. She wasn't married to him yet, and as far as Ryan knew, she wasn't engaged either. If Kenneth were this dilatory in securing his claim on her – or if she were hesitating in committing herself – then he, Ryan, had a better than fair chance of winning her over. With that positive thought, he finally fell asleep.

In the morning, Alys's request for two days off so she could have a long weekend at home disturbed him only momentarily. While his courtship had to be postponed for four days, he could use that time to plan his strategy. The first maneuver would be to have her apartment filled with flowers when she returned. The second would be to get box seats for whatever musical or dramatic offering was being presented at one of the theaters. He'd never been an aficionado of opera, ballet, drama, or symphonies; but if that was what Alys liked, he would take her to everything she wanted to see or hear.

After she'd left, he began going through the mail. Fortunately there was nothing that had to be answered immediately by letter. A few he put aside that he could handle by phone. With the others, he jotted notes on the bottom, securely aware that Alys would know exactly what to write when she returned on Monday. With three of them, he wrote out more complete paragraphs. While doing this, he was moved to write a love letter and slip it in among them. Reaching for a sheet of paper, he began scrawling out a few rambling sentences in which he tried to tell Alys how he felt about her. Only after he read over what he'd written did he realize the adolescent idiocy of what he was doing. He crushed the paper into a tight mass and heaved it in a one-handed basketball toss toward the wastebasket. It missed by three inches. Disgusted with himself and frustrated because Alys wasn't there, he got up and carefully dropped the paper into the basket.

Earlier he'd fixed a pot of coffee, having not the slightest idea the proportions of water he'd added to the coffee; and after pouring himself a cup, he grimaced at the too strong, bitter taste.

Damn! he thought. Why the hell did Alys have to take these particular two days off? The rest of today, all day tomorrow, and the weekend to have to get through before she'd return. The afternoon passed in more frustration when he finally settled down to taking care of things that needed his attention, and he found he couldn't even make simple decisions or add up a single column of figures.

He dreaded spending the evening alone. He could have called one of the people he'd met since coming to Liège; but considering the mood he was in, having to keep up a witless conversation with a mere acquaintance would be even worse. He took as long as possible eating the dinner that the concierge's wife, who cooked and cleaned for him, had left warming in the oven. After shifting from one chair to another and trying to read, he finally decided that maybe he needed fresh air. Twice around the block, and he thought that if he were going to spend the whole time wondering what Alys was doing at home right now, he might as well be spending it in a comfortable chair. By eleven, after slowly sipping two tall bourbons with water, he thought maybe he could sleep. But he couldn't.

At midnight, he fixed himself another drink, but instead of putting him to sleep, it made him more wide awake. At one o'clock he found an old American magazine and reread three boring articles. Back in bed, in spite of his body's being too tired even to turn over, he still couldn't fall asleep. At two, he got up and read over some notes he'd been making all week. Then he took nearly an hour meticulously arranging them in order of importance. Dissatisfied with the result, he spent another hour completely rearranging them in alphabetical order by topic.

Finally, for no apparent, logical, sane reason, he pulled a small suitcase out of the closet and packed it with shirts, underwear, socks, a pair of his oldest, most comfortable shoes, extra shaving gear, and a spare toothbrush. Strangely satisfied that that's what he should have done earlier, he went back to bed and immediately to sleep.

Ryan remained in a deep sleep until nearly dawn, when he was attacked by a series of fitful dreams. In all of them he was searching for something, although he was never quite sure what that something was. In each succeeding dream it varied from being a place to a person to a small object like a book. Whichever, it constantly eluded him. Just as he was about to find it, someone or some thing would appear to turn him back. In the final dream, he was running after a faceless young woman who, as he reached out to touch her, darted into a forest. When he tried to follow, thickly entwined vines and dense underbrush impeded his way. No light filtered through the branches overhead, and the only sounds were the moaning of a mourning dove and the mordent cries of a screech owl.

With his eyes still closed, Ryan turned off the alarm and continued to come awake slowly. His natural waking-up confusion was augmented by a vague feeling of not knowing where he was. With as much traveling as he did, this was not a unique phenomenon. Usually, however, he would have himself oriented in a minute or two. But now it was as if his mind had become disjoined, and the pieces were in several different places. He couldn't focus on any one of them. It wasn't as if the room were unfamiliar to him. He recognized it as his room, so he knew he belonged here; but where was here? Gradually his mind came together, and he knew he was in his apartment in Liège.

Then he realized he was shivering with cold. His body was covered with sweat and entangled in sweat-soaked sheets. Gradually he recalled bits and pieces of his frustrating dreams that must have had him fighting with the bedclothes. After a hot shower and brisk rubdown, he felt physically better; but he was still in a state of mental fatigue and frenzied agitation. He felt like one possessed by a demon that until now had lingered tauntingly on the perimeter of his life for nearly three years. It was the uncontrollable urge to find and reclaim the lost months. All yesterday and last night, he'd thought only of Alys. He'd tried to stifle his impatience for her to return so he could tell her he loved her, so he could court her in the old-fashioned way with flowers and candy, take her out to dinner, and spend evenings with her and Minette and Amalie.

Now he knew he must first discover who he'd been during the months of amnesia. He might soon be free from Janet, but he would still be encumbered by an obscured past that needed to be revealed before he would be totally free to offer a future with himself to Alys.

He wouldn't go to the office today. So strong was the need to recover his memory, he thought only of getting in the car and driving in any direction he felt impelled to go. While applying after-shave lotion, he was startled to discover he'd shaved off his mustache without being aware of what he was doing. He looked in the mirror and saw the man he'd been when he found himself on the road to Liège. The act in no way enlightened him, and yet he felt it was a beginning. As he dressed, he forced himself to recall the various and unusual hints he'd experienced in the past that each time, he thought, were trying to reveal something. The odors of certain flowers; Louise's little, hand-carved wooden horse that made him ask where the other wooden animals were; wondering where his pipe was when he didn't remember ever having smoked a pipe; the feeling when he was in bed with the flu of having had a tube in his throat; the image of a cemetery by a river while he was watching the Citadel cadets parade; and the oft-recurring visions of a young woman. He thought about the dried flower he'd found in his trouser pocket before he was given a uniform; and he was overcome by a bleak sadness, as if that flower alone could have led him to the answer he sought.

Having ended his trek on that fateful day in May 1945, at American Army Headquarters, he drove there first. It seemed as good a starting point as any. He paused for a few minutes, looked through the wrought-iron gate, and thought about the woman he'd seen standing there. He thought today as he'd wondered often since then if she were a part of that shadowed existence he was now determined to infiltrate with light.

Then he turned the car around. He imagined a long road ahead of him stretching toward a frontier at which there were gates forbidding him to pass. Beyond that barrier were the lost months, and somehow he had to force his way through to them. He had no idea where he was going. He knew only he had to get out of Liège and start driving in some direction.

As if propelled by a force stronger than he could control, Ryan headed away from the city. It was as if his will had been anesthetized and he were being directed by a will outside himself, by an invisible guide. With his conscious mind in no way directing his movements, he had no idea which road he had taken, but it kept beckoning him on. Nothing about the road or the countryside looked familiar to him, yet he knew instinctively that he'd been on it before. He drove through small villages and passed farmers working their fields. In each village he slowed down, all his senses alerted for a clue as to where he was, as to whether he should stop; but always he felt the magnetic pull that sped him onward.

Ryan ignored most crossroads, but at one he was mysteriously impelled to turn right and follow the narrow road down into a village of no more than seven houses and a church. From there he drove along a lane that bisected fields freshly harrowed for planting. Into his memory came the day he had bumped over just such a rutted dirt road in a wagon on his way to Liège.

As one country road led to another, he began to wonder if he weren't crazy, driving along like this on some madcap, meaningless venture or if he were really finding his way back. It had taken more than two days of walking, seeking rides in wagons, and finally being picked up by a truck to get from where he'd regained his memory to Liège. How long if one went directly by car? But he wasn't going directly. He was running a maze of dirt roads and country lanes, more than one of which ended up at a dead end in farm yards.

From a mountain range of thunderheads banked against the horizon, massive black storm clouds began to spread with hurricane force across the sky. Within minutes the light rain became a downpour that reduced visibility to less than a foot beyond the windshield. Ryan had no idea where he was going. Not that it really mattered, he supposed. He wasn't following a map; but then, he didn't want to miss a curve and end up among a herd of sheep. Through the murky dusk of rain and near darkness, he saw the faint halos of light a few yards away. Easing the car off the road, he heard the crunch of gravel as well as the splashing of water beneath his tires, and he allowed himself a long, pent-up sigh of relief. He had with luck or good guesswork managed to end up in a driveway.

In the wind, a small sign banged erratically against the side of the building, and Ryan was able to distinguish that he'd stopped at an inn. Blessing the strange power that had been guiding him all day or leading him here, he pulled his shapeless Irish hat farther down on his head, wrapped his all-weather alpaca coat around him, and dashed for the entrance. It was as good a time as any to stop and have lunch. With luck he could wait out the storm here. These sudden, heavy squalls seldom lasted more than an hour or two. The proprietor greeted him cordially, led him to a table, and assured him that monsieur was welcome to stay until the skies cleared.

It rained for nearly four hours; and even then the sky remained hidden by a gauzy scrim of gray clouds as Ryan started off again. Through the humid, late-afternoon haze, the sun glowed like a burning coal. For a while Ryan stayed on this main road. He saw clumps of spring flowers in bloom, and into his mind floated the image of a little girl in a field of wild flowers. The face was shadowed, but he could detect a welcoming smile beckoning him on. The image remained with him until he reached a fork in the road where he turned off the main highway and onto another country byroad. Now he was quite certain he was following in reverse his earlier route to Liège.

Another image appeared, and desperately he grasped and held on to it for more than a minute. The little girl again, but now she was playing on the floor with a jumping jack. No, he must be confusing the image with Minette and his gift to her, although in some strange way the child in his mind appeared much younger.

For a while the road followed a stream, and overlying the peaceful scene like a transparency was the vision of a young woman sitting by a tree. Her face was turned away from him, and she appeared to be looking across the stream toward distant forested hills, with an expectant tautness to her body, as if she were waiting for someone.

Now image after image raced through his mind with such speed he could neither grasp nor comprehend them. It was like the books he'd had as a boy, books in which he flipped so rapidly through the pages, the pictures on them actually seemed to move. The same young woman in a blue dress with a bouquet of flowers in her hands. An older couple sitting by a tiled stove. The child again, running toward a bridge and his trying to call out to her. The young woman speaking French and his responding. Ryan found himself talking aloud and was amazed to discover he was speaking whole sentences in French. Was the woman in the vision the one who had taught him to speak? Who had gone to Liège and told the authorities he had stayed with her family during those months?

All this while he was trying to recall the faces of the woman and the little girl, but all that emerged were the soft brown hair of the one and the blond curls of the other. Gradually he was able to acknowledge the truth. Louise had been right. There was someone he'd been in love with, and it was she he had to find. It was strange how this knowledge in no way diminished his love for Alys nor in any way appeared as an unsolvable dilemma. Ryan's world had long since ceased turning on a logical axis. With the rediscovery of the lost months would come the solution.

Propelled now by a conscious desire to find the woman he had once loved as well as by the unknown power directing his movements, he drove on. In his haste, he passed a turnoff. Unaware he had missed it until he began feeling irritable and confused, he turned around. How, he wondered, was he going to know when he reached the right road? But as with other turns and deviations, he recognized the fork as he approached it. Now, though still not knowing where he was going, he began to feel suffusing through him the calm, tranquil peace of mind he'd so long been seeking.

Slowing down for a curve, Ryan saw that the road now paralleled a river. On either side, the hills and forests of the Ardennes closed in on him, not like a threatening force but as if assuring him he was coming to the end of his long journey into the past. His body tensed and his breathing became more rapid when on his left he saw a stone bridge; and almost immediately afterward, a cemetery to the right of the road. Suddenly apprehensive about what might be waiting for him if he continued on, Ryan stopped the car and got out.

Bedeviled by the tormenting conflict between the inescapable urge to continue on and the more comfortable desire to turn back, he walked slowly across the fields toward the river. The sound of the wind soughing through the trees on the nearby hills hovered over the placid scene like muted echoes of voices long-since stilled. There, on that hillside, among those trees, he had relived the agonies of the war and wrestled with his conscience before choosing the road to Liège. His present quandary offered him alternative decisions almost as difficult to choose between as the previous ones. Yet choose he must. He knew as certainly as he recognized this river that just ahead lay what he'd been seeking for nearly three years: the five lost months. Taking two deep breaths, he looked one last time at the hills, turned, and walked back to the car, impelled by an inexorable force. There was no turning back.

Another two hundred yards and he approached an isolated, three-story, stone hostel. Light streaming from the windows fell across the road in an inviting path to the door.

Guided again by the alien will, he walked around to the back instead of ringing the bell at the front entrance. Stopping by a window, he saw through the opaque curtains the silhouettes of a young woman and two children sitting at a table. He had no idea why he had stopped here, although the place gradually began to assume the familiarity of one visited briefly in childhood then never seen again and almost forgotten. As he looked at the group around the table, he had a vague, eerie feeling that they had been waiting for him for a long time, and yet at the same time he was uncertain if he'd be welcome. In spite of that apprehension, he knocked.

Listening to Amalie's explanation that she couldn't eat all of her supper because an invisible elf on the plate had told her not to, Alys jumped involuntarily at the sound of someone knocking at the door. Rarely did anyone but the family use the kitchen entrance. Memories of other nocturnal visitors flooded through her mind: a drunken tourist who had lost his way and who insisted this was where he had a reservation; the constant invasion of German soldiers searching the house; Ryan being carried in by his two comrades.

No, those were foolish thoughts. A tourist she could handle; the Germans had long since gone; and Ryan was now Mr. Middleton in his apartment in Liège. Still, she shivered with fear, as with an icy draft from an open door, and she wished Jolie and Émile would return from the village. Nonsense, she chided herself, she was still merely a bit unnerved after the violent storm that had momentarily knocked out the lights. Whoever was knocking could be a neighbor who'd chosen to come around to the back and who wasn't able to walk right in because the door was locked. Or perhaps the storm had disconnected the front bell; and a prospective guest, seeing the kitchen lights, hoped he would find someone in here.

After all, Alys thought, as she stood up and walked to the door, this was an inn and visitors did expect to be made welcome.

When the door was opened, Ryan backed away as if from a place forbidden to him. Whirling through his mind was a kaleidoscope of dizzying images, and he had to grasp the doorjamb to keep from falling. When he tried to force his eyes to focus on the present scene, standing here, waiting for him to enter were two Alyses. The one in front wore a skirt and sweater he'd often seen at the office. But behind her, surrounded by a pale aura of light and wearing a blue silk dress, was the shadowy figure of another Alys, the young woman of his dreams whose face was now clearly visible. He wiped a hand across his eyes; and as his double vision cleared, the two women merged into one.

'Alys?' He was unsure which one he was speaking to. 'Alys, I've come back.'

'I know, my love.' She walked unhesitatingly toward him and into his arms. 'Welcome home. Oh, welcome home, darling.'

'It's you, isn't it?' he whispered, holding her close and unable to believe what was happening. 'It's been you the whole time.'

'The whole time, Ryan. Waiting. Wondering when you'd remember. Wanting you to love me as much as I love you.' Why he had remembered didn't matter, only that in remembering he had returned to her.

'I do love you.' He nestled his face in her hair and inhaled the fragrance of a thousand blossoms. 'I know now I never stopped loving the Alys I married, I simply fell in love with you all over again the minute we met in Brussels.'

'Hold me close, Ryan. Hold me very close and say you'll never leave again.' She felt his heart beating as rapidly as her own.

'Never. Finding you here is the most wonderful thing that's ever happened to me.'

Alys turned her head in the direction of the table where the little girls were squirming impatiently in their chairs. 'Minette,' she asked, 'do you know who this is?'

'It's *Papa*!' She scrambled down out of the chair and ran across the room. 'I knew you'd come home. I told *Maman* you would, but I don't think she believed me.'

Ryan gathered Minette up in his arms and held her close against his shoulder. 'She didn't, huh? But I'm glad you did.'

Only then did Ryan look at Amalie, who seemed undecided whether she should run to him, too, or wait for him to speak to her. He glanced inquisitively from her to Alys.

Picking Amalie up, Alys put her in Ryan's arms, from which Minette had descended to dance ecstatically around the room. 'She's yours, Ryan. I didn't know until sometime after you'd left.'

'Oh God, Alys, why didn't you tell me? At the hospital when she was so sick? Or when I came to the apartment? How I envied you having her, even when she was ill, because I so desperately wished I had a little girl of my own. And to think she's mine and I didn't know it.'

With Amalie in his arms, Minette hugging his legs, and Alys's eyes reflecting the same love and joy that swelled within him, Ryan let the tears flow unheeded down his cheeks. He'd found his lost months. The days of lonely uncertainty were over.

Through eyes still misty with her own tears, Alys watched as Ryan seated himself on the floor between Minette and Amalie while they played with the animals he'd carved those long, tortuous months ago. She couldn't decide who was enjoying the game more, he or the girls. Time enough for them to be alone, to rediscover their own special ways of pleasing each other, to come together in the perfect merging of love and physical passion.

There was much to tell each other, but they had years ahead of them in which to say it. Alys curled up on the chair. She felt like a doll that had been loved, tossed aside, found again, and cherished the more for having once been abandoned.

Ryan looked up as if to make certain she was still there, and his smile was all the assurance she needed that she could dismiss all fears of ever being abandoned again.

THE PASSIONATE SAVAGE

Constance Gluyas

Lucien Marsh was a loner, a man who wouldn't settle down in any one place with any one woman – however beautiful she might be. And he had two women who loved him with all their hearts and would shatter their lives to lie in his arms –

FLAMING DAWN the fiery Indian princess who broke her people's trust by giving herself to the white hunter and following him into a white man's world.

LADY SAMANTHA PIERCE the sophisticated society lady who broke her marriage vows to possess Lucien, restlessly seeking to capture her true love and desire.

THE PASSIONATE SAVAGE is the unforgettable romance of two magnificent women raging from the untamed American wilderness to the aristocratic world of Victorian London.

HISTORICAL ROMANCE 0 7221 3901 2 £2.25

Snatched from safety and her husband's harbouring arms by the lawless corsairs of Algiers, fiery but tender Lorna Singleton is forced to obey a pirate captain's bold lusts. But Ahmed's animal passion does not lack barbaric splendour. As a Christian slave in brutal Muslim hands, Lorna must find a protector to save her from the torment and degradation that awaits her in the casbah . . . even if the price of salvation is her virtue.

SO WICKED THE HEART is a gale-force story of surging passion and turbulent love, an unabashed tale of a woman's struggle to defend the storm-wracked fortress of her heart against an onslaught of unparalleled savagery and betrayal.

HISTORICAL ROMANCE 0 7221 7363 6 £1.95